C000184007

# The Rise of Cromwell Jones

## ROY CLEWS

**WARNER BOOKS**

A *Warner* Book

First published in Great Britain by Warner in 1995

Copyright © Roy Clews 1995

The moral right of the author has been asserted.

A CIP catalogue record for this book
is available from the British Library.

ISBN 0 7515 1228 1

Typeset by Hewer Text Composition Services, Edinburgh
Printed and bound in Great Britain by
Clays Ltd, St Ives plc

Warner Books
A Division of
Little, Brown and Company (UK)
Brettenham House
Lancaster Place
London WC2E 7EN

# Introduction

For evil to triumph, it only needs good men to do nothing . . . This is a story about events which have yet to take place. A story of good men fighting back against evil . . . Someday it may become a reality . . . And that day may not be so very distant . . .

# *England – the near future*

The gang of youths roamed the streets of the city
seeking prey. They were a hunting pack of feral
beasts, arrogantly secure in their numbers, enjoying the fearful reactions of those individuals they
pushed and jostled as they swaggered through the
echoing concrete and glass shopping malls. Some
of the youths were white, others black, but they
were uniform in their brightly coloured shell-suits,
expensive trainers and the baseball caps they wore
with peaks turned to the rear. In a noisy menacing
phalanx they swarmed through the aisles of the big
department stores, pilfering goods from counters,
acting without any attempt at concealment, contemptuously defying the frightened shop assistants
to challenge their actions.

In the central mall a cashpoint machine had a small
queue of customers waiting their turn to use it. As
the swaggering gang neared the machine, the people
waiting fearfully abandoned their patient queue and
moved quickly away. Only one stockily built, middle-
aged man remained. Ivor Jones was intent on sorting
out his credit cards and was unaware of the youths'
approach as he stepped up to the cashpoint screen
and inserted his card. The gang of youths suddenly
crowded around him, their bodies crushing hard to

trap him, and he felt the point of a knife-blade pressing painfully into the side of his throat.

He cried out in mingled shock and fear and the black youth holding the knife hissed warningly, 'Don't look at us. Just keep your fuckin' mouth shut and do what I tell you.'

Jones stood motionless, afraid to move, and the sharp pointed steel increased its menacing pressure.

'Take out the maximum,' the black youth instructed, and the man obeyed, his trembling fingers tapping the keys and his fear causing him to make an error in the code.

'Don't try coming the cunt,' the youth warned angrily, and the knife-point jabbed painfully.

Breathing in short shallow gasps Ivor Jones again tapped out codes, and this time to his relief he got it right.

'Please remove your card and wait for your cash . . . Your cash is being counted . . . Please wait . . . Please remove your cash promptly . . .'

The green-lettered messages flashed in sequence and the inner workings of the machine whirred metallically as first his credit card reappeared and then the slender sheaf of new banknotes.

The youth snatched the card and banknotes, while others rifled through Jones' jacket and trouser pockets, taking his wallet, keys, and the small amount of loose change that they found. The black youth took the watch from Jones' wrist and jeeringly told his companions, 'This cunt only buys cheap stuff,' he held the watch high for them to see. 'It's crap, this is.'

The knife-blade slashed down Ivor Jones' cheek, leaving a streak of hot agony, and he shouted in pain as jeering and whooping the gang surged on.

Jones sagged forward against the ledge of the machine, his hands pressing against the bleeding flesh, blood dripping between his fingers. Sick and faint, he fought to steady his reeling senses. Then he turned to find a semi-circle of faces staring at him, some with horror, some with curiosity, some with disbelief.

'Help me!' he pleaded. 'Please help me!'

The faces became guarded and hostile, and some turned away. The pain in his cheek was now excruciating and he felt near to vomiting.

'What's all this?' A helmeted policeman pushed through the semi-circle, his fresh young face excited as he studied the bleeding man. 'What happened to you?'

'I've been robbed.' Jones could only speak with difficulty. 'A gang robbed me!'

The young policeman spoke hurriedly into his chest radio, then attempted to examine the bleeding wound in Jones' face.

'Are you hurt anywhere else?'

'No.'

'The ambulance will be here shortly. Try to keep calm.'

Another policeman, accompanied by a uniformed store security guard, came pushing through the crowd. The newcomers spoke briefly with the first officer, then the second policeman turned to the onlookers.

'Did anyone see what happened?'

Heads shook in negation, and when he pressed individuals voices were raised in angry denials.

'I didn't see anything.'

'He was already like this when I got here.'

'I've only just come.'

3

The disbelief showed clearly in the policeman's expression, and he growled aggressively.

'Somebody must have seen something?'

Some of the crowd walked away, others continued to shake their heads, and one man stated flatly, 'Anybody who gets involved in this needs their heads seeing to.'

Green-smocked para-medics arrived and helped Ivor Jones through the shopping mall, their progress creating curious comments and attracting staring eyes. The youngest policeman went with them, leaving his colleague to continue his fruitless attempts to find someone prepared to admit that they had witnessed the robbery and assault.

In the hospital casualty department a tired-eyed Asian doctor cleansed and stitched Ivor Jones' wound, and clucked his tongue sympathetically when told that his patient was a victim of muggers.

'So many people are being attacked these days. The streets are no longer safe to walk upon at any hour of the day or night. I myself was attacked and robbed two weeks since when I was on my way home.' He shook his head in despair. 'The young people of today have no respect for anything or anyone.'

He finished dressing Jones' face and then went to attend to another casualty.

'Do you feel up to telling me exactly what happened, Mr Jones?' the young policeman asked.

Although it pained him to speak, Ivor Jones related the facts as he could remember them.

'What chance is there that they'll be caught?' he asked when he had finished.

The constable pursed his lips. 'Well, you'll need to come to the station when you feel up to it, and look

4

through some pictures to see if you can identify your attackers.'


Detective Sergeant Denis Matthews sighed wearily when the young constable reported to him.

'Where have you put him?'

'In number two interview room, sergeant.'

The sergeant's heavily lined features frowned doubtfully and he ran his hand through his grizzled hair. 'Is he in a fit state to help us?'

The younger man grinned admiringly. 'He's a tough bugger. I offered to get him home so he could have a rest before he came down here, but he wouldn't have it. He says he wants to have the ones who robbed him put away as soon as possible.'

The sergeant chuckled cynically. 'And pigs might fly!' He rose from his desk. 'Ah, well, I suppose I'd better get on with it. Any details about him?'

The constable scanned his notebook, and recited from it. 'He's a preacher, named Ivor Jones, aged fifty, widower, address Tabernacle Cottage, Meadowpark Gospel Chapel, Meadowpark Road.'

The older man grinned sardonically. 'A bloody parson getting mugged. What's the world coming to?'

The constable shook his head. 'I don't think he's a proper parson, Sarge. I reckon he's one of them cult preachers by the look on him.'

Matthews pursed his lips and said reflectively, 'Wait a minute ... Ivor Jones ... that name rings a bell with me. Have we got anything on him?'

The younger man shrugged. 'I don't think so, Sarge. I can check it out if you like.'

'Never mind.' The detective casually dismissed the matter. 'It'll come to me, it always does.'

*  *  *

Ivor Jones presented a sorry sight: his dark ill-fitting
suit and roll-necked sweater covered with blood, his
face half hidden by the thickly plastered dressing
upon his slashed cheek. He was hatless, and his
sandy, greying hair was sparse upon his shiny scalp.
But the detective's shrewd eyes noted the thick mus-
cularity of the shoulders beneath the cheap cloth of
the jacket, and the fiery piercing quality of the blue
eyes, and could not help but think that this was an
unusual type of preacher man. Jones had more the
look of a soldier than a cleric.

After introducing himself, Denis Matthews began
to flash faces upon the computer screen and Ivor
Jones frowned in concentration as he studied the
images. After three successive re-runs of the tape he
sighed in exasperation and shook his head.

'I'm sorry, I can't pick out anyone for certain. It
all happened so quickly.' His accents were those of
the city and his voice harsh-timbred. 'Number eight
could have been the one who had the knife, but I
didn't really get anything like a good look at him.'
He touched the plaster on his cheek and finished
ironically, 'This was a distraction.'

The detective was not unduly concerned by the
admission. 'Yeah, all right, Mr Jones, it can't be
helped. That'll be all for the present, thank you. I'll
get in touch with you if there're any developments.'

The other man's blue eyes sparked angrily. 'What
do you mean, if there're any developments?' he
challenged. 'Surely you can question number eight
at least? And there must have been a lot of people
who could indentify the gang. The mall was full.'

'We can bring in the one you've pointed out

for questioning,' the detective acknowledged, 'but whether we'll be able to bring any charges against him is doubtful.'

'Why?' Jones demanded.

The other man shrugged uneasily. 'We need more than just your possible identification of him to be able to bring any charges. We need impartial witnesses. We're trying to find some.'

'And if you find some witnesses, what then?' Jones asked grimly.

Again the policeman shrugged uneasily. 'It's not up to me, Mr Jones. We have to pass on the papers to the Crown Prosecution Service for them to decide whether the case is brought to trial.' He grimaced dispiritedly. 'And just between you, me and the gate-post, I sometimes wonder whose side the CPS is on.'

Jones sat frowning as he mulled over what he had been told.

Matthews forced a smile. 'Anyway, Mr Jones, I'll do the best I can for you, and of course I'll let you know what develops.' He rose to his feet. 'Now I'll leave you for a moment while I arrange for one of our cars to take you home.'

Ivor Jones shook his head. 'No, that won't be necessary, thank you. I prefer to walk.'

'Are you sure?' The other man's lined features showed concern. 'You've had a nasty shock, you know. It might be best if you were to let us see you safely home.'

'No, really, I'll be fine, thank you.' Jones was adamant.

'Will there be anyone at home who can look after you, Mr Jones? Delayed shock can sometimes hit you harder than you might expect,' the detective persisted.

'Yes, my sister's there.' Jones was simultaneously experiencing impatience at the man's persistence, and appreciation for the obvious concern. 'She's recently lost her husband, so she's come to stay with me for a while.'

The detective accompanied him to the front doors of the police station, and when they parted offered his hand. 'Go carefully now, Mr Jones.'

He felt the immense strength of Jones' grip and again was struck by the thought that this was an unusual type of clergyman. As Jones walked away Denis Matthews stood looking after him for a brief while, then shook his head and turned back inside.

'You ring a bell with me, Ivor Jones. Where have I heard of you before?'

Back in his office he sat for some seconds restlessly toying with the papers on his desk, then on impulse went to the computer and keyed in certain files, searching for any mention of Ivor Jones. He found the reference for which he had been looking and, leaving the office, went down into the cellar where the old records were stored. After another search through the jumble of dusty files he again succeeded in his quest. He blew the thick dust from the blue covers of the slender folder and quickly read its contents, grinning with satisfaction at what he found there.

'I knew I'd come across Ivor Jones before!'

He replaced the folder and, wiping his grimed hands with his handkerchief, returned to his office.


Ivor Jones traversed the bustling streets of the city centre engrossed in his own bitter thoughts, heedless of the curious stares directed at his bloodstained clothing and plastered face. He was now beginning to

8

experience the reaction to his ordeal, and he was sick at heart and weary in body and mind. He was thankful to leave the city centre behind him and to come to the road leading to the great ramshackle edifice that was Meadowpark Gospel Chapel. Tabernacle Cottage adjoined its western wall, the conjoined building stood in its own grounds, which once had been meticulously maintained shrubbery and lawn but were now a sadly neglected mass of tangled bushes. The grounds were surrounded by streets of terraced houses which had been built to shelter the artisans and workpeople who swarmed to work in the myriad factories and workshops when the entire district throbbed and pulsated with the noisy, grimy vigour of production. Now, the vigour had departed from the district. The factories and workshops were no more, and the streets once vibrant with life now were dull and lifeless, shabby and run down.

Ivor Jones' heart sank when he saw the group of youths and girls lounging on the corner of the street which he must cross to reach his home. He felt a tremor of apprehension and for a brief moment he considered turning around and walking in the opposite direction. Then he was suddenly angry and ashamed of his own timidity, and he forced himself to continue on.

Their eyes swung to him, and as he neared the silent group he moved to the outer edge of the pavement. As he passed them one asked, 'What's happened to you, Grandad?'

His heart thumped and he was near to panic.

'I've been mugged,' he blurted, and quickened his pace.

'What did they get?' the voice demanded.

'Everything.'

9

He kept on walking, and the voice jeered, 'Don't worry, then, it aren't worth us mugging you again, is it?'

Raucous laughter applauded this gibe, and then he was past them.

Not daring to look back, he strained his ears for any sounds of pursuing footsteps, and the pounding of his heart only eased when he had travelled some scores of yards and reached his own home.

Outside the front door he hesitated. Iris, his sister, was much older than him and in frail health, and he was nervous about the sudden shock to her of seeing him like this. He drew a deep breath and knocked on the door, calling out as he did so:

'It's only me, Iris. I've lost my keys.'

As she opened the door he kept his plastered cheek turned from her, telling her quickly, 'Now I've had a bit of an accident, Iris, but I'm all right. There's nothing to worry about.'

He moved past her into the sparsely furnished, austere room, trying to soothe her fearful agitation with reiterated assurances that he was perfectly all right and that his injury was very minor.

But despite his words the shock of seeing his plastered face and bloodied clothing triggered a painful thudding of her diseased heart, causing her to gasp for breath.

The grey pallor of her features alarmed Ivor Jones and he seated her in the small armchair flanking the fireplace and hastened to find the tablets which she carried in her handbag for use in such an emergency.

With sips of water she managed to swallow two of the small capsules, and slowly the grey pallor of her complexion became tinged with colour as the thudding of her heart eased and slowed.

'I'm sorry, Ivor,' she panted weakly. 'Sorry to be such a nuisance.'

'Now don't be so silly,' he told her warmly, and patted her shoulder. He sat facing her, leaning forward to hold her thin hands between his own until he was satisfied that she was fully recovered. Then he told her, 'You just sit quiet now while I get myself cleaned up.'

Jones smiled fondly at her anxious expression. He cared deeply for his elder sister, remembering how she had always loved and protected him when he was a child. Upstairs in the small cottage he changed his bloodied clothing and carefully washed his face and neck. While he did these things he pondered on the possible effects upon his sister if he told her the truth about what had happened to him. The recent death of her husband had all but destroyed her, and it was only now that she was beginning to display some signs of recovery from that bereavement. Ivor Jones knew that the knowledge that he had been brutally assaulted and robbed would cause her immense distress. And so he decided that for the present he would keep it from her. Instead, he would say that he had tripped and hit his cheek against a wall or something.

A fierce anger ignited within him as the vivid recollection of the mugging assailed him, and his big hands clenched into fists as the savage lust for revenge surged through his being.

Then he heard his sister's voice calling him from the room below.

'Do you want some tea, Ivor?'

He forced back his anger, and went down to join her.

11

# *Chapter Two*

After a night of fitful sleep and terrifying dreams of blood and violence which had continually jerked him into clammy-sweated wakefulness, Ivor Jones rose late from his bed weary in mind and body. His cheek was stiff and sore and he winced with pain as he flexed his facial muscles in tentative exploration. He took a bath, then very carefully shaved around the plaster dressing and brushed his teeth.

On the table downstairs was a note from his sister to tell him that she had gone to do some shopping. He frowned uneasily; he did not want her to risk overstraining herself by carrying any loads. Yet he was pleased that she was once more beginning to try to lead a normal life after the trauma of her recent bereavement.

While he was sipping a cup of tea he thought about what he must do that day. He had reported the theft of his various credit cards to the bank's emergency phone number during the previous evening. 'I'll need to change all the locks. They might have just chucked my keys away, but it's better to play safe. I'll have to go to the bank and draw some more money out as well. And I'll pop into the police station and explain to that sergeant that I don't want Iris to find out what happened to me before it's absolutely necessary.'

Once more his anger flared as he thought about the assault, but after a few moments he realised the futility of dwelling upon the incident and tried to concentrate instead on the day ahead of him.

Before leaving the cottage he wrote a note to his sister to explain his absence and laid it upon the table. He let the lock of the front door spring home as he left, knowing that Iris had her own key.

Detective Sergeant Matthews was not at the police station when Jones called there, so begging a sheet of notepaper from the desk constable he wrote a note of explanation for his call and left it with the constable to be delivered to the detective. The remainder of his errands took much longer to complete than he had anticipated, and the early dusk of the winter day had fallen before he trudged wearily up to the front door of Tabernacle Cottage.

There were no lights shining from any of the windows and Ivor Jones experienced a sudden sense of foreboding. Iris should have been home long since.

The front door was locked and he knocked upon its weathered panels, calling loudly, 'Iris, are you in there? Iris?'

There was no reply, and his foreboding intensified. He moved to the window, cupping his hands around his eyes to peer into the dark interior. At first he could see nothing, but then as his eyes accustomed to the gloom his breath suddenly caught in his throat. The table had been upended and its top rested against the inner ledge of the window. He stepped back to the door and without any hesitation slammed his shoulder against it, bursting the lock from its screws and sending the door crashing open.

The breath rasped in his throat as he switched on the light and saw the shambles of overturned furniture, books ripped from their shelves, drawers and their contents hurled across the floor.

'Iris?' His cry echoed through the silent house. 'Iris?'

She was lying on her back on the floor of her small bedroom. Her eyes were wide, mouth open, features twisted in a frozen mask of terror; blood congealing on her lips, chin and throat showed black against the white dentures and pallid grey skin.

Ivor Jones groaned in agonised shock and grief and, slumping to his knees beside her, sought desperately for any signs of life remaining in her still warm flesh. But there were no such signs to be found. Iris, his beloved sister, was dead.

# Chapter Three

During the weeks that followed Iris's death, Ivor
Jones' initial grief became increasingly overlaid by
a sense of bitter frustration. Despite all efforts by
the police no one was brought to book for the crime.
Indeed, there seemed to be considerable uncertainty
amongst officialdom as to exactly what the crime was.
The post mortem had found that his sister had died
of a massive heart attack. The blood upon her face
had resulted from a superficial injury to her mouth,
caused by 'an impact'. What had impacted could not
be clearly ascertained – fist, boot, blunt object, or
some other thing. Whether that injury had brought
on the heart attack also could not be proved. The
medical expert stated that such was the condition
of the dead woman's diseased heart that she could
have dropped dead at any time. The theory of
the investigating police officers was that Iris had
disturbed a thief, or thieves, and that one of them
had struck her in panic as she tried to prevent his
escape. There was no physical evidence of forced
entry, but the police were not able to establish if
the thieves had used Ivor Jones' stolen keys to obtain
access, or if Iris herself had opened the door to them
and let them enter.

The thought that the thieves had used his own keys

to get into the cottage, and then subjected his sister to an unknowable period of terror, caused Ivor Jones many, many sleepless nights.

After the funeral he went away from the city to an isolated rented cottage in Wales where no one knew him. The dual shock he had suffered – the brutal assault on him and the terrible death of his sister – had shaken him to his core, and he could not bear to listen to any more condolences from well-meaning people. Above all else he needed to be alone, and in the solitude of the bleak windswept hills he privately grieved, and brooded bitterly on what had happened.

In scant weeks the tragedy was all but forgotten by the world at large, and Jones returned to his home, ready to resume his work.

He rose early on the morning of the day after his return, and was sitting at the table drinking a cup of tea when a thunderous knocking pounded his front door. He started in shock, his suddenly nerveless fingers lost grip of the cup and it fell on to the table, and with dismayed eyes he watched the steaming tea spread its brown stain over the clean white cloth.

The knocking thundered again and this time a man's voice called, 'Mr Jones? Are you in there, Mr Jones? Can I have a word with you, please?'

His gaze flickered desperately around the small room, and he suddenly realised that he was seeking for a way of escape. Self-disgust surged through him and he slammed down his clenched fists on the table-top.

'What's the matter with me? I'm behaving like a frightened child!'

The self-disgust fuelled a self-directed anger, and that emotion served to steady him, and to drive out the unreasoning panic that had so suddenly predominated.

He swallowed hard and called, 'Just a minute. I'm coming.'

He noted that his hand was still trembling as he unlocked the door and opened it. Then his tension dissolved and he invited, 'Come on in, Sergeant Matthews.'

As the policeman entered Jones shamefacedly indicated the stained tablecloth. 'I've spilt some tea. I'll just change it and brew a fresh pot. Will you have a cup?'

'I'd be glad of one, thanks.' The policeman smiled and gazed around him, appreciating the cleanliness and order of the austere room, its only bright colours the spines of the hundreds of books ranged on shelves which almost filled all the vacant wall space.

'I see you're a book-lover like myself, Mr Jones.' He moved to examine the titles. 'Oh, yes, I've read that one, and that. They're very good, aren't they?'

Knowing what he now knew about Ivor Jones, Denis Matthews was not surprised to see how many of the books were devoted to military history. He stooped to look more closely at one particular shelf, and asked, 'Are you an English Civil War buff, Mr Jones? You must have nearly everything that's been published about it in this collection.'

Jones was laying out cups and saucers on the fresh tablecloth. He nodded. 'Yes, I'm interested in that period. But to tell you the truth, it's Oliver Cromwell who really interests me. He's a bit of a hero of mine.'

The policeman nodded. 'Yes, I've always had a soft spot for "Old Noll" myself. What was it they called him . . .? "God's Greatest Englishman", wasn't it?'

'That's right,' Jones confirmed. 'And he really was a great man, wasn't he? We could do with him today, couldn't we? He'd soon put this country to rights.'

Matthews laughed, and joked, 'I reckon there's quite a few who'd agree with you there. I'm sure if he came beating his drums down that road right now, I'd be more than a little tempted to trail a pike after him myself.'

'I'd follow him without any hesitation. This country could do with a taste of fire and sword. It needs purifying.'

Jones was savage in his tone, and the policeman looked at him curiously for a couple of seconds, then said in an attempt to lighten the charged atmosphere so suddenly engendered, 'Well, you being a distinguished soldier like you are, Mr Jones, I don't doubt but that Old Noll would give you a warm welcome.'

He saw the questioning stare that this statement brought to the other man's face, and explained hastily.

'I've been reading the old newspaper reports about you, Mr Jones. One of the Falklands War heroes weren't you? The only chap from this city to get decorated for bravery in that campaign. Parachute Regiment, wasn't it, that you were in? Battle of Goose Green and the rest.'

'It was a long time ago, Sergeant.' Jones was quick to dismiss the subject. 'I've put that part of my life behind me. I follow another path now.'

Matthews' curiosity about his companion had been burning for weeks, and now he questioned eagerly, 'I can't help but wonder what made you become a preacher after you'd served for such a long time as a combat soldier?'

18

Jones frowned uneasily. 'I'm not an ordained minister of any church, Sergeant Matthews. I live here as resident caretaker, for which I receive this rent-free cottage. And I lead the services as a senior member of our congregation. The Chapel funds don't run to employing full-time preachers any longer.'

'But it's still a tremendous difference in life-style, isn't it, Mr Jones? Paratrooper to preacher,' the other man persisted.

'Not really,' Jones contradicted dourly. 'I was a Christian before I joined the Army, Sergeant. And I remained a Christian during my service. God has always had warriors to fight in His name; they make the finest sort of fighting men, Sergeant.' He smiled grimly. 'I would have thought that admiring Oliver Cromwell like you do, you would have appreciated that fact. He was one of God's warriors, after all.'

'He certainly was that,' Matthews agreed, then went on quietly, 'Well, what I've come about is your sister's case, Mr Jones. I'm sorry to say that we aren't having a great deal of luck with it so far. In fact, we aren't having any luck at all. To be frank, we're at a dead end. So, unfortunately, my superiors are going to scale down the enquiry.'

He saw the surprise in the other man's expression, and added hastily, 'The enquiry isn't being closed, Mr Jones . . . only scaled down . . . We've got such a heavy workload, you see, and we just don't have the resources. Since your sister's death we've had two more killings in the city, and we have to put men on them. But I'll still do whatever I can to track down the scum who caused the tragedy.'

With real regret he went on, 'I'm only sorry that I haven't got better news for you.'

The other man sighed heavily. 'It's not your fault,

Sergeant. It's the way the world is nowadays. People like me and my sister don't really count for anything. We're nobodies in the eyes of the authorities.' There was a harsh, bitter undertone in his voice.

Jones was silent and reflective for a few seconds, then he asked casually, 'That gang who stole my keys. Have you any ideas about who they are? You must be able to make a shrewd guess about their identities.'

Matthews looked stern. 'Now you know that I can't give you that sort of information, Mr Jones. I can't indulge in guesswork and speculation.'

'Why not?'

'Because I'm an officer of the law, and I'm bound by that law. I have to deal in proven fact, not guesswork.' He hesitated for a moment, his eyes troubled as he stared at his companion's grim features. Then he added, 'I've questioned several people that I suspected might have been involved in the mugging, but they've all got alibis for the time when you were robbed, and also for the estimated time of your sister's death . . . But if I was to tell you who they are, then you might well be tempted to take the law into your own hands, and try to have a go at them yourself to break their alibis.'

'And would that be such a wrong thing to do?' Jones demanded heatedly. 'To teach them a lesson by giving them a taste of their own medicine? You and I both know that for thugs like them alibis are very easy to arrange.'

The policeman hesitated, and considered his words very carefully. 'Off the record, Mr Jones, I personally would have every sympathy with you if you did that. But on the record, I would have to arrest you and charge you if you abused or hurt any of them in any way. No matter what you think they may have done to you, or to your sister, you are not allowed to take the law into your own hands. That way we would have anarchy in this country, and not the rule of law.'

Jones smiled bitterly. 'And what is it that we have in this country today, Sergeant Matthews, if it is not anarchy? No man or woman can walk the streets in safety any more. Nobody is even safe in their own home. The criminals ride roughshod over all of us, and the law does nothing to prevent them doing so. And the law protects the thugs by punishing people who fight back to protect their own family and property. I'd call that state of affairs anarchy.'

Inwardly Denis Matthews found himself agreeing with the other man's bitter statement. Outwardly he was forced to disagree. He shook his head.

'You're wrong, Mr Jones. We still have crime under control in this country. The rule of law still stands.'

He replaced his cup on the table and rose abruptly to his feet, eager to terminate this encounter which was forcing him to take uncomfortable stock of his own position and profession.

'I have to get along, Mr Jones. I hope I'll be able to bring you better news by and by.'

Jones nodded, and said quietly, 'Thank you for taking the trouble to call on me, Sergeant Matthews. Believe me, I truly appreciate what you're doing on my behalf.'

There was no irony in his tone, and the detective was touched by these thanks.

'It's my job, Mr Jones. There's no need for you to thank me.'

When the policeman had gone Ivor Jones sat down and stayed almost motionless for several hours, deep

21

in thought. During the past weeks of solitude he had become increasingly conscious of the fact that his sister's death had had a catalytic effect upon his psyche. Certain aspects of his character which had long lain dormant were once again rousing to savage life. The lust for revenge on those who had so mercilessly destroyed his beloved sister was burgeoning uncontrollably within him. He wanted to destroy them, to wipe them from the face of the earth.

'They made my poor Iris a victim. They showed her no mercy. And they made me a victim as well. A pathetic terrified victim, who couldn't defend himself. A victim who surrendered to them like a coward, and made no attempt to fight back.'

His fists clenched so that the knuckles bulged white, and his body shook with a terrible fury.

'I'll avenge you, Iris! I'll make the murdering bastards pay for what they did to you! I'm not a coward! I'm not a pathetic snivelling victim. And I'll show them that I'm not . . . I'll show the whole world that I'm not!'

He rose from his chair and started to pace restlessly up and down the cramped spaces between the sparse furnishings of the room. His thoughts were racing, wild ideas coming and going in rapid succession – ideas that made him simultaneously nervous and elated because of their audacity.

Later, when he felt calmer, and the wild ideas had – with increasing familiarity – begun to seem a little less wild and a little more feasible, he took a book from the packed shelves and sat down to read it, devouring the printed words as if they were food set before a man who was starving with hunger.

Hour after hour he read feverishly, taking down

other books, switching from one volume to the next and back again. Finally he closed the book on his lap and placed it on the small pile that had grown by the side of his chair.

His piercing blue eyes blinked in jerky, rapid succession and his head throbbed fiercely. Outside his window the dawn was paling the sky, and although he was very weary and his eyes ached for lack of sleep, he knew that he would not be able to rest. As he got out of the chair, his stiff joints creaked painfully. Taking his old overcoat from the wardrobe in his bedroom, he went out into the cold air and began to walk, leaving the terraces of houses far behind him as he headed towards the centre of the city.

At this hour of the morning only the occasional car hummed past him, and once a huge trailer lorry with French titles on its massive sides and Parisian number plates. He frowned after its roaring progress, resenting this reminder of the present foreign domination of his ancient nation, whose laws could now be overridden by European bureaucrats, and whose own ruling politicians, in his opinion, constantly placed foreign interests above those of the British people.

The city centre was a characterless mass of glass and concrete: cold, cheerless and inhuman. Propelled by the gusting wind, litter danced along the dirty pavements and was blown into doorways and alleyways where homeless human derelicts lay huddled in shapeless heaps beneath piled ragged coverings and cardboard tenting, snatching what uneasy sleep they could until the onset of the working day would drive them from their temporary havens.

A terrible sadness oppressed Jones as he walked slowly through the city centre, gazed at the crude defacing graffiti which covered every surface, and saw the shoddy ugliness on all sides.

'Oh, my God, who has done this to my home?'

Bitter resentment overlaid his sadness, and his anger burned against the glib politicians, the greedy speculators, the soul-less developers, the faceless bureaucrats who had taken from him the centuries-old city of his birth that he had known and loved so well, and had erected this monstrous creation in its place.

He retraced his footsteps out from the city centre and back towards Meadowpark Gospel Chapel. But now again his mood had changed. The sadness, resentment and burning anger had become channelled into a grim resolve. He kept on thinking about the man Cromwell, the man who had transformed a weak, corrupt, despised, godless nation into a great and feared power.

'Am I going mad?' Jones asked himself over and over again. 'How can I do anything at all to change what's happening here in this country? I'm an under-educated, fifty-year-old man, who preaches to a handful of people in a chapel that's falling down. Who would ever listen to me? I must be going mad. I really am mad!'

Yet despite all his self-castigation the insane conviction that he *could* do something persisted in his thoughts. And by the time he had reached his home and was lying exhausted on his narrow bed the grim resolve that he would fight back somehow, in some way, against those whom he conceived to be the destroyers of his country had hardened like steel in his mind.

# Chapter Four

Meadowpark Gospel Chapel was a relic of past glories. When it had first opened its doors in the heyday of Queen Victoria's Empire, its congregation had packed the serried pews of the vast main hall and balconies to listen to the hellfire-and-brimstone preachers thundering the words of the Lord from the high mahogany pulpit. Now the congregation once numbered in many hundreds had dwindled sadly. Instead of the prosperous shopkeepers, clerks and artisans, it was now the poor, the ageing, the unemployed, the dispirited remnants of a way of life that had all but disappeared who came on the Sabbath Day to huddle in the cavernous emptiness of the hall, and sing their hymns in praise of a God who seemed to have no real relevance in this modern world.

There were no hellfire-and-brimstone preachers thundering from the tall pulpit now. Instead Ivor Jones, as resident caretaker and unpaid preacher, led the services, and from time to time other members of the small congregation would take his place.

But despite the steep decline in numbers, in one sense the Chapel brotherhood had widened. West Indians had joined the shrunken ranks of the faithful. But they were only a small minority, because the majority of their fellow countrymen preferred the livelier services of the various Pentecostal churches which were scattered throughout the city.

Ivor Jones had been a member of the Gospel Chapel since childhood, and even while in the Army had retained his links with it. He and his wife had met and married there, and when they were children his two daughters had belonged to the Chapel Sunday School. Jones' relationship with the grim God he had been brought up to worship had altered from the blind faith of his childhood days. He had watched his beloved wife die slowly and foully with cancer; his daughters had both married men who were godless, and had themselves been only too eager to break free of the restrictions imposed by their religion. Since the death of their mother, both had virtually broken all contact with their father. Now, in his fiftieth year, Jones had all but lost his faith in God's ability, or even inclination, to intercede directly in human affairs. But he still believed that there was a God, and that he himself was a creature of that all-seeing divinity. This alteration in faith he kept to himself. But there were many times when he mounted to the pulpit on the Sabbath Day that he asked himself what he was doing there, mouthing platitudes to blank faces.

Tonight on this Sabbath, however, when he stood in the pulpit the faces beneath him were not blank. They were gazing with avid interest at his face, as if seeking for what the ordeal he had undergone had done to him.

He stared down at the scattered congregation, their numbers made to seem even smaller by the shadowed vastness of the hall, and ran his fingers nervously through his sparse, greying sandy hair. Then he tugged at the lapels of his ill-fitting black

26

suit, as if to draw it tighter around his stocky body. His piercing blue eyes blinked several times in rapid succession and he swallowed hard, causing his glottis to rise and fall jerkily.

'Brethren . . .' His voice sounded hoarse and cracked, and he coughed into his hand to clear his throat. Then he drew a deep breath, and for a few moments stared up at the damp-stained whitewashed ceiling, his lips moving soundlessly as if he were praying.

His gaze shifted back to the people ranged below him, and all his apparent nervousness appeared to leave him. When he spoke again his voice was full and firm, and his manner radiated a fervour which those who knew him had never seen him display before, despite his undoubted eloquence as a preacher.

'Brethren, I'm not going to preach about God. I'm not going to preach about Jesus Christ. I'm not going to talk about the Blood of the Lamb, and the redemption of sinners. And above all, I'm not going to tell you that the meek shall inherit the earth. Because it's very plain that they will never do that.'

As his voice rang out his listeners exchanged startled glances, and uneasiness and shock and doubt were in their eyes. This man was not the familiar Ivor Jones that they were accustomed to.

'You can all see this . . .' He pointed to the scar on his face. 'This happened on the day before my poor sister was so brutally murdered, when I was robbed in broad daylight in the centre of our city. There were many people in that shopping precinct at that time, brethren. But there was no Good Samaritan among them. People passed by, or stood to watch as if it were a show. No one offered to help me. Not while I was being attacked and robbed. Not when it was

27

over and the thugs who did it were running away. I was alone in that crowded place, brethren. As alone as if I were in the middle of a desert . . .'

He paused, and his voice dropped so that his audience was forced to listen hard to hear him.

'While the knife was being held against my throat, I called on the Lord to help me . . .' He shook his head slowly. 'But the Lord didn't heed my call.' Again he shook his head and his voice throbbed with sadness. 'I don't doubt that my sister also called on the Lord to help her, when her killer stood before her, poised to strike her down . . .'

By now the congregation was straining expectantly to hear him, engrossed completely in his words, and he smiled at them.

'I know that among you here today there are those whose homes have been broken into and robbed; in some cases three or even four times. I know that there are those who have been assaulted and beaten by thugs; those who are afraid to venture outside their doors after nightfall, who are even afraid to open their doors to any callers. I know that at some point in our lives most of us here today have been abused and threatened, and have had our lives made a misery and a burden by the actions of the lawless and the ungodly.'

Chorused murmurs of agreement ran through the pews, as Ivor Jones continued in a conversational tone.

'I'm sure that like my poor sister, and myself also in that moment of fearful need, you too have called upon the Lord to come to your aid.'

Heads nodded vigorously and Jones smiled sympathetically, then abruptly he scowled, shook his fists above his head and roared, 'But was your cry for help answered? Did the Lord come in all His power and majesty to save you? Did the heavens open? Did the fiery chariot appear? Did the Lord smite your enemies?'

His audience reacted with a stunned silence, and Ivor Jones lowered his clenched fists and said softly, 'Of course He did not come, brethren. The Lord cannot act in that way. He can only act through us. We have to be his instruments. His will has to be done through our minds and our bodies.'

Again he paused for long seconds, and his eyes swept challengingly across the upturned faces before him.

'I was a man who after experiencing the horrors of war turned towards the ways of peace. I tried to follow the teachings of Our Saviour. I tried to accept His command that if someone should strike me on my right cheek, then I should turn my left cheek to them also. I truly believed that some day the meek and the righteous and the godfearing would inherit the earth. Now I know how misguided my belief was.

'Since the day when my sister was murdered, I've been thinking very deeply about what is happening in our country, about the killings, the rapes, the robberies, the assaults. I've been thinking about the greed and corruption, about the continuous destruction of all that is good and decent in our way of life. I've been wondering why it is that we can no longer walk our streets in safety. Why we cannot even sit in our own homes in safety. I've been wondering why do the wrongdoers walk free? Why do the wicked prosper? Why have the evil inherited the earth?'

He pointed with outstretched arm at different people in the audience, his fingers shaking visibly.

'Do you know why?'

'Do you?'

'Do you?'

'Do you?'

'Do *you* know why?'

He clutched the rim of the pulpit with both hands and leaned over its edge, thrusting his head towards his listeners.

'The answer is very simple, my friends. Evil is triumphing because we are allowing it to do so. Even though the Lord God has given us minds to think with, and strength to strike with, we still sit waiting for Him to do what He has given us the right and the power to do for ourselves. We are expecting Him to do for us that which He wants and expects us to do for ourselves . . .'

He fell silent and his eyes switched from face to face as if inviting comment. Some of those faces looked puzzled, others doubtful and uncertain, a few hostile, and some turned away from his eyes. Then his gaze came to the pleasant, motherly features of Wisdom Maclure, a West Indian woman whose own life had been shattered by tragedy when her son was murdered by drug-dealers. Her eyes were narrowed and she seemed to be thinking hard, then she questioned him.

'Are you telling us, Brother Jones, that we ought to be fighting back against the wicked people ourselves?'

He nodded. 'Yes, Sister Maclure. That's exactly what I'm telling you. We must start to fight back against the evil ones, or we shall all be destroyed.'

'But we're only ordinary, simple people. What can we do about all the wickedness in the country today? The government should be doing something about it. That's their job, isn't it? To tell us all what to do, and to make the rules.'

Again he nodded to her, and smiled as if with satisfaction. 'You're quite right, Sister Maclure. It is the government's job to rule this country – to make the laws and to enforce those laws. But the government aren't doing their job, are they? That's why we have to do something about it ourselves.'

He straightened and stretched his arms wide, turning his upper body from side to side as if to embrace his audience. 'And I'll tell you all what we can do. We can unite! We can join together! Alone, we are powerless, but united we are strong. And when we are strong we will be able to strike back at those who oppress us, those who ill-treat and abuse us.'

His voice throbbed and his eyes gleamed with fanaticism.

'We must unite in the name of the Lord. We must raise His banner on high, and meet force with a greater force, and violence with a greater violence, until it is the wicked who walk the streets in fear, and the righteous who walk in safety.'

'But that's against the teachings of the bible,' a man objected.

'That depends on how we interpret the bible,' Jones retorted. 'Didn't Jesus use force to cleanse the temple? If he could do that, then we can use force to cleanse our country.'

'Vengeance is mine, saith the Lord,' the same man argued.

'We are acting as the Lord's instruments if we take vengence in His name,' Jones stated with utter conviction, and when the man would have answered he shouted him down.

'It will not be the first time in this country's history that the Lord has used a man to take His vengeance for Him. He used a man named Cromwell. He came

31

to Cromwell in a dream and told him that he must do the Lord's work. And Cromwell raised and trained an army. He saw a country that was wicked and corrupt, a country where evil was triumphant and good trampled down, and Cromwell led his army against the Lord's enemies and destroyed them. And he restored peace, and good government, and righteousness in the land.'

'But we're not an army,' a woman objected shrilly.

'We can become an army.' Fervour and absolute conviction glowed in Jones' eyes and pulsated in his voice, and to those who watched him he seemed to have grown in stature. 'We can become an army! All over this country there are millions of people just like us. Simple ordinary people who want only to lead their lives in peace, and in freedom from fear. Who want to bring their children up in decency. Who want to have their loved ones able to walk the streets in safety. Who want to get rid of all the filth and corruption that is polluting our land. All those millions of people are out there waiting for someone to show them the way to bring this about.

'We can show them that way! All we need is the faith and the courage to take the first steps on that journey.'

'But where will that journey lead us?' a voice questioned doubtfully.

'It will lead us into a land where good rules in triumph over evil,' Jones stated quietly.

For over a minute silence reigned in the hall, and Jones was content to see faces furrowed in thought. Then he went on softly, 'I am going to leave you now, brethren. I want you all to think very carefully about what I've said to you tonight. If any of you want to talk to me, then you know where I live, and you are welcome to call on me at any time.

'I intend to begin to fight back against the evil that is destroying this country. I want you to join me in that fight. Some of you may think that you are too old to fight. Too weak or ill. Too poor. Too ordinary to be able to make your voices heard, and your wishes heeded . . . If you are alone, then perhaps that is true . . . But if you all join together, if you stand united, you will no longer be too old, too weak, too ill, too poor, too ordinary. If you stand united you will be strong. And if you stand united under the banner of the Lord God, then you will be invincible!'

He turned from them, came down from the pulpit, and ignoring all efforts to catch his attention walked out of the hall.

Behind him he left silence. And then a babble of excited voices erupted, and the sound reached Jones' ears as he stood in the darkness of the Chapel grounds, and he smiled.

He felt elated and charged with energy and on impulse he left the grounds of the Chapel and began to walk the streets. The shabby terraces of Victorian houses gave way to the vast stretches of the Meadowpark Estate, a massive council development built to replace the festering slums which had once covered its site. Now its tall blocks of flats and rows of houses were beginning to resemble the slums it had superseded. Rusting wrecks of abandoned cars lined the streets, and the open stretches of grass and flower-beds which had been designed for children to play on and people to enjoy were now wastelands littered with rubbish, used condoms, discarded needles of addicts, empty cans and smashed bottles of cheap alcohol. The rows of shops were for the most part boarded up and left derelict, and those few which still remained in business were virtual fortresses with steel-meshed windows and doors, and watchful keepers.

Ivor Jones walked slowly past the neglected houses, the front gardens strewn with rubbish and filled with weeds. Only here and there did he pass a house and garden where some effort had been made to clean and trim and cultivate, and he found himself admiring the people who made that effort when surrounded on all sides by apparent abject surrender to hopelessness.

'It's here that I'll find my army,' he told himself. 'Behind these doors are the people who will follow me. There's still courage here, there're still people who refuse to give in.'

His brain was now beginning to plan ways and means of reaching these potential recruits.

'I need to let them know what I intend to do,' he told himself. 'I need to attract people who've been robbed or assaulted or worse, and who want to get even. I need to bring people to me who want to change the way things are.'

Abruptly he swung on his heels and began to walk quickly back in the direction of his home.

# Chapter Five

Sleep had eluded the woman, and she had lain in silent misery through the long hours of the night, dreading the coming of another meaningless day.

'Lisa, are you awake?' her husband whispered hoarsely, and then she felt his hands upon her breasts, and his mouth hungrily sucking her lips.

Her body went rigid with horror as the awful memories of that other man's hands, and mouth, and savagely biting teeth surged into her brain, blotting out all else.

She screamed and fought desperately, heaving and jerking to free herself from the imprisoning weight of that hot sweaty body; and then the crushing bulk lifted, the light came on, and she saw her husband's angry face glaring down at her.

She screwed her eyes tightly closed as the scalding tears brimmed, and choked out over and over again, 'I'm sorry. I'm sorry.'

The man rolled away from her and got out of the bed. Standing naked, his erection already beginning to soften, his features displayed a mingling of anger and despair as he studied her rigid body and distorted face.

The alarm clock on the side table began to bleep, and the man swore and cut off the monotonous, irritating noise with a swift movement of his hand. He grimaced and shrugged.

'Oh, well, I'd have had to finish too quickly anyway, so we wouldn't have had time to enjoy it.'

She made no reply, only continued to lie rigid and motionless, her full breasts rising and falling as she dragged in ragged breaths, her eyes still tightly screwed shut.

The man sighed heavily and left the room, and moments later she heard the rushing of water as he turned on the shower. Now the rigidity of her body relaxed a little, and she opened her eyes.

Wearily she swung her feet to the floor and stood up, catching sight of herself in the full-length wall mirror as she did so. She regarded her reflection with bitter eyes. The mirror showed her a shapely dark-haired woman in her mid-thirties: full-breasted, round-hipped, a handsome face with the olive skin of her Mediterranean ancestry. A woman whom many men desired. Once she had been proud of her looks and body. Now she felt something akin to loathing for them.

Lisa snatched up her thick woollen dressing-gown, dragging it on with frantic haste so that the voluminous folds would hide those breasts and hips and soft smooth skin.

She ran her fingers through her thick dark hair. Not so very long ago it had been long and lustrous, and many men had wanted to touch its heavy silken waves; but she had hacked off those long lustrous waves, leaving this grotesquely ragged crop. She wished desperately that she had the courage to scar her smooth skin, and to mutilate her full rounded breasts, so that never again would any man desire her.

While her husband showered and shaved she went downstairs to the kitchen and began to percolate coffee and to cook bacon and eggs.

The man frowned as he came into the room.

'I don't want anything to eat. Just coffee,' he snapped, and she cringed inwardly in expectation of what was to come – knowing that she must endure the same angry, scathing words, listen to the same glib clap-trap that he had gleaned from the Sunday supplements.

She went to leave the kitchen, but he moved to block her and told her harshly, 'No! Sit down. We've got to talk about this, Lisa.'

Realising the futility of protest she sat down on the chair facing his across the table, and with hands clasped on her lap and head submissively bowed, set herself to endure.

'You've got to pull yourself together, girl. You're ruining my life and your own. If the boys weren't away at school, you'd be ruining their lives as well.' His voice was high-pitched and querulous, and from beneath lowered lashes she covertly studied his smooth plump face, pink skinned and fresh from razor and aftershave.

'Good God above, Lisa, it's been nearly two years since it happened, you've had more than enough time to put it behind you. I've been patient, haven't I? Do you know of any other man who would have been half so patient?'

The querulous tone was now laced with self-pity.

'But I'm a man, Lisa. With all a man's natural needs and appetites. Why won't you get help? I'm willing to pay for the finest treatment that can be bought. With skilled help you could come to terms with what happened ... There's a chap in our

London office whose wife suffered the same as you did. She took therapy and counselling . . .'

His voice reverberated through the woman's skull, and mentally she mimicked the familiar tirade '. . . she took therapy and counselling, and now everything is back to normal . . .', the throaty chuckle . . . 'in fact, the chap tells me that their sex life is better now than it ever was . . .', the sly smile . . . 'we could be like that, Lisa . . . we could have wonderful times in bed, just like we used to . . . even better than we used to . . .'

Tiring of her inner mimicry, she mentally blocked out his voice. She was sick of hearing its smooth oiliness, just as she was sick of his smooth pink face and his smooth plump body, and his smooth soft hands, and his smooth suits and smooth shirts, and smooth ties and smooth socks and smooth bloody everything.

'Right, I'm off. If I wait any longer I'll get caught in the rush. Now give that chap that I told you about a ring. The number's on the hall table. I've already spoken to him about your case.'

He was on his feet now, considering whether or not he could risk kissing her goodbye

She remained with her head bowed, now feeling guilty that she loathed him so. Because in fairness to him, he had been a good husband and a caring father, and what had happened to her had not been his fault.

She experienced a sudden impulse to rise and go to him, and to throw her arms around him and tell him how sorry she was for him, and for the boys, and for what she was doing to their marriage.

'Look, Lisa.' The hectoring tone had re-entered his voice, and her impulse to comfort him shrivelled and died instantly. 'You just think about what I'm telling you, because I'm getting sick and tired of your behaviour. And I don't think that I can put up with it much longer. If a man can't satisfy his needs with his own wife, then he looks elsewhere. Remember that.'

The threat galvanised her into fierce reaction and she shot a venomous glare at him, causing his plump pink face to look shocked as she hissed, 'That filthy animal is free again. He's walking the streets of this city. You know that, and you do nothing about it!'

For a moment he frowned, then he flushed hotly and retorted defensively, 'But what can I do about it? He's served his sentence. He's been punished. It's all over and done with now.'

She came to her feet, shaking her head and pointing her trembling hand at his face.

'No! It's not all over and done with. I ran into that filthy animal last Saturday, when I was shopping in the city.' Her voice cracked. 'And he grinned into my face, and did this.' Using both hands, she made the obscene gestures which denoted sexual intercourse. 'I told you what happened, and you've done nothing!'

Now his lips became petulant, and he blustered, 'I reported the matter to the police, didn't I? And what did they tell me? They told me that there was nothing they could do unless he actually laid hands on you, or openly threatened you in front of witnesses. You must just ignore him, if you run into him again. He'll soon get tired of baiting you if you ignore him.'

Suddenly her body sagged, and she let her hands fall to her sides. She nodded dispiritedly and turned away.

He smiled brightly, as if satisfied that he had made her see sense. 'That's better, darling. You know that I'm right, don't you? Look, I really do have to go now. Don't forget to ring that psychiatrist chap, will you?'

As the front door slammed behind him, and she heard the car engine splutter into life and move away, Lisa Keegan slumped down on to the chair and, burying her face in her hands, allowed the maelstrom of seething emotions she was experiencing to overwhelm her. Hatred, anger, grief, pity, regret, remorse, bitter frustration swirled and pullulated within her brain until she feared that she would go mad.

She fought back, trying to impose rationality and order upon her thoughts, and gradually she calmed and slowly her chaotic jumbling of emotions soothed.

'Clive's right,' she accepted reluctantly. 'I do need help.'

But that realisation was not enough to impel her to go to the phone and call the number of the psychiatrist. Lisa had a lifelong prejudice against the jargon and glib theorising of the practitioners of what she considered a sadly flawed profession.

She moved slowly to the dresser and from one of its drawers took a sheaf of leaflets that she had accrued during the period since her terrible ordeal. Many of them were from militant feminist groups, Women Against Rape, Take Back the Night, Sisters in Arms. Others advertised the services of various therapists, counsellors and psychiatrists.

As she riffled through them, Lisa smiled wryly. It was amazing what a flourishing counselling industry the physical and mental abuse of women had given rise to. Before she herself had been so brutally raped and beaten, she had had no conception of the vast numbers of people involved in trying to help abused women. Her wry smile became bitter as she thought: 'What a pity they don't do more to prevent women being abused in the first place, instead of devoting all their energies to putting together the shattered pieces afterwards.'

She shook her head and scowled, castigating herself aloud. 'No, Lisa! That's enough! Don't go down that road again! Stop blaming the world for what happened to you. Do something about your own condition yourself!'

Almost in desperation she selected one leaflet, for the Victims' Mutual Support Group, and went into the hallway. After some moments of hesitation she lifted the phone and dialled the number printed on the bottom of the sheet.

'Hello, Lisa, welcome to our group. My name is Jeffrey Harper, but all my buddies call me Jeffy.' He smiled invitingly. 'I hope that you'll regard me as one of your buddies, Lisa. Because I think that you and I will get on really well together.'

The man who greeted her so fulsomely at the door, and grabbed and held her hand, was tall and painfully thin, and Lisa was forced to hide a smile. Jeffrey Harper was the 'Social Worker' of caricature; every inch of him proclaiming that he was a 'caring person' with his beard and sandals, his floppy sweater and designer-ragged jeans. Even his fluting, mid-Atlantic voice fitted the image, with its concerned, phoney-sounding warmth.

Still clasping her hand he led her into the centre of the large room, and she blushed with embarrassment as she felt curious eyes boring into her.

'Listen up, everyone,' Jeffrey fluted. 'We have a new buddy joining the group this evening. This is Lisa. Let's give her one of our group hellos, shall we?'

41

The next instant Lisa cringed physically and her embarrassed blush deepened uncontrollably as complete strangers crowded around her, hugging her affectionately, and telling her:

'Welcome, Lisa.'

'I'm so happy that you've joined us.'

'Welcome, new buddy.'

'You'll find peace and healing here, new buddy.'

'Welcome, Lisa.'

'Happy healing, new buddy.'

'Okay, people, let Lisa up for air. Go on, shoo, shooo!' Jeffrey playfully drove the cluster back, and directed Lisa to sit on one of the circle of easy chairs that dominated the floor space.

'Now you just settle yourself comfortably, new buddy, and relax. You're amongst buddies here. Good and true buddies.' He spoke to the rest at large. 'Who is she with, people?'

'Good and true buddies,' They chorused enthusiastically.

'And what do we do here, people?' Jeffrey questioned.

'We find healing and peace by understanding and forgiving those who caused us pain.' Their voices rang out, and some of them nodded and smiled encouragingly at Lisa.

Lisa felt constrained to smile also, but experienced the disconcerting certainty that those watching her so intently would easily discern that her smile was forced and false.

'Okay, let's all sit down and prepare, good buddies. Let's relax, open our minds, and let the good vibes flow,' Jeffrey fluted and clapped his hands as if in signal.

While the members of the group were settling

42

themselves into the easy chairs, and sitting back with closed eyes and beatific smiles wreathing their faces, Lisa seized the opportunity to take a closer look at her new companions. She saw that they were mostly women of varying ages, while the minority of men who were present looked to be of a uniformly older age group. There was nothing in the group's dress or bodily appearance to mark them out as victims. They appeared just a normal cross-section of people.

Lisa found herself feeling strangely comforted by this normality of appearance and dress. Since her brutal rape ordeal there had been many times when she had feared that because she had been a victim, there must be something about her that marked her out from the mass of her fellow citizens; some visible sign that proclaimed to the world at large, 'I am a victim!'

'All these people here are victims,' she told herself, and they all appear to be perfectly normal. I must look the same as them to anybody who passes me by in the street.'

She started to feel more at ease in these new surroundings, and her inner tension slackened.

After some time had elapsed Jeffrey again clapped his hands, and the group opened their eyes and smilingly began to hug and cuddle their immediate neighbours in the circle.

Lisa was again included in these physical demonstrations, and felt increasingly uncomfortable. She was not a tactile person at the best of times, and these repeated close contacts with complete strangers disturbed her.

'Okay, good buddies, let's begin,' Jeffrey instructed jocularly. 'I think it's your turn, Janine.'

Janine was a short plump woman wearing a voluminous brocaded kaftan. She stood up and with a nervous tremour in her voice declared, 'My name is Janine, and I am a victim.' She flushed and hesitated, staring beseechingly at Jeffrey, who urged, 'Go on, Janine, go on, good buddy. We want to share your pain with you.' He spoke to the gathering at large. 'What do we want to do, people?'

'We want to share our good buddy's pain with her,' they chorused.

Jeffrey once again directed his full attention towards the standing woman. 'Now just you go ahead, Janine.'

It was a command rather than request, and flushing more deeply the woman stammered, 'But I feel so embarrassed.'

'There's nothing to feel embarrassed about here, Janine. You're among your good buddies. We want to share your pain, and to help heal it.' Jeffrey was beginning to sound impatient, and the woman regarded him nervously, then began to stammer out an account of the rape which two men had committed upon her when she was returning home late at night after visiting friends.

Lisa found herself pitying Janine for the ordeal the woman had undergone, but also pitying her this further ordeal she was now undergoing in revealing yet again the intimate degradations to which her attackers had subjected her.

Covertly studying the other people around the circle, she was horrified by what she saw. While some of the faces mirrored a genuine concern and pity, others were more excited than concerned, more avidly prurient than pitying.

When Janine had finally faltered to the end of her

44

harrowing story, Jeffrey invited the other members of the circle to question her about aspects of the rape. Janine made a weak protest about being forced to endure fresh probing, but Jeffrey told her sternly, 'It's like lancing a poisonous boil, Janine. You must mentally squeeze the last traces of poison out, before you can begin the healing process.'

As the questions began to be hurled at the woman, she became greatly agitated and near to tears, and her distress was very clear to see. But the questioners were merciless in their interrogation. It was not until Janine actually broke down and began to sob that Jeffrey called a halt. Then, from the briefcase at his feet, he produced a folder.

'This is the transcript of the trial of Janine's attackers. And a profile of both of the guys. When I read it to you, you'll begin to understand what made them act as they did. Please, sit down, Janine. And I want you to pay particular attention to the profiles that I'm going to read to you. I think you'll find yourself able to understand why they attacked you, and with that understanding will come forgiveness.' He smiled around the circle. 'And what comes with understanding and forgiveness, people?'

'Peace and healing,' they chorused.

He began to read out what were virtually potted biographies of the two young men, placing great emphasis on their deprived childhoods, broken homes and lack of education. He traced their youthful criminalities, and the lack of any real parental love and guidance in their lives, and finished by saying that because of these deprivations it was inevitable that they would be driven to commit serious offences against their fellow citizens – that they were in fact more sinned against, than sinners.

Lisa sat listening to the muted exclamations of sympathy emitted at intervals during the reading by one or another of her companions, and began to feel that she was surrounded by simpletons and idiots. With the bitter memories of her own rape still raw and agonising, she could feel no sympathy or understanding for any rapist, and certainly not the faintest desire to forgive them. She felt her anger smouldering, and when Jeffrey began to tell Janine that she must try to understand and forgive her attackers, Lisa suddenly exploded.

'I think this is bloody monstrous, what you're doing to this poor woman,' she shouted at Jeffrey.

His thin face was utterly amazed as he stared at her.

Lisa jumped to her feet. 'And I think that the rest of you are bloody fools to listen to his garbage.'

'What do you mean, garbage?' he blustered indignantly.

Her dark eyes glinted with fury. 'No, it's not garbage.' She shook her head violently. 'I should have used a stronger word. It's shit! Complete and utter shit!' Her furious gaze swept around the circle of shocked faces. 'And I think that the rest of you are complete bloody shitheads to sit here listening to it. It's not understanding and forgiveness that's needed for rapists. It's castration!'

With that, she turned and hurried from the room, leaving a stunned silence behind her.


Clive was sitting in the living room watching television when Lisa got back to her home.

'Well? How was it? Has it helped you?' he demanded to know as she entered the room.

She stood silently staring at him. Even at a distance she could smell his expensive after-shave. And her lips quirked into a sneer as she took in the fact that he was freshly bathed and shaved, wearing a dressing gown, which she knew from experience was covering only nakedness.

Indignation surged through her as she realised: 'The bloody fool really thought that I was going to come back from that meeting and throw myself down with my legs wide open for him.'

The urge to cruelty swept over her, and she shook her head with open contempt. 'The meeting was a waste of bloody time. A collection of fools wanting to understand and forgive the filthy animals who'd hurt them!'

Disappointment spread across his smooth pink features. 'But I thought . . .'

'Don't bother trying to think, Clive,' she cut in witheringly. 'You haven't got the equipment for it.'

Petulant anger replaced the disappointment. 'Now look here, Lisa, I assumed that this would help you. And I'm not prepared . . .'

'No! *You* look here!' Again she shouted him down, and her body was shaking with the force of her anger against his perennial arrogant assumptions. 'I'm not prepared to go on allowing myself to be browbeaten by you, or anyone else, into seeking understanding for the animal who raped me. I don't want to understand him! I don't want to pity him! I don't want to forgive him!' She paused to draw in a sharp breath, and for an insane moment she felt like shrieking with laughter at the bemused expression on her husband's normally smugly complacent features.

'I only want one thing from the bastard who raped

me, Clive. I want his balls on a bloody plate! I want revenge!'

She turned away, telling him, 'I'm going to sleep in the spare room from now on. The door will be locked, so don't try coming in to me.'

'You've no right to sleep apart from me,' He blustered angrily.

'I've every right,' she retorted flatly, and left him puffing and blowing with impotent rage.

# Chapter Six

Chris Thompson was a very ambitious young man who considered himself to be too big a fish for this small pond he was currently swimming in. He lusted for the kudos and riches of his profession, which meant working for one of the great national newspapers instead of the provincial journal he was now with, the *City Gazette and Advertiser*. All his waking hours were dominated by his lust for 'the Big Story!' which would bring him national recognition, and gain him entrée to editors' offices in the grade of newspaper that he aspired to.

He was sitting at his desk, having just completed his piece on the Rotary Club's Annual Dinner and Dance, and he yawned and stretched, and glanced at the old wall clock – grimacing to see that it was still too early for him to sneak off for a lunchtime drink at the new wine bar which had just opened near to his office, and which boasted some very attractive young barmaids.

Sighing despondently, he allowed himself to become immersed in his favorite daydream. He had just achieved an exclusive on the story of the century, and was receiving the award for 'Investigative Journalist of the Year' from a great newspaper magnate who, while shaking his hand amid the admiring applause of thousands, was inviting him, Chris Thompson, to come and discuss his future career at the magnate's stately home.

'I hope I'm not disturbing you, Mr Thompson?'

Tony Prendergast, the assistant editor, rudely shattered the dream, and Thompson scowled and opened his eyes.

'What is it, Mr Prendergast? Can I be of service to you in any way?'

The two young men displayed their mutual loathing for each other with an elaborately sarcastic courtesy of address.

'I think that perhaps you might be able to help me with a small matter, Mr Thompson. But only if you're quite at liberty to do so, of course. I know that you're a man of affairs, and have very little time to spare from them.'

Thompson smiled charmingly. 'For you, Mr Prendergast, I shall create that liberty, and cast all other matters aside.'

Smiling equally charmingly, Prendergast offered profuse thanks, before continuing, 'I want you to do a feature for me. A guy got mugged in the shopping precinct down on Elmer Street a few weeks ago, and the very next day his sister got killed by burglars. You may have heard about it?'

Chris Thompson nodded his head. 'Yes, I did hear about it. But if you recall I was on holiday when it happened, so I didn't cover the story. And if you want me to do a feature on the number of killings and muggings taking place in the city these days, may I make so bold as to respectfully remind you that I did an article on the current epidemic of such crimes only three weeks ago.'

'Yes, I know you did, Mr Thompson.' Prendergast

assumed an air of humbleness, 'And believe me, I was very, very grateful to you for doing so. The article was quite brilliant. But this is a new assignment I'm giving you, as a follow-up. The guy I'm talking about is named Ivor Jones. He's a local war hero, decorated for gallantry in the Falklands campaign. I want you to go and see him, and do a feature on him. About fifteen hundred words or so. 'Hearts and flowers' treatment, Mr Thompson. Touch our readers' hearts with the pathos of this case. An old war hero assaulted and robbed, and his sister killed, in his home town where he was enjoying his well-deserved rest after the glories of his youth. How is he coping with his tragedy? Is there still life after it? You know the sort of thing I want. Use that purple prose that you do so well.'

Thompson rose to his feet and salaamed respectfully. 'To hear is to obey, Mr Prendergast.'

Abruptly tiring of the exchange, the assistant editor dropped a piece of notepaper on to the reporter's desk. 'Here's his address. He's a preacher of some sorts now. So make sure that you play up that angle. You can use Charlie for the pics.'

He turned and walked away, adding as he did so, 'And I want it by tomorrow noon at latest.'

Thompson scowled and lifted two fingers in a lewd salute to the other man's retreating back. And then he grinned and winked at the young girl junior who was wide-eyed in amazement at such a display of defiance.


Chris Thompson brought the car to a halt outside the grim edifice of the Gospel Chapel and grinned at the anorak-wearing man in the passenger seat beside him.

51

'If I had to live next to that, I'd rush out and beg somebody to mug and kill me.'

The photographer smiled politely, but said nothing.

'Do you know this guy, Ivor Jones?' Thompson queried.

The other man silently shook his head.

'Jesus!' Thompson thought wryly. 'It's no wonder the art of conversation is dying. I'm sure this guy is going to be one of the pall-bearers.'

Aloud, he said, 'Come on, then. Let's get to work.'

He got out of the car and waited while the photographer loaded himself up with camera and satchels, and then led the way up the broad entrance drive of the Chapel and around the side of the gaunt building to the front door of the adjoining Tabernacle Cottage.

There was a chill wind blowing and Thompson felt its biting edge through his thin silk designer suit. He shivered involuntarily and envied the dour photographer his warm anorak.

He hammered the warped panels of the door, muttering impatiently under his breath, 'Come on . . . come on . . . come on.'

The man who opened the door was of middle height and stockily built, his muscular shoulders and chest straining against the roll-necked sweater that he wore. His greying sandy hair was sparse on his shiny scalp, and his weathered features frowned at the two men on his doorstep.

'Good afternoon, sir. It is Mr Jones, isn't it? Mr Ivor Jones?' The reporter enquired with an ingratiating smile.

The man nodded curtly.

Thompson could not help but stare at the long

red scar on the man's cheek. Still angrily red and raw-looking.

'That's a nasty wound you had there, Mr Jones,' he stated sincerely.

'I'll live,' Jones replied gruffly. 'Now, who are you?'

'We're from the *Gazette and Advertiser*. My name's Chris Thompson.' The reporter proffered his press card. 'I'd like to talk to you about what happened to you and the tragic death of your sister. I've been doing a series on local crime. I expect you've been reading it?'

Jones shook his head. 'No, I don't read the *Gazette* any more.'

Thompson grinned, as he shook his finger and said archly, 'You naughty man, you! Everybody should read the *Gazette*. You have to support your local paper, you know.'

He saw the scowl of irritation cross the other man's face, and mentally chided himself: 'Steady, Chris, boy. You're taking the wrong tack with this guy.'

'Can we come in and talk to you, Mr Jones, and take a couple of pictures? You'll want our readers to hear your story, I'm sure.'

He began to move forward, but Jones remained standing blocking the door, and the younger man was forced to halt uncertainly.

'Is anything the matter, Mr Jones?' He was becoming increasingly aware that this man was not what he had expected to find. With his fiery blue eyes, hard features and powerful body, he was an unusually tough-looking physical type for a preacher.

Jones shook his head. 'No, nothing is wrong. I just don't want to talk to you just now.'

'Don't you want to let the people of this city know your story?' Chris Thompson demanded.

Again Jones shook his head. 'No. It's not their concern.'

'Excuse me, Mr Jones, but I think that violent crime is everybody's concern,' the young man asserted vehemently.

He saw the sudden glint of anger in the keen blue eyes, and was puzzled by this reaction. For a brief instant he was tempted to accept defeat and leave now; he wasn't very interested in doing this feature anyway. Then in his mind's eye he saw the face of the hated Tony Prendergast, and decided mentally, 'Oh no, you bastard. I'm not going to give you the opportunity to crow over any failure of mine to interview this awkward sod.'

He assumed a sympathetic smile, and tried a softer approach. 'The thing is, Mr Jones, what happened to you and your poor sister was a disgrace. I know that so far nobody has come forward to identify your assailants. Maybe, when we publish the feature about you, someone will feel sufficiently ashamed of themselves to do so. I'm sure a lot of people will feel sorry for you.'

He was taken aback by the wild glare that sprang into Jones' eyes, and the clenching of the man's big fists.

'That's the very reason why I don't want this story in the paper,' Jones gritted out. 'I don't want anybody to feel sorry for me. I don't want them to regard me as a helpless victim. And I don't care about trying to make any witnesses feel ashamed they haven't come forward.' He paused, and seemed to be trying to come to a decision. As if making that decision, he continued abruptly, 'It's me that's feeling

54

ashamed. Do you understand that? I'm ashamed for allowing those thugs to do such a thing to me. I'm ashamed for behaving like a coward, for letting them rob me in broad daylight without even trying to put up a fight. If I'd kept my keys, then perhaps my sister would still be alive.'

Chris Thompson's veneer of worldly-wise cynicism was penetrated by the obvious sincerity of this impassioned outburst. He experienced a sudden sympathy for the other man.

'But you shouldn't feel like that,' he declared with genuine conviction. 'God only knows, with your military record no one could ever begin to think that you're a coward. And all the experts say that when a mugger attacks you, then the correct thing to do is to simply give him whatever he wants and not to try and resist. That way you avoid serious injury.'

'Like I avoided it,' Jones challenged furiously, and pointed to the long red scar on his face. 'Like my sister avoided it?'

'Your sister's death wasn't your fault, Mr Jones. And if you'd put up a fight then the chances are you might have been very badly hurt, or even killed.'

'Yes, I might have been badly hurt, or killed. But on the other hand I might have managed to badly hurt or even kill one of them.'

'But then you would have been in serious trouble yourself, wouldn't you, Mr Jones?' The reporter spoke as if he were lecturing a stupid child. 'The police would have arrested you, and you would have been facing a charge of murder or assault.'

A bitter smile twisted Ivor Jones' lips, and he nodded slowly. 'Exactly so, young man. I'm living in a country where if a man breaks into my house to steal my property, or mugs me on the streets, I'm not allowed to hurt him. I'm expected to submit to whatever he chooses to do to me, and then report him to the police.'

'Oh, come now, I don't believe that that is the case at all,' the reporter chided. 'You're entitled to use reasonable force to defend yourself, or your property.'

'And that is exactly what I intend doing in the future.' Jones' bitter smile was again in evidence. 'Only I shan't be bothering to stop and wonder what constitutes reasonable force. I shall use whatever force I think is needed, and I'm hoping to persuade many other people to join me in that aim.'

Chris Thompson's highly developed instincts for a news story reacted instantly to that final sentence.

'What do you mean by that, Mr Jones? You're hoping to persuade other people to join you in that aim?'

Jones seemed on the verge of replying, then he suddenly checked the hovering words, and shook his head. 'It's a bit too soon to tell you that,' he replied. 'Now I'll say goodbye to you, young man. I'm sorry if you've had a wasted journey, but I'm not ready to talk to you yet.'

He stepped back inside his cottage and firmly closed the door.

Thompson lifted his hand to knock on the panels, then changed his mind and shrugged.

'Goodbye then, Mr Jones.' He knelt and pushed one of his business cards under the door, and called out, 'There's my address and telephone number if you change your mind about talking to me.'

Back in the car he fired the engine, then sat for a few moments turning over in his mind what the man had said. He turned to the photographer beside him.

'What did you think of him?'

The photographer shrugged non-committally.

Chris Thompson sighed with exasperation, but persevered. 'Did you hear what he said, about using force and persuading other people to join him?'

The other man nodded.

'Well, what do you think?' The young reporter's instincts were telling him that Ivor Jones would in some way or other become the subject of a newsworthy story. 'Do you reckon he's going to set up as a vigilante?'

His companion shrugged non-committally once more, and accepting defeat Chris Thompson drew away from the kerb. But he could not shake off the strange conviction that Ivor Jones was going to do something sensational.

Unknown to him, the confirmation of that conviction was passing him on the pavement as he drove away.

Dorothy Chapman, a small, shabbily dressed, worn-faced woman in her mid-thirties, came to the Gospel Chapel entrance and stood for some moments summoning up the courage to go up the entrance drive and knock at the door of the cottage.

When she finally did so, Ivor Jones opened the door with a menacing scowl on his face, and in alarm she flinched back from him.

The moment he saw her he instantly apologised. 'I'm sorry. I've just had a reporter pestering me, and I thought he'd come back again.'

He smiled, and that smile transformed his hard features, making him appear kindly and approachable. 'Did you want to see me, Mrs?' His voice became a question.

'Mrs Chapman. Me name's Mrs Chapman,' the

small woman informed him timidly. 'I'm a neighbour of Mrs Maclure. She said that you might be able to help me.'

'Oh, Wisdom Maclure, you mean. Yes, she's a good friend of mine.' He stepped back. 'Come on in, Mrs Chapman.'

Inside she gazed with awe at the serried shelves of books, and murmured, 'You must read a lot, Mr Jones.'

'Too much,' he confirmed, with a rueful smile. 'Please, won't you sit down. Would you like a cup of tea?'

'Oh, no, thank you, Mr Jones,' she flustered, as she seated herself on one of the straight-backed wooden chairs and perched on the edge of the seat, tense and fluttery-breathed, like a frightened bird ready to fly from danger.

'Now, how can I help you?' Jones' kindly manner put her more at ease.

'It's me daughters, Tina and Jenny, Mr Jones. They've got into bad ways, and I can't do nothing with them. Since their Dad run off and left us, they've got more and more wild. And there's nothing I can do or say which seems to make any difference to 'em.' Her voice faltered and broke and she started to sob. 'I'm sorry,' she choked out. 'I'll be all right in a minute.'

Ivor Jones waited patiently until she had recovered herself sufficiently to be coherent, and then asked her puzzledly, 'But what is it that you think I can do to help you, Mrs Chapman? I'm sorry naturally to hear that your daughters are playing you up so badly, but how can I help in the matter?'

Her small worn face was woebegone and tear-stained as she stared beseechingly at him, and he found himself pitying her from the bottom of his heart.

'Wisdom Maclure said that last weekend in the Chapel you was telling them how we'd all got to join together to fight them who was doing bad to us, Mr Jones.' She spoke rapidly, in a tremulous voice.

'That's right, Mrs Chapman,' he confirmed readily. 'And I meant every word that I said. We must unite and stand up for ourselves, because nobody else is going to stand up for us if we don't.'

'Well, that's just it, Mr Jones. I've got nobody to stand up for me. My girls have got in with bad company. They'm out all night and every night. They've started taking drugs, Mr Jones. They goes to the Rec. and gets drugs from the dealers there. A lot of the kids from the estate does it. The dealers are there nearly every night. They needs to be drove away, Mr Jones – Drove away from my girls and the rest of the kids.'

Ivor Jones regarded the woman with a sombre expression on his face. 'And you want me to drive the dealers away from the Rec., do you, Mrs Chapman?'

She nodded slowly. 'Wisdom Maclure told me that you said you was going to start fighting back against the evil people, Mr Jones. And I thought that if you was going to fight against them, then I could help you, and you could help me to drive them drug-dealers from off the Rec.'

Ivor Jones pursed his lips and sat deep in thought. The 'Rec.' the woman talked about was a stretch of recreation ground on the Meadowpark Council Estate which had been designed for games pitches and contained a children's playground in one corner of its expanse. During the last few years the Rec. had gained an unsavoury reputation; it had become the haunt of child molesters and other types of pervert, and a favourite meeting place for teenagers up to mischief.

While Jones sat silently thinking over what he had heard, Dorothy Chapman started anxiously at him with red-rimmed eyes made puffy by tears. Finally he drew a sharp hissing intake of breath, and smiled at her.

'Come to the Chapel for the Sunday evening service, Mrs Chapman,' he instructed. 'I'll help you.'

When the small woman had gone, tearfully thanking him even as he closed the door after her, Ivor Jones went to stand for a long time staring out of the window at the dull overcast skies. Then he suddenly slumped down on to his knees, and clasping his hands before him began to pray fervently to the grim God of hellfire that he had been indoctrinated to believe in as a child.

# *Chapter Seven*

During the days that followed Mrs Chapman's visit to him, other people came to call on Ivor Jones, and all of those who called wanted to know how exactly he intended to fight back against evil?

To this question his answer was to ask them, 'Do you think it is right to use force against evil?'

The majority affirmed that they did, and then Jones asked them, 'Are you prepared yourself to personally use force against evil?'

About a third affirmed to this too, and to these Jones said, 'Then come to the Chapel next Sunday evening. If you have friends or acquaintances who think as you do, then bring them along also.'

To those who answered that they personally were not prepared to use force, he said, 'I respect your views on this matter, but I do not agree with them. However, let us part as friends.'

Jones also spent many hours in the city's central library poring over the bound volumes of previous years' *Gazette*. From these he extracted the names of victims of various crimes and noted them down, together with the details of the crimes committed against them. He also extracted the names of those accused or convicted of committing those crimes and entered those details too. Then he asked for the electoral registers and tried to match as many of the names as he could to current addresses.

He spent Sunday morning re-reading a biography of Oliver Cromwell, and the afternoon in praying to his God for guidance. Then, tense and nervous, he went into the Meadowpark Gospel Chapel in the early evening.

The hall was almost a third filled and when Ivor Jones climbed into the pulpit a susuration of voices greeted him, and rows of curious eyes stared up at him. He stood for some moments silently surveying the congregation. There were all ages represented here, from the old to the young, both white and coloured. His initial nervousness evaporated and excitement burgeoned within him as he realised that these people had gathered together because of *him*. That all these people before him had come to listen to what he had to say. A sense of power pulsed in his brain, and he felt as if he were expanding both physically and mentally in strength and ability.

He drew a long, deep breath, and then his voice rang out across the hall.

'Brethren . . . Friends . . . It is our turn to make our voices heard. For too long we have sat in silence and allowed vociferous minorities to dictate what happens in our country. For too long the "do-gooders", the "bleeding hearts", the self-styled "carers and sharers" have been dictating how we should deal with the thugs and murderers and rapists who infest our land. And what have they achieved?'

He paused, then answered his own question.

'A land where no one is safe. A land where the interests of the criminals are put first, and their victims are forgotten! A land where millions of pounds are spent to ensure the comfort and wellbeing of convicted criminals, but where the old, the sick and the poor must endure cold, and hunger, and hardship . . .'

Heads nodded agreement, and voices sounded in encouragement.

'You're right!'

'That's the truth!'

'Speak out for the Lord's people!'

'Amen!'

Ivor Jones nodded back, and then declared ringingly, 'Well, I for one am sick and tired of being told by these do-gooders that criminals who rob and rape and murder are just pathetic victims of their environment! That the thugs only need love and attention and they will reform and become good citizens!

'I am sick and tired of seeing thieves, rapists and murderers being set free to rob and rape and murder again and again and again!'

Now shouts of agreement and plaudits rang out from the rows beneath him and as his eyes ranged across the eager excited faces a sense of exultation caused his chest to swell and his own excitement to soar.

'We must unite, friends. We must form our own organisation to fight against the evil that is flourishing all around us. If we stand together we shall be strong. As individuals alone, we are powerless to influence anyone in power. But if there are sufficient numbers of us standing together, then we can make those in power listen to what we have to say.

'As individual citizens we are powerless to influence, or even to question effectively the actions and motives of whichever political party happens to be in control at the time. As members of an organisation

. . . as our numbers grow . . . then we will be able to question our political masters. They will no longer be able, as they do now, to ignore with impunity the ordinary members of our society who want to know why the government is so soft on criminals.'

Loud clapping and applause momentarily drowned his voice, and he waited for the noise to subside before continuing. Then, very sombrely, he told them, 'But it's no use merely to talk, and to ask questions, and to plead for someone else to take action on our behalf. History shows us that those who merely talk, and plead, and wait for others to act, achieve nothing. Anyone who joins me in my organisation must be prepared to take militant action if needs be. They must be ready to stand in the front line if that is necessary.'

He noted that some of his audience appeared doubtful at this idea that they themselves might be placed in any danger, but there were many others to whom the idea appeared to appeal judging from their nods of approval. He hesitated for a second or two, then decided to put into effect the idea that had suddenly sprung into his mind while he was speaking.

He went on in a quiet, calm voice. 'Just about three-quarters of a mile away from this hall, there is a children's playground. At least, that is what it was originally intended for when this estate was first built. There are swings there, and roundabouts and climbing frames and see-saws. All those children's playthings have been vandalised now. But children still go to that playground. Only they don't go there to play on swings and roundabouts any more; they go there to sniff glue, and to buy drugs from the dealers who've taken over there. Even now as I'm talking to you, the drug-dealers are selling their filthy wares to our children on that same play area.'

There was a rumbling of anger from his audience.

'I know that the police have done their best to stop the drug dealing there. But because of the obstacles placed in their path by recent legislation, there is not much that they can do to take the drug-dealers off the streets. And so, day after day, week after week, month after month, year after year, our children are being corrupted, degraded and destroyed by evil men. And the evil men can do this with impunity, because good men are doing nothing to stop them!'

Jones stretched himself to his full height, and his blue eyes gleamed as he invited, 'Which of you good people will come with me now, and drive those evil men away from that play area? As Jesus cleansed the temple, let us now cleanse our own place.'

There were brief moments of silence, then the small shabby figure of Dorothy Chapman rose up, and she shouted 'I'll come with you, Mr Jones! I'll help you!'

Other men and women rose from their seats as he came down from the pulpit and walked up the central aisle towards the entrance door. Then a cheer erupted and from all over the hall more men and women came out from the pews to follow him.

Outside, the yellow sodium lamps cast their baleful light over damp, dark roads, and the air was chill. The long strip of glistening macadam stretched before them as they walked in straggling procession with Ivor Jones in the lead. After only a few paces, Jones threw back his head and sang out in a powerful baritone the first words of the 'Battle Hymn of the Republic'.

'Mine eyes have seen the glory of the coming
    of the Lord;
He is trampling out the vintage where the grapes
    of wrath are stored . . .'

Behind him his followers took up the refrain and
the roaring of their voices echoed out along the
night-shrouded street:

'He hath loosed the fateful lightning of His
    terrible swift sword; His truth is marching
    on . . .
Glory, glory, Halleluiah
Glory, glory, Halleluiah
Glory, glory, Halleluiah
His truth goes marching on . . .'

In most of the houses they passed the sound of the
television drowned out any noises from the streets
outside, but there were several curtains twitched back
on the line of march and people peered out at the
passing singers and wondered what was happening.

As they neared the wide-open space of the recreation ground where the play area was situated, Jones
held up his hand in signal to halt and gathered his
followers around him.

'Do any of you know these drug-dealers?'

'I know some of their faces,' a young woman
declared.

'My kids pointed one out to me the other day,'
a man informed Jones. 'I'll know him again if I
see him.'

Now that the moment for action had arrived, Ivor
Jones experienced the sickening realisation that by
acting as he had on the spur of the moment, he had

led these people here without any plan of action, and without really knowing what should be done. He felt confused and helpless. He stared across the grass and was able to make out the clusters of dark shapes around the vandalised artefacts of the play area. There were a lot of those shapes, numbering more than his followers. For a brief moment he was tempted to call this action off, but even as the wish tempted he realised that should he do so, then the tenuous domination he had achieved over these people would instantly disappear, and he would become a figure of fun to them. A man who could only speak empty words. A charlatan who could not perform deeds to match his promises.

He was acutely conscious of the dawning doubt in the faces around him as he hesitated, and in his mind he begged. 'Oh, Lord, help me . . . Please help me . . . Don't let me fail these people now.'

'Well, what are we going to do?' a voice challenged him impatiently.

A sudden sense of certainty surged up in Ivor Jones' mind, and his brain cleared of all extraneous thoughts. It was as if the words that now flowed from him came from a source outside his own being.

'We are going to drive the evil men away from our children, brethren. Follow me and let them know the wrath of the Lord's people.'

In an unwieldy mob they surged behind Ivor Jones across the open ground towards the distant play area, roaring out their new-found battle song.

'Mine eyes have seen the glory of the coming
    of the Lord.
He is trampling out the vintage where the grapes
    of wrath are stored . . .

At the play area where the shadows were only lightened by the distant street-lamps, Leroy Murchison heard from the distance the approaching echoes of the roaring hymn, but paid them no attention. He was too intent on haggling over the price of an 'Ecstacy' pill with a young customer. Around the pair other groups clustered about the vandalised swings and seesaws, some likewise haggling prices with Murchison's friends and helpers. The acrid scents of 'joints' hung heavy in the air, and large paper bags rustled as glue was shaken up to release its toxic fumes, while youthful voices bantered and laughed and swore and flirted sexually.

Money changed hands and Leroy Murchison completed his business. He fingered the plastic bag in his pocket, savouring the feel of the rocks of 'Crack' it contained. There was no market for that here, the price was too high for his school-aged customers. But he knew that later he would be able to dispose of it easily in the illegal late-night drinking clubs around the city centre.

Now, though, he was feeling hungry for sex and he moved through the clusters of teenage boys and girls like some feral beast seeking prey. He found the girl he saught, under-aged, but big-breasted and firm-fleshed, and he drew her aside and talked in low-pitched urgency.

'Come on, Jenny, come with me. I've been really missing you.'

At first she resisted his advances, but he persisted and judiciously fed her tablets and shared his joint with her and at last she went with him away from the play area and across the open grass into the deeper shadows further from the street-lights.

He was about to pull her to the ground when he heard the roaring voices . . .

'He hath loosed the fateful lightning of His
   terrible swift sword:
'His truth is marching on . . .'

'What the fuck?' He peered around him and sighted a mob of dark figures coming towards the play area from the road on the far side of the recreation ground.

'What's up, Leroy?' the girl asked. 'Who're they?'

'Shut your fuckin' mouth!' he told her roughly.

Frightened by his abrupt change of manner Jenny Chapman tried to pull free of his grip, but he hissed threateningly at her to stand still as he watched the dark figures.

Then, from the mob of advancing people there came loud shouts of . . .

'Police! Police! Stay where you are!'

There was instant pandemonium as the teenagers panicked and scattered in all directions, girls screaming, boys shouting and cursing.

Leroy Murchison kept his head. Snatching his switch-blade knife from his pocket, he knelt and cut a flap of turf which he lifted. He stuffed the plastic bag containing the rocks of 'Crack' and the other drugs under the flap, and put his knife there as well. Then he stood and stamped the flap down, mentally memorising his position in relation to the road and play area as he did so. He turned and quickly looked all about him, and saw that the way to his car parked at the farthest end of the area was still clear. He began to run, and the young girl shrieked in fright.

'Don't leave me, Leroy! Wait for me! Wait!'

He kept on running and she tried to follow him, but her long stiletto heels twisted beneath her ankles and she fell to the ground.

Around the play area the mob had collided with some of the fleeing teenagers; punches were thrown and threats, curses and shouts filled the air.

'Jenny? Tina? Jenny? Tina?' Shrieking out their names over and over again, Dorothy Chapman stumbled through the darkness seeking her daughters.

A man bellowed out in pain as a kick took him between the legs and he slumped to his knees, and a woman squealed as a fleeing teenager elbowed her savagely in the face. Blood spattered as one of the dealers fought desperately to free himself from clutching hands, and as he was borne to the ground by sheer weight of numbers he screamed out, 'Leroy! Leroy! Help me, Leroy!'

Panting heavily, Leroy Muchison reached the car and snatched at the door-handle. As his fingers clutched the cold metal, he turned to look behind him and saw that no one was in pursuit.

'It can't be the fuckin' pigs!' Suddenly he doubted.

As he screwed up his eyes and peered back through the darkness, he could make out the seething mass of bodies around the play area. For a brief instant he pondered whether or not to return and confront the intruders, then dismissed that idea. There was always the chance that they might be the pigs, after all.

He jumped into his car and roared away from the estate.

Back at the play area the scuffling had ceased, all but two or three of the teenagers had made their escape. The captured youngsters were held motionless by many hands, and one by one Ivor

Jones faced them as matches were lit to illuminate their youthful, frightened faces.

'That's one of them. That's the one my kids pointed out,' a man's voice shouted. 'He's one of the dealers!'

The youth who had been so identified was white, and he began to struggle violently against the imprisoning hands. Then from behind he was gripped in a choking stranglehold and he subsided, gasping out, 'I won't make no trouble. You're hurting me. You're hurting me!'

Those who held his arms loosened their grips, and the arm around his throat was withdrawn.

'What shall we do with him, Mister Jones?' a man asked.

'Let's turn him over to the police,' a second man suggested, and others agreed.

Ivor Jones frowned and thought for a few moments. Then he instructed, 'Search him.'

The youth made no resistance as hands went through his pockets and clothing.

'Nothing! He's got nothing on him, Mister Jones.' The searcher almost groaned with disappointment.

Jones sighed. 'Let him go. And let the rest go as well.'

As the men drew back Jones stepped forward to stand facing the drug-dealer. 'We know you now,' he snapped curtly, 'and if you ever show your face on this estate again, you won't get away so lightly. Tell the rest of your friends, too, that the next time any one of them so much as shows his face around here, we'll finish what we've started tonight.'

He signalled for the captors to release the youth, who immediately loped away into the darkness, while the other teenagers ran off in different directions.

71

'Look at this lot,' a woman declared jubilantly, and indicated a tiny pile of glue-bags, half-smoked joints and assorted tablets.

People began to crowd around Ivor Jones, their voices babbling excitedly as they congratulated him on his generalship. He hid his own grave doubts concerning the way he had led them and told them all, 'We've done well tonight. We've carried out the Lord's work, and dealt the drug-dealers a blow. I don't think that they'll return here in a hurry.'

His listeners cheered, and one volunteered, 'I'll take this lot and burn it, shall I?' He pulled out a handkerchief and carefully gathered the tiny pile into it.

'Has anyone been hurt?' Jones questioned, and was relieved to find that the injuries suffered by his followers were only superficial cuts and bruises. Then he instructed, 'We'd better split up now, before we have the police arriving to see what's going on. Many thanks, and God bless you all.'

They parted, some in small groups, others walking singly, and dispersed into the night talking and laughing excitedly – jubilant at what they saw as a victory.

But Ivor Jones, walking slowly alone, was not jubilant. Instead he felt angry at himself for what he considered to have been his crass leadership.

'I won't make this mistake again,' he promised himself. 'From now on I'll organise. I'll get the priorities in the correct order. By acting so stupidly tonight, I nearly lost this war before it's even properly begun. If I'm to win, then I need an army. A properly trained and disciplined army. I need men who are accustomed to violence. And most of all I need to plan carefully. To map out every single step before I take it . . .'

# Chapter Eight

As the designated crime reporter of the *Gazette and Advertiser* Chris Thompson had cultivated contacts among the city police, and each working morning he would phone the Central Station and ask what was happening on the crime front.

On the Monday morning following the clash between the drug-dealers and Ivor Jones' followers, the young reporter made his usual telephone call, and spoke to Detective Sergeant Denis Matthews. After an exchange of good-natured banter, Thompson asked if there was anything for him, and the policeman gave details of the normal weekend fights, burglaries, car thefts etc.

'Jesus! Haven't you got a juicy murder for me, Denis?' Thompson complained jokingly. 'I'm sick of the same old boring stuff every Monday morning. I'm desperate for something different.'

The policeman chuckled, and sifted through the pile of reports in front of him. Then he lifted one out, and briefly scanned it. 'There's something here that might interest you, Chris. We've had a report of a bunch of people having a go at some teenage yobs on the Recreation Ground at Meadowpark Estate last night. The station received an anonymous phone call saying that there was a real battle going on in the

73

Rec. One of our cars checked it out, but when they got there everything was quiet.'

'Well, thanks for nothing, Denis. That sounds like the non-event of the year. Should make a great story. Police car reports that the Rec. was empty!'

The policeman chuckled, but then added, 'Something had gone off though, Chris. When our lads made a few enquiries some of the locals told them that a gang of people had gone charging across the Rec. singing bloody hymns, and there'd been a fight.'

Instantly Chris Thompson's interest was sparked. 'Singing hymns?'

'Yeah, singing hymns. Probably a Salvation Army recruiting drive,' Matthews joked.

Thompson laughed dutifully, and after thanking the policeman rang off. Then he sat drumming his fingers on the desk in front of him.

'Ivor Jones said he was going to do something, didn't he? He said he was going to get others to join him. Who else would be singing bloody hymns?'

Thompson knew the unsavoury reputation of the Rec. And he knew that teenagers gathered there to take drugs and have sex, and generally create an uproar.

'I wonder if Jones has got a bunch of vigilantes together? I wonder if he decided to have a go at cleaning up the Rec.?'

On impulse Chris Thompson jumped up and hurried from the office.

Ivor Jones opened the door of Tabernacle Cottage to Chris Thompson's insistent knocking, and frowned in surprise when he recognised his visitor.

The reporter had already decided on his course of

action during his journey across the city, and he gave the other man no chance to speak.

'I've come about last night, Mr Jones. I'd like to know your side of the story.' He nodded confidently. 'I know for certain that it was you who led those people on to the Rec. You've formed a group of vigilantes, haven't you?'

For long moments the stocky man stood silently frowning, and Thompson began to wonder if he had jumped to the wrong conclusions. Then Jones stepped back and invited, 'You'd better come in, young man.'

The reporter entered with relief, and when Jones asked him if he would like a cup of tea he readily accepted. While the other man was brewing the pot Thompson stared curiously around the small, austere room. He was surprised at the numbers of books, and even more surprised when he studied the titles to discover that Jones' reading tastes, while very definitely biased towards military subjects, also seemed to be directed towards the cultivation of intellect and the acquisition of a broad base of knowledge.

When they both had cups of tea on the small table between them, Chris Thompson's professionalism came to the fore, and he began to probe for details of what had happened the previous night. Ivor Jones answered without hesitation, and certain aspects of what he said both delighted and intrigued the reporter. Even as he made notes he was visualising various headlines:

'CHURCH LAMBS TURN INTO WOLVES.'

'BIBLE PUNCHERS PUNCH OUT DRUG-DEALERS.'

'ARMY OF THE LORD IN ACTION.'

When he had obtained the material for his story,

Thompson asked, 'Do you realise that you could get into trouble with the police for doing what you did, Mr Jones?'

The piercing blue eyes were steady upon him.

'Of course I realise, young man.'

'Naturally you'll not do anything like this again, will you?'

'I most certainly shall,' Jones declared firmly, and with no hint of bombast continued, 'I have declared war on the criminals who infest this nation, Mr Thompson. Last night's effort was only the firing of the first shots in this war. It was amateurish, I know, and in all honesty very ineffectual. But future operations will not be so amateurish or ineffectual.'

Chris Thompson sat up straighter in his chair and stared hard at Jones. The conviction he had experienced before concerning this man now flooded through him afresh.

'Go on, Mr Jones. I'm very interested to hear what you intend to do?'

Instead of talking immediately about his future plans, Ivor Jones began to repeat almost word for word what he had said to the congregation in the Gospel Chapel. His eyes were fiery with fanaticism, his harsh voice pulsed with fervour, and his powerful physique seemed to increase in size and stature before the young man's astonished eyes.

Despite his habitual cynicism, and his veneer of world-weary sophistication, Chris Thompson felt himself being overwhelmed by the other man's impassioned words, and he found that he was accepting all that he was being told, and supporting the aims that Jones projected. He sat as if mesmerised until the speaker fell silent, then for some time remained in frowning concentration, trying to analyse the effect that Jones had had on him.

'Would you like some more tea, Mr Thompson?'

The harsh voice broke in on his thoughts, and he nodded and stared wonderingly at the stocky figure now turned away from him.

'What the hell did he do to me? Did he put something in the bloody tea? Did he hypnotise me?' Although Thompson asked himself these questions with an effort at self-mockery, he knew that what had happened to him had nothing of the facetious in it.

'This guy is a bloody potential demagogue.' The young man felt a rapidly increasing excitement as ideas began to thrust into his mind. 'And if he can whip up a bunch of chapel deadbeats to have a go at drug-dealers, then what could he do with an audience from the "flog, hang and draw 'em" persuasion?'

Ivor Jones returned to place fresh cups of tea on the table, and reseated himself facing the reporter.

'This organisation you talk of forming, Mr Jones?' Thompson questioned eagerly. 'Have you already got the blueprints for it?'

Jones shook his head. 'No, not completely. I haven't fully worked out yet how I am going to do it.' He smiled wryly, and that smile made him appear kindly and avuncular. 'I have decided on a name for it, though . . . It will be known as "The Cromwell Movement".'

Chris Thompson considered briefly, then smiled congratulations. 'I like that name, "The Cromwell Movement". It carries the connotations of strength and discipline, and success.' Again he paused and thought for some moments, considering how he could turn this situation to his own advantage.

Ivor Jones sat silently watching the younger man,

his features now once more dour and hard, his keen blue eyes wary and speculative.

'The Cromwell Movement will need publicity to get it off the ground, won't it, Mr Jones?' Thompson stated eventually.

'Of course,' Jones concurred. 'But it must be the right sort of publicity.'

'I can help you there, Mr Jones. I can give you that publicity, and maybe help you to meet the contacts you'll need to expand your movement. It takes a lot of money to finance any organisation. I know a few people who might be sufficiently interested in what you intend to do, to help you with the financial side of things.'

Jones' piercing blue eyes blinked rapidly several times in succession. Then, staring grimly at the other man, he demanded harshly, 'And what's in it for you, Mr Thompson? What do you hope to gain out of helping the Cromwell Movement?'

Chris Thompson instinctively knew that this was a crucial moment, and that the wrong answer would distance him for ever from Ivor Jones. He paused and pondered briefly then opted for the unembellished truth.

'I want to further my career in the newpaper business, Mr Jones,' he said firmly, meeting and holding the other man's searching regard. 'To do that I need exclusive coverage of good stories. I have the gut feeling that the Cromwell Movement will turn out to be a good story, and I want the exclusive coverage of it from the inside.' He waited for the older man's reaction, and Jones nodded.

'Go on, Mr Thompson.'

'To generate the necessary publicity and to get maximum news coverage, you'll need to pull a few stunts. I could help you there as well, I've got all sorts of ideas about that. I know I can dream up the kind of stunts that will ensure the maximum news coverage for you.'

He saw Jones scowl, and instant misgivings filled him. 'What's the matter, Mr Jones? Have I said something wrong?'

Still scowling, Ivor Jones slowly nodded his head. 'Yes, you have, young man. You should understand that although I am prepared to listen to advice from people who have expertise in fields that I'm ignorant about, that is all that they can do: to advise me. Any actions taken are taken under my direction. There will be no stunts, as you term them. No publicity! No inside stories! Unless I decide that there will be. Any work that you do for the Cromwell Movement will be done under my direction. Now if you cannot accept that, then I'll understand, and we part with no hard feelings. But if you decide to help me, then you must be very clear that this is the way it is going to be. I give the orders concerning anything to do with the Cromwell Movement. I direct its publicity. I direct its course of action. I plan its strategy and tactics. I *am* the Cromwell Movement!'

There was an instant dichotomy in Chris Thompson's mind. One side of him wanted to jeer and scoff at this display of arrogant egoism, but the other side acknowledged the aura of strength, power and absolute confidence that radiated from Jones as he spoke.

Some moments elapsed as the young man considered whether or not he was prepared to accept orders from Ivor Jones. He weighed possible future advantages to be gained, against present acceptance of a submission to the will of this man before him.

'There could be some great stories here,' he told himself, then argued, 'But why should I take orders from him? He's just a nobody after all . . .' Then it was as if a strange voice invaded his mind to tell him, 'But he's going to be a somebody very, very soon . . .' And impelled by a force beyond his control, Chris Thompson nodded slowly.

'All right, Mr J. We'll do it your way.'

Jones snapped curtly, 'My name is not J, young man. My name is Jones.'

After a short hesitation, the younger man apologised. 'Of course. I'm sorry, Mr Jones. Now what is it that you'd like me to do?'

'I want you to make it plain in your story that I accept full responsibility for what happened last night. I want you also to emphasise that I intend to go on fighting against the criminals that are infesting my country. But make no mention of the Cromwell Movement.'

'But why not?' Thompson exclaimed in surprise. 'I thought that you wanted people to know about it?'

Jones shook his head and explained quietly, 'Not yet, Mr Thompson. I've already learned one lesson from what happened last night. And that is that every step that is taken from now on must be carefully thought about and, above all, well planned.'

'Yes, I take your point, Mr Jones, but this story would be a great opportunity to get publicity for the Cromwell Movement,' Thompson argued.

'Just write the story as I want you to. The time hasn't yet come to publicise the Cromwell Movement,' Jones ordered flatly, and realising the futility of further argument the reporter concurred.

Jones took a thin sheaf of notepaper from the inside pocket of his jacket and handed it to the younger man. 'I've noted the details that I want you to use for the story. I shall leave you to arrange it in the proper manner.' He rose to his feet. 'Come to the Chapel next Sunday evening, Mr Thompson.'

It was simultaneously a dismissal and a command, and the young man walked from Tabernacle Cottage feeling somewhat disoriented by what had happened during the brief spell of time he had spent with Ivor Jones.

As he drove away, he asked himself in puzzlement, 'Why the hell did I agree to everything so tamely?'

But even though he questioned his actions, he knew that he was going to do as Jones had instructed.

It was many hours later when the disconcerting thought occurred to him that Jones had displayed an uncanny prescience in writing out the details of the story as he wanted it to be published. Thompson could not suppress a shiver of apprehension. Could the man be possessed of some type of mental powers that enabled him to foresee the future? Could he have known in advance that he, Chris Thompson, would be coming to interview him?

'Stop thinking such bloody nonsense!' He jeered at himself, yet the incredible concept persisted in disturbing him throughout a long night.

# Chapter Nine

'Are you coming to see the boys?' Clive Keegan made the question seem like a challenge, and Lisa reacted irritably.

'Of course I am. Why should you need to ask me that?'

His lips puckered petulantly. 'Well, you've stopped being a wife, so I naturally wondered if you'd decided to stop being a mother as well.'

She rose to the bait. 'If I've stopped being a wife, it's because you haven't been behaving like a husband.'

'How have I stopped behaving like a husband?' he demanded blusteringly. 'I still work and support you and the boys. I still want you to share my bed. It's you that want to sleep apart from me, isn't it?'

'If you acted like a real husband you'd do something about that animal. He's started phoning me here now.'

'You don't know that it's him, it could be anybody. All that you've heard on that phone is someone breathing and giggling, so how can you be sure that it's him?'

'Oh, I'm sure. I'm very sure,' she stated dogmatically. 'If you were a real man, you'd deal with him, and make him stop pestering me.'

Clive Keegan rolled his eyes heavenwards and raised his plump, smooth hands as if beseeching some divinity for help.

'We're on that track again, are we,' he said with a long-suffering air. 'I'm supposed to go and confront a man who has served his sentence for what he did, who has already been punished for his crime. I'm supposed to go and accuse that man of making phone calls to you – even though you haven't got the slightest shred of evidence that he's the one who's doing it.'

'I know it's him. I just *know* it is,' she insisted sullenly.

'Look, if you're coming to see the boys you'd better get ready.' He turned away from her and went to sit in the easy chair. Lifting up his newspaper, he took cover behind its spread pages.

Lisa stared angrily at the printed news sheets, itching to go and tear them from his plump, smooth hands, and to see the outrage on his plump, smooth face as she did so. But then guilt suddenly assailed her.

'I'm being a bitch! He doesn't really deserve this. It's not his fault that that animal is pestering me.'

She went upstairs and began to take a shower. The hot stinging spray soothed her irritation, and she resolved that she would make a special effort to be pleasant to Clive during the trip to their sons' school.

The Forest Glade Preparatory School was situated some miles to the north of the city, and educated boys from seven to thirteen years of age for entry to various public schools. To send one's children to Forest Glade was a social cachet in the city, although it had to be confessed that the public schools its pupils

83

finally went to tended to be the minor and less august establishments.

Lisa had made a special effort to dress simply yet smartly for this visit. She knew that parents were vetted by the boys, and an over-dressed or flamboyant parent was a source of great embarrassment to the unfortunate son, who would be ribbed unmercifully by his schoolfellows. Primarily the visit was an annual occasion when the parents would be given the opportunity to socialise with each other and with the school staff, and receive informal reports on their child's progress and general performance in school life. Until she had been raped, Lisa had enjoyed these gatherings. But since that assault she had found them an ordeal to be endured and curtailed as soon as politely possible. She felt that the men and women she met there were looking at her speculatively, their minds busy with the sordid details of what had been done to her. Although she tried her best to cast such thoughts from her mind, still they persisted and disturbed her greatly, causing her to act stiffly and awkwardly in the various groups which collected and dispersed throughout the afternoon.

Because of the nature of the visit she was only able to spend a brief period of time with Robert and David, her twin boys aged eleven, thin and gawky, but showing promise of a handsome maturity to come.

Clive Keegan was in his element at this gathering. He loved an audience, and because he was one of the most successful businessmen in the city, he was assured of an eager coterie of attentive listeners as he pontificated about a variety of topics.

Lisa stood by his side, wearing a fixed smile on her face, her thoughts roaming. She was aware of the covert glances from the men surrounding her husband, and the admiration and desire in those glances as they lingered on her lush figure. Once, not so very long ago, she would have flirted demurely with these admirers, allowed her own eyes to meet and briefly hold theirs. She would have enjoyed the effect that she had on them. But now, she felt only an angry contempt for their desire.

The visit completed, she sat by her husband in the warmth and comfort of his expensive executive saloon and stared out at the bleak winter fields. That bleakness matched her mood as she listened to her husband congratulating himself on the triumphs of the day.

'Did you see Toby Jenkins' face when I put him right about the last round of GATT talks? I thought the bugger was going to explode, he was so mad. Bloody fool! The man's basically a cretin!'

Not for the first time Lisa noted how many of Clive Keegan's acquaintances were bloody fools, and cretins, and imbeciles, and half-baked idiots, and not worth the air they breathed.

Having fumbled in her bag for her pack of cigarettes, and found that she had none, she swore under her breath and asked her husband, 'Can you stop at the next shop? I need to get some cigarettes.'

He clucked his tongue against his teeth impatiently. 'Can't you wait until you get back home? You must have at least a dozen packs there.'

'No, I can't,' she retorted, and counter-attacked. 'If you needed cigars, you'd stop quickly enough!'

'All right, all right.' He sighed wearily, and when the next filling station appeared he pulled in.

As she hurried towards the small shop attached to the filling station, Lisa noticed the *Gazette and*

*Advertiser* board outside the door. In big black letters it proclaimed: 'VIGILANTES IN THE CITY'.

Made curious, she bought the paper with her cigarettes. When she opened it, Clive Keegan sneered, 'I don't know why you bother to read that cheap rag.'

She ignored the gibe, and found the article she was seeking. It was a short report of how a group of vigilantes had driven drug-dealers from the Recreation Ground of the Meadowpark Council Estate the previous Sunday evening.

Lisa mentally shrugged. 'Big deal! Just another flash in the pan.'

Then she saw another brief article under the report about the vigilantes. It concerned the man who had led their attack, Ivor Jones. After a brief résumé of his military career, the article stated that Jones had declared his intention of leading a fight against crime in the city. One sentence in particular struck a chord in Lisa Keegan's mind. Jones declared that victims of crime had the right to seek revenge against those who had harmed them.

She folded the paper carefully, held it on her lap, and spent the rest of the journey home deep in thought.

# Chapter Ten

'For God's sake, Chris, if I hear another word about this man Ivor Jones I'll bloody well scream.'

Shelagh Perrot tossed her glossy blonde hair in exasperation, and as Chris Thompson opened his mouth to reply, she shouted angrily, 'I mean it, Chris. One word and I'll scream the bloody house down.'

'All right, all right. I'm sorry.' He raised his hands in a placatory gesture.

Paradoxically, after making such a threat it was she who spoke about Ivor Jones in her very next sentence.

'I don't know what this man Jones has done to you, Chris, but you've talked about nothing else for the last three nights.'

He grinned ruefully. 'I know . . . I'm sorry, sweetheart.'

She got up from the low-slung overstuffed chair in a lithe, catlike motion, and began to stalk restlessly around the large room.

Chris watched her, and thought how feline she was in her movements. She reminded him of some beautiful exotic cat, with her lean taut body, almond-shaped green eyes, and glossy mane of blonde hair. She reminded him of a cat also in the way she treated him: demanding affection and attention when she required it, and at other times acting with a cool contemptuous disdain of his needs. She reacted like a cat when he did something to annoy or offend her, flaying him with the cruel savagery of her verbal assault – biting, scathing words which she used like hooked, sharp talons to rend and tear at his emotions.

He had lived with Shelagh Perrot for a year now, a year which had been simultaneously the happiest and the most miserable twelve months of his life.

She was a freelance feature writer for women's magazines, and was beginning to make something of a name for herself in that field on a fact which pleased Chris Thompson, but also depressed him. He feared that once she became established, then she would leave him and strike out for the big city, that the lights of London would take her from him. This was one of the reasons for his own ambitions in that direction. He thought that if he could achieve success and fame, it would keep her with him. Selfish and greedy as she was, she would stay with him if he could provide her with the status and riches she coveted.

With the sudden change of mood which never failed to delight and disconcert him, she came to perch herself on his lap, and began to nuzzle his cheeks and ears with her soft, moist lips. Through his shirt he could feel the pressure of her hard nipples against his chest and he began to become tumescent as his excitement fired.

She drew back and her white teeth gleamed in a broad smile as she saw the effect she was having, and she whispered invitingly, 'Let's fuck.'

Clasping her close, he struggled to his feet and began to move towards the bedroom with her in his arms, but she broke free, shaking her head.

'No! Not there. Let's fuck here.'

With deft fingers she unbuttoned his shirt and took it from his body, then unbuckled his belt and let his trousers fall. Even as he stepped out of them her long fingers were cupping his genitals, and stroking his throbbing manhood. He went to grab her, but she evaded his clutching hands and, deliberately tantalising, she slowly removed her own clothes and then stood naked before him, breasts full and firm, waist and hips slender and rounded, thighs long and sleek.

He groaned with wanting and reached for her again, and this time she allowed him to enfold her and to draw her hard against him, as he sank with her down on to the thick, soft carpet. So intense was his hungry need that he entered her with almost brutal urgency, but as he drove deeper and deeper into her hot moistness she arched against him, and her long scarlet-painted fingernails raked cruelly over his skin, leaving weals that stung painfully; but immersed in his passion the pain only served to heighten his pleasure, and he panted and moaned as he drove himself frantically into her. He cried out as the shuddering ecstacies of climax overwhelmed him, and she hissed and dug deep into his flesh with her nails as her own climax took her and enmeshed her in a mindless thrall of physical sensation.

Spent, he went to gently kiss her lips, but she jerked her head to avoid his seeking mouth and wriggled out from under him. Ignoring his pleas to remain, she went to the bathroom, and locked the door behind her, and he heard the rushing of water as she ran a bath.

Although satiated with passion, he could take no joy in remembrance of what they had just done together. Always, after making love, she immediately distanced herself from him both physically and mentally, and he was left feeling unhappy and rejected.

As he lay listening to the sounds of water rushing from the taps, his thoughts turned to Ivor Jones, and he grinned ruefully.

'I wonder what you would make of Shelagh, Mr Jones? How would a woman like her fit into your puritanical life?'

He felt a sudden desire to see and to hear Ivor Jones. He wanted to listen to the impassioned words, and to look into the fiery, piercing blue eyes. Above all else he wanted to experience again that sensation of utter absorption, that absolute sense of faith, trust and belief that he had felt when Jones had talked to him.

Shelagh came from the bathroom smelling of perfumed soap and fresh, youthful skin. She had wrapped a towelling robe around her slender body, and her long blonde hair was tied up in a turban fashioned from another towel. Even in these shapeless coverings she managed to look glamorously alluring. The young man waited warily to discover her mood, unconsciously steeling himself for mockery and scorn. But then she smiled warmly and came to snuggle against him.

'Chris, tell me why he's made such an impression on you, this Ivor Jones?'

He mentally examined her tone of voice, wary of ambush. He had lost count of all the times in the past when she had lured him into confession and intimate confidences, and then laughed in his face and used those confessions and confidences as weapons to wound him.

'Tell me,' she urged softly. 'I really do want to know.'

'All right.' He surrendered, and thought carefully before telling her, 'I think it's because he has an absolute certainty. And when he talks he radiates strength and purpose, and you believe completely in what he is saying, and you know without any doubts that he is the type of man who will lead to the cannon's mouth and beyond.'

'That's very flowery.' She giggled, and repeated mockingly, '. . . to the cannon's mouth, and beyond . . .' Then she giggled again and queried teasingly, 'He's not a survivor of the Light Brigade, is he?'

Chris felt disgusted with himself for having been so easily drawn into her ambush, and he shook his head and scowled down at her green eyes, alight with mischief.

'I want to meet him,' she declared. 'When will you be seeing him again?'

'Next Sunday, I suppose,' he told her sulkily.

'Then I shall come with you. I'm very curious about Ivor Jones. I want to see this wonderful person who's got you so entranced.' Her tone brooked neither argument nor refusal, and Chris Thompson nodded in reluctant agreement.

# Chapter Eleven

The newspaper report about Ivor Jones had been read with a good deal of interest by very disparate people in the city. Policemen, criminals and victims all studied the brief paragraphs and reacted in their various ways to what the report had to tell them.

George Faraday, leader of the City Council, chairman of the Police Authority, and an advocate of the hardline approach in the war against crime, immediately got in touch with senior police officers of the City Force to enquire what they knew of this man, Ivor Jones?

For the most part they knew little or nothing, but took steps to have him checked out. The orders for this action circulated downwards through the ranks and eventually ended up on the desk of Detective Sergeant Denis Matthews. The grizzled detective sighed wearily, and decided that he would join the congregation of the Gospel Chapel on the following Sunday and see for himself what Ivor Jones was getting up to.

Most of the criminality who read of Jones only sneered and laughed with contempt. They were well accustomed to would-be crusaders, who blustered and threatened but in the end did nothing. One criminal, however, took a different view. Leroy

Murchison was still smarting at the way he had allowed himself to be chased off the Rec. by the motley crowd of vigilantes. The newspaper report gave him the identity of the man who had led them, and Leroy vowed that he would take revenge on Ivor Jones personally.

He went to see the man known as 'Big Winston,' a major gang boss in the city, and also its main pimp and procurer. A towering, massively built, full-bearded man who had employed Leroy Murchison many times as a strong-arm man and enforcer, he listened sympathetically to Murchison's request. When Leroy left the luxury flat of Big Winston he was smiling with the knowledge that the gun he had asked for would be supplied to him later that same day.

Many victims of crime who read of Ivor Jones wondered if at last they had found the man who could give them what they wanted above all else: vengeance on those who had harmed them. Other victims of abuse and harassment suddenly began to hope that here was a man who could give them what they wanted more than anything: freedom from fear, and protection from threatening violence.

Several of both types of victim came to call at Tabernacle Cottage, and Ivor Jones received them courteously, and listened sympathetically to their harrowing stories. He sent each person away with the promise that he could and would show them the way to achieve what they wanted, and told them all to come to the Gospel Chapel on the next Sunday evening, and to bring with them any others who felt as they did.

# Chapter Twelve

The weather was cold and there were frequent down-pours of rain throughout the day, but nevertheless, when Ivor Jones entered the Gospel Chapel on the Sunday evening, he found to his gratification that newcomers had come in sufficient numbers to fill three-quarters of the pews, and the hall was clamorous with voices.

Some of the Chapel Elders intercepted him before he could mount the pulpit, and hiding his annoyance he followed them into the vestry room behind.

'Well, what is it that you want to speak to me about?' he challenged impatiently.

It was Alan Tims, the senior Elder, a tall, cadaverous-featured, elderly man, who spoke out.

'We don't like what's going on, Brother Jones. This is the Lord's house, and you're turning it into some sort of circus.'

'In what way?' Jones demanded.

'Bringing all these strangers here, like this,' Tims said angrily. 'There's none of them have ever set foot in here before. And they're acting like hooligans. Just listen to them!'

He gestured towards the door and the loud noise coming from the hall beyond it.

'It's disgraceful!' He spluttered, and saliva spattered

from between his badly-fitting upper and lower dentures. 'They're behaving like hooligans. They should be showing respect for us, and behaving properly.'

The other three Elders in the room voiced their agreement.

Ivor Jones' fiery blue eyes glinted with temper, but when he spoke his voice was low and gentle.

'Brothers, I'm sorry if these people who've come here tonight are causing you any distress. Believe me, I had no intention of that happening.'

'Oh, I'm not blaming you, Brother Jones,' Harold Isaacs, a short, plump-bodied, middle-aged man told him. 'But you can see what Brother Tims is all aereated about, can't you?' In his turn he also gestured towards the door and the hubbub beyond it. 'I mean to say, Brother Jones. This is a place of worship, isn't it? It's not right to have this racket, is it?'

'It's a disgrace, Brother Jones!' Tims did not like anyone else usurping his position as spokesman. 'Do you know that some of the brethren have threatened to leave the Chapel if this continues?'

'If what continues, Brother Tims?' Jones asked innocently.

'You know very well what!' Tims lost his temper. 'If you keep on bringing all these non-believers into the house of the Lord.'

Jones turned to the other men. 'What do you gentlemen think? Will you leave the Chapel if this continues?'

There was a hard edge to his voice, which made them a little wary of him.

'No, I'm not saying that I'll leave the Chapel, Brother Jones,' Harold Isaacs denied uneasily. 'But there has been talk among the brethren and some are saying that they'll go.'

Jones smiled, but that smile resembled a snarl.

'Well, I shall be sorry to lose any of our congregation, Brother Isaacs. But if that's what they decide, then it's up to them, isn't it?'

They stared at him in shock, and Tims was the first to recover himself, immediately declaring open warfare.

'Oh no, Brother Jones, it won't be they who leave this congregation,' He snapped heatedly. 'You'll be the one who goes, if you don't stop bringing this rabble into our Chapel.'

All pretence now disappeared, and Ivor Jones' face became a mask of fury, which caused the other men to nervously edge further away from him. Through clenched teeth he gritted out, 'Before you made that threat, Brother Tims, you would have been well advised to ask the opinions of all of the members of this congregation. I've taken the trouble of doing just that, and you'll find that the vast majority of the brethren support what I'm doing. Under the charter of this congregation, the majority vote carries the decision on any matter concerning this Chapel. I know that I can get that majority vote in my favour. If you want proof, then let's go out there now and put it to the test, shall we?'

The Elders exchanged anxious glances. His voice had carried the ring of conviction, and they were very hesitant to accept his challenge.

From the hall slow-handclapping started up, and there were shouts for Jones to make his appearance.

He grinned savagely. 'It seems that I'm urgently needed, Brothers. So I'll leave you now. But just remember one thing. If it comes to the vote, it won't be me who is expelled from this congregation; it'll be those who oppose me. So think very carefully about what you are going to do.'

He walked through them and they parted to give him passage.

Alan Tims' face was suffused with anger as he demanded, 'Well, are you lot going to stand by me?'

An outburst of cheering sounded from the hall to greet Ivor Jones' appearance in the pulpit. And one by one the Elders shamefacedly walked back into the hall and took their seats on the elevated pew to the side of the pulpit, leaving Tims seething in impotent fury, and alone.

Chris Thompson was sitting with Shelagh Perrot towards the rear of the congregation, and he watched closely the faces of those around him as Ivor Jones began to speak. He wanted to observe this audience objectively, to see what effect Jones would have on them.

The gist of the speech was very similar to the others that Jones had made previously. He talked of crime, and the lack of punishment. He played on the fears and the justifiable resentments of his listeners. He talked of weakness, and of strength. He spoke of separation, and of unity. He talked of betrayal, and of trust; of wrong and right, of justice, and of vengeance. He played upon the emotions of his listeners, like a consummate musician playing upon an instrument. He seemed to exert a spell upon them which held them in thrall to his voice, and when he finally came to an ending, his audience roared their applause and shouted out their support.

Despite his intentions to remain watchful and uncommitted, Chris Thompson found that the spell of Jones' voice drew him inexorably into an almost mindless state, and the young man bellowed his cheers with the rest when the speech came to an end. By his side Shelagh Perrot was feeling angry with herself, because she had also cheered and shouted uncontrollably.

'I'm becoming as silly as bloody Chris!' she thought. But then she found herself straining her ears to listen to what else Ivor Jones might have to say.

In other parts of the hall, Lisa Keegan, Dorothy Chapman, Wisdom Maclure and hundreds like them gazed at Jones as if he were some Messiah come to lead them from the darkness they dwelt in. In yet another part of the hall, Denis Matthews was experiencing an emotion that in his cynical and world-weary middle age he had never expected to feel again: a dawning hero-worship for the man in the pulpit.

Face reddened, and dripping with sweat, Ivor Jones stood silent and unmoving until the roaring plaudits slowly died away. Then he gripped the lapels of his jacket and leaning forward, demanded ringingly, 'Brethren . . . Friends . . . Are you ready to fight?' He paused, and then in a voice which dripped contempt questioned, 'Or will you remain as you are now? Content to moan, and groan, and weep and wail, and let others do your fighting for you?'

There were murmurings of resentment from among the audience, and a man shouted resentfully, 'I do my own fighting!'

Jones had noted the part of the hall where the shout came from, and he threw out his hand to point in that direction as if at the man who had shouted.

'Well said, Brother,' he roared in congratulation.

'Well said! A man like you will always be welcome to join my movement. To join the Cromwell Movement.'

A concerted gasp of excitement came from around the hall, and Jones smiled grimly and slowly nodded his head.

'Yes, my friends, that is the name we shall be known by . . . "The Cromwell Movement" . . . A movement dedicated to fighting against those who would destroy us. But those whom I allow to join my movement must be ready to fight shoulder to shoulder with me.'

His hand moved and the pointing fingers picked out faces in the crowd. 'Will you fight, Brother? Will you fight, Sister? Will you? Will you? Will *you* fight? Because if you will not fight, then there is no place for you with us. You will not be allowed to join our ranks. Because the Cromwell Movement is a fighting movement; it is a movement that is ready to do battle with evil wherever that evil is to be found. And in this city we know where to find it, don't we, Brethren . . .'

He beckoned to a small group of people sitting in the front row to stand up and face the congregation, and when they had done so he went on in a voice which was modulated now, but still carried to every quarter of the hall.

'These good people before you live in our city. Last week an old lady was killed by joyriders in Flowerbank Road. That old lady was the mother and grandmother of these good people standing before you.'

One of the standing women burst into loud sobs, and an outcry of pity sounded from the hall.

'Brethren, even now as I am talking to you, joyriders are racing stolen cars on Flowerbank

Road. They are racing those cars on the very place where they slaughtered that poor defenceless old lady!'

Jones' voice shook with furious outrage, and that sense of outrage was shared by his audience.

'Those vile, callous, heartless thieves are even now creating havoc! Terrifying innocent people! Defying the law! Treating all of us who try to live decently with contempt.' He drew a long breath, and let his words sink fully home before asking. 'Who among you will go with me now, and put a stop to this outrage?'

He came down from the pulpit and, looking neither to left nor right, marched down the centre aisle towards the entrance doors. The family of the old woman who had been killed followed behind him, the women among them weeping heartbrokenly.

Even before Jones had walked half-way along the aisle men and women were standing and pushing forward to follow him.

Outside in the roadway, Jones stood flanked by the family and watched the crowd pouring out of the Chapel entrances. They filled the roadway from pavement to pavement and stretched back in a dense column.

Jones turned and began to march up the road, and they surged after him. He threw back his head and sang out the opening lines of the 'Battle Hymn of the Republic', and within seconds massed voices had joined in thunderous unison.

'Mine eyes have seen the glory of the coming
    of the Lord.
He is trampling out the vintage where the
    grapes of wrath are stored.

100

He hath loosed the fateful lightning of his
   terrible swift sword.
His truth is marching on . . .'

As the column marched on, filling the air with their battle song, Chris Thompson and Shelagh Perrot marched with them. Dorothy Chapman, Lisa Keegan and Wisdom Maclure strode out in the roaring ranks. Denis Matthews told himself he was only there to observe, and gather evidence, but he also raised his voice in song, and a fierce exultation pulsed through his mind as for the first time in many years he let his emotions rule him.

Approximately half a mile from the Gospel Chapel, two stolen cars were roaring up and down a length of a residential road of semi-detached houses. Tyres screeched and smoked as the two fourteen-year-old boys who were driving sent the cars spinning in handbrake turns and racing slides, and a small crowd of teenagers whooped and cheered the displays of recklessness, egging on the youthful drivers to take greater and greater risks.

Jones gestured his followers to silence long before they came within sight and hearing of the road where the cars were skidding and screeching. He divided the column into two halves, and issued detailed instructions.

As the procession of silent marching people came into view, the teenage spectators stood and gaped, and ignored the roaring cars.

Like a human river, and maintaining absolute silence, the two halves of the column split apart and flowed along the pavements to opposite ends of the road. Then they flooded across the roadway and linked arms, forming a dense mass of human chains which stretched across the full width of the carriageway and pavements.

Slightly in advance of the front of the leading chain in his section of the column, Ivor Jones lifted his arm and waved in signal, and still maintaining silence the serried ranks started to pace steadily towards each other, trapping the roaring cars between them.

The teenage spectators stared in nervous puzzlement, retreating from the oncoming chains and clustering together midway between. One of the young drivers killed the engine, jumped out of his car and ran to where the teenagers clustered and tried to hide himself among them. The other driver stared unbelievingly at the advancing masses, then revved his engine fiercely and the car's tyres screeched and smoked as he gunned it straight at Ivor Jones, who was now five paces in advance of his leading chain. Jones shouted. 'Don't stop, brethren! Don't give way!'

Some of the women screamed as the car came roaring down on the soliary figure, and behind Jones the human chains eddied and threatened to break as the frightened ones tried to halt or to scramble aside. But the more steadfast grimly clutched their arms and refused to let them break away. The engine's roar crescendoed and still Jones paced steadily onwards, and more screams echoed out as the car seemed almost on the stocky figure. Then, with a long-drawn-out screeching of smoking tyres, the driver spun the car. It skidded sideways, the engine cut out, and the vehicle rocked to a halt. The driver burst out of it and went running frantically across the road and in between the houses, scrambling over fences and gardens to get away. As if galvanised into movement by his example the rest of the teenagers followed suit, ignoring the shouts and dodging the clutching hands of the angry householders who had come to their doors and windows to see what was happening.

Jones' followers began to cheer and clap hysterically, and came swarming around him.

'You see, brethren?' he shouted exultantly, his arms raised high in a salute of victory. 'You see what you can do when you stand united? You become invincible. Invincible!'

He waited until the first tumult of excitement subsided and then told them. 'When you go out into the city, to your homes and to your work, tell them what you have done here tonight. Tell them how the Cromwell Movement has shown you that by standing together, by standing united, wickedness can be overcome.'

'When can we join the Cromwell Movement?' a woman demanded.

Jones smiled benevolently at her. 'I shall tell you when, Sister.'

He turned to the faces pressing in on him. 'Go now, all of you. The Lord's blessings be upon you.'

He began to move away, and reluctant to part from him, many of the people still followed.

From an upstairs window of one of the houses a man had been filming everything with a camcorder: the roaring cars, the whooping teenagers, the arrival and action of the silent columns led by Ivor Jones.

As the crowd was dispersing, talking and laughing excitedly, Jones passed beneath the film maker's window, and the man leaned out and shouted: 'Excuse me, but who are you lot? Where did you all come from?'

Jones halted and stared up at the questioner, then

smiled and replied, 'We are the Cromwell Movement. And we come from everywhere.'

He walked on, and the cameraman hurriedly squinted through the viewing lens and shot more film.

Ivor Jones felt as if he were soaring through the air with elation; he felt almost godlike. Although he had known the pleasures of command during his Army service, tonight's experience had gone far beyond anything he had ever known before. As an NCO he had merely transmitted and carried out the orders of his superiors. When he led troops in combat he had been following the instructions and plans of his superior officers. But tonight he had truly been a leader. He had planned, and led, and directed, and been obeyed, and above all else he had been victorious! He felt intoxicated with power.

In the group of people still dogging his footsteps, there were others feeling intoxicated with emotion. Chris Thompson was one of them. He had become separated from Shelagh Perrot when the ranks of human chains had formed, and found himself directly behind Jones when the car came roaring against them. His first impulse had been to break and run, and then silhouetted by the headlights of the oncoming car he had seen Ivor Jones' powerful stocky figure marching on – fearlessly confronting a roaring mass of metal that could have smashed him to a pulp, and winning that confrontation!

The experience had had a traumatic effect upon the young man, an effect that he was still in the early stages of evaluating. But of one thing he was already sure. If it had not been for Jones' example and fearless leadership, he, Chris Thompson, would have broken and run like a coward.

'He's a true leader,' the young man told himself over and over again. 'He's a true leader. I'd follow him anywhere.'

Others in the group were thinking along similar lines. Lisa Keegan was staring at Jones' stocky figure with a profound sense of gratitude. At last she felt that she had found the man who would put right the wrong done to her; who would help her to wreak the vengeance she craved to inflict upon her rapist.

Wisdom Maclure was possessed of similar thoughts. Her younger son had been murdered by 'Yardie' drug-dealers. Ivor Jones would surely destroy those evil men.

Dorothy Chapman had worshipped Ivor Jones ever since he led her against the drug-dealers on the Rec. She would follow him without question, to the death if needs be.

Denis Matthews, for so long bitterly resentful of the political decisions which tied his hands in the fight against crime, still kept on telling himself that he was only trailing after Ivor Jones to gain evidence and information. But in his heart of hearts he knew that he was there for quite another reason. In Ivor Jones he had found the man who was doing the things that he had long wanted, but never had the courage, to do himself.

And all the rest of the group shared similar motives. At last they had found a man who possessed the courage to lead them along a path where they had long wished to go . . .

# *Chapter Thirteen*

The story of what had happened in Flowerbank Road was widespread throughout the city by the next day's afternoon, and the amateur cameraman who had filmed the episode took his film to the local television station. It was used on the evening regional news programme, and created a minor sensation. Hundreds of viewers phoned in to voice their support for what Jones and his followers had done; only a handful called to condemn such foolhardy action.

The film was used again for the late national news, and on the Tuesday morning Ivor Jones awoke to find himself a local celebrity. All through the morning there was knocking at his door, and his phone kept ringing as people tried to contact him. At last he felt driven to leave his cottage and go for a long walk to escape the continuous badgering. He used the long walk to good effect, in carefully thinking out his next moves. It was dusk when at last he returned to Tabernacle Cottage, relieved to see that there did not appear to be any reporters or others waiting for him.

As he neared the Chapel and crossed the road a car engine suddenly fired into life, and from out of the line of parked cars along the street a set of headlights flashed three times as if in signal.

Suddenly Ivor Jones was wary and alert. He could sense danger. It was as if the years had rolled back and he was once again on the murderous streets of Belfast trying to outwit the hidden snipers of the IRA. He glanced quickly all around him. The street appeared deserted, but he knew instinctively that hidden eyes were watching him. The car that had flashed its headlights remained stationary with its engine running, but it was too far away for him to make out its occupants. All the lessons learned in his long Army service flowered afresh in his mind, and he let his instincts direct him.

He was certain that there had been an ambush prepared, and he slowed his pace while his eyes ceaselessly raked the surrounding area. He did not waste time in trying to reason out who might be lying in wait for him; that information could be sought later. Now, in this instant, he must concentrate on foiling his would-be ambushers. Mentally he cursed his lack of any sort of weapon, then quickly knelt in the shadows of a parked car and, taking off his shoe, pulled his thick woollen sock from his foot. Retying the shoe, he felt in his pockets and drew out all his loose change, dropped the coins into the sock and tied them into the toe. He hefted the makeshift cosh.

'Not too bad! It'll do a bit of damage.'

Keeping the weighted sock concealed he began to cross the road towards the Chapel entrance, watching for any movement from the car further up the street. When it stayed stationary, he thought with satisfaction, 'You're waiting for me in the Chapel yard, aren't you?'

There was a solitary old-type street-lamp overlooking the yard entrance, and its globe was the only illumination for the yard itself, with its overgrown tangle of shrubs and weeds. Ivor Jones knew that he could reach the low globe by standing on the wall that fronted the Chapel grounds.

As he crossed the road and walked to the entrance of the Chapel, he glanced quickly around himself to make sure that no one was surreptitiously closing on him. Then, with surprising agility for a man of his years, he jumped up on to the wall and smashed the globe and bulb of the lamp with his weighted sock. As the shattered glass cracked to the ground and darkness plunged on the area, he came off the wall and ducked low through the entrance and into the dense tangle of shrubs and weeds. There he stayed motionless, waiting for his eyes to accustom to the darkness, listening for movement.

The movement came within brief moments; there was a brief threshing in the bushes further into the grounds, and then a shadowy figure came down the driveway. Ivor Jones cautiously blended further back into the shrubbery, and the shadowy figure moved up and down the drive several times, then ejaculated an angry curse, and went into the roadway.

The car came roaring down the street, and Ivor Jones moved to watch it halt. The headlights picked out the man waiting for it, a young Afro-Caribbean, and Jones scowled as he caught a momentary glimpse of the handgun he was carrying. The gunman got into the car and it roared away.

'What's up, Leroy?' the driver questioned. 'What went wrong?'

'The bastard's smarter than I thought. He got in among the fuckin' bushes. I couldn't risk going in after him.' Leroy Murchison suddenly broke into loud swearing in Jamaican patois, and the driver wisely kept his attention fixed firmly on the road ahead, hiding the malicious pleasure he was deriving from the other man's failure.

In the Chapel grounds Ivor Jones remained hidden for quite a long time, until he was fully satisfied that no other attackers were waiting for him. In his cottage he sorted out his old Army-issue sleeping-bag, and then slipped out and went into the Chapel itself. He went up to the balconies and selected a place to sleep, then improvised some noise-making booby-traps so that no one would be able to creep up on him unawares.

Once he had taken these precautions he made himself comfortable in his sleeping-bag and for the first time gave thought as to who the would-be ambusher might be.

'It's got to be one of the drug-dealers we chased off the Rec.,' he concluded.

As he settled himself to sleep he decided it was time he organised some personal security for himself; he would go and look up Will Rimmer the next day.

109

# Chapter Fourteen

The long narrow room was overheated and the air was thick with tobacco smoke and rank with the stench of unwashed flesh. Two rows of tables flanked by tubular steel chairs filled almost the entire floor space, and at one end of the room a hatchway opened on to a small kitchen, from which a pair of elderly Salvation Army officers were serving mugs of tea and hunks of bread and cheese to a queue of men.

Ivor Jones entered the doorway set in the wall opposite the kitchen and stood for some moments regarding the motley collection of shabby, down-at-heel men sitting at the tables. His nostrils quivered as he drew in the smell of the room, and his lips twitched with disgust. At most of the tables knots of frowsty heads were pushed close together, and talk and laughter and hoarse bouts of coughing resounded. But at one table a man was sitting alone, staring morosely down at the mug of tea on the table before him, and it was towards this solitary man that Jones made his way.

Unlike the rest of the men, the solitary man was neat and clean in appearance, greying hair close-cropped, his lean cheeks and muscular throat well-shaven. He wore a clean white shirt and neatly knotted tie, and his threadbare suit was brushed and pressed. He did not look up when Ivor Jones reached the table and, seating himself on a chair opposite, leaned across the stained formica top.

'Hello, Will, it's been a long time.'

William Rimmer's head lifted abruptly and he stared hard at the other man. Then he scowled, and jerked his head in dismissal.

'I've nothing to say to you, Ivor. So spare me your bloody preaching and just be on your way.'

Jones was not rebuffed by this greeting. Instead he smiled wryly and acknowledged, 'Yes, I used to get up the lads' noses when I tried to tell them about the Lord, didn't I, Will?'

Rimmer's hard-etched features softened a fraction, and his thin lips quirked in the merest suggestion of a grin. 'And you used to get up my nose most of all, you sanctimonious bleeder. You always had the gift of the gab.'

Jones' smile broadened. 'Good job for me that we were mates, wasn't it, Will? Or I might have found myself sitting with my head in my lap more than a few times.'

The grim face of the other man softened, and he chuckled huskily and held out his hand.

'Yes, we were good mates, Ivor. And it's good to see you again.' As their hands clasped he went on, 'But I wish we could have met again when I was up, and not down.'

Their hands parted, and Rimmer said, 'I read about you in the paper. I'm really sorry about your sister.'

Both men were silent for a few moments, then Rimmer grinned and said banteringly, 'I saw that television news the other night. You're getting to be famous in your old age, aren't you? So what are

111

you doing in a stinking dump like this? Working as a missionary to the down and outs, are you?'

Jones shook his head. 'No, I'm not working as a missionary to the down-and-outs, Will. I came here to see you.'

'How did you know where to find me?' Rimmer asked curiously.

'It was easy enough.' Jones shrugged, then went on quickly in a low voice, 'In a way I suppose I am like a missionary. Only I'm not trying to save any souls. I'm a missionary for something else altogether. Something that I think you might be interested in . . .'

Just then a big shambling man came to the table, reeking of methylated spirits and stale sweat.

Rimmer motioned Ivor Jones to stay still, and snapped, 'This is a private talk. Find somewhere else to sit.'

The big man's bleared eyes blinked owlishly, as if he were struggling to comprehend what had been said to him. Then he scowled menacingly and lifted his filthy hand in threat. 'I'll put your fuckin' lights out!'

William Rimmer's pale amber eyes were colder than ice as he rose lithely to his full lean height of six feet four inches. 'You'll never be able to reach the switch, you stinking animal.' He hissed, and jerked his head. 'Now do yourself a favour, and fuck off!'

The big man stared hard at Rimmer, and in the depths of his drink-deadened brain recognised that he stood in mortal danger. After a momentary indecision, he turned and shambled away, mouthing incoherent threats and curses.

Rimmer shook his head in disgust, and said, 'We can't talk here. Let's go and get some fresh air.'

For a time the two men walked in silence, but it was a comfortable silence during which they both mentally travelled back through the years that they had known each other, and the many memories they shared.

It was Ivor Jones who eventually broke the silence. 'I was disappointed that you didn't come to see me when you got out of prison, Will. I could have helped you.' He grinned wryly at his much taller companion. 'But I knew that your pride wouldn't let you ask for any help from anybody. I just hoped that when you'd got back on your feet again, then you'd have come to see me.'

'I wanted to see you, Ivor,' the tall man said quietly, 'but not down like this.'

'You needn't be down any longer, Will,' Jones told him, 'because I've got a job to offer you.'

His friend frowned uneasily. 'This isn't charity under another name, is it, Ivor?'

Jones chuckled grimly. 'No, it's anything but that. I can only offer you small wages, and a lot of hard work and risk. But it's a genuine job, Will, and not charity.'

The other man didn't hesitate. 'I'll take it.'

Jones shook his head. 'Don't you want to know what it is first?'

It was the other man's turn to chuckle grimly. 'I can already guess that it's got something to do with what the papers were saying about you.'

'Do you know, I'd forgotten what a shrewd sod you can be at times.' Jones laughed with genuine amusement, then he sobered abruptly. 'Yes, it's got everything to do with that. I'm ready to start recruiting for my movement, Will. It'll be known as the Cromwell Movement. Now last night a guy came to sort me out. I think he was one of the drug-dealers that we chased from the Rec. There are bound to be a lot more like him when we really get going and I'm going to need some good men with me. Men like you. To act as security, and also to do the secret, dirty jobs that will have to be done if I'm to succeed in what I'm setting out to do.'

Rimmer's lean features were speculative, and he said quietly, 'You'd best give me the full sitrep then, Ivor, about exactly where you're heading with this movement of yours.'

'All right, that's fair enough,' Jones agreed, and began to talk with urgent intensity.

Rimmer listened without interruption, his eyes gleaming as his friend's impassioned words fired his own enthusiasm. And when Jones finally finished speaking and waited for a reply, Rimmer threw back his head and laughed uproariously with delight, then told him, 'I think that's bloody brilliant, Ivor! Bloody brilliant! I'm with you all the way. God! It'll be just like old times, won't it! When do you want me to start? And how many blokes do you want me to recruit to begin with?'

'A dozen should do. But you'll have to make it clear to them that at first they'll only be paid a small wage. I'll be using the money that I got for my house, to pay you all with.' He saw the unspoken question on Rimmer's face and explained, 'After my wife died, I sold up everything and moved into the cottage at the Gospel Chapel. The cash has been in the bank ever since. Poor Iris left me a bit of money as well. But I shall have to budget it carefully because a lot of other things need to be done to get the Cromwell Movement off the ground. But I reckon that once the movement gets going, then finances won't be a problem, and the lads you have in your section will be better paid then.'

Rimmer nodded, then frowned doubtfully. 'But listen, Ivor, who's going to be watching your back while I'm out finding these recruits?'

Jones grinned and pulling back his coat showed the other man the semi-automatic pistol he was carrying in a shoulder holster.

'Souvenir from Goose Green, Will. I always knew it would come in useful one day. But I don't think that the black guy will be back just yet. He knows that he's missed his chance of an easy kill, and that I'll be on my guard from now on. I reckon he'll leave it for a while before he tries again. And we'll be organised in plenty of time to handle him or any others who try it on when the movement takes off.'

'Okay, then,' Rimmer accepted.

Jones handed him an envelope. 'There's enough money in there to do your recruiting with, Will.' He became brusque and authoritative in manner. 'From now on, first names are for use only when we are alone, and in private. Until further notice you address me as Mr Jones in public, and I address you as Mr Rimmer.'

The ingrained discipline of years instantly showed in Rimmer's stiffening of posture, and ready response. 'Very good, Mr Jones.'

'Good!' Jones nodded. 'I'll expect regular progress reports from you. I want the men ready for use within a fortnight.'

The two men parted and went their separate ways.

William Rimmer's cold amber eyes were gleaming as excitement bubbled through him. What had happened seemed almost like a miracle. Just when he had reached what seemed to be the end of any kind of worthwhile existence, Ivor Jones had appeared from nowhere, and had given him this chance to rebuild his shattered life. A smile of pleasurable anticipation slowly spread across his lean, dour features, and for the first time in many years he experienced the stirring of happiness.

Rimmer had been a young and ambitious soldier when he met and married his German wife, Trudie. At first they had been happy, and when a son was born it had set a seal on that happiness. His Army career had entailed frequent and sometimes extended separations from his small family, but his wife had appeared to be able to cope with this. And his returns were always joyful and passionate.

Then, during the Falklands War while Rimmer was fighting on those distant islands, his infant son had been knocked over and killed by a speeding truck, and Trudie had had to face the tragedy alone. Of course the Army had rallied to try and support her, but the welfare officers and the other soldiers' wives were not any use in helping Trudie to bear her grief. She wanted her husband with her.

After the War, when he returned, she had changed towards him. Unjustly, she blamed him for not being with her when their son had died. William Rimmer loved his wife very deeply, and had adored his son, and his own sense of guilt was torturing him. He could not help but blame himself for his son's death – tormenting himself with the thought that if he had not been in the Army, if he had not gone to war, then his son might still be alive.

The years passed and their marriage continued. But now when Rimmer was away on training exercises, or foreign postings, Trudie sought solace and pleasure in bars and night-clubs. She began to drink heavily, and other men came into her life, many of them. Rimmer came to know of this, and there were terrible rows between them, but because he loved her he could not bring himself to break from her. And so he suffered the torments of her infidelities and heavy drinking year after year, hoping against hope that if he continued to love and care for her, then someday the Trudie that he had first known would come back to him. Then, during one of his tours in Northern Ireland, she met the man who would become her pimp, and when Rimmer returned to England she had disappeared.

He had finally managed to trace her here, to the city, only to find that she was working the streets as a prostitute. Rimmer clashed violently with her pimp, and in the fight he killed the man. He received a long sentence of imprisonment, and was thrown out of his beloved Army. After his discharge from prison he had been inexorably drawn back to the city, to search for his wife. Eventually he found her, and had stared at her with horror. She had degenerated into a raddled, diseased hag, shambling the streets with the meths drinkers and half-insane, the alcoholics and drug addicts, her own mind all but destroyed by drugs, drink and the brutal mistreatment of pimps and clients through the years.

Badly shaken by the encounter, Rimmer had spent long hours sitting in his small bed-sit, brooding on all that had happened in his marriage. Then he went in search of her again, determined to try to do what he could to help her. But before he could find her, she had been discovered battered to death in a stinking corner of a rubbish-tip. Her killer had never been traced. Rimmer had claimed her body and given her a decent burial. He then tried to continue with his own life, but had sunk into a morose and lonely solitude; unable to find work, he was unwilling to surrender the vestiges of pride and self-respect and allow himself to become a parasite living off the state, and the proceeds of crime. And so his bleak pauper existence had been dragged out until today . . . until the moment when, like a guardian angel, Ivor Jones had come to find him.

William Rimmer drew a deep hissing breath of sheer exultation. His back was ramrod straight, his head held high and proud, as he marched with a snap and a hint of swagger back into a purposeful life.

# Chapter Fifteen

When Clive Keegan returned home after a long and taxing day, the first thing he heard as he entered his house was the sound of women's voices and laughter. He frowned, assuming that it was the television with the volume turned high. Then he realised that the noise was coming from his study where he kept his computer graphic and word-processing equipment.

As he walked towards the open door of the room he heard his wife talking excitedly, and shook his head in puzzlement. He had not heard her sound so happy since long before she had been raped.

The printer was purring, and when he looked through the doorway he saw a coloured woman feeding fresh sheets of paper into the holder.

She saw him and looked shocked, and he demanded angrily, 'What the hell do you think you're doing? And who the hell are you?'

He moved into the room and saw his wife and another, shabbily dressed, small-statured woman, arranging printed sheets of paper into boxes.

'What's going on, Lisa? And who are these people?'

'They're my friends,' she told him coldly. 'And I'll thank you not to take that tone with me.'

He picked up one of the printed sheets and studied it. On the top it bore an emblem of the head and shoulders of an Ironside trooper of Cromwell's New Model Army: a hard, hatchet-edged face wearing the distinctive iron helmet with its long lobster-tailed neckguard. Beneath this emblem was a title in capital letters: 'THE CROMWELL MOVEMENT'. Under this in smaller capitals was the proclamation: 'CRUSADE FOR BRITAIN'.

Clive Keegan glared at his wife. 'What is this rubbish?' He read aloud from the leaflet:

'"People of Britain, we must act. For too long we have sat silent while ever-increasing crime rages unchecked. Now we must unite and fight against those who commit outrages upon innocent men, women and children. One voice can be ignored by our political masters. A million voices cannot be ignored. JOIN THE CROMWELL MOVEMENT . . ."'

At the bottom of the leaflet was printed the address of the Meadowpark Gospel Chapel; only now it was not termed the Gospel Chapel, but instead altered to 'Cromwell House'.

Clive Keegan stared bemusedly at his wife, and asked again, 'What the hell is going on?'

'We're printing leaflets for Mr Jones.' There was a mischievous sparkle in her dark eyes. 'Do you want to help us?'

He thought hard for a few moments, then recollection came. 'Do you mean that chap who was on the television the other night? That bloody cretin who is leading a bunch of half-baked vigilantes?'

He became aware of the furious scowling faces of the three women.

'Mr Jones is not a cretin!' It was the coloured woman, Wisdom Maclure, who first sprang to Ivor Jones' defence, but the other two women were quick to add their voices.

120

'Mr Jones is a wonderful man!' Dorothy Chapman's worn face was flushed with indignation.

'Don't you call him a cretin. He's worth ten like you!' This last was from his wife.

The final sheet came from the printer and its loud purring clicked into stillness.

'I think that's all we need for now, Mrs Maclure.' Lisa Keegan smiled at the other woman. 'We'll parcel them up and take them to Cromwell House. We can use my car.'

'What about my dinner?' her husband demanded. 'Have you got anything ready for me?'

She shook her head. 'You'll have to see about your own meals from now on, Clive. I'll be working full-time at Cromwell House.'

'You'll be what?' He could not believe what he was hearing.

She smiled into his angry scowl. 'Yes, working full-time, and most evenings as well, I expect. Mr Jones has asked for volunteers, and I'm one of them.'

The three women ignored him and bustled around, arranging the leaflets into piles and boxing them up.

He tried another tack, protesting petulantly, 'And who gave you permission to use my equipment?'

'Oh, Clive, stop pouting like a spoiled brat,' his wife chided witheringly. 'You hardly ever use this stuff as it is. And I bought most of it for you anyway.'

'Yes, with my bloody money,' he retorted.

As the women began to carry the boxes out of the house to Lisa Keegan's car, Clive trailed after his wife, asking in a whining voice, 'Well, what time will you be back, Lisa? How long do you think that you'll be away?'

She sighed impatiently. 'I'm not going away, Clive. I'm only going to Cromwell House.'

'But I thought it was a chapel that you've been spending so much time at lately?'

'Oh, I haven't time to explain everything now.' She dismissed his question and brushed past him.

He stood by the car and watched them load all the boxes. As Wisdom Maclure got into the rear seat she told him, 'You should come and listen to Mr Jones sometime, Mr Keegan. He's a great man, he would inspire you.'

He scowled into her pleasant, motherly features and told her sourly, 'I think one fool in a family is enough, don't you? My bloody wife is making an idiot of herself again from what I can see of it.' He vented a sharp exclamation of anger, and told them, 'Bloody Cromwell Movement! You ought to be locked up, the bloody lot of you!'

The women ignored him and drove away, leaving him standing glaring after them.

The newly renamed Cromwell House was a blaze of lights when the three women reached it, and what appeared to be swarms of people were scurrying about, engaged in scores of different tasks.

Ivor Jones had announced the launch of the Cromwell Movement on the previous Sunday evening, and had called for volunteers to help with the publicity and enrolments, and also to clean out, paint and refurbish the maze of cellars which lay beneath the flooring of the main hall. The Chapel had been built on a steep slope which fell sharply away from the road, and the builders had cut into that slope to lay the foundations and cellar floor.

Ivor Jones himself was in Tabernacle Cottage – which he was using as his office – and with him was

Chris Thompson. Jones was on his feet pacing up and down the cramped room, and was thinking aloud.

'Now we've got the correct forms for enrolment and registration of members, we can start taking members from tomorrow. Will you be able to come along and give a hand with that, Mr Thompson?'

The young man nodded readily. 'I'll be here, Mr Jones.'

Even as he agreed he was aware of the by now customary dichotomy in his mind. One section of it was sneering, 'Here you go again, you bloody idiot. More time lost from your real work, and that'll mean another row with Tony Prendergast'; while another section was only too eager to begin the work of taking in members for the Cromwell Movement.

'The enrolment fee for adults can be £25, payable by cash or cheque. For juniors and old-age pensioners, £10. That will also cover their membership fees for their first twelve months membership of the movement.' Jones paused for a moment, then smiled brightly as if he had just thought of something pleasurable. 'Do you know what we'll do, Mr Thompson? We'll set up a social club for our members, with a bar and other amenities. And we'll have a youth club for our juniors. As we expand, there's no reason why we shouldn't be able to set up a whole lot of other benefits as well. Special bulk insurance deals, cheap holidays and stuff like that.'

He became aware of the young man's questioning stare, and he smiled confidently at him.

'Trust me, Mr Thompson. I am being guided in all this by the Lord.' His fiery blue eyes were burning with conviction. 'Each night I pray for guidance, and each night the Lord gives me that guidance.'

123

For an uncomfortable moment Chris Thompson found himself wondering about Jones' sanity, but then mentally shrugged with sardonic humour: 'Are any of us completely sane? I still want to go along for the ride. Normality would be too dull to bear after this.'

There was a knocking at the door, and Lisa Keegan called, 'Can we come in, Mr Jones? We've brought the leaflets.'

'Come, Mrs Keegan,' Jones called back, and the three women came in.

'We've left the boxes in the Chapel, Mr Jones. But I've brought you this one to see.'

Lisa Keegan handed him one of the printed leaflets, which he scanned with every appearance of satisfaction.

'Excellent!' he told them. 'You've done a marvellous job for me, Sisters.'

All three women fluttered and blushed and preened themselves under his warm praise.

'Look at this, Mr Thompson.' Jones handed the leaflet to the younger man, indicating the face of the Ironside trooper. 'That man's face radiates strength and purity and courage, doesn't it? He makes a fine symbol for the Cromwell Movement.' Jones' eyes took on the fire of fanaticism and his voice was strong and vibrant. 'The Cromwell Movement must be like the Ironside troopers of the Lord Protector. A shield and protector for its members. It must be the rock in their lives, the rock which they can trust in, and stand firm upon even when everything around them is sinking into the depths of ruin. The Cromwell Movement must defend its own people at all times, and at all costs. It must become the most important thing in their lives: a father to the fatherless, a mother to the motherless, a sanctuary and safe haven for those who are lost . . .'

The three women were staring at Jones with shining, adoring eyes, and Chris Thompson could also feel himself being swept up by the man's rhetoric.

Jones began to pace up and down the room punching the air with his clenched fists to give emphasis to the points he made.

'The people who'll come to us are the solitary, the lonely, the frightened, those who think that they are failures, who feel embittered by what life has done to them, who haven't achieved what they feel they could have achieved had life given them a better deal. We shall have the envious, the misfits, the defeated, coming to our doors. Every dead-beat and no-hoper with even a spark of spirit left in him or her will want to join us once we are on the march. And above all, we shall attract every victim. Everyone who at some time or other in their lives has been brutalised, or terrified, or robbed or raped will see in us their chance of obtaining revenge.'

He halted; his piercing blue eyes seemed to be staring at something beyond the confines of this shabby room as he whispered hoarsely, 'And I shall give them that chance. I shall give them their time of vengeance!'

He blinked rapidly several times, then his eyes moved to the three women and he told them, 'And you Sisters will obtain your vengeance on those who have harmed you or yours very, very soon. I promise you.'

'Thank you, Mr Jones.' Lisa Keegan's full lips drew back from her white teeth in a savage snarl, and she said fervently, 'God bless you, Mr Jones. God bless you!'

'Amen to that!' Wisdom Maclure's normally pleasant features were bitter and angry, while the worn face of Dorothy Chapman was twisted with hatred as she muttered, 'Amen, Mr Jones. Amen!'

# *Chapter Sixteen*

Detective Chief Inspector Henry Thomas, red-faced, heavy-bellied, and seething with anger, sent for Detective Sergeant Denis Matthews, and when he appeared tossed the copy of the *Gazette and Advertiser* across the desk and demanded loudly, 'Why wasn't I informed of this, Matthews?'

Denis Matthews sighed wearily, and enquired respectfully, 'Informed of what, sir?'

'That! Look, there on the front page.'

Matthews leaned to turn the newspaper, and studied the headlines with eyes that were bleary from the previous night's heavy drinking.

'Ivor Jones launches Cromwell Movement. Modern Crusader opens his campaign. My movement will combat evil wherever it is to be found, Ivor Jones promises . . .'

The detective cleared his sore throat, and informed his superior officer, 'With all respect, sir, you were informed of this development. I stated in my report that such a movement was shortly going to be launched by this man, Jones.'

'I've had George Faraday on the phone to me already this morning.' Thomas ignored Matthews' statement. 'It makes me look a bloody idiot when a member of the Police Authority knows more about a man under our investigation than I do myself. Your detail was to check out this Ivor Jones, and to report back to me.'

Matthews again exhaled a muted sigh of utter weariness, and respectfully informed his superior, 'My report on Ivor Jones was placed in your "In" tray ten days ago, sir. I put it there myself.'

The other man's rubicund cheeks became puce-coloured with temper. 'If that was so, then why haven't I seen it?'

Denis Matthews shook his head. 'I really can't say why you haven't seen it, sir. Unless perhaps someone removed it from the "In" tray before you had a chance to read it.'

'Don't get smart with me, Matthews,' the Chief Inspector warned. 'Don't forget that I was walking a beat before you ever thought of joining the force.'

'No, sir, I won't forget,' the detective answered submissively, and mentally lifted two fingers in lewd salute.

The show of submissiveness did nothing to soothe the fat man's liverish temper. 'It's no wonder that the force is being criticised so much these days. There are too many like you in it, Matthews. Sitting on your arses waiting for pension day to arrive. But you'd better watch your step in future, because I'll be watching you very closely from now on, and if I catch you slacking off again I'll have those bloody stripes off you and you'll find yourself in very serious trouble. Understand?'

Denis Matthews allowed none of the bitter resentment he was feeling to show on his impassive features; he only nodded. 'Yes, sir, I understand. And I apologise if I've let you down on this matter.'

The fat man's temper was mollified slightly by his

subordinate's meek acceptance of the rebuke, and he nodded and ordered curtly, 'Fill me in on this man, Jones. What was the gist of your report on him?'

'I stated that in my opinion Jones was just another nine days' wonder, sir. An irate citizen who won't do any real harm.'

'Is he anti-police?' the other man wanted to know.

Matthews shook his head. 'No, sir, definitely not. Bit of a publicity hound, I think. Likes to see his name in the papers. But he's harmless.'

'I'm just wondering if we should take any action at this time?'

Again Matthews shook his head. 'Not in my opinion, sir. He's got a lot of public sympathy at the moment. We don't really want to be seen to be harassing a law-abiding citizen who is only trying to fight crime, do we?'

'No, of course not. We should be encouraging public-spirited citizens like Ivor Jones, not harassing them. You keep that in mind, Matthews. We've got to get the public on our side, remember that.'

The detective sighed wearily. 'I will, sir.'

'You can go. Keep an eye on this chap Jones, though, and keep me informed of any new developments.' It was the turn of Henry Thomas to sigh wearily. 'I really shouldn't have to check on petty details like this, Matthews. Not with all the other responsibilities I have on my back.'

'No, sir,' Matthews replied submissively. 'I'm sorry you've been inconvenienced, sir. It won't happen again.'

'It had better not, or you won't be seeing any pension,' Thomas grunted, and Matthews made his escape.

As he closed the office door behind him, resentful

fury shuddered through him. 'You fuckin' wanker, Thomas. It's lazy useless bastards like you that have fucked up the force.'

Not for the first time during the last few years, Denis Matthews wondered whether he had misplaced his loyalties.

'I've got eighteen years' exemplary service behind me. Three commendations for bravery. I've been one of the best thief-takers that this city has ever had, and I still have to stand and take shit from a fat, incompetent sod like Henry Thomas. Ivor Jones has got the right idea, hasn't he? He's bypassing the useless wankers like Thomas, and doing the necessary himself.'

He went back to his own office and checked through the current newspapers which were there until he found the copy of the *Gazette and Advertiser*.

Carefully he studied the report of the launching of the Cromwell Movement, then took his Burberry from its hanger and went out into the coldness of the day.

He found Ivor Jones in the main hall of the Chapel, talking to a small group of men and women, while other men and women stood queuing in front of two trestle tables on which there were piles of printed forms. Seated behind the tables were three women and one man, asking questions, filling in the forms and taking money and cheques from those standing before them.

When he saw the policeman enter, Jones said a few words to the group, who then filed out of the hall, some nodding and smiling pleasantly in acknowledgement as they passed Matthews.

The policeman mentally estimated the amounts of money in the open cash-boxes on the table-tops and when Jones came to him warned jokingly, 'You ought to have an armed guard standing over those cash-boxes, Mr Jones. There looks to be a lot of money there.'

'The Lord is the only guard we need, Mr Matthews,' Jones told him very seriously. Then in a lighter tone he asked, 'What brings you here at this hour? Have you come to join my movement?'

'Not on this occasion, Mr Jones. But I have come to talk to you about it.'

'Come into the vestry. There's an electric kettle there and we can have a cup of tea.'

There was an ebullient air about Jones. He seemed somehow taller and leaner, and he smiled readily as he busied himself in brewing the pot of tea and laying out cups and saucers.

When they both had their drinks in front of them, Jones asked, 'Now then, what is it you want to know about the Cromwell Movement?'

'Everything, including where you keep the dirty linen,' the policeman quipped drily. Then he went on, 'But to speak seriously, Mr Jones. This Cromwell Movement you've launched sounds very much like a vigilante organisation. My superiors don't like vigilantes, people taking the law into their own hands.'

'I can assure them, and you, that I've no intention of doing that.' Jones' ready smile had disappeared, and a hard edge entered his voice. 'But on the other hand, I've no intention either of continuing to sit and do nothing while the country goes to rack and ruin, and while evil men and women walk the streets and commit their crimes with impunity.'

'No one commits any crime with impunity, Mr Jones.' Matthews resented this aspersion on

131

his profession, and he answered sharply. 'We police do our job. It's not our fault that crime is increasing. We're starved of the necessary resources that we need.'

'Exactly so, Mr Matthews.' The smile reappeared on Jones' face. 'And what the Cromwell Movement intends to do is to put pressure on the authorities to give the police what they need. It seeks to work with the police, not against them. Ideally, I'm hoping that my movement can perhaps help them out in certain . . . shall I call them, grey areas, where perhaps the police might find difficulties in ensuring that justice is done. Here, look at this.'

He handed one of the Ironside leaflets to the policeman, who studied it with great interest and then handed it back with the comment, 'It's very striking, but it doesn't give any details about how you intend to achieve your objectives.'

'The Lord will show us the way,' Jones told him gravely. Then with apparent casualness he remarked, 'You're the sort of man that I'd hoped to recruit into my movement, Mr Matthews.'

The policeman stared steadily at him, and there was ambiguity in his expression as he replied, 'I must admit there's something that appeals to me about the Cromwell Movement, Mr Jones. But it's early days yet, isn't it? I'll have to wait and see what develops, won't I?'

'Of course you must,' Jones agreed warmly, 'but bear it in mind, Mr Matthews, that there will always be a place for you here if you ever decide to join me. A man with your experience could rise high in my movement.'

'Thank you.' Matthews was genuinely appreciative, and after a slight hesitation told the other man quietly, 'I'm very sympathetic to what you are trying to do here, Mr Jones. And if there's ever anything that you might think I can help you with . . .' He paused and then said meaningly, 'Advice on legal matters, etcetera, then don't hesitate to call on me, will you?' He smiled, and winked. 'It's better sometimes not to have all your friends openly associated with you, you know.'

'I'll remember that, Mr Matthews. I'm really pleased that you and I can understand each other so well. And as a matter of fact there is a small thing that you might be able to help me with. There are a few people that I'd like to get in touch with, but I'm having trouble finding their present whereabouts.'

The policeman's eyes were knowing. 'Well, Mr Jones, if you'd like to give me their names, I might be able to help you.'

Jones frowned regretfully. 'I know some of their names. But there are some others where I only know what they do for a living.'

The policeman pursed his lips and reflected for some moments, then shrugged. 'I'll tell you what. You write down the names that you know, and what those others do for a living, and I'll see what I can do.'

Jones experienced a fast-burgeoning tension as he wrote on a sheet of notepaper. He was gambling on his judgement of the other man's character, and taking a risk by giving Matthews this clue as to his intentions. He handed the sheet of paper to the police officer, who glanced quickly at it and, with a smile quirking the corners of his mouth, nodded.

'Yes, that'll be all right, Mr Jones. Now I'll have to be on my way. Good luck with your new venture.'

133

Ivor Jones visibly relaxed, and felt a rush of satisfaction that he had judged the policeman correctly.

They parted with a genuine warmth of regard, and when he was alone once more Jones smiled broadly and murmured, 'I like you, Mr Matthews. You're a man after my own heart.'

Jones went back into the main hall and stood watching the four people working at the makeshift desks: Lisa Keegan, Dorothy Chapman, Wisdom Maclure and Chris Thompson. If all went as he intended, the Cromwell Movement would be needing many executive officers to deal with its administration. There would be an extended command structure, and he would need loyal and trustworthy subordinates – people who would carry out his orders without question. The three women he was sure of, and had already earmarked them for full-time salaried employment within the movement. But he still had some doubts about Thompson. The young man had ability and intelligence, and had shown courage when confronting the joyriders; but Jones was unsure of his loyalties. Now he decided that he would put the reporter's loyalty to the test as soon as possible.

His gaze moved to Lisa Keegan. He had already decided how he would bind her completely to himself. He would give her what she craved above all else, revenge on the man who had so brutally raped and abused her. Wisdom Maclure and Dorothy Chapman were already his creatures, and he would reward them for their unquestioning loyalty by striking back at the drug-dealers who had caused them both so much misery. Again he stared hard at Chris Thompson, now laughing and joking with one of the men registering for membership.

Jones smiled bleakly and decided, 'I'll take you with us, Thompson, when we go to deal with Lisa Keegan's rapist. That should make a good test for you.'

# Chapter Seventeen

On the morning of the second day after his brief talk with Detective Sergeant Matthews, Ivor Jones received a plain brown envelope in the post. It contained only a list of names and addresses, with extra notations besides some of them. There was nothing to indicate who had sent the envelope to him, nor where the information it contained had originated.

Jones smiled happily, and during the cause of the day went into the city centre and made some purchases of similar types of articles, but from different and widely dispersed shops.

When he returned to Cromwell House, William Rimmer was waiting to report to him on the progress made in his specialised recruitment.

'I've got nine prime ones so far. And there's another half a dozen that are keen to join us. Do you want me to stick to the orginal number we decided on? Or shall I take on the extra lads as well?'

Jones considered briefly, then told him, 'Take on the extras. You never know, there might be a couple who'll get cold feet when they hear what we're going to do. It's okay if they all decide to come in with us anyway. Registration has gone better than I expected, so money won't be a problem for a while.'

Before Rimmer left he instructed, 'I want you to come back here at nine o'clock tonight. I've got a little job on.'

During the course of the day Jones had a word with Lisa Keegan, who was working in the main hall, and then phoned Chris Thompson at the *Gazette* office and told him to come alone to Tabernacle Cottage at nine o'clock that night.

'You can't go out tonight! I ran into Tom in town this afternoon and I've invited him and Alison round for drinks. It's ages since I've seen Alison. We've lots of gossip to catch up on, so you'll have to look after Tom.' Shelagh Perrot's imperious tone brooked no argument, and Chris Thompson sighed unhappily.

'I'm sorry, darling, but I do have to go out.'

'No, you don't *have* to go. You have to stay here and help me to entertain them; they're your friends as much as mine.' Her beautiful face betrayed a petulant determination to get her own way.

For a moment Chris Thompson almost did as he always did, and surrendered to her will. But then a mental image of Ivor Jones' fiery blue eyes entered his mind, and he wondered if those eyes would fill with contempt if he failed to keep their appointment because he was fearful of his girl-friend's petulance. An unfamiliar stubbornness invaded the young man, and he shook his head.

'No, darling, I've got to go and see Mr Jones.'

He steeled himself to face the contemptuous tirade she would hurl at him, but to his surprise Shelagh said nothing abusive, only stared questioningly at him.

'Why does he want to see you tonight?'

He could only shrug and tell her, 'I don't know, but he said that it was important.'

The young man would have been even more surprised if he could have read Shelagh Perrot's thoughts. Although she would never have admitted it to any living soul, she had been greatly impressed with Ivor Jones. The man was totally alien to her own world of suave sleek men and brittle fashionable women. When, with all those others, she had followed Ivor Jones to confront the joyriders, she had thrilled to see him go fearlessly forward against a roaring, hurtling mass of metal. It had irresistibly reminded her of the childhood stories about mythical heroes and legendary knights. And although she found his middle-aged stockiness physically unattractive, on that night he had radiated strength and power and charisma.

Beneath her surface materialism, and obsession with self, Shelagh Perrot possessed much imagination and capacity for poetical fancies. She was able to picture Jones as some ancient warrior monk of the Crusades. She was also able to imagine herself as the object of his devotion, and had amused herself with the fancies of trying to seduce him.

Now, she suddenly smiled and told Chris Thompson, 'Well, if it's Mr Jones, then of course you must go.' She paused and as if the idea had just occurred to her, suggested, 'I'll come with you, shall I?'

He gaped in amazement. 'But what about Tom and Alison?'

'What about them?' She laughed dismissively. 'I can see them any time I want, can't I? And frankly I'm beginning to find them both very boring.'

Accustomed as he was to her lightning changes of mood and fancy, the young man could only smile wryly. But then he told her, 'I'm sorry, darling, but you can't come with me tonight. Mr Jones was quite explicit that I was to come alone.'

She tried to argue, but he was adamant. Then she tried to coax and cajole, but although he was charmed by her affectionate advances, he still would not give in. And at last she accepted defeat, but with a customary flash of thwarted temper.

'Go, then. But don't expect me to be here when you get back!' She flounced away into the bedroom, slamming the door so hard behind her that the walls trembled.

He felt miserable as he stared at the closed door, and normally at this stage of the argument he would have gone after her, offering to do what she wanted, asking for her forgiveness for having angered her. But the mental image of Ivor Jones' fiery blue eyes persisted in his mind, and to his amazement he found that the compulsion exerted upon him by that mental image was greater than that of the tempestuous young woman in the bedroom.

Shelagh Perrot heard the flat door open and close behind her lover, and could hardly believe that he had dared to defy her. Perversely she smiled, strangely gratified by this proof that the charisma Ivor Jones exerted over those who came close to him was indeed a tangible and powerful force.

'If he can make a worm like Chris turn, then he really is quite something,' she told herself. 'It's not just in my own imagination, is it? Ivor Jones is really a hell of a man.'

Humming gaily she began to prepare for her friends' arrival, making up her face with great skill, and satisfied with the reflection of her own beauty in the dressing-table mirror. Already in her mind she had discarded the hapless Chris Thompson, and had become the adored mistress of Ivor Jones, the all-powerful leader of the Cromwell Movement.

In the home of Lisa Keegan, a dispute was taking place.

'You've been there all day! Why must you go back there tonight?' Clive Keegan's plump pink face wore an expression of exasperation. 'I come home after a hard day's work and there's no meal ready, the house is a shambles, and all you can say is that you've been too busy to do anything! What in hell's name is happening to you, Lisa? You were difficult enough before, but now you're bloody impossible!'

Lisa Keegan's attitude was one of supreme indifference. 'I told you before, Clive, that you'll have to look after yourself for a while.'

With an immense effort he controlled his urge to hit her, and attempted to be reasonable and understanding. 'Look, Lisa, I know that it's been very hard for you to come to terms with what happened. And I know that since that man has been released you've been upset by him again. But why do you have to take it all out on me?'

Lisa regarded her husband with mingled feelings: guilt at the way she was treating him clashed with irritation for his lack of any real understanding of how she felt, dislike of his blustering seethed against acknowledgement that he was trying to behave as a caring husband. But above all else, contempt for what she perceived to be his weakness of character and his cowardice over-rode all the other emotions pullulating within her.

His self-pitying whine drilled into her brain.

'I was happy when you joined this Cromwell Movement, Lisa. I thought that it would help you to be like you used to be. I thought that it would help you to come to your senses, and be a proper wife to me again. But it just seems to have made you worse. You've no interest in the boys, you've no interest in your home, you've no interest in our marriage any more. All that seems to fill your mind is this bloody Cromwell Movement, and that cretinous idiot, Ivor Jones! Who does the bloody fool think he is? Moses? Does he think he's bloody Moses leading the bloody fools who follow him through some bloody wilderness or other?'

Clive Keegan threw his arms skywards, and shouted. 'What sort of man does the things he does? What sort of man goes chasing bloody drug-dealers across lousy council playing-fields? What sort of man takes a hundred half-baked morons and puts them in front of speeding cars? I'll tell you what sort of man, Lisa. A bloody madman! A bloody lunatic! That's what this Ivor Jones is, a bloody lunatic! And you're as moronic and crazy as he is.'

All the blood drained from Lisa Keegan's face, and her dark eyes glittered murderously. Her husband stared aghast at the transformation in her features, and momentarily feared that what he had accused her of being was in fact true. At this moment she looked like a homicidal maniac.

But when she spoke, her tone was icy cool, her words clipped and modulated and perfectly controlled.

'Well, if that is what you believe, Clive, then divorce me. I'm more than willing to give you your freedom. So just let me go, and you can lay all the blame for our marriage breaking up on me.'

He peered searchingly at her, and asked disbelievingly, 'You don't really mean that, do you?'

'I've never meant anything more in my life,' she retorted bitingly, and then before he could react, she was gone.

He listened to her car engine start up and move away, and tears stung his eyes. But then anger forced him to dash those tears away as he muttered, 'I won't divorce you, you bloody cow. I won't let you go. If I can't have you, then I can make sure that nobody else will either.'

As the distance between herself and her husband rapidly increased, Lisa's own inner maelstrom of thought swirled and eddied, and eager expectation filled her.

She knew that tonight her most consuming desire was to be satisfied. Tonight, Ivor Jones had promised to give her what she had lusted for during so many weary months; he had promised her revenge on her rapist. This obsession was so all-encompassing that she gave no heed as to what he might require of her in return . . . because she knew that whatever he might ask from her, she would give it, and give it gladly and willingly. In him she had found a man that she could trust and revere, a man she was prepared to follow without hesitation or question wheresoever he chose to lead.

She drove too fast for safety through the dark, drizzle-wet streets, goaded by the hungry compulsion to satisfy her terrible need for revenge.


When Chris Thompson reached Tabernacle Cottage he found Ivor Jones and Lisa Keegan there, together with another man who was a stranger to him. He stared curiously at the stranger, noting the lean, hard appearance, and sensing the aura of potent menace he exuded. This stranger made him nervous and tense, and he felt relief when Ivor Jones introduced him.

'This is Mr William Rimmer, Mr Thompson. He is a member of my movement. I hope that you and he will come to be friends as well as colleagues.'

The young man thought, 'I'm glad to hear he's on our side,' and took the chair that Jones indicated.

Jones moved to stand facing the three seated people, and began quietly to speak.

'You have all become associated with my movement for your own individual reasons. Now that the Cromwell Movement has been launched I shall be requiring full-time executive officers. Those whom I select to join me in my crusade must give themselves over to the service of the movement completely. They must put it before their own pleasures, their material comforts, even their loved ones and families if needs be. They must in effect belong to the Movement body and soul; they must give it their total loyalty.'

Chris Thompson's initial reaction to this preamble was a secret wry snigger, and the thought that Ivor Jones was asking for a hell of a lot. He risked a covert glance at his companions, expecting to see some hint of what he was feeling himself in their faces. But to his surprise he saw that they were both nodding at Jones in eager acceptance.

Jones' gaze fixed on his face, and he felt as if the fiery, piercing blue eyes were penetrating his mind, and noting the wryly cynical reaction. Flustered, he also nodded and tried to assume an expression of eager acceptance. Jones frowned slightly, and to the young man's relief transferred his attention to Lisa Keegan.

As he smiled kindly at her, Lisa felt as if she were being enfolded by loving and protecting arms, and she experienced a surge of gratitude towards him.

'Mr Rimmer has already been appointed as a movement officer. Tonight I have made the decision to appoint you as an officer of my movement also, Mrs Keegan.'

Pride and joy welled up in her at this confirmation of his high regard, and she exclaimed. 'I only hope that I'll prove worthy, Mr Jones.'

Jones nodded, then threw back his head and began to declaim sonorously. 'Vengeance is mine, saith the Lord. This is true. But the Lord also knows that to exact that vengeance he must use the bodies and the minds of men and women. We shall tonight become the intruments of the Lord's vengeance. We shall be the swords of the Lord, which he will take in His hand to smite the evil ones.'

Chris Thompson's throat tightened apprehensively, and he began to wonder what was to happen. A sense of foreboding crept over him.

'Mrs Keegan, will you tell us what happened to you?' Jones invited, and Lisa felt her colour rise as embarrassment flooded through her.

'Speak, Mrs Keegan. We are your brethren, and have the right to know.'

She stared into his eyes, once more experiencing the sensation that loving and protecting arms were enfolding her. All reluctance to speak left her, and she was able to relate her experience calmly.

'I was attacked and raped by a man who broke into my house one night when I was alone there.' Tears brimmed in her eyes, but her voice remained clear. 'The man didn't simply beat and rape me. He did other things to me as well . . . filthy, bestial things.'

She swallowed hard to dispel the lump that had suddenly formed in her throat. 'I have never felt clean from that night onwards.'

'Tell us what happened to your attacker, Mrs Keegan,' Jones ordered.

Anger rose in Lisa, and her face twisted with hatred as she spat out, 'He was sentenced to only four years' imprisonment. But he didn't serve even half of that before he was released. And now he is back in the city, and he has twice waylaid me, and made obscene gestures and threats. He is also telephoning me regularly.' Now she started to tremble with the force of her rage and hatred. 'The police say that they can do nothing, because there are no witnesses. They say that he actually has to attack me before they can touch him.' Her voice suddenly went high in wailing outrage. 'And my husband is too much of a coward to deal with the situation! So that evil animal can keep on torturing me for just as long as he wants, and then when he's ready, he can come for me again one night, and do the same things, or worse than he did to me before. And there is nothing that the police or my own husband will do to stop him . . .'

'Thank you, Mrs Keegan, there's no need to go on.' Jones intervened to save her from further distress, then his eyes switched to Chris Thompson. 'Now, Mr Thompson, are you prepared to go with me and to deal with this evil man?'

Doubt clamoured and Chris Thompson hesitated, then slowly nodded. But the fiery blue eyes continued to stare hard at him, and he was driven to ask, 'Is anything wrong, Mr Jones?'

Jones nodded slowly. 'I'm not sure that you possess the necessary dedication to belong to my movement. You seem hesitant and unsure.'

Chris Thompson imagined that the other man and the woman were looking at him with contempt, and he felt driven to wipe that contempt from their eyes.

'I have the dedication, Mr Jones. I'll do whatever anyone else will do to prove that fact.'

Even while he was voicing this defiant declaration, a part of his mind seemed to be divorced from him, demanding, 'What are you saying? What are you doing? Have you gone crazy?'

Jones continued to stare hard at him for some time, then appeared satisfied and asked, 'You have your car here, don't you, Mr Thompson?'

'Yes.'

'Good, then we'll use it. Now let's prepare.'

He went into the other room, to reappear almost immediately carrying a large plastic bin liner from which he took out some one-piece boiler-suits, rubber boots, black balaclava helmets with eyeholes cut into them, and sawn-off baseball bats.

'We shall put these on. Take off all of your own clothing. Mrs Keegan; you may change in the other room.' He smiled grimly. 'Don't be concerned about the fit, Mrs Keegan, this isn't a fashion show.'

Lisa Keegan's answering smile was one of exultation. At last her time had come, and she gloried in that fact.

Chris Thompson's sense of foreboding pressed heavily upon his spirits as he changed, but he felt that he had no other choice but to obey Ivor Jones. He seemed to be acting without any volition of his own, and had the weird sensation that Jones possessed complete dominance over his mind and body.

In Chris Thompson's sporty, high-powered car they headed towards a district close to the city centre, and Jones directed, 'The man we want lives

146

in a bed-sit in Elmer Street. Do you know where that is?'

Chris Thompson nodded, and swallowed hard to ease the nervous constriction in his throat, then he asked, 'Will the man be there? In the bed-sit, I mean?'

'No, not at this time of night. He'll be in a pub a short distance from Elmer Street, the Boilermakers' Arms. Do you know it?' Jones spoke confidently.

Chris wondered how Jones could be so sure, but only confirmed, 'Yes, I know the pub. It's an awful dump. There's trouble there most nights.'

They travelled through the concrete canyons of the city centre, bleak and almost deserted under the cold sodium lamps, and rain began to spatter against the windscreen of the car.

'Good,' Jones breathed. 'This will help us. It'll stop anybody hanging about in the streets.'

From the centre they entered the district they sought: close, huddled terraces of grimy, run-down red-brick houses and decaying industrial buildings. At one time a project to rebuild had been started here and many of the terraces of houses had been bulldozed and cleared; but then government funding had dried up, the project had come to a halt, and now only the scattered stretches of weed-grown wasteland were left to bear testimony to vanished dreams.

Jones directed Chris Thompson to halt the car on one of these stretches of wasteland near to the brilliantly lit façade of the Boilermakers' Arms. From their parked position they had a clear view of the pub entrance, and could see who came and went.

Despite the long recession there seemed to be no shortage of people able to afford to drink, judging by the constant stream of men and women passing in and out of the pub's doors, and even at this distance they could hear clearly the thudding beat of the music that increased in volume each time the doors swung ajar.

Now that the car's engine had been killed the inner surfaces of the windows started to mist over, and Chris Thompson was forced to continually wipe the glass clear. He was glad to have something to do which helped in a small way to relieve the tension he was under.

His companions were all silent, the only sounds in the car the hissing of their breathing and the occasional clunk of metal as the engine cooled and contracted. Thompson was again asking himself what he was doing here? Why was he sitting in this car in the company of virtual strangers, waiting to ambush a complete stranger whom he had never seen before in his life, and who had done no harm to him personally?

'I must be insane,' he thought over and over again. 'I *must* be insane.'

Waves of apprehension washed over him, causing his throat to tighten and his mouth to dry and parch. Yet at the same time there was excitement in him, and the anticipatory bloodlust of the hunter. Thinking of what the young woman had told them, he felt a sexual frisson in his groin as he remembered her full breasts rising and falling. A sharp mental image came into his mind of her lying naked and defenceless before him, and for one brief instant he could share the ravening instincts of her rapist. Then he was attacked by acute self-disgust that he could entertain such imaginings in his mind, and he tried to push the shamefully obscene thoughts

148

from him, but still they persisted in spite of all his efforts.

'There he is!' Jones' sibilant whisper brought them all from their private reveries, and he sought confirmation. 'That's him, isn't it, Mrs Keegan?'

Lisa stared hard at the man illuminated by the garish lights of the pub, and terrible memories assailed her, momentarily making it impossible for her to speak. Once again she experienced the terror she had known, and her body trembled uncontrollably. Then the furious lust for vengeance overpowered all else, and she hissed venemously, 'That's him, Mr Jones. That's the filthy animal who raped me!'

Chris Thompson was surprised at how young, clean-cut and neatly dressed the man appeared, and such was his surprise that he muttered aloud, 'He looks too respectable to be a rapist, doesn't he?

Jones laughed softly. 'In nature it's often the most beautiful creatures who turn out to be the most poisonous, Mr Thompson.'

They watched as the young man walked in their direction on the opposite side of the roadway, continually disappearing and reappearing between the parked cars, vans and lorries that lined the gutters.

When he neared them Jones tapped Thompson's shoulder and instructed, 'Pull out, go down the road and take the second turning left.'

Thompson obeyed, and they travelled a couple of hundred yards further on from their quarry and turned into a short street of derelict industrial buildings. The street-lamps here had all been smashed, and it was dark and deserted.

Jones issued quick instructions and all of them got out of the car, pulled the balaclava helmets over their heads and took up the sawn-off baseball bats. Then they hid themselves in the shadows and waited.

They could hear the young man whistling as he neared them, and as they watched he kicked an empty beer-can and sent it clattering along the deserted roadway. Then he was passing them, and Jones shouted, 'Get him!'

Chris Thompson had been engaged in silent troubled debate while he waited in the shadows, doubts as to what he was doing weighing heavily upon him. But when he heard Jones shout and saw the quarry turn in sudden shock, all those doubts and fears fell from him and he exploded forward, weapon raised high, shouting gutturally.

'Bastard! Bastard! Bastard!'

His raised arm chopped down savagely, and he felt the impact jarring through his wrist bones as the bat cracked against the young man's skull.

The young man fell on to his hands and knees, and the four jostled each other in their eagerness to get at him. As their arms rose and fell, the cracking and thudding of the blows created a staccato rhythm.

The fallen man screamed out once only, then that scream was choked as a bat smashed into his mouth – bursting lips, breaking teeth, drowning his outcry in a rushing of blood and agony.

'Pull his legs open,' Jones ordered, and Chris Thompson and Rimmer each took hold of an ankle and wrenched the almost senseless man's legs wide apart.

Jones gripped Lisa Keegan's arm and whispered urgently into her ear, 'Make sure he can never rape again.'

Bloodlust was raging in her brain, and she needed no second bidding. She positioned herself and began

150

to batter his unprotected groin and genitals with an almost methodical precision, the heavy bat clubbing and crushing, and smashing.

Then Jones was ordering, 'That's it, leave it. Get back to the car.'

He was forced to bodily pull away both Lisa Keegan and Chris Thompson.

Thompson's eyes were wild and staring, and he felt that he was peering through a red mist. Then his senses returned, the mist cleared, and the urge to get away, to escape, overwhelmed all other emotions.

They crammed into the car, Thompson slammed into gear and the tyres screeched as he sent the vehicle screaming down the dark street.

'Slow down, you fool!' Jones ordered curtly; his fingers clamped and painfully squeezed Chris Thompson's shoulder, causing him to wince as he brought the speed down.

As the car travelled sedately through the city centre, its occupants listened to Jones' voice caressing them, telling them how well they had done, how splendidly they had carried out the Lord's work, and had won the Lord's blessings.

At Tabernacle Cottage they changed back into their ordinary clothes and Jones took away the other clothing, rubber boots and baseball bats. Then he told them to make their separate ways home, adding that if they should be asked any questions, the four of them had spent the evening here in Tabernacle Cottage having a bible reading and discussion group.

Chris Thompson drove slowly through the streets, the pavements deserted beneath the cheerless light of the towering concrete lamps, and tried to rationalise what he had done that night. Now he thought back with amazement and disbelief at his own savagery.

During that brief span of vicious attack all the veneer of sophisticated civilisation had been ripped aside, and a primitive atavistic beast had come howling forth from the buried depths of his psyche. Even now he found it difficult to accept that he had behaved in such a manner.

'What the hell is Jones doing to me?' he questioned. 'What's happening to me?'

Then, as if from some source outside himself, a voice whispered in his mind. 'But you enjoyed battering that man tonight, didn't you? You enjoyed hunting him down and battering him to a pulp. You enjoyed it!'

The civilised repulsion against what he had done was gradually being infiltrated by an obscene yet thrilling exhilaration, and he was forced to surrender to its insidious impulsion.

'Yes, I did . . . I did enjoy it.'

His lips drew back from his teeth without his conscious volition, and he grinned like some ferocious animal. 'I enjoyed it . . . I *enjoyed* it.'

Lisa Keegan left with the others, but then made an excuse that she had left something behind, and returned to the cottage.

Jones opened the door to her soft knocking, and although surprised at seeing her, invited her in. He turned away from her and her eyes widened as she saw him slip a pistol beneath the cushion of one of the chairs.

When he turned back to her he realised from her shocked expression that she had seen the weapon and he smiled reassuringly. 'It's only a safety precaution, Mrs Keegan. I have enemies who wish to harm me.'

He waited expectantly, and she fumbled for the words to tell him of her gratitude for what he had done for her that night. She felt purged of her shame; she felt clean again. She gazed at him with worship in her dark eyes, desperately wanting to give herself to him fully; to merge with him both physically and spiritually. Yet she hesitated from offering him her body. She could not bear to risk rejection of any sort from him.

He listened in silence to her halting, fumbling words, then smiled kindly at her, and reached out to pat her shoulder in a fatherly manner.

'You've become one of my closest and most trusted aides, Mrs Keegan. Tonight we've forged a bond between us that nothing will ever break.'

Tears of happiness filled her eyes and as he gently ushered her out into the night she snatched his hand to her lips and covered it with passionate kisses.

'God bless you, Sister,' he told her quietly. 'Rest well, because tomorrow we have much to do.'

As she drove home Lisa Keegan revelled in her sense of new-found contentment. She had found peace of mind for the first time since she had been raped, and she owed this wonderful feeling to Ivor Jones.

'I'll serve him, and honour and obey him, until the day I die,' she vowed fiercely. 'And whatever he commands me to do, I'll do it gladly.'

The house was in darkness when she arrived back home, and she was grateful that she would not have to face her husband.

In the silent living room she saw a note on the table and when she picked it up and read it, she threw back her head and laughter pealed from her. Almost hysterically, she laughed and laughed and laughed.

The note had been left by her husband, to tell her that he had gone back to his mother's house and would stay there until she, Lisa, came to her senses.

When she went to her bed she slept well and deeply, and her dreams were of strong, comforting, protecting arms enfolding her in safety . . . and in love.

The flat shared by Chris Thompson and Shelagh Perrot was in an ultra-modern luxury block largely lived in by the young and upwardly mobile. The block was situated in the opulent Highfield suburb on the northern outskirts of the city, with a backdrop of wooded hills and moorlands.

Thompson pulled into the garage area and looked up at the flat's windows. He saw Shelagh's head and shoulders briefly outlined in the bedroom window as she stared down towards him, and he felt a sudden pulsing of sexual excitement in his groin.

By the time he had parked and locked the car that sexual excitement had intensified to a fiercely throbbing torment, and he cursed the slowness of the lift that bore him up to the top floor of the block.

He hurried into the dimly-lit bedroom and found Shelagh lying in bed.

'I sent Tom and Alison away early,' she told him. 'Now, what did Ivor Jones want you for?'

With fingers made clumsy by haste he tore off his clothing, and she chuckled huskily as she saw his immense erection.

'You've really missed me then,' she joked.

He made no reply, only dragged the sheets down from her slender body and fell upon her with ravenous greed.

She cried out in protest as he savagely bludgeoned her rounded thighs apart with his knees, and drove his manhood into her moist heat.

At first she resisted, tearing at his back and shoulders with her hooked nails, jerking her hips in a fruitless effort to slip him out from her body. But then his driving passion brought an answering response, and she began to gasp and cry out; her hands and arms and legs clutched and held, and she sucked his mouth with a greed that matched his own. As he pounded his hips harder and harder against her soft silkiness, the young man's mind was filled with the images of baseball bats smashing down, breaking bones, crushing flesh, sending blood flying and splattering. He felt all-powerful, all-conquering, and his lust was a madness enslaving his body. The woman screamed in climax and writhed and shuddered in his arms, but still he drove himself harder and harder into her; when she lay spent and exhausted his sensation of dominance, of mastery, only served to increase his already unbearable excitement, and he became a creature of solely fleshly sensations, his mind conscious only of the need to satiate himself in the body beneath him. He was no longer even aware that this was the woman he loved, she had become a nameless being, who existed only to satisfy his rampaging hunger.

And then, abruptly, it was over, without climax, without the exquisite pleasures of orgasm. He had simply had enough, and had exorcised whatever demons had controlled him.

He rolled off her and lay on his back, sweating heavily, panting for breath, utterly content.

After a time Shelagh raised herself on her elbow and stared wonderingly at him.

'What got into you, Chris? I've never known you like that before.'

He could only shake his head wordlessly, not even meeting her eyes.

She stared hard at him, and then gasped and pointed to his hands. 'You've got blood on them!'

In sudden alarm she sat up and got off the bed, peering down at her body and hurrying to the mirror to examine every inch of her smooth skin. But there were no bleeding wounds on her body, and she came back to stand staring down at him with wide eyes in which lurked fearful uncertainties.

'What happened tonight, Chris? What did you and Ivor Jones do? Where did that blood on your hands come from? What have you been doing? Tell me, Chris! Tell me!' The anxious questions tumbled from her lips in a frantic torrent.

He met her frightened eyes, found himself despising what he saw in them, and felt a sudden urge to hurt her physically and mentally – to repay her for all the pain and humiliations that she had caused him during their relationship. But that urge disappeared as quickly as it had come, and now a delightful sense of intoxicated lassitude stole over him. He felt as if he had been drinking fine wines, which had mellowed and cheered him, and filled him with well-being.

When he finally answered her his voice was slurred, as if he really was drunk. Smiling, he told her, 'Tonight I've experienced the greatest thrill that I've ever known in my entire life.'

She stared in perplexed incomprehension, and almost pleaded, 'But what have you *done*, Chris? Won't you tell me what you've done?'

'That is none of your business!' he stated flatly, and turned over on his side to fall instantly asleep.

Shelagh Perrot stood for a long time listening to his snores. Slowly her own anxieties and fears lessened, and her curiosity became all-dominant.

'What is Ivor Jones up to? What's he doing to make Chris behave like this? What sort of a man is he? How has he managed to change Chris so much? I have to get to know him. I must get to know him.'

Eventually she lay down by her lover, and with her mind full of Ivor Jones slowly drifted into sleep.

# *Chapter Eighteen*

Chris Thompson awoke with the same sense of pervasive well-being with which he had gone to sleep the previous night. Shelagh was not in the bed, but he knew that she would have gone on the early train to London to see her agent.

He showered and shaved, then drank several cups of strong sweet coffee. Afterwards he dressed with care and, whistling light-heartedly, journeyed to the *Gazette* offices in the city centre.

Because he had arrived early, he made a special point of going to wish Tony Prendergast good morning, and after the usual exchange of elaborate sarcasms, he went to his desk and phoned the Central Police Station.

As the calling tone repeated, he was invaded with the tension of anticipation. He felt his stomach fluttering with nervous excitement.

'Central Police CID, Detective Sergeant Matthews. Can I help you?'

'Hello, Denis, it's Chris Thompson. Have you got anything interesting for me?'

'Only the usual, Chris.' There was a pause and then the policeman began to recite a list of crimes ranging from burglary to auto theft to assault.

The reporter listened tensely for mention of the

battered rapist, but none was made. He couldn't understand how such a serious assault could have gone unreported, but he dared not draw the policeman's attention to the omission. Then, just as he was about to say thank you and ring off, Matthews added, '. . . Oh, yes, and there was a possible hit-and-run in Stokesay Street. It doesn't look as though the guy is going to survive.'

Chris Thompson swallowed hard and tried to sound bored and uninterested. 'Oh, yeah. Well, I suppose I'd better make a note of it. What's the guy's name?'

'Ray Benton.' Matthews sniffed disparagingly. 'He won't be much of a loss if he does snuff it. He's a convicted rapist, and he's got enough form to run a book on. Whoever hit him must have a bloody big dent in their car, though, because he was really smashed up.'

'Any ideas about it?' Thompson asked with assumed casualness.

'Probably kids in a nicked motor.' Matthews chuckled grimly. 'Perhaps you should get Ivor Jones down there with his movement. He'd soon stop the joyriding around Stokesay. Do you know, we haven't had another complaint about it from Flowerbank Road since he took his people up there.'

Chris Thompson was able to laugh easily, and to joke, 'I'll give him your suggestion, Denis. I'll probably be seeing him later today.'

'You're getting very involved with the Cromwell Movement, aren't you, Chris? I'm surprised about that.'

'Why?' Thompson was instantly defensive. 'Why should you be surprised?'

'Well, I wouldn't have thought that something like

that was really up your street, Chris. You've always seemed more of a wine-bar and club merchant, rather than a latterday crusader.'

The young man found himself resenting the veiled mockery in the other's tone, but he only replied lightly, 'You know me, Denis, I'll mix with anybody for a good story.' He could not resist a swift barb. 'Even with the police ... Bye now, and thanks a lot.'

He put the phone down and sat drumming his fingers on the desk, his thoughts racing.

The rapist wasn't expected to live! If he died that would mean that they had murdered him! That all four of them were killers!

Fear lanced through him, and he felt a clammy sheen of sweat start out upon his skin. Desperately he tried to recall everything that had happened the previous night, trying to think if they could have left some clue which would betray them. He racked his brains for long, long minutes, and could remember nothing that might lead to their discovery. He sought to draw comfort from what Denis Matthews had said, that it looked like a possible hit-and-run. Surely if the police had suspected anything else, then Denis would have mentioned that fact to him. At the very least dropped a hint that deliberate foul play was suspected?

'Mr Thompson, I'm most awfully sorry to interrupt your thoughts, which I am sure are of the most sublime content, but could you possibly drag yourself away from your desk for a teensy-weensy while, and go and see our revered leader of the Council? He has specifically requested your esteemed presence at his audience chamber in the Council Palace!'

Tony Prendergast was standing in front of Chris Thompson's desk, humbly crouching in supplication.

Under too much strain to bother to make any flowery reply, Thompson merely nodded absently, stood up and went away silently, leaving the other man staring in puzzlement after him.


George Faraday, leader of the City Council and Vice-Chairman of the Police Authority, was a product of the city slums who, by sheer determination and perseverance, had risen far above his lowly origins. But to his credit, he had never forgotten the people from whom he had sprung, and for whom he had a genuine concern. His aged mother still lived in an old people's flat on the vast Meadowpark Council Estate, and stubbornly refused to let him take her from there; his two sisters and their families also lived on the estate. Faraday was a man of considerable intelligence and attainments. His family had been too poor to afford to keep him at school beyond his fifteenth birthday, and had put him to work as a builder's labourer. So he had enrolled in the city night schools, and over the years had succeeded in educating himself and gaining the necessary qualifications to win entrance to a university and to obtain a good degree. His life had been a hard and gruelling struggle, and he had known bitter poverty as a child and young man. Now, in his sixtieth year, he was wealthy and successful, with many business interests, and regarded himself – with perhaps justifiable conceit – as being one of the 'kings' of the city.

In contrast to many of his fellow local politicians, George Faraday was basically an honest man, but like many other honest men he could at times deviate from the straight and narrow path of moral probity to gain his own ends. These deviations he excused on the grounds that there were times when those ends justified the means.

Now, when his secretary showed the young newspaper reporter into his luxurious office, Faraday briefly considered whether he should deviate from the path of moral probity, and decided against it.

His association with Chris Thompson was of several years' standing, and was one of mutual benefit. Faraday would feed the reporter with juicy titbits of inside news, and in return Thompson would slant certain newspaper stories favourably towards George Faraday. Both men had considerable respect for the other's shrewdness, and both trusted each other up to a certain point.

Thompson had managed to thrust his worries into the recesses of his mind. Now, wondering why Faraday had summoned him here, his acute brain was examining various possibilities.

'Chris, thank you for coming so quickly.' Faraday rose and came out from behind his vast, leather-topped desk to shake the young man's hand warmly. He was a big man, still robust and fit-looking, and his well-barbered white hair was thick and luxuriant. 'How are you, my boy?'

'I'm fine, thank you, Mr Faraday, and you and Mrs Faraday are well, I hope?'

'In the pink, Chris! In the pink,' Faraday assured him heartily. 'Sit down, my boy, and make yourself comfortable. Would you like some coffee or tea? Or perhaps something stronger?'

'No, thank you.' Chris Thompson seated himself in the expensive leather armchair in front of the desk, and relaxed back against its opulent cushioning. He always enjoyed coming here to this office. The warm welcome and the trappings of power and influence made him feel that he was accepted by those who wielded that power and influence, and that he himself was on the upward path.

'Try one of these, Chris. They're just in from Cuba.' Faraday proffered a box of thick, fragrant-smelling cigars, and the young man accepted and allowed the other man to supply him with a light from the solid silver table lighter

When both men had their cigars burning well, and were relaxed, Faraday asked, 'This chap Ivor Jones. What can you tell me about him?'

Chris Thompson stared in surprise, and the older man grinned, displaying expensive dentistry.

'It's all right, Chris. I know that you're involved with him. Whatever passes between us here today remains strictly confidential.'

'Oh, I know that, Mr Faraday. It's just that I'm surprised by your interest in Mr Jones.'

The shrewd older man noted the use of the prefix, and nodded wisely. 'I see you've got respect for him at any rate, Chris.'

Thompson nodded readily. 'A great deal of respect, Mr Faraday.'

'Good! If a fly young chap like you has respect for him, then he must be worth it. Tell me all about him. What's he like. What does he intend doing? Why is he doing it? Do you think he *can* do it?'

The younger man thought for some moments and then began to speak, and George Faraday listened intently to the long recital. When Chris Thompson at last fell silent, Faraday nodded as if satisfied with what he had heard.

'I'll be getting in touch with your Mr Jones, Chris.

I might be able to help him in some way or other. But that information is strictly confidential – with the exception of Mr Jones himself, of course.'

Chris Thompson accepted without demur. 'Certainly, Mr Faraday.'

Realising the interview was at an end, he stood up and took his leave; then at the door he halted and turned.

'Can I ask you something, Mr Faraday? Strictly confidential, naturally.'

The other man nodded his permission.

'Why are you so interested in Mr Jones? And why are you prepared to help him?'

The older man's expression was sombre, and his tone was harsh when he replied, 'For a long time now I've been watching this country dragged down into ruin by the self-serving, gutless bastards who rule it. I'm an old-fashioned patriot, Chris. I love this country with all its faults. If a man like your Mr Jones is prepared to stand up and fight to bring back some decency to our land, then I'm ready to help him . . .'

As Chris Thompson drove back to the *Gazette* offices he thought about the fact that twice that morning men had referred to his involvement with Ivor Jones. It was as though he was now being thought of as an Ivor Jones disciple by those who knew him. He felt both disturbed and gratified by this. Disturbed because he himself could not fully understand how in such a short space of time Jones had managed to influence him so much. Gratified, because if a man like the powerful George Faraday considered Ivor Jones was becoming an important figure, then Thompson himself could only gain kudos by being closely associated with him. The thought of Ray

Benton, the man who might be dying, suddenly no longer bothered him. He was invaded by the bizarre conviction that Ivor Jones was invulnerable, and that that invulnerability also encompassed himself.

His good humour was completely restored by the time he returned into the *Gazette* offices, and when Tony Prendergast enquired what Faraday had wanted to see him about, Thompson grinned and tapped the side of his nose with his forefinger.

'I'm not allowed to tell you, Mr Prendergast. Even though it grieves my heart to have to refuse you anything.'

Pleased by the aggrieved look on the assistant editor's face, Thompson sat down at his desk, and as he did so his phone rang. It was Denis Matthews.

'Hello, Chris, just thought I'd pass on a bit of news. That hit-and-run case, Ray Benton, died about an hour ago without regaining consciousness. Good riddance to bad rubbish, I'd say. What would you say?'

Warning bells rang in the reporter's brain. Something in the policeman's tone of voice suggested that he knew much much more about the real causes of Ray Benton's death than he was revealing.

The young man tried to sound casual and uncaring. 'Well, I couldn't really give any opinion about that, Denis. I never knew the man.'

Matthews chuckled drily. 'No, but you know the woman he raped, don't you?'

'Do I?'

'Yes, it's that pretty woman who works with you at Cromwell House . . . Lisa Keegan . . . It'll be good news for her, won't it?'

Chris Thompson was beginning to feel toyed with, and he replied a trifle heatedly, 'I don't know what

165

sort of news it will be for her, Denis. She's never talked to me about what happened to her.'

'All right, Chris, if you say so.' The other man was openly sceptical now. 'Anyway, you can say in your report that I'll be heading the search for the hit-and-run driver . . .' He paused and then emphasised, 'The hit-and-run driver, Chris. Goodbye now.' The phone clicked and the empty line hummed.

'He bloody well knows that we did it!' The conviction hit Thompson with the force of a hammer blow. 'The bastard knows what happened!'

Panic welled up, but before it could unman him completely, another thought came into his mind. 'He kept on telling me that he's looking for a hit-and-run driver. He's made very sure that I know that he's heading the investigation.' More recollections flooded into the young man's memory. 'Mr Jones knew Ray Benton's address, and he knew exactly where Benton would be that night.' Suddenly understanding burst upon Thompson, and he drew a sharply audible intake of breath. 'It was Matthews who told Mr Jones where Benton was. Matthews set it up for Mr Jones. Matthews is one of us!'

At first he could not fully accept these ideas. But the more he considered all the aspects, the more the conviction strengthened. Finally he relaxed and sighed with deep relief. 'We're safe. We're really safe . . . Nothing can touch us . . .'

Even as the jubilant conclusion came, so simultaneously did the realisation: 'I'm really committed to Mr Jones now. I really am one of his disciples . . .

# *Chapter Nineteen*

During the weeks since the launch of the Cromwell Movement, Ivor Jones had been constantly addressing meetings of the new recruits at Cromwell House. To give them a sense of purpose he had organised them into 'observation patrols', groups of half a dozen or so people who would spend several hours during the day and evening walking around their own home areas, noting any suspicious or illegal behaviour. Each group carried a mobile phone, and if they came across anything which appeared criminal they were instructed to immediately contact the police. So as not to bring any charge of vigilantism upon them, the observation groups were under strict instructions not to attempt in any way to intervene physically against any sighted wrongdoing unless it was absolutely imperative to save a life. However, since a large proportion of the observation groups were old-age pensioners, the image of violent thuglike vigilantes was not what the public was presented with.

Although the senior city police officers praised this display of public-spiritedness, privately they resented what they considered to be an encroachment on their personal domain, and the lower ranks of the force were very unhappy at the extra work which the continual reports from the patrols made for them.

But the response of the people living in the selected areas had been enthusiastic, and because of this the police were forced to put a good face on things, so outwardly the relationship between police and observation patrols was amicable.

There had been further developments on the recruiting front also. Some of the national newspapers had carried reports of the launching of the Cromwell Movement and there had been many enquiries thoughout the country from people wishing to form branches in their own towns and districts. Ivor Jones had vetoed this, but had then offered an alternative. For a fee of £10, such interested people could become a member of the 'Cromwell cadres', embryo branches of the Cromwell Movement which in due course would be fully activated when Jones was in a position to establish a Cromwell House and a command structure in their area. This had proven surprisingly popular and now there were several such Cromwell cadres in existence throughout the country.

Here in the city, premises for both a youth and an adult social club had also been found, and the leases signed. Both buildings were close to Cromwell House; one had been a licensed hotel, the other an Army Cadet drill hall, and both would need only the minimum of conversion for their designated purposes.

Another matter, for which Chris Thompson took full credit for himself, was having Cromwell Movement lapel badges and brooches manufactured, in the form of the Ironside trooper's head and shoulders. Also, there were sweaters, tracksuits, tee-shirts and ties with the emblem printed or embroidered on them.

These were headily exciting days for the new

movement, and for its ever-increasing membership. But Ivor Jones did not allow himself to be swept into any premature euphoria. He knew that he had taken only the first steps in a very long and arduous journey, and now he was ready to take another very important step in his chosen direction. He instructed William Rimmer to gather the newly recruited Security Section at Cromwell House late one night, believing that it was now the correct time to activate that part of his organisation.

The hours before the meeting with the Security Section, Ivor Jones spent on his knees praying in the vestry at Cromwell House. He was begging his grim and fearsome God for guidance, and for help. There were times when Jones was awestruck by what had happened to him during these last weeks. Everything had moved so quickly, and sometimes he felt that he had been wrenched from a safe, secure cocoon and thrown into the chaos of a storm. There were moments when his strength and confidence threatened to desert him, and he wondered at his own sanity for doing what he had done. There were many more moments when he wondered at the radical changes within his own nature of which he was conscious. And in all these moments he would call upon his God to help and to guide him, and lately his God had always spoken to him. It was as if the more daring he became – the more reckless in his actions, the more audacious in his plans – then the more ready God was to speak to him, to come to his aid, to guide him. Jones' faith in his special relationship with God was now absolute. He was convinced that God had chosen him to become His striking arm, His instrument of vengeance, His true prophet and priest here on earth.

In his new-forged intimacy with God, Ivor Jones found much to be sardonically amused at. He was continually amazed by God's roguery and cynicism. He listened to God's voice telling him how to act, and could not help but chuckle wryly at how devious and cunning God could be. There were times even when he was shocked at God's ruthlessness, when God urged him to instigate certain actions which could only bring grief to members of the Cromwell Movement and other innocents. At such moments he questioned and argued these directives which were shortly to be put into practice. But then God would sternly reprove him, and tell him to remember that the ends justified the means; that it was necessary for him, Ivor Jones, to become more ruthless, more merciless, more cunning, more devious, on occasion more wicked even, than the forces of evil, if those dark forces of evil were to be destroyed and the light of God was to shine over this country.

Tonight, Jones was seeking confirmation from God that the time was ripe for him to launch two simultaneous operations: one overt, one covert, but both interconnected.

He prayed long and hard, at times rocking backwards and forwards on his knees, his low voice rising and falling, his eyes tight closed, his hands gripped together so strongly that the blood was squeezed from his fingers. At last he fell silent and remained motionless, his head cocked to one side as if he were listening. For long, long minutes he waited, anxiety causing him to frown. Then, faintly at first, he heard God's voice, and as he concentrated hard that voice became ever stronger, ever clearer. A broad smile spread across Jones' features, and exultation exploded within him.

'Halleluiah! Halleluiah!' he shouted aloud. 'Thank you, Lord. Thank you. Thy will be done, Lord. Thy will be done . . . Amen . . . Amen . . . Amen.'

He rose with a smile on his face and went into the main hall to wait for the other men to arrive.

For William Rimmer, the enlistment into the Cromwell Movement had given his life fresh direction and purpose, and he had thrown himself into his new role with all the zeal and enthusiasm that he possessed. His personal loyalty to Ivor Jones was total, and he was ready and eager to do whatever his new commander ordered without question or doubt.

The men he had recruited for the Security Section had had to satisfy certain strict criteria laid down by Ivor Jones. They must have no dependent family; be free of domestic entanglements; be physically fit and robust; possess a proven capacity and relish for extreme violence; be disciplined and obedient, and prepared to obey orders without question. They must swear absolute loyalty to the Cromwell Movement, and above that to Ivor Jones personally; and, most important of all, they must be bitter; they must have a deep sense of grievance against the politicians who sat in the Houses of Parliament, and against the ruling establishment of the country.

William Rimmer had known exactly where to find such men. The latest swingeing cuts in defence expenditure had cast tens of thousands of highly trained and disciplined servicemen adrift. And many of these men were either unable, or unwilling, to come to terms with their new civilian lives. Rimmer had relied on personal knowledge and recommendation for each man he had selected. The fifteen he had finally recruited were all ex-Special Forces. Commandos, Paratroopers, SAS. He could easily have recruited scores, even hundreds more, because it seemed that the country was awash with ex-service personnel embittered by being cast aside by a government which, in their opinion, had callously consigned them to the scrapheap.

Jones stared closely at each recruit as he was introduced, making mental evaluations of them, and was satisfied with what he saw. Rimmer had selected well. Each man looked fit and hard, was well-groomed, and carried himself with an air of confidence. An individual dossier had been prepared on every man, and Jones had studied those reports very closely. Some of what he had read would have made most potential employers shudder, but Jones had only smiled grimly.

They seated themselves on the first row of pews while William Rimmer made a quick security check of the hall, ensuring that all doors were locked and that there was no one lurking anywhere. He returned and nodded to Ivor Jones, who then moved to stand facing the seated men.

'I want to welcome you all to my movement, gentlemen,' he said quietly. 'I know that Mr Rimmer has told you a great deal about what will be expected of you. But there are certain points which I want to emphasise immediately. To begin with, if you now remain here to listen to what I have to say, then there will be no turning back for you. You will not be able to resign from my movement. You will be bound body and soul. So if anyone among you has any reservations or doubts, I would ask you to leave now. Your expenses will be paid to wherever you need to go, and you will be recompensed for the time you have been kept on standby.'

He paused and waited for several minutes, giving

them time to think over what he had said. They remained motionless, staring stolidly at him.

Jones nodded in satisfaction. 'Good, then I'll begin ... As you know Mr Rimmer has hand-picked every one of you, and I have carefully studied your individual dossiers. I know what you are capable of. I know your worth. I know that some of you have experienced savage fighting in the Falklands and the Gulf, that many of you have served in Northern Ireland and Bosnia and other trouble spots. You have all proved yourselves in combat, and have repeatedly demonstrated your courage and toughness. Your loyalty to your regiments and your country has been matchless, and that loyalty has been shabbily rewarded by this country's rulers.

'If you give an equal degree of loyalty to the Cromwell Movement, then be sure that unlike the scum who rule this country, I shall not abandon you. I shall not cast you out. I shall not betray your trust as the ruling establishment has done. And above all else, I shall not throw you to the wolves as the politicians did when they allowed some of you to be charged with murder because you shot and killed terrorists, or enemy soldiers. You were charged and imprisoned for doing your duty. You were unjustly punished because of political expediency, and to save the worthless skins of treacherous and gutless politicians . . .'

Resentful scowls had appeared on some of the faces facing Jones as bitter memories were goaded, and old wounds reopened. He was now warming to his task; his voice was throbbing with fervour and his fiery blue eyes flaming with conviction.

'I will *never* betray you. I will never abandon you. I will remain true to you, even unto death!

'There will be times when I shall ask you to break the present law of the land, but I don't think you need worry too much about the morality of such law-breaking. We have witnessed these past years how there are two codes of law in this country: one code for the great and powerful, and another for us. The code for the great and powerful is a set of rules which enables them to cheat, and steal, and lie with impunity. And the code for us is a set of rules enforced by the police and the judiciary to allow the establishment to live in luxury and privilege on the bowed backs of a docile population.

'The law in this country has nothing at all to do with truth and justice. The legal profession itself is the biggest obstacle to obtaining such truth and justice, as some of you here know to your own bitter sorrow . . .'

The faces before him were no longer stolid and expressionless. All were angry and resentful, and all showed an eagerness to hear more.

'. . . You men here today are the vanguard for all the thousands, tens of thousands and hundreds of thousands who will one day march beneath the banners of the Cromwell Movement. But you are the elite, because you are the first to be chosen. You will some day be the leaders of those marching men. We are embarking on a great crusade, gentlemen. We are going to cut out the rottenness that has festered for too long. We are going to burn out the filth and corruption that lies thick in the corridors of power and privilege. Our present rulers – while ensuring that they and their families are protected from the criminals – allow us and our families to go unprotected and, what is worse, forbid us to act in our own defence. They pay hypocritical lip service to

174

the idea of rehabilitating the scum that prey upon the weak and helpless, but do nothing to put an end to the depredations that are constantly committed against the decent people of this country by that same scum. The evil flourish and grow fat upon the sufferings of the rest of us, and our rulers' mealy mouths vomit only lies and platitudes, while they do nothing . . .'

He paused and his flaming blue eyes swept across their faces, momentarily catching and holding each man's gaze. Then he went on.

'But now all that is to be brought to an end. We are going to restore honour and decency to this nation; we are going to make it a place where people can dwell in safety. Where instead of good and honest folk being afraid to walk their own streets, afraid at night to answer the knock on their door, it will be the wrongdoers who walk the streets in fear, the criminals who tremble at the knock on the door. And if the high and mighty political masters of our country try to prevent us from cleansing it of the evils that afflict it, then they also will become our enemies, and we shall know how to deal with them!'

He fell silent and William Rimmer cheered loudly, then all the others joined in cheering, punching the air with their fists and stamping their feet.

Jones allowed them to applaud for some time, then he gestured for silence and was instantly obeyed. Pleasure gleamed in his eyes at this disciplined response.

'Thank you, gentlemen. Now I shall tell you of some of the ways I shall be using you during these early stages of our crusade.' He grinned conspiratorially. 'Needless to say, this information will remain strictly classified.'

They reacted to his sudden lightening of mood, and visibly relaxed, smiling appreciatively.

He spoke for a long time, and they listened intently, and when he had finally finished their applause was long-drawn-out and wildly enthusiastic.

He left them talking and laughing excitedly among themselves, and accompanied by William Rimmer walked out into the cold drizzle of the night.

'You've done a fine job, Will.'

'Thanks. They'll do, I think. So, when do we start?'

'Very soon, Will. Very soon. I just have to go and see a man first.' Jones smiled grimly into the darkness. 'And as soon as I've seen him, we can start the ball rolling . . .'

# *Chapter Twenty*

Ivor Jones had been giving much thought to the question of secure areas such as the IRA possessed in Northern Ireland: certain districts in the cities and towns, certain villages in the countryside where the population was under the domination of the IRA; where the terrorists were guaranteed safe haven and assistance, where the police and security forces met only hostility and hatred.

Jones' intention was to turn the vast Meadowpark Housing Estate into a secure area for the Cromwell Movement. The estate was a notorious hotbed of crime and delinquency, and had long been used by the City Council as a dumping ground for problem families. But still the majority of people who lived there were fundamentally law-abiding and decent. They lived in fear of the lawless gangs and the violent families, and so tried to keep a low profile and not draw the unfavourable attentions of the troublemakers to them. Jones was prepared to gamble on the fact that if his movement used strong-arm tactics to drive the criminals, the delinquents, the troublemakers and problem families from the estate, then the silent and terrorised majority would at best actively support his movement's actions, and at worst turn a blind eye.

Once the estate had been purged of its worst elements, then families who belonged to the Cromwell Movement could be moved into the vacated dwellings, and the flats and houses that now stood empty and vandalised could be lived in again. Once that task was completed, the movement would have acquired both a powerbase and a safe area. But to bring this plan to fruition he would require the active co-operation of certain officals in the City Housing Department, and another set of information from Detective Sergeant Denis Matthews.

The latter was easily obtained. A discreet phone call to the policeman's house brought within a few days the delivery of another plain envelope containing lists of names, addresses and notations. As before, there was nothing to indicate who had sent the list or where the information it contained had been culled from.

Jones photostatted some copies of the list and passed them on to William Rimmer. Soon afterwards an anonymous rusting old van made several journeys around the Meadowpark Estate. Secreted in its rear compartment was a man with a high-powered camera equipped with long-range lenses. Within the space of a few days the list of names and addresses had been augmented with pictures of men, women, teenagers and younger children.

In the meantime Ivor Jones had been talking to a wide variety of Cromwell Movement members: pensioners, young people, married couples, families, singles. To all of them he made the same suggestion, and in all but two or three cases received the response he sought.

Then he called in Chris Thompson and asked the young man to ensure that a specially written article be published in the next issue of the *Gazette and Advertiser*. Only then, after all these tasks had been completed, was he ready for his first encounter with George Faraday. He phoned the man at his home and they talked guardedly for some time, then arranged a meeting.

They met on neutral ground in a large bustling pub in a town many miles from the city, where it was unlikely that either of them would be readily recognised. In order to aid that anonymity, both men were dressed in the nondescript donkey jackets and flat caps of workmen.

After settling themselves in a corner recess of the bar they eyed each other, much as two boxers might do when standing waiting for the opening bell of the first round.

It was George Faraday who was the first to challenge. 'I take it this is some of your work, Mr Jones?'

He pulled a copy of the *Gazette* from the capacious pocket of his jacket and opened it to the article by Chris Thompson. Then he ran his fingers down the printed lines and began to read aloud: 'Seven thousand homeless people have been on the waiting list for more than two years, yet there are many houses and flats standing empty on the Meadowpark Estate. There can be no justification for the City Council's neglect of these vacant properties, which are being allowed to fall into decay because of the gross inefficiency of the City Housing department. The *Gazette* would like to know what the councillors who make up the City Council Housing Committee propose to do to rectify this disgraceful state of affairs. Is it not time that instead of claiming grossly inflated expenses for drinking endless cups of tea and indulging in idle chatter, these councillors set about doing what they have been elected to do? . . .'

Faraday laid down the paper and chuckled. 'Of course, it's true. But what do they expect the council to do about the Meadowpark Estate? It's become a rubbish tip, and every problem family in the city eventually gets rehoused there. And as soon as we rehouse them, they smash the places up again. The flats in the blocks are standing empty because no decent person will go to live in them. And I can't blame them for that. I wouldn't live in that bloody hell-hole myself.' He sighed and grinned wryly. 'And yet my old mother lives in one of the sheltered bungalows down Dahlia Crescent and refuses to move. She says it's perfectly safe down there.' He laughed and added, 'Of course, the fact that I pay out of my own pocket for a twenty-four-hour private security patrol on Dahlia Crescent might have something to do with that!'

Ivor Jones smiled, and found that he was rapidly warming towards the other man. He liked his frankness, his lack of bluster, and his wry humour.

'I have a proposition to put to you, Mr Faraday, which will at least save you that expense,' he said quietly.

Faraday sobered and told him, 'We can speak openly to each other, Mr Jones. What is said here stays between us.'

Jones accepted the invitation. He instinctively knew that he could trust this man's word.

'Very well, I will speak openly. Those empty flats and houses on the Meadowpark Estate – I can get you tenants for them.'

'Oh, yes,' Faraday scoffed dismissively, 'it's no trouble finding tenants for them. We could fill them tomorrow, if we took in all the dossers and squatters and nutcases, and let them live rent-free.'

Jones eyes glinted, but he controlled his rising impatience.

'Hear me out, Mr Faraday . . . I can find good, respectable tenants for the empty flats and houses on the Meadowpark . . . I can even create vacant flats and houses on most of the other council estates in the city for the people on your waiting lists.'

Faraday looked keenly at the other man, recognising that he spoke with a confident certainty which contained no hint of bombast or braggadocio.

'Explain how you can do that, will you please, Mr Jones,' he invited quietly.

'It's very simple. I've got members of my movement who are ready to move into the Meadowpark Estate, just as quickly as you can get the empty flats and houses refurbished. I also have other members living in council properties in other parts of the city who are willing to exchange with tenants on the Meadowpark Estate, or to take any vacant property that is available there. So that will give you vacant properties in more desirable parts of the city where people want to live, won't it?'

'And how do you think I would be able to help you to move your members on to the Meadowpark?' Faraday challenged.

'Because I know that when you say "Jump", the Council members and the officials says, "How high?"'

There was no obsequious flattery in Jones' tone, merely a factual statement.

'And why should I help you, Mr Jones?' Again there was a challenge in Faraday's voice.

Ivor Jones' fiery blue eyes stared levelly into the

other man's questioning gaze. 'Because you want the same things that I want, Mr Faraday. Streets where women and children and old people can walk safely. Streets where decent people can live their lives without fear.'

'Yes, I'll go along with that,' Faraday accepted. 'But now let's be realistic, shall we? As my old man used to say, nobody really ever does "'owt for nowt". What's in this for you? And what's in it for me?'

Ivor Jones did not hesitate. 'I want to make Meadowpark Estate into the home base and safe area for the Cromwell Movement. When my campaign against crime really gets going, my members will become targets. So I want us to have an area which we organise so that no one can get at us when we're off guard and relaxing in our own homes. Meadowpark is almost ideal for that purpose. The layout of the housing and the access roads makes it comparatively easy to set up a good observation system, so we can monitor what's going on in the area. That's basically what's in it for me . . .' He paused, seeking for some sign of reaction from his companion, but the big old man's features remained impassive, betraying no reaction other than concentration. 'Now as to what's in it for you, Mr Faraday . . . You still have ambitions to become our local MP, don't you? Well, my movement's membership is increasing rapidly. By the time the next elections come around, I'll have enough votes in my control to virtually guarantee you a majority, when my votes are added to the party votes you're already sure of. But that of course, is still only pie in the sky, isn't it? So let's look at the immediate future instead.

'That article that I had Chris Thompson write is only stating what's common knowledge in this city. Your housing policies have failed miserably, and the housing situation is a shambolic disgrace. This article gives you the opportunity to step in and take control of the housing problem yourself. It gives you the excuse that you need. You can announce publicly that you are personally going to deal with the problems of Meadowpark Estate, and regenerate it. You can make a big show of being the new broom. In the meantime, I will clean the estate up, using my own methods. All you have to do is to ensure that it's my people who get given the vacant tenancies on the estate. You gain all the kudos for the reclamation and regeneration, and I will secretly do all that is necessary to ensure that everything goes to plan. A success like that will guarantee that you get the nomination as candidate for the local seat when the time comes for the election. It will also improve your party's showing in the local elections – and, quite frankly, you're in desperate need of a boost in that direction, aren't you?'

Faraday nodded. 'Yes, that's true enough. If the local elections were to be held tomorrow morning, I could well be out on my ear by tomorrow night.'

He pondered for a considerable time, and Ivor Jones made no atempt to press his case any further but sat silently, occasionally sipping from his glass of beer.

At last George Faraday grinned, and nodded. 'When can you let me have the names of your people who are going to move in to Meadowpark?'

'Right now.' Jones slipped a sheaf of papers across to the other man, who stowed them in his pocket.

The older man got to his feet. 'I'll do my part,' he promised. 'And I'll leave it to you how you do your part. I don't want to know anything about that . . .'

183

They shook hands very briefly, then Faraday left.

Ivor Jones remained in the bar for some time, buying and drinking several more glasses of beer. He felt very relaxed, and very content, as he told himself, 'Now that's settled, I can start the ball rolling in Edgeton . . .'

# Chapter Twenty-One

'I'm sixteen now, and I can do what I want!' Jenny Chapman faced her mother defiantly. 'I'm sick of living with you in this stinking dump. You never let me have any fun! All you do is nag at me and pick on me all the time.'

Dorothy Chapman's worn face was despairing. 'I'm only trying to do what's best for you, Jenny. You're too young to leave home. How will you live? You haven't got a job.'

The girl tossed her long mane of dyed blonde hair back from her face. 'Leroy's going to look after me. We're going to get married.'

At the mention of that name the woman exploded in a fury that was fuelled by real fear and dread. '*Leroy*? Leroy Murchison? That's that bloody nigger who sells drugs, aren't it!'

Although her mother's fury made the girl feel a trifle nervous, her own defiance heightened. 'There, you'se said it now, en't you! You called him a nigger, didn't you! You're just a fuckin' racist, like all the rest of the bleeders around here.'

Aware that she was only making a bad situation worse by losing her temper, Dorothy Chapman tried to reason more quietly with her daughter. 'No, Jenny, I aren't a racist. How can you call me that when one of my best friends is Wisdom Maclure? But that bloody Leroy Murchison is a bad bugger! It's him as gives you them bloody filthy drugs, aren't it? You and our Tina. He's no good, Jenny, and he'll only ruin you.'

The girl's fresh, pretty features were sullen as she refused to let her momentary moral advantage slip from her. 'Leroy's never give me no hard drugs. He wun't let me touch 'em. The only things I takes is what all the other kids takes, and they don't do us any harm. We just has a bit o' fun with 'em, that's all. You're just against Leroy because he's black, that's all. You're just a bleedin' racist!'

The small, frail-bodied woman was trembling uncontrollably now, and was fighting to hold back her tears. 'Is that where you're going to live? With that blackie?'

'It's none of your bleedin' business!' Jenny shrieked hysterically. 'I'm going, and that's that!'

She snatched up the two black plastic bin-liners into which she had crammed her clothing and scant possessions, and tried to storm out of the room.

'No, Jenny.' Her mother moved to stop her. 'Don't go, love. I don't want you to go!'

Despite her desperation, her frailty was no match for her daughter's youthful strength, and the girl was able to shove her aside with almost contemptuous ease, and then was gone from the shabby flat leaving only the scent of her cheap perfume in token of her presence.

'No . . . No, Jenny . . . No . . .' Dorothy Chapman slumped down on to her knees and harsh, guttural animal-like sobs tore from her throat.

Her youngest daughter, Tina, already beginning to resemble her sister with her fast-budding breasts and long blonde-dyed hair, came out from the bedroom where she had been listening in mingled excitement and fear to the clash between her mother and Jenny. Her breath quickened as she stared fearfully at her mother's terrible anguish, and then her natural instincts asserted themselves and she went to kneel by her mother's side.

'Don't cry, Mam. Our Jenny 'ull be all right. Don't cry, Mam.'

'Oh, Tina, what am I going to do? What's going to happen to our Jenny? That blackie 'ull ruin her, I knows he 'ull! He'll bloody well ruin the silly little cow!'

Tina's fearful distress at her mother's grief caused her to suddenly burst into tears. Dorothy Chapman reached out for her youngest daughter, and the two of them stayed crouched in tight embrace, their tears mingling.

187

# Chapter Twenty-Two

In Tabernacle Cottage Ivor Jones was entertaining two visitors – Wisdom Maclure and her eldest son, Darren, a tall, handsome young man who had just been discharged from the Army.

'So, Darren, what do you want to do now?' Ivor Jones was mentally examining various ideas of his own concerning the young man.

Darren Maclure smiled easily and shrugged his broad shoulders. Jones was struck by what a fine physical specimen he was, and thought, 'You'd have no trouble making a living as a gigolo, with your looks and body . . .'

'I haven't given it a lot of thought yet, Mr Jones. I never expected to be a civilian. My redundancy came out of the blue.'

Jones nodded sympathetically. 'Yes, I can understand how you must be feeling. This government is insane, the way it's destroying our armed forces.'

'I hope you won't think I'm being too pushy, Mr Jones,' Wisdom Maclure put in diffidently, 'but I was wondering if there might be something for Darren to do in the movement? I've told him all about it, and he's very interested, aren't you, Darren?'

'Oh, Mum, you're embarrassing me now,' the

young man protested mildly. 'Mr Jones is going to think that we've only come here job-hunting.'

'Well, and what's wrong with that?' the woman retorted sharply. 'It's better to be job-hunting, rather than dole-hunting, isn't it?'

Jones grinned inwardly, and intervened to save the young man any further embarrassment. 'As a matter of fact, Darren, I was thinking along the same lines as your mother. A fine young man like you, with your background, could be an asset to my movement.'

'Well, thank you for saying so, Mr Jones, and I am very interested in what you're doing. But to be honest, I'm not really a religious man.'

'You was brought up in a Christian home, young man!' Wisdom Maclure reproved sharply, and turning to Jones she told him, 'He went to Sunday School regular when he was a boy, Mr Jones. Him and his brother Clent, as well. They was both real good little Christians.'

At the mention of his murdered brother's name a grimace of both pain and anger fleetingly crossed Darren Maclure's face, and Ivor Jones' sharp eyes saw it and assessed what it might mean. He came to an instant decision as a result of that lightning evaluation.

'I don't expect, or require, all the members of my movement to be religious people, Darren. But naturally I do expect them to respect their colleagues' beliefs. I also expect them to conform to certain standards of behaviour. Would you like to hear what those standard are?'

'Certainly, Mr Jones,' the young man confirmed readily.

Jones nodded. 'Very well, let me explain how

I visualise the general morals and mores of my movement.'

He leaned back in his chair and steepled his hands in front of his chest, touching the point of his chin with his fingertips. Then with eyes intent upon the young man's face, he continued, 'We're embarking upon a great crusade against evil. Therefore we have to conduct ourselves accordingly, and our way of life must be seen to be decent and law-abiding. I've no objection to alcohol or tobacco, and the members of the Cromwell Movement can use both as they wish. But habitual drunkeness is not acceptable. The general behaviour of my members must also set an example to the public. I want to see courtesy practised, and honesty in dealings, and cleanliness in body and dress. I'd like my members to show a readiness to assist people in difficulties; to display charity and tolerance. I want this type of behaviour to become the hallmark of the Cromwell Movement.'

He smiled with a hint of cynicism. 'Older people like myself always look back nostalgically to a mythical childhood when decency and courtesy and good neighbourliness were part of the normal way of life. When people could leave their doors unlocked and their goods unattended in perfect safety. That belief, is of course apocryphal – but not entirely so, perhaps. The days of my childhood were more secure and not as lawless as the present day. But I'm hoping that the Cromwell Movement will come to represent the hope that that apocryphal past can be brought to a present reality.'

It was Darren Maclure's turn to nod. 'Yes, I can accept what you've told me so far, Mr Jones. I'm in sympathy with it.'

'Good!' Jones' relaxed manner became suddenly

decisive. 'Mrs Maclure, will you leave us alone please? I want to have a long talk with your son in private. 'He smiled warmly at her pleasant features.' I want to see if there's some way I can persuade him to accept a position within the Cromwell Movement.'

Greatly pleased by this development, Wisdom Maclure was only too willing to leave the two men to talk alone.

It was nearly two hours later when Darren Maclure left Tabernacle Cottage. He was now a member of the Cromwell Movement, and he was looking forward with keen anticipation to carrying out the task that Ivor Jones had allotted to him.

His mother was waiting anxiously back at her small flat on the Meadowpark Estate.

'Well? Have you joined us?' Her face beamed when he nodded.

Then he told her, 'But I'm not going to be known as a member yet, Mum.'

She looked puzzled. 'What do you mean by that, Darren?'

'Mr Jones has got a secret job for me. It means that I have to go away again for a while.'

She shook her head in bafflement. 'I don't understand.'

'Some day I'll tell you all about it,' he assured her gently. 'But for now you must trust in Mr Jones, and in the Lord. And you must tell anyone who wants to know where I am, that I'm working abroad.'

She still could not understand, but her faith in both Jones and God was absolute. And she accepted without further argument.

* * *

It was fairly late in the evening of that same day when Dorothy Chapman came seeking Ivor Jones' help to recover her daughter, Jenny.

He listened intently to her harrowing account, and inwardly he praised his fearsome God. 'You are indeed mighty and all-seeing, Lord. You have aided me this day above my wildest expectations, in sending me Darren Maclure, and now this woman. Thank you, Lord. Thank you.'

He felt awestruck at how God had once again moved to present him with the human weapons he needed to launch his assault upon that bastion of evil, Edgeton. But now he must make the best possible use of those weapons, even if it meant using them so ruthlessly that they might be placed in danger themselves.

When the woman reached the end of her story, Jones informed her pityingly, 'Sister Dorothy, at sixteen years of age your daughter can legally leave home. I can't force her to return to you. I would be breaking the law, if I did so.'

The woman's grief-shadowed eyes mirrored her bitter disappointment, and all the childlike trust that she had placed in this man's infallibility threatened to desert her.

He had anticipated this reaction, knowing that at times it was necessary to almost destroy a faith in order to then restore it and make it even stronger.

'But aren't there nothing you can do, Mr Jones?' she pleaded desperately, tears falling down her worn cheeks. 'Aren't there nothing you can do for me?'

He deliberately and slowly shook his head. 'I cannot break the law, Sister Dorothy,' He told her sternly. 'Jenny is legally entitled to leave home.'

'But that bloody nigger 'ull ruin her, Mr Jones!' the woman cried out piteously. 'He's a bad, wicked sod, and he'll ruin her and give her a life of misery. I know he 'ull!'

Jones' expression became troubled and he lowered his head as if he were being pressed down physically by an unbearable load. He was mentally questioning the morality of what he intended doing, but despite his misgivings knew that he had no real choice but to continue. He was fighting a war, and in war there was always the risk of casualties.

'Please help me, Mr Jones!' the woman begged in a tear-choked voice. 'Please . . . Please . . .'

He allowed her to go on begging and pleading for long, long minutes, then suddenly slammed both hands hard down on his knees, and shouted, 'Enough, Sister! Enough!'

Shocked into silence, she stared at him with open fear. Instantly he softened his voice and manner, and leaned close to her. 'Peace, Sister. Peace. I shall help you.'

She moaned in relief and a dawning joy curved her lips.

'But you must do exactly as I say, Sister Dorothy,' he ordered grimly, and as she nodded in eager agreement he went on in a low, anguished voice: 'Because I am prepared to break the laws of this land, and to become a sinner myself, in order to help you.'

She slumped down on her knees before him, her hands clutching at his legs, babbling brokenly.

'Bless you, Mr Jones. Bless you . . . Bless you . . . Bless you . . .'

He sent her away after swearing her to silence, and then sat back in his chair and breathed admiringly, 'Oh, Lord, how mighty you are. And how cunning, Lord! How devious and cunning you can be. Blessed be your name, Lord. Blessed be your name.'

He rose from his chair and went out of the cottage, stopping for a brief word with the man from the Security Section who was patrolling the Chapel grounds, then carried on into the main building.

Lisa Keegan was sitting at one of the makeshift desks in the hall, talking to some women; Jones waved and smiled to her, then went though a side door and down a flight of narrow stairs which led to the cellars beneath. These cellars were of differing sizes and were dissected by a virtual labyrinth of narrow passageways. As Jones made his way towards the largest of the rooms, he could hear the gasps, grunts, loud panting and thumping bodily impacts of exercising men.

He stood in the doorway for a few moments watching what was taking place within the secretive long room, with its blank whitewashed walls. The floor was covered with padded gym matting, and the tracksuited men inside were practising armed and unarmed combat under the tutelage of William Rimmer.

Jones enjoyed the expertise displayed by the men as they used knives, clubs, hands, knees, feet and heads in savagely lethal attack and defence.

Rimmer saw him and called the men to order, but Jones indicated for them to continue, and beckoned Rimmer to him.

'When you've done here, Mr Rimmer, I'd like you to take me on a conducted tour.'

'Where to, Mr Jones.'

'Edgeton, Mr Rimmer.' Jones smiled mirthlessly. 'I think it's time to reconnoitre our next target area . . .'

194

# Chapter Twenty-Three

Edgeton bordered the city centre. In the heyday of Victorian industrial prosperity its villas and town houses had been the homes of successful manufacturers, merchants and professional men, and its wide tree-shaded streets had been thronged with the horse-drawn carriages of its residents. Now the villas and town houses were shabby and down at heel, and most of the vehicles that cruised the streets did not belong to the residents, but carried men who came here in search of sexual adventure and relief. Edgeton was now the city's 'red-light' district, and at all hours of the day and night women and girls patrolled the pavements or stood on street corners to offer their bodies for sale.

The vast majority of the respectable residents of Edgeton had initially remained apathetic when the first protitutes began to work in the section of Edgeton nearest to the city centre. Those residents living furthest away from the affected streets were noticeably the most tolerant.

'The girls have got to work somewhere,' they would point out. 'And at least they make the streets safer for decent women, don't they? No man is going to try raping a decent woman when he can get what he wants just down the road there.'

Some even took vicarious pleasure in living so close to the scene of depravity and wickedness, and would regale their absent friends and relatives with highly-coloured stories about the happenings. But then the encroachment widened. Gradually at first, then with ever-increasing speed, street after street became the working beats of prostitutes. As the fame of the growing 'red-light' area spread, their clientele and the thrill-seekers, the voyeurs, the perverted from other towns and cities were attracted to the tree-shaded streets. And the residents found that their own womenfolk, their own wives, daughters, sisters, mothers, had also become targets for the men who came seeking readily available female flesh.

Belatedly the residents tried to fight back against the invasion. They wrote letters, laid complaints, organised ineffectual and short-lived Residents' Associations. They badgered the local police, and the local councillors, and the local Member of Parliament. There would be spasmodic official reaction to the residents' protestations when for a few brief days police presence in the area would increase, and prostitutes would be arrested, charged and fined for plying their trade. Then other more pressing matters would lead to the withdrawal of the police, and the prostitutes and their pimps and clients would once more dominate the streets.

Those residents who could afford to take the loss entailed on the sale price of their homes sold up and moved away. Those who could not afford to take a loss, or even to move away, were forced to stay and endure the torment that their lives had become. To listen to the nightly cacophony of revving car engines, slamming doors, screeching altercations, and the shouts and screams of savage fights and beatings.

To have their womenfolk solicited and sometimes physically molested. To find the writhing bodies of prostitutes and clients in their doorways and driveways and gardens. To walk over the debris of used condoms, blood-stained needles, broken bottles, urine and excreta.

William Rimmer knew Edgeton well. He knew it by day, and he knew it by night. He had walked its streets in sunlight, moonshine, rain, sleet, mist and snow, in heat and in cold. He hated Edgeton.

It was here that he had found his wife working as a prostitute. Even after her squalid death the memory of her and her life in Edgeton tormented him constantly. He began to stalk the streets of the 'red-light' district, obsessively watching the prostitutes and their pimps. He saw women and girls being drugged and abused, brutally beaten, degraded by the men who made their living by selling women's flesh, and during each incident of ill-treatment that he witnessed he found himself superimposing the face of his wife upon the suffering victim. A terrible hatred grew in him for the pimps, and he lusted to take revenge on any man who worked at this filthy trade, because he blamed all of them for what had happened to his beloved Trudie.

Rimmer and Ivor Jones travelled to Edgeton in the same rusty old van which had been used at the Meadowpark Estate, and Jones talked as they went.

'I've been approached by some of the residents of Edgeton, Will, who want to see their streets cleaned up. I think that an operation like that will keep us in the public eye, and also give our people something to occupy themselves. We must have mass support and sympathy in every public action that we undertake.' There was concern in the look he gave Rimmer.

'And the cleaning up of Edgeton will be very popular among the general public.'

Rimmer's hard-etched features were exuding hatred. 'It'll be popular with me as well, Ivor.'

'Exactly. It will be vengeance for what happened to your poor wife, won't it?'

Jones ran his hand through his sparse, greying sandy hair, and pursed his lips as if seeking for words. Then he went on, 'But I want us to fail this time, Will.'

The other man stared in surprise. 'To fail?'

'Yes, to fail initially, Will,' Jones confirmed. 'I also want that failure to give our movement its first martyr.'

'Martyr?' Rimmer could not understand.

Jones nodded, grim-faced. 'Every movement needs martyrs, Will, and sometimes they are provided by the course of events. But we haven't the time to wait and trust to luck. So we shall have to make sure that we get our martyr by our own efforts.'

Rimmer was still baffled. 'But why? How? What do you really mean, Ivor?'

'Later, Will. I'll make it fully clear to you later.'

When they reached Edgeton they parked the van on its outskirts and slowly strolled through the tree-lined streets. It was still possible to discern something of what this once opulent area had represented; but now, on every corner, women and young girls were offering their bodies for sale to the drivers of the constant stream of slow-moving cars cruising along the pavement edges. The women's watchful eyes examined the two men walking past them; they noted the hard features and the confident air, and decided that these two were best left alone to make their own approaches if they so chose.

'It's a shame to see such a nice area brought down to this level, isn't it, Will,' Jones remarked. 'I can remember when I was a boy, that this place seemed awesomely grand to me. I used to imagine that the people who lived in these houses dined off gold plate, and had dozens of servants at their beck and call.'

Rimmer sniffed disparagingly. 'They'll all be eating Chinese takeways from cardboard boxes now.'

As always when he walked these streets William Rimmer's bitterness welled up within him, and his face mirrored the hatred he felt for the area.

Pimps clad in shoddy elegance and heavily bejewelled stalked watchfully, most of them black but with the occasional white man among their number. They also stared at the two men strolling past them, but made no challenge.

Ivor Jones had noted the disproportionate numbers of coloured men, and remarked casually, 'I wonder why it should be, Will, that most of these local pimps are black?'

'Because most of the white pimps have been scared out of business by the blacks,' Rimmer growled. 'When my wife was working these streets most of the pimps were white. At least they were mainly bloody Maltese and Cypriots, so I suppose that counts as white, doesn't it? The bastard who put my missus on the game was white anyway, he came from Bradford.'

'You'll really enjoy getting to grips with the pimps here, won't you?' Jones observed, and his companion scowled savagely.

'I'll love it! The sooner the better!'

'That's a thing we'll need to guard against,' Jones said reflectively. 'Any suggestion that we're prejudiced against coloured people.' He chuckled grimly.

'Though I know some of our members are. But we must try to recruit as many people from the ethnic minorities as we can. Naturally, we continue to proclaim ourselves as a Christian organisation, but we must explore the possibility of having Muslim and Hindu sections. And with all these Hong Kong refugees flooding in, we might try to recruit some of them. I don't care what a man's colour is, Will. Or his race or creed. I'm on the side of decency, and that's how I judge a man. This movement's not just for the whites. It's here to defend the Pakistanis and Indians in their corner shops, and the Chinaman in his restaurant, and the African and West Indian. It's here to defend every decent, hard-working man and woman in this land from the evil scum that prey on all of us.'

By now they had covered nearly all of the district, and Jones nodded. 'I've seen enough. Let's go back to Cromwell House.'

On the return journey he went into more detail concerning his plan of action. Firstly he told Rimmer about Dorothy Chapman's daughter, Jenny.

'This chap she's run off with, Leroy Murchison; he's on the list that Matthews gave me. He's down as a drug-dealer, but he's also one of Winston Otway's strong-arm men. And Otway is the main pimp and procurer in this city. So I think it's a safe enough bet that sooner or later, and more likely sooner, young Jenny Chapman is going to be touting for business on one of these corners. So I'm going to come down here with Dorothy Chapman and a few of our women to search for her daughter. While we're here, we can try to persuade these whores to give up what they're doing.'

He chuckled at the doubt in Rimmer's face.

'I know that that will be useless, Will. But just think how much sympathy we'll gain, when the pimps set about us. If any of us are seriously maimed or killed, that gives us our martyr. But what I'm really hoping for is that this Leroy Murchison puts Jenny Chapman out to work the streets, and we can set up a confrontation between Jenny and her mother – poor pathetic woman that she is. Public sympathy will really be aroused when people see what a pimp has forced her daughter to become.'

'Will our women be prepared to risk getting beaten up by the pimps?' Rimmer questioned doubtfully.

The light of fanaticism sparked in Jones' eyes. 'I shall ask for volunteers to follow me. And I'll tell them the risks that they'll be running. They'll follow!' He sounded absolutely sure of what he said.

'What happens then?' Rimmer questioned grimly. 'When you've got your martyr?'

Jones drew in breath a sharp hiss, and his hands clenched into fists. 'The forces of evil will learn that they have roused the whirlwind against them. They will learn what the wrath of God really means!'

## Chapter Twenty-Four

Life in Edgeton with Leroy Murchison was initially all that Jenny Chapman had envisaged it would be. The first few days and nights were wonderfully exciting. She was fêted like a princess. Leroy made love to her constantly, he bought her presents and clothes, and fed her drugs so that she floated on a cloud of dazed happiness. She spent night after night dancing in clubs that throbbed with heavy, deafening music. She met real gangsters who carried real guns, and she thrilled because it was as if she had become a star in a TV movie. There were moments when she became annoyed because the men surrounding her spoke in West Indian patois which she could not understand, and there were many times when she had the uncomfortable sensation that they were mocking and jeering at her. But always Leroy laughed her misgivings away, and took her back to his flat and kissed and stripped and screwed her into ecstatic oblivion.

But when she asked him when they would be getting married, he always evaded giving any direct reply. Instead he would tell her. 'Soon, baby. Soon.'

Sometimes thoughts of her mother and her sister, Tina, would cause her to feel sharp pangs of sad regret, and it was at these moments that she would wish most desperately that she and Leroy were married, so she could go back and see her mother and sister with a brand-new wedding ring on her finger, and a brand-new husband, and show her mother how wrong she had been about Leroy.

Then, not quite two weeks after she had gone to live in Edgeton with Leroy Murchison, Jenny Chapman was introduced to 'Big Winston'.

She and Leroy were drinking in a small smoky club when she saw a towering figure, wearing a broad-brimmed hat, with an ankle-length fur coat draped like a cloak from his massive shoulders, loom over their table.

'Hey, Leeroy!' The high-pitched voice issuing from such a massive bulk would have seemed ridiculous, were it not for the tangible air of menace that the man generated.

'Hey, Big Man.' Leroy jumped to his feet, and the men touched clenched fists, then those clenched fists opened and hands circled and entwined and fingers clutched and held.

'Respect, Big Man.'

'Reespect, Leeroy.'

Jenny stared hazily up at the newcomer, and blinked at the sight of his full beard which to her frenzied stare appeared to be a thick black veil covering half of his face and falling down to his massive chest.

'You bludclahh maann, Leeroy. You bin keeping this sweet little bitch all to yourself.' Big Winston's red-rimmed eyes roamed greedily over Jenny's jutting young breasts.

Leroy Murchison's face twisted in a forced grin. 'Raasss, Big Man. I bin waiting to see you.'

'Well, you've seen me now, bludclahh. Bring her to my place tonight.'

203

Flanked by his entourage of aggressive-looking young men, Big Winston moved on like a visiting monarch surveying his domains.

Jenny Chapman had heard the big man's last command, and despite the fuddle of drugs and drink in her brain, it had disturbed her.

'What's he want me at his place for, Leroy?' she questioned doubtfully.

'Shut your fuckin' mouth!' Her lover snarled at her, and she felt a sudden surge of fear.

'But, Leroy . . .' she began, and his hand whip-lashed into her mouth, the impact of the blow jolting her head backwards.

'Shut your fuckin' mouth, bitch!'

She tasted the saltiness of blood, and half-stunned by shock tentatively explored the moist inside parts of her lips with her tongue, finding the cut that his blow had inflicted. Sheer fear kept her rigidly motionless, and her frightened eyes were huge in her blanched face as she stared at her lover's furious scowl.

'It's your fuckin' fault, you fuckin' slag!' He snarled at her, and brandished his fist beneath her nose, causing her to flinch and cower back from him. 'If you hadn't put yourself about like a fuckin' slag, he'd never have noticed you. You give him the fuckin' come-on, didn't you? You fuckin' slag!'

Murchison lusted to smash her face into a pulp, but did not dare mark her now that Big Winston had ordered him to bring her to him that night.

'I aren't done nothing, Leroy,' the young girl protested tearfully. 'I never even saw that big man until tonight.'

'Well, you're going to see plenty of him now, you fuckin' slag. Because he'll be fuckin' you tonight.'

As the words penetrated her drug-dulled brain

Jenny Chapman's face filled with horror. She shook her head. 'No! I wun't go with him! I wun't!'

Murchison's fury was such that he could not stop himself backhanding her viciously across her face, and she fell sideways off her seat and lay on the floor sobbing bitterly.

The young man jumped up and, grabbing her long hair with both hands, dragged her bodily upright, ignoring her shrieks of pain. The men and women around them glanced across to see what was happening, then studiously ignored the couple. It was just another bitch being taught how to do what she was told to do without argument.

Murchison dragged the shrieking girl out of the club and into the alleyway. There he shoved her back against a wall, and punched her in the stomach with all his strength. She jack-knifed almost double, a high-pitched moaning coming from her gaping mouth as she fought to draw breath. Again he grabbed her long blonde hair with both hands and dragged her upright to ram her head back against the wall.

'You fuck Big Winston tonight, bitch! And when he's had enough of you, then you'll fuck whoever we tell you to fuck. You start earning from now on, you fuckin' slag. Or I'll shove my fuckin' blade down your fuckin' throat.' Again he savagely slammed her head against the wall. Then a flick-knife appeared in his right hand and he sprang it and held the blade in front of her terrified eyes. 'Got that, bitch? You fuck who we say, or you're dead meat.'

Suddenly she began to vomit and he cursed and sprang back from her. She crouched low to the ground, helplessly retching, and he waited until she had emptied her stomach and was sobbing

205

and moaning. Then he started to drag her down the alley, cursing because he must now take her back to his flat and clean her up ready for Big Winston Otway's pleasure. His fury was abating a little now. He had known that it was inevitable that sooner or later he would have to turn Jenny Chapman over to Big Winston. But he had hoped to have a few weeks' earnings from her entirely for himself, before Big Winston came to know that he had turned out a fresh young bitch.

'Ah well, Leroy,' he consoled himself now, 'at least you'll get a percentage from the big man. That's better than nothing, 'ent it.'

As he pulled Jenny Chapman along the pavement he saw a young, light-skinned, well-built man approaching, and he grinned and waved.

'Hey, Darren. How's it smokin'?'

'Sweet, man,' the other replied.

When they met their clenched fists rose and touched, then fingers opened, the hands curled around each other, fingers clutching and holding.

'Respect, Leroy.'

'Respect, Darren.'

And it was with real respect in his eyes that Leroy Murchison regarded the man before him. Darren Maclure was fresh on the local scene, and had moved into Edgeton about two weeks previously. But already he had made a name for himself as a 'bad ass', a 'mean bludclahh', a 'crazy dude'.

With a cool daring that Leroy Murchison wished he possessed himself, the newcomer had fronted Big Winston and asked him for a job as a minder, or a dealer, or a bitch keeper. When the Big Man had told the brash newcomer to fuck off, Darren Maclure had pulled out a piece and threatened to blow Big Winston's head off. One of the big man's minders had tried to intervene and Darren Maclure had coolly blown his kneecap away.

Then, grinning, he had said, 'Look, Big Man, there's a job vacancy now in your organisation, 'ent there? Please let me fill it. I'll be the best guy you've ever had working for you . . .'

Big Winston had stared down at the man writhing and screaming on the floor, blood pooling out from his shattered knee, and had suddenly roared with laughter and told the newcomer, 'You a mean bludclahh, man, and you got balls. You a bro now. You can join my team.'

Then the laughter had died and Big Winston's black eyes had become coldly menacing as he growled, 'But if you fuck with me, bludclahh, I'm going to take that piece from you and shove it up your ass and pull the trigger.'

Darren Maclure had reacted with such cool daring that Leroy Murchison had been struck speechless with admiration. The newcomer had handed the piece butt first to Big Winston, and told him quietly, 'It's a heavy trigger, Big Man, so when you fire it allow for that.'

Big Winston had taken the gun and held its muzzle against the front of Darren Maclure's head, and growled, 'You a real shithead, man. You come in here and cripple one o' my boys and then expect to work for me. You a real shithead. But now you a dead shithead.'

Everyone in the room had tensed expectantly, waiting for the explosion of blood and brains and bone. But Maclure had shown no sign of fear; he had only shrugged, then grinned wryly. 'Well, okay, Big Man, if I've got to go, then I've got to go . . .

But you must admit, it's been a cool job interview, 'ent it!'

Big Winston had stared hard, then his mouth had opened and he had laughed uproariously, shaking his head and spluttering, 'You a cool bludclahh. You a fuckin' crazy dude.'

He had slipped the piece into his pocket, and asked the newcomer, 'Who you got to vouch for you, man?'

Maclure had mentioned several names.

Big Winston had nodded thoughtfully. 'They heavy stuff, man.'

'I'm heavy stuff meself.' Maclure grinned. 'My bro was a mean bludlahh as well. He was one o' your bloods: Clent Maclure.'

'You Clent's bro?' Big Winston questioned with surprise, and blew out a gust of whistling breath. 'Well, why din't you say so in the first place, you fuckin' bludclahh. You could ha' got yourself killed here acting crazy like you did.'

'Because I din't want to come in on Clent's rep, Big Man. Like I told you, I'm mean stuff meself.'

'All right,' the big man nodded. 'I'll give you a try-out.'

The try-out was for Darren Maclure to punish a couple of a couple of London 'smack' dealers who had been annoying Big Winston during the previous few days by surreptitiously trying to sell in the city. Both men were known as 'heavies' who went armed at all times. They also claimed to have 'Yardie' connections, which had made Big Winston reluctant to clash openly with them; he didn't want to risk offending his own 'Yardie' connections by damaging their contacts.

But something had to be done about the situation,

because it threatened the fear and respect with which himself was regarded in the city. He could not afford to have anyone muscling in on his territory.

This crazy newcomer, Maclure, was expendable, and Big Winston could deny any knowledge of him. So he was ideal for the job of dealing with the two Londoners.

Leroy Murchison had been ordered to identify the two men for Darren Maclure, and instructed to then hang back and watch what happened.

It had been a revelation of controlled lethality. Maclure had walked up to the two dealers in broad daylight, carrying an iron bar rolled in a newspaper. Scant seconds later the two men had been left lying senseless in the gutter, their legs and arms broken, their faces smashed and bleeding. Maclure had calmly strolled away still carrying his iron bar, with the dealers' guns in his pockets, and their money and store of 'smack' also.

Three days later word came to Big Winston from London that the two dealers had also been in bad odour down there, and that their contacts with 'Yardies' had been a myth.

Following the receipt of that news, Darren Maclure became a member in good standing with Big Winston's organisation. And now he was one of the big man's minders and enforcers.

Now, as Darren Maclure passed a few remarks with Leroy Murchison in the street, he covertly studied the young blonde-haired girl. He thought that she was the Jenny Chapman that Ivor Jones had intructed him to look out for. He felt a flash of pity at seeing how sick and ill and frightened she appeared, and he said casually, 'Your bitch looks a bit rough, Leroy.' Murchison agreed readily. 'And

Big Winston wants her tonight, as well. I'm going to have to clean her up and get her looking better for him, Man, or he'll fuckin' well slay me.'

Darren Maclure assumed a lascivious leer. 'She's tasty. I wouldn't mind laying some pipe in her meself. You going to turn her out?'

'Yeah.' Murchison nodded glumly. 'I was going to work her private, but now that Big Man's seen her she'll go into the team and all I'll get is the percentage.'

'Never mind.' Maclure grinned commiseratingly. 'You'll easy find another sweet bitch.'

Murchison cackled with high-pitched laughter. 'She's got a sister as looks just like her!'

Maclure was now certain that this was indeed Jenny Chapman, even though the photo that Ivor Jones had shown him had been taken when she was much younger. But he gave no indication of any further interest, and instead strolled away with a word of farewell.

Darren Maclure was obtaining a fierce satisfaction from what he was presently doing, which was building up a complete dossier of information about Big Winston Otway, his gang and his operations in Edgeton and the city. Although it had not been Big Winston or his gang who had murdered Clent Maclure, nevertheless Darren hated and despised them all, and lusted to see them destroyed.

The death of his beloved younger brother had affected him very deeply. But, unlike his mother, the young man did not idealise the dead youth. Wisdom Maclure still refused to believe that Clent had been anything other than an innocent caught up against his will by evil forces. Darren knew, however, that Clent had been a willing and eager

210

gangster, and he partially blamed himself for what he had become. As a young teenager Darren himself had hung around the drug-dealers and the gangsters of the city, and had filled Clent's childish mind with stories of 'glamorous' lawlessness. But Darren had then quarrelled with his mother and had left home to join the Army. Deliberately he had cut off all contact from his small family for several years, stupidly trying to punish his mother for all the quarrels they had had in the past. Then, when he had been reconciled with her, it was to discover that his younger brother had become a gangster and drug-dealer. Only weeks after their reconciliation, his mother had written to tell him that Clent had been gunned down by rival drug-dealers.

Darren Maclure blamed himself for not having stayed with his family to watch over and guide his brother. He did not try to make his mother face the truth about her youngest son; he accepted that it was her way of finding some shreds of comfort. But now he was determined to do everything he could to destroy all gangsters and drug-dealers wherever he might find them – this was *his* way of finding some shreds of comfort.

During the long private conversation he had had with Ivor Jones, he had realised that he was with a man who was setting out on a ruthless crusade against the very people that Darren Maclure himself lusted to destroy. He also very quickly realised that Jones was the most formidable man he had ever met in his life – a man who was ready to dare anything to achieve his aims. And those aims were of an audacity that took Darren Maclure's breath away.

By the time Ivor Jones had finished talking to him, Darren Maclure was wildly excited, and eager to enlist in the Cromwell Movement. And when Jones offered him the chance to act as a spy, to infiltrate the gangs and obtain all the information about them that Jones needed, he accepted without a moment's hesitation.

Now, as he strutted down the street, Darren Maclure's mind was filled with the image of Jenny Chapman's tormented young face.

'I've got to get you away from these bastards,' he thought pityingly.

The throbbing rhythm of the music enfolded Darren as he entered the smoke-filled club, and his eyes sought and found Big Winston Otway.

'Hey, Darren.'

'Hey, Big Man.'

'Reespect, Darren.'

'Respect Big Man.'

'How's it going, my main man?' Otway grinned. 'How's your life?'

Darren chuckled. 'It's smooth and sweet, Big Man, like a young whore's pussy.'

The huge man giggled and waved to the chair beside him, and Darren sat down and slipped a wad of notes from his pocket into the other's hand.

'Here you go, Big Man. The Paki paid up.'

Otway chortled in delight. 'You the best collector I got, Darren. It was the best day's work I done in years when I took you on my payroll.'

Darren Maclure's handsome features wore a gratified smile, but inwardly he jeered at his companion. 'Oh no, Big Man. It was the worst day's work you ever did. And you're going to find that out very, very soon . . .'

# Chapter Twenty-Five

Ivor Jones was in the old vestry room at Cromwell House, awaiting the arrival of the people he had sent for. While he waited, he sat enjoying what had become his favourite daydream. Thrilling mental visions of massed banners, beating drums, shrilling trumpets and the boots of marching men ... Thousands, and tens of thousands, and hundreds of thousands of men, their boots crashing down in unison, creating a thunder of disciplined, directed advance ... Jones' lips parted slightly, and his breathing quickened as once again he saw himself at the head of that mighty host of marching men.

'Mister Jones? Mister Jones?' Chris Thompson's voice jerked him from his daydreams.

'Oh, there you are.' The young man came smiling through the door. 'I'm sorry I'm late, Mr Jones. I got held up at the office.'

'That's all right, Mr Thompson.' Jones smiled away the apology. 'Now, I wanted to have a few words with you before the others arrive.'

The young man frowned worriedly. 'There's nothing wrong is there?'

'No.' Jones shook his head. 'I've been thinking about your position within the movement, that's all.'

Again the worried frown creased the other man's brow, and Jones smiled reassuringly.

'I've come to value you very highly, Mr Thompson. So much so that I'd like you to become a full-time salaried officer of the Cromwell Movement.'

He watched the young man's reaction closely.

Aware of that keen regard, Thompson tried not to show the conflicting emotions that this offer had aroused within him. On the one hand he was thrilled at the thought of becoming a full-time officer of the movement; but on the other hand, to accept the offer would entail putting his own long-cherished ambitions to become a national journalist into abeyance.

Jones watched the young man for some seconds and then with a display of uncanny percipience said, 'You're thinking that if you become a full-time officer, then you must forget your journalistic ambitions, aren't you, Mr Thompson?'

Ruefully Chris Thompson admitted to the truth of this and the other man nodded understandingly.

'That's a very natural reaction. It's hard to lay aside cherished dreams, isn't it? But let me tell you what sort of job I have in mind for you here. At first you will become the Press Officer of my movement, and also handle all our publicity. Then, when the time is right, you will also be responsible for the movement's journal. I'm not envisaging a small newsletter type of operation there, Mr Thompson, but a glossy, professional publication, with a wide circulation and influential articles. A publication which will be on public sale, challenging the other journals and magazines for their readership. Surely to be editor-in-chief of such a journal would be preferable to being a mere reporter or columnist? After all, you would be commissioning such people to work for you. Naturally, you would also be contributing articles and editorials yourself, if you so chose.'

Again his fiery blue eyes stared penetratingly at the reporter, and he smiled secretly as he saw the effect of his offer.

Chris Thompson beamed delightedly. 'What can I say, Mr Jones? It sounds wonderful.'

'I take that to be an affirmative answer then?' Jones queried drily, and the young man enthusiastically agreed.

'Good, that's settled then.' Jones was satisfied. 'You begin your new duties immediately.'

There was a flash of doubt in Thompson's eyes, and Jones chuckled. 'It'll cause your Mr Prendergast some annoyance when you tell him what he can do with your present job, I take it. So why bother to work a month's notice?'

'All right, Mr Jones. I'll tell him tomorrow.' Chris Thompson beamed happily.

They waited a few minutes more and then Lisa Keegan and William Rimmer arrived almost simultaneously. Now that they had all gathered, Jones wasted no time in idle chatter. After informing them about Chris Thompson's new job he addressed Lisa Keegan.

'Mrs Keegan, you are now promoted to become my chief administrator. You can immediately recruit the necessary full-time staff, but that staff must be drawn from members of my movement.'

The woman's handsome face glowed with pleasure. 'Thank you, Mr Jones.'

He nodded a brusque acknowledgement of her gratitude and then informed her, 'I want to form a youth branch of the Cromwell Movement. A type of cadet force, if you like, with the emphasis on physical

215

fitness, adventure training, martial arts, that sort of activity.' He spoke directly to William Rimmer. 'Do you have anyone in the Security Section capable of organising and running such a branch?'

The man pondered dourly. 'I'll have to check on that, Mr Jones.'

'Let me know as soon as you've done so,' Jones ordered. Then to all of them he said, 'I'm very concerned about the youth of our country, and I want to set up our youth branch as soon as possible. So we must all involve ourselves in its formation. Initially I see us providing them with somewhere to go in the evenings, and with something to do which will be more appealing than roaming the streets. So we must set up a type of youth club where they can meet, and feel free to enjoy themselves and let off steam with the very minimum of supervision.'

He grinned with a hint of slyness. 'This of course is a very standard and ordinary type of youth club, isn't it? But we shall introduce something a little different from usual. As soon as we have a regular attendance then we shall carefully select the more naturally dominant individuals amongst them and invite them to take part in more exciting and unusual activities, which the movement will finance.'

He broke off suddenly and stayed silent as if in thought, then requested, 'Mr Rimmer, will you tell us how elite soldiers such as paratroopers and commandos are motivated to undergo such a gruelling training, and to take such risks as they do?'

'By being told over and over again that only the cream of them can get through the training and win their berets,' Rimmer answered without hesitation. 'And by being tested to their mental and physical limits, so that it really is only the best of them who get through the course.'

Jones nodded slowly. 'Yes, exactly, Mr Rimmer. As I just said, we must form a special grouping within the youth branch. We can train them physically and mentally as the recruits for the elite regiments are trained. We can indoctrinate them to believe that they are an elite among the young people of the nation; that they are superior to other members of the youth branch who have not been invited to join this inner grouping. And we can most certainly make them believe that they are immeasurably superior to all those young people who do not even belong to my movement.'

He rose to his feet and briefly paced up and down the cramped room for a time, then halted and went on, 'We shall all have to involve ourselves very closely in this inner grouping of the youth branch. They are the future of my movement, and in some ways the most important part of it.'

Lisa Keegan had listened with utter absorption, sitting completely motionless, her face rapt. Now she abruptly held up her hand, as if she were a child in a classroom asking the teacher for permission to speak. 'Please, Mr Jones?'

Jones regarded her kindly. 'Yes, Mrs Keegan, what is it?'

'Excuse me for saying this, but I can't help thinking that this youth movement sounds more like an army. You talk of training them as if they were soldiers?'

He chuckled. 'That's exactly what they will be, Mrs Keegan. Soldiers in the Army of the Lord.'

A fanatical gleam came into Jones' eyes as he drew himself up to his full height, and fervour throbbed in his voice. 'I see the Cromwell Movement as the sword of God, His weapon against the men of evil. But every sword needs a cutting edge, and our young Ironsides will be that edge. Brave young men and women, eager to confront the thugs and hooligans who plague our streets; trained and ready to destroy our enemies.'

Lisa Keegan and Chris Thompson stared at him as if they found it difficult to credit what they were hearing, and he smiled down at them.

'Let me tell you something, my friends. Every religion, every great movement, every political grouping, every revolution throughout recorded history, has begun with a solitary man having an idea. Having a dream. A dream of change, a dream of his own destiny. That solitary man has then shared his dream with a handful of others, who themselves have dreamed of changing their own destinies. All that we need to do is to have the courage and the faith to follow our dream. To grasp our time of opportunity. I am going to alter the course towards self-destruction that this nation is presently set upon.'

His fiery blue eyes were blazing with conviction as he caught and held their gazes. 'And if you have the courage, and the faith, and the belief to follow me, then together we will build the New Jerusalem, and make this poor sick country of ours into a land fit once again for good, decent people to live in.'

He paused, before asking, 'Will you follow me?'

And each one whispered in turn, 'I'll follow you, Mr Jones. I'll follow you.'

Jones took a leather-bound bible from one of the shelves. 'Will you swear on this holy book to give me your total loyalty, and obedience?'

One by one they solemnly took an oath on the bible that they would give total loyalty and obedience to Jones, and to the Cromwell Movement.

As each completed the oath, Jones took them in his arms and embraced them.

Then he reiterated at length his own fervent belief in the future of the Cromwell Movement and when they finally left the great gaunt structure of Cromwell House, each of the three were convinced that they were irrevocably bonded with a man who was truly destined for greatness.

## *Chapter Twenty-Six*

While Ivor Jones was waiting for his carefully laid preparations regarding Edgeton and Meadowpark Estate to reach the stage when he could launch his attack, he busied himself with the continuing recruitment for the movement. He held nightly meetings in Cromwell House, feeding his eager audiences the messages they wanted to hear: telling them that their time was coming, that they would soon be putting the forces of evil to rout; exhorting them to use this waiting time in preparing themselves both mentally and physically for the battles to come.

The observation patrols continued to operate in certain designated areas, and now positive results were beginning to show in those areas in the diminution of burglaries and other crimes. He continued to lead masses of his followers in sweeps of the Rec. on Meadowpark Estate, and here also they had achieved success in keeping away the drug-dealers, child molesters, perverts and also the mischief-seeking teenagers.

Meanwhile he sent Chris Thompson to several major towns and cities throughout the country where there existed sizeable Cromwell cadres, to book halls and arrange advance publicity for a speaking tour by Ivor Jones.

The lightning tour duly took place, and Jones was received by wildly enthusiastic audiences wherever he spoke. He repeated his familiar theme, and promised that as soon as possible he would establish Cromwell Houses in each area. He continued to veto any activation or unilateral action on the part of any of the cadres.

His reasons for this veto were multi-faceted: reluctance to risk losing complete control of his movement; his desire not to see the enthusiasm now displayed frittered away with ineffective actions; his instinctive feeling that the longer he delayed his coming, then the more eagerly awaited he would become; his knowledge that he must come with a successful, strong and established power-base behind him, so that when he eventually did establish a Cromwell House in any of the areas, he would possess the necessary resources to make a dramatic impact on the local crime situation.

The lightning tour was something of a triumph, and the numbers of people enrolled in the Cromwell cadres almost doubled as a result.

When he returned to the city, the confidential information waiting for him gave him further cause to rejoice. All was now in place for him to launch his simultaneous operations against Edgeton and the Meadowpark Estate.

He called a meeting with William Rimmer, Lisa Keegan and Chris Thompson, and issued lengthy and detailed instructions. Some of those instructions brought protests from Lisa and Chris, but he overruled them sternly, and they were forced to accept without further argument. A short time later he had a private meeting with William Rimmer, and again issued long, detailed instructions which Rimmer accepted without question.

It was late at night when that second meeting ended, and when he was alone once more in Tabernacle Cottage, Ivor Jones went down on his knees and entered into a communion with the God whom he was now beginning to conceive as being more of a senior partner in his personal crusade, rather than his all-powerful Master. But still, when God spoke to him, Ivor Jones listened and obeyed. And now, tonight, God spoke to him for many hours, and Ivor Jones did not dispute anything that he was being told to do. When he finally rose up from his knees and went to his narrow bed to sleep for a few hours, he felt exultant, and eager for the next day to come.

# *Chapter Twenty-Seven*

Sharon Chambers stared at the man and woman and demanded disbelievingly, 'What did you say?'

'I said that I want you to stop doing this, and to tell me where Jenny Chapman is,' Ivor Jones repeated quietly.

The young girl grinned and her eyes, thick with mascara, flickered up and down the street. Three other girls worked this beat, and she could see women talking to each girl. She shook her head and, still grinning, told Ivor Jones, 'Fuck off!'

'No.' It was Jones' turn to shake his head. 'I'll go when you agree to stop doing this and to tell me where Jenny Chapman is. This is her mother.'

Beside him Dorothy Chapman's frightened face was grey and drawn, and Sharon Chambers scratched her broken nose with badly bitten fingernails. 'Listen, love, I don't know where your daughter is. If I was you I'd go on home.' She turned to Jones. 'I don't know where you comes from, mister, or what you thinks you're doing. But I've got a living to make. I don't know anybody named Jenny Chapman.'

She frowned as she glanced towards a car cruising slowly down the street, and stepped past the couple to stand on the pavement's edge. She ran her hands up her bare thighs and slowly lifted the hem of her mini-skirt to display her black briefs. The car halted alongside her, and the driver opened the passenger door.

'How much?'

'Depends what you wants,' Sharon told him, and leaned low so that her pushed-up, half-naked breasts were displayed to their best advantage.

The man swallowed. 'I want the lot.'

'Twenty quid.'

He nodded. 'All right, get in.'

Before the young girl could enter the car, Ivor Jones bent down and coolly informed the driver, 'I've made a note of your car number. I'm going to report you to the police for soliciting a minor for immoral purposes.'

He produced a small flash camera and took a photo of the man's shocked glare.

'What the bloody hell?' the driver ejaculated, and then slammed the passenger door shut and drove quickly away.

Sharon Chambers swung round cursing in fury, and spat a torrent of verbal filth into Jones' face.

He remained unmoved, and when the girl finally exhausted her extensive repertoire, said calmly, 'I'll do that to every man who approaches you.'

The girl brandished her fist threateningly. 'I'll smash your fuckin' face in, you old cunt!'

Jones shook his head. 'No, you won't. I'm bigger than you, and far stronger. And so are most of my friends here with me tonight.'

As if to prove his claim there came the sounds of a heated altercation further down the street, as another car which had stopped suddenly roared away, and the prostitute who had lost her customer turned on the woman with her and viciously swung out.

The assaulted woman, who was very large and fat, closed with the prostitute and wrestled her down on to the ground, then simply sat on her. The hapless prostitute screamed and raved in impotent fury, helpless beneath the weight.

The other girls working their beats came running to the aid of their friend, but Ivor Jones' women also came at a run and the prostitutes, seeing that they were heavily outnumbered, were forced to vent their anger in tirades of abuse and threats.

As the fat woman ponderously raised herself from her captive, the girl snarled and came off the ground flashing a knife which she had snatched from inside her high boot. The woman moved with amazing speed for such bulk, and in split seconds had disarmed the screeching girl and rendered her powerless with an armlock.

Ivor Jones could not help but smile at the expressions on the other prostitutes' faces, and he informed them. 'My colleague used to be a judo instructor in the Military Police. So I shouldn't advise any of you girls to try what your friend did.'

Sharon Chambers beckoned the other prostitutes to her and whispered urgently to them. Then she asked Ivor Jones, 'What is it you really wants?'

'I want you to tell me where Jenny Chapman is. I want you to stop what you are doing. I want you to get out of Edgeton, and stay out.'

'But why are you picking on us? There's girls working every other street, so why pick on us?'

'We're not picking on you,' Ivor Jones informed them quietly. 'You just happen to be the first. We're going to clear every one of your friends out of this district.'

'But who the fuck are you?' the girl screeched in baffled rage.

'We're the Cromwell Movement,'Jones told her.

'You'll be the fuckin' dead movement when Big Winston gets hold of you. You'll be fuckin' dead!'

Another car came cruising slowly along the pavement's edge, and one of Jones' women went to speak to the driver. After a couple of seconds that car also roared away.

'You bastards!' another of the prostitutes shrieked. 'You're ruining our business!'

Sharon Chambers again beckoned the other girls into a huddle and talked rapidly to them, punctuating her words with short chopping gestures of her arms.

Then she came back to face Ivor Jones. 'Let me mate go, and we'll leave.' She pointed to the girl still held in the armlock.

Jones nodded to the fat woman, who immediately released her captive.

The girl spilled filthy insults from her lips as she massaged her arm, and tottering on their high heels, buttocks waggling furiously beneath their scant miniskirts, the four prostitutes hurried away. As they reached the corner Sharon Chambers shouted defiantly, 'Big Winston 'ull sort you bastards out. Just you wait. He'll do the bleedin' lot of you!'

Jones smiled at his twelve companions.

'We've made a good beginning, Sisters. Let's move on to the next street, shall we? Same tactics.' To the worried-looking Dorothy Chapman he said gently, 'Don't distress yourself, Sister Dorothy. We'll find Jenny and restore her to you.'

Across the roadway from Ivor Jones and the group of women, Chris Thompson asked the two men with him who were both carrying camcorders, 'Did you get all that?'

One nodded. 'Yeah, I got it.'

Thompson allowed the group of women to disappear around the corner of the neighbouring street and then ordered, 'Right, let's go.' And he led the two men to follow the women.

An hour passed, and by now three streets had been cleared of the beat-patrolling girls. A couple of the prostitutes had become violent, but had been quickly overpowered by the Cromwell Movement women. A good many potential customers had also been frightened off and, as if they were spreading the word of what was happening to other potential clients, there were now no cars at all cruising the cleared streets.

Some of the residents had also come out from their houses to find out what was happening, and their plaudits and profuse expressions of gratitude were also recorded by Thompson and his two assistants.

Then Jones and the Cromwell women entered the fourth street, to find that the prostitutes who worked it were standing in a small group at the far end. As Jones led his party towards them, a luxurious American-model stretch limousine came slowly around the far corner, and halted briefly by the group of girls. The women bent to its open windows and there was a quick exchange between them and the car's occupants. Then the car started up again, and with ear-splitting rap music reverberating from its open windows cruised slowly towards the oncoming Cromwell group. Halfway along the street the car halted and the music switched off. The Cromwell group moved steadily onwards, and then the car's doors swung open and five men got out – all black, and all carrying baseball bats. Then a towering figure emerged from the car's interior, wearing his customary broad-brimmed hat and ankle-length fur coat. He moved his hands and in the street-lamps' light the rings flashed and glittered on his fingers.

'I think it's the one the girl called Big Winston,' Jones informed his followers, and he saw their nervous faces, and encouraged, 'God is with us, Sisters. God is with us.'

He walked steadily on, and the men spread out to block his way. He halted a few paces from them, and demanded, 'Are you going to let us pass?'

Behind him the other women bunched nervously; only the massive ex-Military Policewoman seemed unafraid, as she moved to stand alongside Jones.

The huge black man came directly into the light of the street-lamp, and from a distance Chris Thompson could make out the man's full beard, and appreciate the size and power of his body.

'Now, ladies, and gennulman.' The high-pitched voice issuing from such bulk would have seemed ridiculous, were it not for the tangible air of menace that the man radiated. 'You've had your fun, and I think it's time you went about your business elsewhere.'

'Our business is here,' Ivor Jones stated calmly. 'We've come to fetch Jenny Chapman back to where she belongs. And to save these other poor foolish women from their dreadful fate.'

'Mister, I'm a good guy. You ask any of my bitches if I don't treat 'em right? They'll all tell you what a good guy I am. But you're hurting my business, mister, and I can't have that.' He spoke in a reasonable, good-humoured tone. 'So why don't you all go away, and leave us be?'

'We shall go away when you have given us back Jenny Chapman, and released these other women that you're exploiting so wickedly,' Ivor Jones declared, his voice firm and determined.

'Look.' The huge man smiled and there was a white gleam of teeth. 'How about if I make a contribution to your funds? How will that be?' He pulled a thick wad of money from his pocket, and peeled a few notes from it which he held out towards Jones. 'Now you just take this, mister, and leave me alone.'

Jones shook his head contemptuously. 'I've told you already what we are here for, Mr Winston, or whatever your name is. There is no place here for you and your filthy trade any longer. We are on God's work.'

The big man roared with deep-throated laughter. 'Is that so, mister? God's work, is it? And you think that God is going to help you, right?'

Jones nodded positively. 'Yes, the Lord will help us.'

The big man slowly shook his head. 'Not tonight he won't, mister. Not tonight.' He turned and went to the long-bodied limousine, and bending low he climbed inside it.

The men with baseball bats exploded forward, the bats swung viciously, and Ivor Jones and the big fat woman took the full force of the savage onslaught. Behind them the rest of the women screamed, and some turned to flee; but the men were on and over them before they could run. The dully thudding impacts of wood on flesh and bone reached the ears of Chris Thompson. He stared with horrified shock as screaming women were smashed to the ground and then he shouted.

'No! No! No, you bastards! You bastards!' And he hurled himself up the street.'

A man came to meet him, baseball bat raised threateningly. Chris Thompson jigged and ducked, but the long length of rounded wood cracked against the side of his head, his eyes were blinded by dazzling flashes of light, and he fell into blackness.

William Rimmer was sitting in the office of Cromwell House when the phone rang, and he answered. He listened in silence for some seconds, then replaced the receiver and hurried out of the building.

The transit van was waiting at the side of the Chapel, and Rimmer got into the passenger seat and told the driver, 'Head for the Meadowpark.'

As the van made the short journey to the estate, Rimmer tuned in the radio receiver he had brought with him, and located the frequency used by the local police.

Staccato messages crackled constantly as police patrols were directed towards Edgeton, and Rimmer chuckled grimly and told the silent men sitting in the rear of the van, 'It looks like Mr Jones has done a good job. Every copper in the city is being sent to Edgeton by the sound of it.'

Meadowpark Estate was quiet, its streets and open stretches of ground deserted. The van slowed and stopped and two men got out of the back, then the van continued on. Twice more it stopped and men got off, then with just Rimmer and the driver left on board it entered a cul-de-sac of semi-detached houses and travelled to the end circle.

'Just pull over there,' Rimmer directed.

When it stopped he went to get out, and the

driver said, 'Hold on a minute while I get me balaclava on.'

'No, there's no need. I'll do this one by meself. Keep the engine running.' Rimmer pulled the masking balaclava over his head, and from beneath the passenger seat he took a wine bottle with a strip of rag dangling from its corked neck, which smelled of petrol, and half a broken house-brick.

The driver grinned savagely. 'This takes me back to bleedin' Belfast.'

Rimmer chuckled. 'Just wait till we really get going. You'll think this *is* bloody Belfast then!'

He walked back to the cul-de-sac circle and stopped outside a house where a strip of light shone through a gap in the drawn curtains of the ground-floor window.

He hurled the half house-brick at the window, which shattered inwards under the impact. From inside a woman screamed, and a man shouted. Rimmer struck a match to light the rag fuse of the Molotov cocktail and sent it hurtling through the smashed window.

It exploded with a roar of flame and the woman shrieked hysterically.

Rimmer ran back to the van and as it drove away he tugged off the balaclava and looked back, grinning, as he saw people running out of the houses adjoining the house where the flames were already flaring out of the broken window.

As they travelled back along the streets leading towards Cromwell House they passed another house where a crowd of people were standing on the pavement, and Rimmer instructed, 'Pull up just past them.'

He left the van and casually strolled to join the noisy crowd.

'What's up, mate?' he asked a man standing slightly apart from the rest.

'I don't know exactly,' the man answered. 'From what they'm saying, a couple o' blokes wearing masks smashed into the house and wrecked the downstairs room. They gave the bugger who lived there a real pasting as well.'

'Who lives there then?' Rimmer asked interestedly.

'Bloody Simmy Court, he's a right bloody tearaway. Them blokes couldn't have picked a better bloke to do over. He's had it coming a long time, Simmy Court has.'

'Oh, yes, I've heard about him.' Rimmer nodded. 'He's a bit fond of beating old folks up, aren't he?'

The man with him laughed, showing decayed teeth. 'He wun't be beating any more of the poor old buggers up for a bit, from what they'm saying. He's inside there waiting for the ambulance to come.' The man winked knowingly. 'That's if the one who went to phone for it made the call. I'm bloody sure I 'udden't lift a finger to help the rotten sod meself.'

'Ah, well, I'd better get off to work,' Rimmer said. 'Good-night, mate.'

In the van he told the driver, 'The lads did a good job there. I hope the others did as well.'

When the van returned to Cromwell House, the rest of the party were already waiting in the vestry office.

Rimmer listened to their reports and nodded. 'Well done, lads. You can dismiss, but remain on standby.'

The men filed out and went down to the cellars where one of the rooms had been fitted out as a communal rest room with television and a small bar. Some of the other cellars had been fitted out as sleeping cubicles for the men on duty watch at Cromwell House, which was now covered by a twenty-four-hour guard roster.

They sat together, drinking, smoking and laughing while the hours passed.

Rimmer remained upstairs until the two men who had been in Edgeton with Chris Thompson came in, half-supporting the injured man between them.

'What's happened?' Rimmer questioned.

'He wanted to be a hero,' one of the men jeered, and went on to explain what had happened.

Rimmer stared at the injured young man with open contempt. 'That's what you get for not obeying orders, Mr Thompson. Next time you'll know better, I hope, and just do what you're told to do.'

He turned back to the other two men. 'How about Mr Jones and the women?'

'They bin battered, but they'll all be all right. We went to the hospital and made a few discreet enquiries. Nobody's on the critical list.'

'Did you get everything?' Rimmer demanded.

The other man grinned and tapped the case in which he was carrying his camcorder. 'Everything, Mr Rimmer,' he confirmed.

'Good. Go downstairs and have a drink. I'll see to Mr Thompson.' Rimmer jerked his head in dismissal, and when the two men had gone, set himself to bathing and dressing Chris Thompson's cut head.

For the first time the young man spoke. 'I was afraid Mr Jones would be killed; that's why I intervened,' he muttered defensively.

William Rimmer grinned mirthlessly. 'It'll take more than a bloody nigger pimp with a baseball bat to kill Mr Jones. Next time, just do as you've been told, Mr Thompson. It's necessary to set an example to the troops, you know. If they see the officers disobeying orders, then their own discipline goes out of the bloody window.'

'Oh, I'm sorry!' Chris Thompson snapped in irritable sarcasm. 'I didn't know we were in the Army.'

Rimmer was unperturbed by the sarcasm. He merely answered dourly, 'Well, you know now, don't you, Mr Thompson. You are in an army. And don't you go forgetting that ever again.'

In the casualty department of the City General Hospital Ivor Jones was lying on a stretcher, his features bloodied, badly bruised and swollen. He had refused to be treated until all his women had been seen first. Anxious Cromwell Movement members who had hurried to the hospital upon hearing the news were standing by his side, and he told them, 'Leave me, and go and help attend to your Sisters.'

Across the large crowded room, filled with injured Cromwell Movement women being treated by harassed nurses and young duty doctors, Lisa Keegan was talking to the senior doctor, who was a personal acquaintance.

Outside in the waiting room a uniformed Chief Inspector and Inspector of the City Police were waiting impatiently to speak to Ivor Jones.

Lisa Keegan finished talking to her acquaintance and came across to Jones' stretcher. Her dark eyes were filled with loving anxiety as she stared down at his swollen, bloodied face.

'Don't look so worried, Sister Lisa.' He smiled at

her. 'You'll have to get used to seeing injuries now that our campaign has begun in earnest.'

'You shouldn't put yourself in danger like that,' she scolded protectively. 'You're too valuable to risk yourself so. What will happen to us if you get seriously injured, or killed even?'

He stared reproachfully at her. 'Would you have me send others to do what must be done, Sister Lisa, and hide away myself like a coward?'

'No, I don't mean it like that. But I love you too much to want to see you harmed in any way,' she retorted without thinking, then flushed deeply as she realised that she had betrayed her feelings for him.

He smiled tenderly and reached out his right hand to take her hand. 'We are in God's care, Sister. He will protect us.'

Letting go her hand, he became brisk and businesslike. 'Now, what's the situation regarding our Sisters?'

Relieved that he had not referred to her unguarded words, Lisa Keegan told him, 'Dorothy Chapman is being operated on now for a depressed fracture of the skull, and Sister O'Hagan has both arms broken. The rest appear to have only minor bruises and surface cuts.' Again a scolding note entered her tone. 'And we shan't know what injuries you've suffered until you allow the doctors to examine you properly.'

He dropped his voice to a whisper. 'Any other news?'

She glanced about her to make sure that no one was listening, and nodded. 'Brother Rimmer told me to tell you that everything went as planned.'

Jones looked satisfied; then he closed his eyes, telling her, 'Thank you, Sister Lisa. Leave me now, please.'

Reluctantly she obeyed and, with a final long loving look at him, went to help the injured women.

Eventually the doctors had finished with the other casualties and Ivor Jones permitted them to examine and treat his own injuries which, apart from badly swollen bruises on his face, head, and body, comprised two cracked ribs and a hairline fracture of his lower left arm.

When his arm had been put into plaster the doctor permitted the policemen access to him.

'I'm Chief Inspector Clayton, this is Inspector Miller.' The senior policeman, a tall, lean, white-haired man, introduced himself brusquely, then demanded angrily, 'What in hell's name were you and your members doing in Edgeton tonight?'

Jones was not fazed by the other man's aggressive manner, and he replied coolly, 'Edgeton hasn't been declared a "No Go" area, has it?' 'Why do you ask that?' the policeman demanded angrily.

'Because if it hasn't been placed off limits, then I and my members have the right to walk its streets, do we not?'

'You haven't got the right to go down there and deliberately provoke trouble,' Clayton declared heatedly.

'Before you continue making these allegations, Chief Inspector Clayton, I'd like to be told in detail what action you have taken tonight. I and my members have been attacked by thugs armed with offensive weapons and badly beaten. One of my members is even now being operated upon for a fractured skull. Have you arrested the thugs who gave her those terrible injuries?'

'All right! All right, Mr Jones.' The policeman swallowed his own anger and became more mollifying

236

in his manner. 'I apologise if I've been a little hasty. Only this is a very serious matter. Inspector Miller, will you give Mr Jones the full details of what steps we are taking?'

'Yes, sir.' Inspector Miller was young and clean-cut, and his accents were those of an educated man. In clipped tones he told Jones that the police enquiries were continuing, and arrests were expected to take place very shortly.

Jones heard him out in silence, then when the young man had finished he questioned sharply, 'These thugs who attacked my members, you know their identities then, do you?'

'As I said, our enquiries are continuing, Mr Jones, and we expect a speedy result from them,' Miller answered smoothly.

'I want to know why you were in that area tonight, Mr Jones?' the Chief Inspector chimed in.

'I was on the Lord's work, Chief Inspector. Trying to save souls,' Jones said gently. 'I don't think that such work is against the law, is it?'

'No, it's not against the law, but it's damned foolishness to provoke the gangs in Edgeton.'

'Oh, I see.' Jones smiled bleakly. 'The gangs of pimps in Edgeton are allowed to flout the law with impunity. Why is that, Chief Inspector?'

'No one is allowed to flout the law in my division, Mr Jones,' Clayton gritted out, and Jones scowled.

'I don't understand your aggressive attitude. You are acting as if my movement has done wrong in trying to do the Lord's work; in trying to save the souls of those poor unfortunate women who are brutalised and forced into their vile trade by gangs of pimps.'

'I'm not saying that your movement has acted wrongly, Mr Jones,' the Chief Inspector protested defensively. 'But I am saying that you acted foolishly in provoking the gang to attack you.'

'If to act in the Lord's name is to act foolishly, Chief Inspector, then I am the biggest fool that you will ever meet. And I'm proud to be called such.' Jones' eyes began to gleam piercingly and his voice to pulse with fervour. 'We are on the same side, you and I, Chief Inspector. We are both on the side of law and order. That is the side that the Lord is on also. When we do his work, we are doing the work of goodness against evil. You say that I and my members acted foolishly tonight? Well, I'll tell you now that tomorrow night more of my members will be acting foolishly, and I shall be at their head. I shall lead them into Edgeton again, and carry out the work of the Lord. Now if you will excuse me, gentlemen, I have to go to my members who are in need of my comfort.'

'No, I haven't finished talking to you!' the Chief Inspector objected, and Jones stared at him with assumed shock.

'Am I under arrest? Am I being detained here?'

'No, of course not,' the policeman flustered.

'Then I'll say good night, gentlemen.'

Jones stiffly levered himself off the stretcher and stood shakily upright. Then he walked unsteadily out into the corridor leading to the casualty department waiting room, and the two policemen hurried out after him.

'I don't want you going into Edgeton tomorrow night, Mr Jones,' the Chief Inspector insisted forcefully.

'I shall do what the Lord commands me to do,' Jones called back over his shoulder.

'I'll prevent you from going there,' the policeman threatened.

'You do that, Chief Inspector!' Jones jeered at the threat. 'That will look good in the newspapers and on the television, won't it? Your policemen preventing my people from carrying out the Lord's work. Your policemen protecting evil pimps, who have already attacked and badly beaten my members. You do that, Chief Inspector.' He halted briefly and swung to face the following men. 'I shall lead my members into Edgeton tomorrow night. And if you try to stop me, then I'll make sure that the world knows how you are protecting the forces of evil.'

Then he walked away, and the policemen stared at each other in consternation.

Inspector Miller grinned wryly at his superior officer. 'I think you made an error there, sir.'

'Oh, you do, do you?' The Chief Inspector scowled fiercely. 'Well then, let's see if you can handle it better, shall we? You'll be in command tomorrow night, and you'll stop that bloody lunatic from going into Edgeton. And for your own sake, you'd better not make any errors . . .'

From the waiting room a cheer resounded as Ivor Jones went in to join his members who were waiting for him.

He told them in ringing tones what the police had threatened, and declared, 'I shall be going into Edgeton tomorrow night. Who will go with me and drive out these evil men?'

A roar of acclamation gave him his answer, and he smiled triumphantly and, throwing back his head, sang out . . .

'Mine eyes have seen the glory of the coming
    of the Lord . . .'

Their massed voices came thundering in to join his.

> 'He is trampling out the vintage where the
> grapes of wrath are stored.
> He hath loosed the fateful lightning of his
> terrible swift sword.
> His truth is marching on . . .'

# *Chapter Twenty-Eight*

'Mine eyes have seen the glory
Of the coming of the Lord.
He is trampling out the vintage
where the grapes of wrath are stored.
He hath loosed the fateful lightning
of his terrible swift sword.
His truth is marching onnnnn . . .'

They marched in a long column and as the massed
voices soared, pedestrians halted, cars stopped and
people came to windows and doors to watch them
pass.

'Glory, glory, Halleluiah
Glory, glory, Halleluiah
Glory, glory, Halleluiah
His Truth is marching on . . .'

Ivor Jones, head bandaged and left arm in a broad
white sling, led the column, and four paces behind
him marched two sweet-faced young girls carrying
banners. One banner was black, the other white;
both were emblazoned with the gold emblem of
the Cromwell Movement, the helmeted head of an
Ironside trooper.

Directly behind the young girls came wheelchairs bearing the injured women, bandaged and bruised, and after them followed the column of young and old, black and white, men, women and children.

Judicious phone calls to various paper and television news editors had ensured a heavy turn-out of cameramen and reporters, some of whom had followed the column from Cromwell House, while others waited at Edgeton.

Inspector Miller smiled sourly as he watched the approach of the column, and grudgingly conceded that Ivor Jones had already out-manoeuvred him. The policeman had deployed his constables to block this main approach road into Edgeton, but as soon as he saw the wheelchairs he realised that he could not prevent the column entering the area. The television and newspaper reporters would have a field day if the police attempted to use force against these injured women. For a brief moment Miller considered bringing in the police vans to form a barrier, but dismissed this idea. If Jones split up his column and tried to use other access roads the police would be made to look ridiculous if they attempted to rush around the area in a race against wheelchairs. In his mind Miller viciously cursed his Chief Inspector for giving him this assignment, and then signalled his accompanying inspectors and sergeants to come to him.

'The column is to be allowed to enter this area. We'll escort it and protect it.' He went on to issue the necessary instructions and when the singing column neared him he stepped out into the middle of the road and walked to meet Ivor Jones.

Lights flashed and reporters, cameramen and sound-boom operators jostled to be near the two

242

men as they met beneath the bleak rays of the tall street-lamps.

'We are on the Lord's work, Inspector Miller,' Ivor Jones declared in ringing tones. 'Let us pass.'

The policeman smiled and answered silkily, 'I have no intention of trying to prevent your work, Mr Jones. My men are here only to keep the peace and to protect your people. We are not here to stop you from going into Edgeton.'

This unexpected answer momentarily disconcerted Jones. He had wanted a confrontation with the police.

Then he smiled inwardly as he realised that by having the police marching alongside his column it would appear to any viewers that the police and the Cromwell Movement were actually acting in concert.

'Very well, Inspector, but you must walk at my side.'

The policeman considered this suggestion briefly, then nodded.

The column marched on, and now the police marched alongside.

'Mine eyes have seen the glory of the coming
    of the Lord. He is trampling out the vintage
    where the grapes of wrath are stored . . .'

The roaring echoes carried far and wide and house-holders came out to stand and watch, and they cheered and clapped as the column passed.

Those prostitutes who were patrolling their beats cursed and swore as the column neared them, but recognised the impossibility of doing any business that night and abandoned their beats. Several pimps stood in a sullen knot glowering and mouthing threats but conscious of their impotence to do anything about this situation, made no overt move.

With a bandage wrapped around his injured head, Chris Thompson and his two men moved with the column, concentrating on obtaining the reactions of the Edgeton residents to this demonstration. Without exception the reaction was jubilant, and resident after resident offered profuse thanks to Ivor Jones and the Cromwell Movement for this effort to clean up Edgeton.

Away on the opposite side of the city the dark-coloured transit van was entering the shabby streets of the Meadowpark Estate. As on the previous occasion it stopped at intervals to decant pairs of men, their faces hidden by balaclavas. Doors were kicked in, men shouted, women screamed, children shrieked, as the masked men carried out their allotted tasks with a ruthless precision. Then they disappeared into the night leaving broken bones and bloodied heads behind them.

In Edgeton the column paraded around and around the streets, their voice's roaring out their battle hymn.

'Glory, glory, Halleluiah
Glory, glory, Halleluiah
Glory, glory, Halleluiah
His truth goes marching on . . .'

Periodically, Ivor Jones would halt the column and address the watching spectators.

'Friends, the Cromwell Movement has come in

answer to your call. Some of our Sisters have been grievously hurt in answering that call. But even if we must lay down our lives, we of the Cromwell Movement will continue to come to your aid. We shall be here every night until these streets are cleansed of wickedness. We shall continue this fight against the evil men who have made your lives a misery and turned your streets into foul sewers of vice. We shall not rest from this battle until we have won the victory and given you back your own streets. We shall give Edgeton back to the decent people who live here. We shall not fail you.'

The spectators cheered vociferously and many shouted out:

> 'God bless you, Mister Jones!'
> 'Well done, well done!'
> 'Good old Cromwell!'
> 'Well done, Cromwell Jones!'

A television reporter seized on those last shouts, and told his audience. 'The crowds here are cheering Ivor Jones, and some of them are calling him, "Cromwell" . . . And that nickname fits this man to perfection. Like Oliver Cromwell leading his psalm-singing troops into battle, Cromwell Jones has led his own hymn-singing army into battle against the pimps and thugs who infest Edgeton. And many of this modern New Model Army have already been wounded in this battle of Edgeton. But they have returned here tonight, in wheelchairs, and on the arms of their comrades, to carry the fight back to their enemies. And at their head has been the new Oliver Cromwell . . . Cromwell Jones . . . This is Henry Winterton, News at Ten, Edgeton.'

The report was televised by the national news networks later that evening, and from that night on Ivor Jones would be popularly known to millions of people throughout the length and breadth of the country as 'Cromwell Jones'.

# Chapter Twenty-Nine

'But you must have heard something, Mrs Willis?' Detective Sergeant Denis Matthews protested aggrievedly. 'It was next door to you, after all. These walls are thin enough to hear a mouse squeak next door, let alone what happened last night.'

'Oh, yes, I did hear summat all right. I heard that bugger giving his missis a good hiding. But I hears that nearly every night, so I don't pay any heed to it any more.'

'No, Mrs Willis.' The policeman frowned dourly. 'It wasn't Mr Leonard giving his wife a good hiding. It was the pair of them getting kicked to pieces last night by two masked men who had smashed their door down to get at them.'

The old woman's lined face grinned delightedly, and her thin lips flecked out saliva as she cackled, 'Bloody good job, then. That's what I says! The pair on 'em are no good. Bloody useless thievin' layabouts. Never done a day's work since he's bin here on this estate, that Leonard 'asn't. And there's my Harold worked all his life, right up to the day he dropped down dead. And for what was he working? I'll tell you for what. He was working hisself to death to pay the bloody taxes to keep rotten scrounging bastards like them two next door laying stinking in their beds all day.'

'All right, Mrs Willis, thank you.' The policeman nodded resignedly. 'If you should remember anything that you saw or heard, then get in touch with me at the Central Police Station, will you, please? My name is Matthews . . . Detective Sergeant Matthews.'

The old woman's rheumy eyes peered slyly. 'Shall I get a reward if I does?'

Matthews chuckled grimly. 'I shouldn't think so, my dear. But you never know, do you?'

Outside in the street his detective constable was waiting for him.

'Did you get anything, Trevor?'

'No, Sarge.' The young constable seemed disgruntled. 'This lot's like the bloody three wise monkeys. See nothing, hear nothing, say nothing.'

The sergeant smiled sardonically. 'Well, at least this time they're not swearing at us, or chucking stones.'

The younger man frowned thoughtfully. 'It's vigilantes who're doing this, isn't it, Sarge?'

His superior shrugged. 'I dunno. What makes you think that, Trevor?'

'Well, it's obvious. There's been seven attacks in the last two nights, one of them a fire-bombing. And each time the targets have been buggers who are on our books for some reason or other. And nobody has even so much as given us a nod in the direction of the ones who're doing it.'

'Since when has Meadowpark ever given us a nod in the right direction?' the sergeant jeered.

'Oh, I know that they don't like us, Sarge. But you'd think that with a fire-bombing on a house that had young kids in it, there would have been somebody ready to tell us something?'

Again the Sergeant shrugged his broad shoulders. 'I've given up thinking about what people might or might not do, Trevor.' He assumed a mock harshness. 'And our enquiries aren't going to get very far anyway, if you keep on standing here talking instead of getting on with the bloody work you're paid for. Start at the far end of the street there, and begin to work your way back to me.'

'But I've already spoken to the houses down there,' the constable protested.

'Then speak to them again, and see if they've managed to remember anything,' the sergeant ordered sharply, and as if to illustrate his point he turned and went back to the old woman's front door.

'What does you want worrying me again?' she demanded angrily when she answered his knocking.

Matthews held up his hand in a placatory gesture. 'I just wanted to ask you one more thing, Mrs Willis. Then I'll go away and leave you in peace.'

'Go on then,' she assented grudgingly, 'but make it quick. I aren't got time to waste talking to you.'

'What do your friends think about these attacks that have taken place here on this estate? There's been seven now you know, in two nights. Aren't you afraid that it might be you who gets attacked next?'

'That's two things you're asking me about,' she grumbled petulantly. 'You said you only wanted to ask me one thing.'

Matthews grinned patiently. 'Well, do me a favour and answer both of them, there's a good girl.'

Her lipless mouth opened wide to display discoloured teeth and she chortled, 'All right then, I'll tell you straight. These buggers that's been set about all deserves whatever they gets, and a bloody sight more as well. Me friends and me think that whoever's doing it, is doing a bloody good job . . . And if you wants to know if I'm afraid o' being attacked by whoever's doing it, then I can tell you straight that I aren't a bit afraid. It's got to be good people who're doing this, not bad buggers. They wun't touch me.'

'How can you be so certain of that?' the policeman challenged.

'I just knows it, that's all. I just knows it,' the old woman stated positively, and slammed the door in his face.

He smiled secretly as he walked back along the street. 'I think I know what you're up to, Ivor Jones,' he told himself. 'In fact I'm bloody well sure that I know what you're up to. You've got William Rimmer doing this stuff, while you're parading around Edgeton making a name for yourself. I'll bet my life on it, that that's the case. It's Rimmer and those tough nuts of his who're hammering these toe-rags. Well, good luck to you, my son. More power to your arm!'

# Chapter Thirty

Every morning a meeting took place in the office of Chief Superintendent Richard Barker at the Central Police Station, the headquarters of the City Force. Normally the members of the senior management team were present, plus the duty Inspector, and the Sergeant who ran the intelligence and information computer. During this meeting, overnight events were discussed and the coming day's problems and possibilities were assessed. Unusually, however, today the Assistant Chief Constable was also present. The reason for this was the immense amount of national publicity being generated by the Cromwell Movement's actions in Edgeton. Every night for the last week they had paraded round and round the streets of Edgeton, necessitating the deployment of large numbers of policemen to prevent any outbreaks of violence. The number of extra duty men had decimated the overtime budget, and the City Force was now badly overspent in that department; which was why the Chief Superintendent, normally jealous of his chairmanship of the daily meetings, had specifically requested the attendance of the Assistant Chief Constable. He was feeling the need to pass the buck on to higher authority concerning these continuing demonstrations.

Barker called the meeting to order and directed Chief Inspector Clayton and Inspector Miller to report on the events in Edgeton. Next he called upon Detective Chief Inspector Henry Thomas to give his full report on what was known about the Cromwell Movement, and its leader, Ivor Jones.

Assistant Chief Constable Simon Street listened in silence as each man spoke, thanking them courteously when they had done, but vouchsafing no comment on what he had heard. He himself had been carefully monitoring the public reaction to what was happening in Edgeton, and had also had a man making enquiries in Edgeton itself amongst the residents there.

He dismissed all the other officers except for Chief Superintendent Barker, and when they were alone he said, 'This chap Ivor Jones is creating quite a stir, isn't he? Public opinion seems to be supporting him very strongly. So, incidentally, are the Authority.'

'He's costing us a lot of money, sir,' Barker pointed out sourly, 'And public opinion isn't footing the overtime bill. I'm doing that, and it's money that my budget can't afford to spend.'

Street nodded sympathetically. 'I understand your difficulty, Richard. However, this is money well spent. I'm told that the public are also applauding your action in protecting the demonstrations by this Cromwell Movement. It makes a nice change for us to be receiving plaudits instead of abuse. Young Miller is a sharp lad. He did well when he went into Edgeton side by side with Ivor Jones.'

Barker was a very shrewd career officer; he instantly divined which way the Assistant Chief Constable was inclining, and immediately took the credit for himself.

'He followed my instructions, sir, and carried them out very well. He should go far in the force.'

Street smiled inwardly, and baited, 'Oh, you'd ordered him to do so, had you, Richard? He rather gave the impression in his report that he had acted on his own initiative.'

Barker smiled avuncularly. 'He's young, sir, and very ambitious. I make due allowance for that when I read his reports.'

'Just so, Richard, just so.' Street nodded, then rose briskly to his feet and took his braided cap, gloves and swagger stick from the table. 'Well, carry on with the good work, Richard. Keep on protecting Mr Jones for the time being. I'll cover the overspending with the Chief.'

The relieved Barker was almost obsequious in his gratitude. Then at the door, as if in after-thought, the other man turned and asked casually, 'Oh, by the way, what's this I'm hearing about vigilantes operating on the Meadowpark Council Estate? There's been a series of incidents, hasn't there. Including a fire-bombing? What's being done about it?'

'I've got some of my most experienced men on the case, sir. To tell you the truth, they're meeting a wall of silence.'

'Oh, come now, Richard! "Wall of silence?" That sounds like the title of a bloody TV serial,' Street scoffed dismissively. 'Don't give me that guff. Your people must know who's behind it, even if they haven't been able to get the evidence yet.'

Barker sighed unhappily. 'Well, sir, it's a very difficult investigation to make. You know what Meadowpark is like, they'd sooner talk to their Maker than talk to us. Henry Thomas thinks it could be a local vendetta. There's a grouping of families there that have been scrapping among themselves for years: the Sweeneys, the Hallorans and the Leonards. It's them and their relatives and hangers-on who've been the targets of the attacks so far. But don't worry, sir, Thomas assures me that he'll soon have the evidence to bang them up.'

'He'd better.' Street frowned. 'The Chief isn't happy about the situation, and neither am I, Tom. We don't like civil wars on our patch. It makes it look as though we're not doing our job. And fire-bombs are bad news. I know that the bunch who were fire-bombed are scrotes, but there were baby scrotes in the house, and the Authority have been bending the Chief's ear about it. And he's been bending mine. So I want a result on that fire-bombing, and I want it yesterday.'

With a curt goodbye, he left an unhappy man behind him.

Barker sat in deep thought for a while, then summoned Detective Chief Inspector Henry Thomas to his office.

'Meadowpark Estate ... Mr Street isn't happy about it,' Barker announced accusingly.

Henry Thomas's fat face darkened ominously. 'And neither am I happy about it. I've had my best man down there, and half a dozen constables for the best part of a bloody week. There's other cases to deal with, you know, sir? I don't know why we're taking so much bother about a bunch of bloody toe-rags having a go at each other.'

'Now calm down, Henry, and hear me out.' Barker grinned slyly. 'The thing that's really getting up

254

Street's nose is the bloody fire-bombing. So, give me a result on that.' He winked broadly. 'There's got to be some available toe-rag we can put in the frame for it.'

The other man sucked his teeth reflectively, then offered, 'I'll have a word with old Denis.'

Barker grinned and nodded. 'You do that, Henry. You do that. Once we've got a body for the fire-bombing, we can forget the rest. And you'll be able to put your chaps on to other things.'

Thomas went directly to Detective Sergeant Denis Matthews' office and had a short talk with him. Matthews' heavily lined features were impassive as he listened. When his superior finished speaking Matthews nodded.

'Leave it with me, sir.'

Later that morning he used a public phone box some distance from the station to get in touch with Ivor Jones. Shortly afterwards he had a brief and apparently accidental encounter with William Rimmer in the Elmer shopping precinct. They exchanged a few words and then parted.

Later in the afternoon of that same day two over-alled Council plumbers carrying bulging toolbags called at the marital home of Dean Halloran on the Meadowpark Estate.

It was Esther Halloran, Dean's wife, who answered the door to the workmen.

'What d'you want?' Her blotchy face was aggressively suspicious.

The younger workman, a tall, good-looking man, stared suggestively at her dumpy body, which bulged in all the wrong places against the skin-tight stretch pants and teeshirt. 'I 'udden't mind you for a start, love!'

Flattered by the admiration in his expression, she preened and retorted, 'If my bloke heard you say that, he'd tear your fuckin' 'ead off!'

'Good job he 'ent here then, darlin'.' The good-looking young man grinned, displaying even rows of white teeth.

'He is 'ere.' She jerked her head backwards. 'Does you want him?'

'I've already told you who I wants, darlin'.' The younger plumber was very cocky. 'I can always have your bloke afterwards if he fancies his chances, can't I?'

Dean Halloran was lying on the battered sofa in the living room, senseless and snoring from drink. The television was blaring, and his swarm of snot-nosed little children were fighting and screaming around him.

'It's a fuckin' good job for you that my bloke's havin' a kip, you cheeky bleeder.' Esther Halloran grinned, showing stained teeth.

'Can we bloody well get on with the bloody job?' The older plumber scowled and grumbled impatiently. 'We'se got another bloody dozen bloody cisterns to check arter this 'un, missus.'

'You check it, Arthur.' The young plumber grinned and winked at the woman. 'I'll stay here and keep this young lady company. I reckon she's lonely.'

She laughed and punched him. 'You cheeky bleeder!'

'Can I go up to your loft then, missus?' the older plumber asked, and she nodded carelessly, her eyes intent on the good-looking younger workman.

He bantered suggestively with her for several

minutes, while up in the loft the older plumber bumped around. The banter was so well received that the young plumber took even bolder liberties. Esther Halloran's struggles were only momentary, then she revelled in being expertly kissed and intimately caressed behind the front door, by a handsome, muscular man whose clean smell and sweet breath contrasted so dramatically with her husband's stench.

When the older man returned from the loft he told Esther Halloran, 'You'll be all right now, missus. I'se renewed the ballcock.'

'She can have another ballcock any time she wants.' The younger man smiled invitingly at her. 'You just give me the word, darlin'.'

'Gerroff, you cheeky bleeder.' She laughed and simpered, and as he whispered in her ear she gurgled with delighted laughter and slapped him playfully.

Then the two plumbers went next door and reluctantly Esther Halloran went back to the living room, and the shrieking swarming children, and her snoring, grunting husband.


Early the following morning Detective Sergeant Denis Matthews and other police armed with search warrants called at several houses on the Meadowpark Estate tenanted by members of the Leonard and Halloran families. In the loft of Dean Halloran's house they found four petrol bombs made from wine bottles, corked and fused with rag strips, and ready for use.

Bawling his innocence, Dean Halloran fought violently against the arresting officers, but was taken away in the police van, while his swarm of children shrieked and cried, and their mother screamed filthy abuse at the policemen. Later that morning Halloran was charged with the arson attack on the home of Terence Sweeney. Bail was refused and he was remanded in custody.

# Chapter Thirty-One

The Sylvan View flats on the Meadowpark Estate were eight stories high and built in four separated blocks around a vast central courtyard. They were the main dumping ground for the city's problem families, and a hellhole for the unfortunate pensioners, single mothers, the unwilling unemployed and the decent families who were forced to live in the vandalised blocks because they had nowhere else to go. Gangs of teenagers and smaller children ran uncontrolled here, and burglaries and assaults were almost a nightly occurrence. Many of the flats had been completely wrecked and left boarded up and derelict. Others were used by squatters and drug addicts, alcoholics, tramps and vagrants of all types. The decent residents lived in a state of virtual siege, bolting and barring their doors and windows – afraid to stir out at night, fearful each time they left their homes that they would return to find doors and windows smashed in and their scant belongings pillaged and vandalised.

It was into Block 1 of Sylvan View that Ivor Jones moved his first member and family from the Cromwell Movement. Two days previously another flat in Block 3, which directly faced Block 1 across the central courtyard, had also gained new tenants: three hard-featured men who ignored all attempts by their immediate neighbours to talk, and whose forbidding appearances made those same neighbours very wary of upsetting them. Under cover of darkness the three men had moved into the flat several packing cases containing expensive video cameras and equipment. They set up the cameras so that the flat which the Cromwell Movement family had been allocated was under complete visual surveillance, and then settled themselves patiently to wait and observe.

When the new family moved into Block 1, curious eyes had watched the removal van arrive and the furniture and belongings of the newcomers being carried up the flights of stairs since the lifts were out of order again. Expert assessments were made of the values of the various articles, and pleasure was expressed at the good quality of the high-priced merchandise.

Damien Foreman, aged twelve, summoned his two lieutenants, aged ten and eight, who in turn summoned the rank and file of the gang, ages ranging from six to nine years.

'We've got a good 'un,' Damien told them.

The gang truanted from school and took up their positions to keep a watch on the third floor of Block 1, where the opulent newcomers had moved into their flat.

They waited patiently until the couple and their two tiny children left the flat, then Damien Foreman beckoned his gang to him.

'Come on, we can do it now. There's nobody left in there, or the one next door. We'll do both on 'em.'

'But what about the other side? Old Grimshaw 'ent gone out, has he?'

Damien grinned and produced a short steel crowbar from under his bomber jacket. 'Don't worry about that old bastard. He knows what's good for him. He won't tell anybody, he's too fuckin' scared of us.'

'What if he does tell somebody, though?' the worried boy persisted, and Damien lost his temper.

''Ull you shut up, you windy cunt! If you'se lost your bottle, then fuck off!'

The other boy pouted sullenly. 'I 'ent lost me bottle.'

'Come on then, let's go.' Damien Foreman led his gang at a fast run across the courtyard and up the dark stairwells stinking of human urine and excreta and strewn with filth and rubbish.

Across in Block 3, the hard-featured men grinned at each other as they saw the gang sprinting across the courtyard, and focused the cameras lenses on the fronts of the third-floor flats opposite.

Damien Foreman attacked the door of the first flat with savage urgency, and in scant seconds had jemmied it open. Whooping and laughing excitedly, the gang swarmed inside and rampaged through the neatly furnished rooms. What they couldn't carry or didn't want to steal they smashed and destroyed: pouring milk and treacle into the interior of the big stereo unit, shattering the television screen, slashing the stuffing of the chairs and sofa, ripping out pages from books and tearing up family photographs, urinating over bedding and carpeting, turning taps full on after plugging the drainholes in the sinks and bath.

After only a couple of minutes the flat had been completely vandalised, and the occupants' hard years of working and saving to furnish and equip their home had been ruthlessly and mercilessly wasted.

'Right, that's enough, let's do next door,' Damien ordered, and they all followed and clustered around while he attacked the locked door. Inside that third-floor flat two other hard-featured men grinned at each other as they heard the crowbar's impact upon the front door, and the cracking splinterings of wood.

Damien Foreman levered the door open and, grinning triumphantly, accepted the plaudits of his gang. Then further down the balcony a door opened and a grey head appeared. Damien brandished the crowbar and shouted threateningly, 'Fuck off, Grandad, or you'll get some o' this!'

The grey head instantly disappeared and the sound of the door being slammed shut echoed along the balcony.

'All right, strip the fucker,' Damien Foreman ordered, and stood aside to let his gang swarm into the flat. He was unconcerned about any of them trying to cheat him. His hold over them was almost absolute, and he kept them in fear of his violence.

He had begun to move away from the front door, intending to terrorise the pensioner next door by smashing the window with his crowbar, when there came high-pitched shouts of shock and terror from inside the flat and the gang members came fleeing, frantically jostling and punching at each other in an effort to get clear of impeding bodies.

Damien Foreman didn't wait to enquire what was wrong, instead he fled himself.

Inside the flat the two men laid aside their shot-guns, then looked at each other and laughed.

'That scared the little bastards, didn't it!'

\*       \*       \*

262

The woman's face was wet with tears when she came to Cromwell House in search of Ivor Jones.

'They'se wrecked me son's place, Mr Jones. They stole what they could carry and just smashed up the rest.' Sudden fury caused her to cry out bitterly. 'Why don't the police do summat about it, Mr Jones? All they'm good for is having us up for not having a bloody dog licence, or some other such bloody nonsense. But they don't do nothing about the young bastards that are smashing people's homes up, does they!'

'There now, my dear, the police are doing their best,' he told her gently. 'But what do you want from me?'

'They says that you're the only one who can help us, Mr Jones. All me friends on the Meadowpark are saying that you can help us.'

Jones returned to the Sylvan View Flats with the woman, and was greeted by a small crowd of residents. The woman's son and his young wife were standing amid the wreckage of their home with shocked white faces, and a youthful police constable was taking a statement from them.

'Did anyone see who did this?' Jones asked the crowd in general, and one middle-aged man answered angrily.

'It'll have been the bloody kids again – that Foreman kid and his bloody mates. They'se bin took to court time and time again, and nothing's bin done to them. This estate is a bloody cesspit. Last night over on Piper Avenue a poor old bloke had his door kicked in while he was watching the telly, and a bunch of bloody yobs ransacked his place and beat him up as well.' The man shook his fists in impotent fury. 'And the best of it is, that we tells the police who the young buggers are who're doing this, and the bloody police never touches 'um. The world's gone mad! Bloody stark raving mad, so it has!'

The young constable had finished taking the statements and was leaving the flat. He saw and recognised Ivor Jones and spoke to him.

'Hello, Mr Jones.'

'Hello, officer, it's a bad business.' Jones nodded towards the wrecked flat. 'Did they break into anywhere else?'

The young policeman shook his head. 'No, not as far as I know. They had a go at next door, but were scared off by some friends of the family who were inside.'

'Do you think you'll catch the ones responsible?' Jones asked and the constable answered in a low-pitched voice, careful not to be overheard by the people around them.

'I know for sure who's done this, Mr Jones – the same little bastards who've done at least fifty other jobs like this over the past few months. And I can't do a dammed thing to stop them. I'm not allowed to lock the young bastards up any more. If I took them to court, nothing can be done to punish them. They're supposed to be too young to know that what they're doing is wrong. It's bloody insane, isn't it? I only wish the bloody fools who make these rules could be here with me on the estate, when I'm trying to explain to decent people like this young couple why I can't do nothing about what's happened to them.'

Jones nodded sympathetically, and the policeman left.

'Can you do something about this, Mr Jones?' The

young husband came with his harshly weeping wife to plead. 'I know you can't get my stuff back, but is there anything you can do to stop the buggers who did this from doing it again?'

Jones reached out and touched the young man's shoulder, as if in benediction. 'They will be caught, and they will be punished. I promise you.'

Turning, he walked quickly away.


In Cromwell House, in a darkened room in the cellars, the video film was played several times, and each time faces were compared with photographs, names and addresses were verified.

The lights were finally switched on, and Ivor Jones told William Rimmer, 'Very well, Mr Rimmer. You have your orders. Carry on.'

Rimmer saluted military-style, but there was no trace of mockery in the gesture. 'Very good, Mr Jones.'

He turned and barked a series of brusque instructions to the dozen men in the room, and in silence they hurried away.

A short time later four dark-coloured vans drew out from the grounds of Cromwell House and, taking separate routes, made their way into the vast Meadowpark Estate.

Each van parked discreetly in different streets, and the occupants waited patiently in the dark-shadowed interiors beneath the cold bleak lights of the tall concrete lamps.

In William Rimmer's van the man with him suddenly nudged his elbow. 'There's the little cunt coming now.'

Along the pavement strutted Damien Foreman.

Rimmer nodded. 'You take him, Ted. Knocker, you deal with the doors.'

As the unsuspecting boy walked past the van, the rear door was flung open and a dark figure launched out from the interior. Before the boy could even realise what was happening a chloroformed pad had been clamped across his mouth and nose, and he was dragged into the rear of the van. The door closed and the vehicle drove sedately away, the whole operation taking place in split seconds.

Similar events occurred where the other vans were parked, and when they finally left the estate the vans were carrying a total of six chloroformed boys.

Damien Foreman woke up with a splitting headache, and a feeling of nausea. He was very cold and stiff, and peering around in the darkness realised that he was lying on the ground at the children's play area on the Rec. Dazed and badly frightened, he tried to make sense of what had happened to him. All he could remember was that he had been walking home, and next instant had been grabbed from behind and a sickly-smelling cloth had covered his face. He lifted his hand to his mouth, where the skin around his lips was sore and blistered.

Then he became aware that other figures were lying around him, and nervously he crawled to the nearest, to find that it was one of his gang members snoring in deep sleep. Another of the figures stirred and sat up with a yell, and Damien went over to him.

'What happened to you, Fatso?'

He stared curiously at the wide strip of tissue

paper stuck across the fat boy's forehead, and then realised that a similar strip was sticking to his own forehead.

'Keep still and shurrup,' he ordered the whimpering boy, and pulled off the strip of tissue paper. He squinted in the gloom and could just make out some lettering. Realisation came in a rush.

'You've bin tattooed, Fatso.' Damien Foreman pulled the strip of paper from his own head and felt with careful fingers. He winced at the pain of the punctured flesh, and moaned with real dread. 'And me, I've bin tattooed as well.'

He rushed to one after the other of the supine figures and found that every one of them had likewise been tattooed across their foreheads.

By now they were coming round from the effects of the chloroform, whimpering, puking, crying out in fear and distress. Damien kicked and cuffed them to their feet, and led them towards the distant lamp-posts.

In the cold harsh light he stared in horror at Fatso's forehead, his lips moving as he slowly deciphered the double row of tattooed words: 'I am a dirty little thief.'

Panting heavily as his own distress rapidly mounted, he grabbed the fat boy's arm and shouted, 'Read me 'ead, Fatso.'

The fat boy was crying, and could not read anyway, so Damien grabbed another of the gang and shook him violently. 'Read me 'ead, you cunt! Read me 'ead!'

The boy stutteringly read out, 'I am a dirty litle thief.'

'Oh, fuckin' hell!' Damien wailed pitifully. 'Fuckin' 'ell! Fuckin' 'ell!'

The boys suddenly erupted with cries and shrieks and sobs, and began to run off in all directions.

Damien Foreman sank to his knees, his fingers clawing desperately at his forehead as if to tear the words from his skin, wailing out over and over again, 'Oh, fuckin' 'ell! Fuckin' 'ell! Fuckin' 'ell . . .'

# Chapter Thirty-Two

The tattooing of the youthful thieves created an uproar. The 'concerned', the 'compassionate' and the 'caring' from all over the nation roared their outrage and demanded that the police hunt down and bring the perpetrators to trial. Journalists from the media brandished cheque-books to obtain exclusive interviews with the boys and their parents. Politicians, social workers, pundits, psychologists and religious leaders joined forces to condemn the boys' unknown attackers.

Ivory Jones, now seen as a leading crusader against crime, was repeatedly approached for his opinion about the incident. Following his usual practice, he refused to give any interviews to press or television. The Cromwell Movement Press Officer, Chris Thompson, issued a statement on behalf of the movement leadership which, although deploring the violence used against the youngsters, nevertheless refused to condemm the perpetrators. The statement also pointed out the long reign of terror that the gang of boys had inflicted on the residents of the Meadowpark Estate, and the failure of their parents, the police and all those others now shouting in outrage to do anything to bring that reign of terror to an end. 'It was therefore only to be expected that sooner or later people would be driven to take the law into their own hands, and strike back against those who preyed upon them . . .' the statement concluded.

The City Police detailed a team of detectives to hunt down the attackers, but their enquiries throughout the Meadowpark Estate were met with silence.

As the days passed it became noticeable at Police Headquarters that the incidence of break-ins and burglaries on the vast estate had dramatically diminished, and many policemen privately expressed their approval of the tattooists. An increasing groundswell of approval also began to be voiced among the general public, when it was revealed by one of the national tabloid newspapers just how many criminal offences the youthful gang had been suspected of committing.

Then six nights after the initial incident three accused paedophiles, out on bail while awaiting trial, were chloroformed and snatched from off the streets by masked men, to be later found lying senseless on the municipal rubbish dump. Their foreheads were tattooed with the words: 'I am a child molester.'

The following night the same thing happened to a convicted rapist, who had been given early release following his second conviction and short term of imprisonment for rape. In his case the words read simply: 'I am a rapist.'

It was very noticeable that these latter incidents did not provoke the same amount of outrage and condemnation as the previous incident with the boys. Instead there were many letters written to the newspapers expressing whole-hearted approval of what had been done, and even calls that all such types of criminal offenders be dealt with likewise.

Meanwhile, the Cromwell Movement continued to make its nightly marches through the Edgeton district, and its sweeps across the Meadowpark Rec.

The movement had also deployed its first observer patrols across the Meadowpark Council Estate, and those patrols were greeted with enthusiastic approval by the vast majority of the estate's residents.

George Faraday was making an impact in his new role as troubleshooter in the city's Housing Department. Under his constant barrage of chivvying the refurbishment of the derelict properties on the Meadowpark Estate was proceeding with unaccustomed rapidity, and as soon as each property was ready, people from the Cromwell Movement took up the tenancy.

A delegation of shopkeepers from the estate came to Ivor Jones, asking him for help in protecting their business premises, and for the first time members of the 'Ironsides', the youth branch of the Cromwell Movement, appeared on the streets in their dark grey hooded tracksuits and bomber jackets with the emblem of the Ironside trooper printed in gold upon their chests, and the word 'Ironside' emblazoned across their backs in massive gold letters. The teenage boys and girls patrolled the three separate shopping areas of the vast estate during the late afternoon, early evening, and weekend opening hours of the shops, which had previously been the peak times for shoplifting and general abuse and vandalism. By sheer weight of numbers they deterred the yobs and sneak-thieves, and many of the estate's children and teenagers stared enviously at the emblazoned tracksuits and bomber jackets, and made enquiries as to how they could join the Ironsides.

But although the Cromwell Movement was striding on to ever greater strength and its leader, Ivor Jones, was fast becoming a widely known figure locally and even nationally, certain of his movement officers were finding their own personal troubles beginning to press upon them.

'We owe three months' mortgage, Chris. We owe the grocer. We owe the butcher. We haven't paid the phone or the electricity. Every time we've entertained our friends during the last couple of months, I've paid for everything – for the food, the wine, the smokes. I'm sick and bloody tired of supporting you financially. I didn't say a word when you walked out of your job, did I? I accepted it. I accepted that you needed to venture into fresh fields. To find fulfilment! But I'll be dammed if I'm going to say nothing now! I've had enough of it, Chris! A bloody belly-full of it, in fact!'

Shelagh Perrot's shrill voice grated irritatingly upon Chris Thompson's hearing. He stared at her frowning face, its beauty made hard and ugly by petulant lines of temper. And he suddenly recalled all those other occasions during their relationship when he had done something which displeased her, or that she did not think was a good career move, and then had been forced to endure similar tirades of petulance until he surrendered to her will.

'. . . Tom and Alison think that you must have had a brainstorm, or something, to go chasing off to join up with this Jones man. They say that anyone in their right mind would recognise immediately that at best he's a self-deluding idiot, and at worst, a shabby little con artist . . .'

The young man was stung by this and interrupted heatedly. 'You've changed your tune all of a sudden, haven't you? A few weeks ago you thought that Mr Jones was the best thing since sliced bread.' He grinned sneeringly. 'But that was before you tried to chat him up, wasn't it? And got ignored by him. That's what your problem is really, isn't it? You can't stand the fact that he's got no interest in you.'

The truth cut deep, and Shelagh Perrot's fury flamed.

'You're a bloody fool, Chris! I've never had any interest in Ivor Jones. Tom and Alison are always telling me that I'm a fool to stay with you; that I could have any man I chose, instead of wasting my time with a born loser like you. And I'm beginning to think that they're right.' She shook her head, causing her blonde hair to flare out around her flushed cheeks. 'I don't understand you, I really don't. What can you possibly see in such a pathetic little man? It's so glaringly obvious to anyone who has a modicum of sense that Jones is becoming a laughing-stock . . . Cromwell Jones!' In her mouth the nickname was an epithet, and she sneered with bitter contempt. 'It's a good job for him that they've closed the lunatic asylums, or he wouldn't be walking the streets for much longer. He'd be where he deserves to be, locked up in a padded cell, and all the pathetic fools like you that he's managed to con into working for him for peanuts would be in there with him. Tom and Alison say that . . .'

'I don't care what Tom and Alison fucking well say!' the young man bellowed in an explosion of fury, and she stood open-mouthed, shocked into silence.

'And I don't care what you think either. So just shut your bloody mouth, or I'll shut it for you.' He

273

rammed his face forward to within inches of the young woman's, and brandished his clenched fist threateningly under her jaw. He saw fear spring into her eyes, and for a brief instant shame rose in him, but then the recollection of her sneering words banished the shame, and his fury raged unchecked once more.

'Mr Jones is a great man, and I'm proud to follow him. Prats like Tom and Alison think they're being very funny when they call him "Cromwell". But the joke's on them, and before very long they'll be laughing on the other sides of their stupid, smug faces.'

He grinned savagely, then straightened and stepped back from her, and she flinched involuntarily at his sudden movement.

'Don't be afraid,' he jeered. 'I'm not going to touch you. In fact I'm never going to touch you, or to come near you again. You can shove your head up Tom and Alison's arses. I'm going to live where I belong.'

He turned away from her and, taking his suitcases from the hall cupboard, went into the bedroom and began to pack.

After a while she came to the doorway to watch him, her eyes wide with disbelief. He completely ignored her, and eventually she was driven to question, 'Are you really going to leave me?'

He made no answer, and she displayed a flash of temper. 'You can't go. We've got a joint mortgage on this place.'

'Excuse me.' He brushed past her to go into the bathroom and collect his toiletries.

Now she began to look worried. 'But what have I done, Chris?'

He smiled mirthlessly. 'You've been yourself, Shelagh, that's all. You've just been yourself.'

'I was only trying to make you see sense. Trying to make you see what's best for you,' she protested indignantly. 'Since you've gone to work for the Cromwell Movement, you've been paid next to nothing. I've been paying all the bills round here.'

He finished packing and locking the cases, then lifted them and moved towards the front door.

'I'll fetch the rest of my things later. Don't worry if you're not here when I come for them. I won't take anything that doesn't belong to me.'

'But why are you doing this?' she wailed, and tears shimmered in her eyes. 'Why are you leaving me like this? We've had rows before, and you haven't left me.'

He stared at her for a long, long moment, then told her quietly, 'I never left you before, Shelagh, because before now I've never had anywhere that I wanted to go to, if it meant leaving you behind. But now I've found somewhere, and I want to be there. I ought to thank you really, because until you started ranting and raving at me just now, I hadn't realised just how much I wanted out from this relationship. I hadn't fully recognised what it was that I really wanted. You've clarified my mind, Shelagh, and I'm very grateful to you for that. Goodbye, and good luck.'

He heard her sobbing as he left the flat, but felt only relief that he was going.

As he drove his car across the city he experienced an eerie sensation of *déjà-vu*. It was as though he was following a preordained pattern of events. And when he arrived at Cromwell House, it was as if he had come to the place which had always been destined to be his true home . . .

\* \* \*

275

Lisa Keegan had been aware for some time that the Cromwell Movement was operating in both overt and covert ways. She knew that the Security Section had been responsible for the incidents on the Meadowpark Estate. But the attack on the gang of child thieves had horrified her; she could not help but mentally superimpose her own sons' faces when she saw the photos and television pictures of the tattooed boys. She had no actual proof that the Security Section had carried out the action, because the group of men were kept apart from the general administration of the movement, but in her own mind she was certain. Her troubled spirit was quickly noticed by Ivor Jones, and one morning he called her into Tabernacle Cottage and confronted her.

'You've changed, Sister, you no longer display the same enthusiasm for our cause,' he stated quietly, and then asked, 'What's troubling you?'

Lisa Keegan's initial reaction was one of fear and guilt, and she opened her mouth to deny that anything was worrying her.

Jones smiled kindly, and told her, 'Don't lie to me, Lisa. I know you too well. Tell me truthfully what it is that's upsetting you.'

She drew a ragged breath, and summoning all her courage said, 'It's what's happened to those children . . . those children that were snatched off the streets and tattooed. I think that Mr Rimmer and his men did it.'

Jones chuckled richly. 'Of course they did it, Lisa.'

She stared at him in shock and horror, and burst out, 'But it was bloody evil, to do that!'

He shrugged his powerful shoulders. 'Perhaps, Lisa, perhaps . . . But I ordered it to be done for a very good reason.'

Anger rose in her and she demanded heatedly, 'No reason can justify doing something like that to children – how can you stand there and calmly admit to ordering it to be done?'

He smiled bleakly, and his voice was very calm. 'Because I thought it necessary.'

'It was wicked! Evil!' she blurted out.

He pursed his lips judiciously, and after a few moments said sadly, 'What a pity! What a pity!'

She stared at him in surprise. 'What do you mean? "What a pity?"'

'That you should have turned against me like this, Lisa.' His blue eyes were accusatory.

She shook her head in denial. 'But I haven't.'

His weathered features became set and hard. 'You've called me wicked and evil.'

Made nervous and uneasy by his manner, she again denied forcefully. 'I haven't turned against you, Mr Jones. I didn't mean that *you* were wicked or evil. Only that what was done to those boys was.'

His fiery blue eyes were becoming increasingly hostile. 'I've trusted you implicitly, and this is how you repay my trust. By taking the part of worthless scum against me.'

Now she was really becoming distressed, and tears stung her eyes as she protested, 'No, Mr Jones. I wouldn't ever support anyone against you.'

He dismissed her protests with a wave of his hand. 'You've made me very unhappy, Sister Keegan. Wait here.'

He left the cottage and Lisa, bitterly regretting that she had spoken out, sat tensely awaiting his return.

When he did come back he was accompanied by a man from the Security Section.

'I think it's best that you should have some time

to think about your future, Sister Keegan.' Jones' manner was terse and businesslike. 'I am suspending your membership of my movement, to give you time to consider very carefully where your loyalties lie.'

She experienced a sense of real dread. 'But why?' She started to question him, and he cut her short.

'There will be no discussion about this. My decision has been made. Mr Fitzgerald here will escort you to clear your desk of any personal belongings. Your salary cheque will be posted to your home address. I suggest that you think very deeply about what you want to do with your life.'

Before she could reply, he turned from her and went out of Tabernacle Cottage.

Bemused by the suddenness of events, she allowed herself to be ushered out by Fitzgerald and escorted to clear her personal belongings from her desk.

As she sorted out the contents of the drawers, the other women and girls in the large office studiously avoided her eyes. Even Wisdom Maclure, who had become a close friend, kept her head averted, and Lisa began to feel like a pariah, a leper. Indignation at this cavalier treatment bubbled up and she told the burly security man, 'I want to speak to Mr Jones.'

The man regarded her with cold hostility, and snapped curtly, 'Just get your things together, and get out of here. You're not going to speak to anybody in this building.'

Her anger rose. 'You can't tell me what to do. I've the right to speak to anybody I choose to.'

His smile resembled a contemptuous snarl. 'Outside Cromwell House, you can speak to whoever you want, lady. But in here, you can't.'

'And who'll stop me?' she challenged defiantly.

His cold eyes gave her that answer, and she could

not suppress a frisson of fear at the malevolence in their stare.

She felt both degraded and somehow guilty as she was escorted silently from Cromwell House and up to the entrance gates.

The man guarding the gates held out his hand. 'Give me your pass, and membership card.'

Her initial instinct was to refuse, but then her escort whispered sibilantly, 'Don't be a fool to yourself, lady. We'll take them from you anyway.'

Outside the gates she felt suddenly fearful, as if all the surety of protection that she had known since she had joined the movement had been stripped from her, leaving her vulnerable and defenceless against the hostile world outside. She turned to stare back at the two men standing in the gateway, but they were engrossed in conversation and paid her no attention. The sensation of being reduced to nothingness unnerved her, and she hurried away, head bent, feet scurrying, to her car parked further along the street.

Driving back to her home Lisa was tearful and confused, asking herself over and over again, 'What have I done to deserve this? What have I done?'

Back at Cromwell House Ivor Jones was deep in thought. What had just occurred had disturbed him greatly. He had believed that Lisa Keegan was his creature, that she would never question anything that he did or said. Her reaction to what had been done to the youthful thieves had come as a tremendous shock to him, a blow to his ever-expanding ego and confidence to find that he had misjudged the woman. Now, the longer he thought about what had happened, the more he was coming to regard Lisa's reaction as an act of treachery against himself. He was also starting to experience a niggling worry that she might voice her suspicions about who had carried out the attack and tattooing to the wrong ears.

As had now become customary with him, he talked aloud to his God. He spoke in conversational tones, because the deity was now as much an equal confederate as He was Lord and mentor.

'I made a mistake about the Keegan woman, didn't I? I wonder how far she can be trusted now to keep her mouth shut?'

'Let it be a lesson to you,' God chided. 'Don't ever trust anybody one hundred per cent. Particularly when it's a woman. Watch your back at all times. Never trust anybody completely.'

'You've no need to keep on telling me that,' Jones retorted testily. 'You're just repeating the obvious. What's important now is to decide what to do about Lisa Keegan.'

'She's a valuable member,' God reminded him. 'She was doing a wonderful job as administrator.'

'Nobody's indispensable, though, are they? I can always find another administrator. Wisdom Maclure could take over the job.'

'Yes, she could. But what effect would that have on Lisa Keegan? You know what they say about a woman scorned, don't you?' God chuckled slyly. 'She might just be mad enough about being supplanted to go and say the wrong thing to the wrong person.'

'I'm not worried about that.' Jones was dismissive. 'She knows nothing really.'

'She knows what you've told her yourself, you damned fool,' God snarled angrily. 'What possessed you to tell her that Rimmer and the lads had had those little toe-rags?'

'All right, all right,' Jones grumbled resentfully. 'It was a mistake. I got careless.'

'It was a mistake all right. And you might pay dearly for it.'

'Lisa couldn't prove anything, even if she did tell the wrong people about what I said.'

'She doesn't need proof, does she?' God pointed out. 'You've made a lot of enemies, Ivor. And they're just waiting to get hold of something like this. You know what folks would say then, don't you? That there's no smoke without fire. The police would really get on your tail, wouldn't they? Denis Matthews wouldn't be able to shield you from that.'

Jones shook his head in confident dismissal. 'I really don't think that I've got anything to worry about with Lisa Keegan. She'll never turn against me to that extent.'

Then he paused for some moments as his thoughts veered off on a fresh tangent. 'Darren Maclure reports that Otway is ready to hit back at us. He's hired a bomb-maker. So we'll make a pre-emptive strike.'

'How?' God questioned curiously.

'We'll use the bombs that Otway's paying for.' Jones smiled. 'It'll be poetic justice, won't it?'

His smile broadened as he heard God's appreciative laughter.

# Chapter Thirty-Three

Lisa Keegan had spent yet another restless night, her sleep beset by troubled dreams. When she awoke she lay staring up at the ceiling, and the keen pain of loss cut sharply. The ringing of the telephone brought her running from her bed and down the stairs with bare feet to answer its summons, wild hope in her heart that it was Ivor Jones who was calling her.

'Lisa, I want to speak to you.'

The familiar voice caused her to scowl in disappointment, and for a brief instant she was tempted to hurl the handset from her.

She drew a long breath and snapped, 'Yes, Clive, what is it?'

'We need to talk, Lisa.' His tone was supplicatory. 'And I mean *talk*, not argue or fight. Please, Lisa. Please let's talk.'

The sadness in his voice touched her deeper feelings. Sad and bereft as she felt herself, it evoked her pity.

'All right,' she agreed quietly. 'You'd better come over.'

'I'll come straight away,' he told her eagerly.

Lisa returned upstairs slowly, already regretting her momentary weakness. She stripped off her long nightgown and stood beneath the stinging-hot spray of the shower for long minutes, reliving in her mind the events of the fateful day when she had challenged Ivor Jones.

'Why did I do it?' she asked herself over and over again. 'Why did I say such things to him? Why couldn't I just keep my mouth shut? What did those young thieves mean to me anyway? They're only scum. Why should what happened to them concern me?'

But then the images of her own sons' bright, youthful faces came sharply into her mind, and she visualised the big black lettering defacing their smooth brows, and despite her bitter regrets knew that she had been right to condemn what had been done to those other boys.

'It was a wicked thing to do, Ivor,' she told Jones in her mind. 'Wicked!'

And then she was racked with sudden weeping at the knowledge that Ivor Jones had cast her from him.

'I love you,' she told him. 'I love you no matter what you might do. I love you . . .'

Reluctant to allow her husband to see the ravages of her grief, she brushed her hair until it shone, dressed in a neat blue two-piece, and made up her face carefully. Then she went downstairs to wait for him.

Clive Keegan rang the doorbell and waited to be let in, even though he still possessed keys to the house.

When she questioned him about this, he told her quietly, 'It's your home now, not mine, Lisa. I don't like to barge in.'

She regarded him curiously, noting that his usual

air of bumptious self-confidence was no longer apparent. He seemed strangely diminished. Still well-dressed, still well-groomed, but somehow lacking the sleek smoothness that he had always radiated.

'Have you lost weight?' she asked suddenly, and he shrugged.

'I've no idea.'

She examined him speculatively, and then nodded. 'I think you have. You look different somehow.'

'I *am* different, Lisa. I've changed.' He suddenly shook his head dismissively. 'I didn't come here to talk about me, I came to talk about the boys. You haven't been to see them lately, have you?'

There was no accusation in his tone, merely a statement of fact.

'No, I haven't. I've been very busy.' She bridled defensively as guilt struck through her.

'I know you have. I'm not criticising you,' Clive hastened to assure her. 'But I think that you ought to know how badly our separation is affecting them.'

Again her sense of guilt caused her to react defensively. 'They haven't mentioned anything about that to me when I've phoned them.'

'I go to see them every week, and I've seen the alteration in them both,' he riposted.

'I see, and you're blaming me because I haven't visited them every week, I suppose,' she challenged him aggressively.

His pink face darkened and he seemed about to reply angrily, then he visibly checked himself, and instead answered in a reasonable tone. 'No, I'm not blaming you, Lisa. I'm not blaming you for anything. I've done a lot of thinking since we parted, and I've realised that I'm mainly to blame for what's happened between us. I was selfish and insensitive, and I accept that fully.'

He held up his hand to forestall her speaking. 'No, please, let me finish what I've come here to say, and then I'll leave.' He hesitated until she gave a slight nod of assent, and then he went on rapidly.

'I want you to give me another chance, Lisa. I want to try and make our marriage work. As much for the sake of the boys, as for mine. If you'll live with me again, I promise that I'll be more sensitive to your needs. I won't object to you being a member of the Cromwell Movement. In fact, I'll even have a shot at being a member myself, if you want me to.'

Again he hesitated, and stared anxiously at her impassive features. 'I want us all to be a family again, Lisa. I love you, and I need you, and the boys love you and need you.' He shook his head. You don't have to give me any answer now. Just think about it . . . Please?'

With that he turned from her and went out of the house.

Lisa remained standing as the noise of his car's engine died away in the distance, and tears trickled slowly down her cheeks. Guilt at the suffering she had caused to her sons gnawed agonisingly, and she bit hard on her lips, breaking the soft moist skin and bringing blood, as if by inflicting physical pain on herself she could in some way atone for the pain she had given to her loved ones. For long minutes she stayed motionless, while her inner being was relentlessly buffeted and torn by a raging maelstrom of emotions.

Later that morning, when she had had time to calm down and think carefully about her life, she drove down to the school to see her boys.

The headmaster was not at all pleased by her coming. He regarded parents who called without a definite invitation from himself as nuisances who disrupted the working day, and unsettled the pupils.

Although irritated at his attitude Lisa had no wish to quarrel with the man, and knowing his susceptibility to a pretty woman she exerted all her considerable attractions and blatantly flirted with him. Flattered and charmed, he finally willingly agreed to her taking the boys out of school for the remainder of the day.

The atmosphere in the car during the drive back home was strained and awkward. Both boys were sullen and monosyllabic, and Lisa talked constantly, desperate to bridge the gap between them. But finally, baffled by their stubborn refusal to make even the slightest effort to respond to her advances, she lapsed into an unhappy silence.

When they reached the house the two boys immediately went up to their shared bedroom, and started to play with their computer games. Lisa wanted to shout at them to stay with her, to make some effort to communicate with her. But with a sense of hopelessness she realised that any attempt on her part to force the boys into her company would only make matters even worse. With an assumed brightness, she looked into their room and asked, 'What would you like me to cook you for lunch? Is there anything that you really fancy?'

They exchanged a long look, and their thin, pale faces bore an expression that was akin to contempt.

Then Robert answered for both of them. 'We're not really hungry, thank you. We'll eat when we get back to school. You'll take us back soon, won't you?'

The cool rebuff was like a physical blow to Lisa,

and she felt a wave of actual nausea shudder through her.

'All right, then,' she muttered and went downstairs, fighting to hold back her tears. She sat in the kitchen, trying to marshall her confused thoughts and to control the burgeoning grief.

'I've lost them. I've lost my boys!' The thought reverberated through her head. 'They don't love me any more!'

A sense of utter desolation oppressed her, and she felt that if death came seeking her at this moment in time she would welcome its dark embrace.

And then the phone rang. She lifted the extension and said glumly, 'Lisa Keegan.'

'How are you feeling today, Lisa? I've been worried about you. I feel I acted too harshly towards you the other day.'

The warmth and concern in Ivor Jones' voice brought a lump to Lisa's throat, and relief made her feel physically weak. All the love and respect that she had for him welled up in her, and she told herself thankfully, 'He loves me. He cares for me. He worries about me.'

'I'm fine, Mr Jones.' The words rushed out of her. 'I'm so sorry for what I said to you. I wasn't thinking straight. Of course what you did was necessary. It had to be done, I know that now.'

'Shhh, Lisa. It doesn't matter,' he soothed fondly. 'I know that you didn't really mean what you said. I was hurt and angry at the time, but let's put it behind us, shall we? Let's forgive and forget.'

'Oh, yes. Yes, please,' she breathed gratefully.

'Right then.' He became brisk and businesslike. 'There's a lot of work piling up on your desk, Lisa. What are you going to do about it?'

287

She was half-laughing, half-crying in thankful relief. 'I'm going to get it done right away, Mr Jones.' Then she remembered the boys upstairs, and explained hastily, 'I've got my boys with me. I'll have to take them back to their school first, so I shan't be able to come into work until later. Will that be all right?'

He chuckled amusedly. 'I've a better idea, Lisa. Treat today as a holiday. I'd like to meet your boys. Why not bring them down here with you, and let them see what it is we're doing? Let them have an inside look at the Cromwell Movement.'

She was delighted to agree, and humming to herself went back upstairs.

Filled with a resurgence of confidence, she told the twins briskly, 'I know you think that I've been neglecting you both lately, but I've been working very hard. You know that I'm a member of the Cromwell Movement, don't you?'

They both nodded.

'What you don't know is that I'm a very important member of the movement. I'm one of its officers. And we've all been invited by Mr Jones, the leader, to go to Cromwell House and have a look round.'

For the first time since she had picked them up from school, their faces registered interest and a hint of excitement.

'Mr Haldane says that Ivor Jones is a dangerous madman!' Robert informed her. Mr Haldane was the boys' housemaster.

'But Mr Smerrick says that Ivor Jones is the best thing to happen in this country since the war,' David chimed in. Mr Smerrick was the school groundsman.

'Well, you'll be able to form your own opinions

about Mr Jones, because he wants to meet you both.'
Lisa's happiness was bounding as at last she made
some progress in interaction with her much-loved
children.

At Cromwell House she was greeted with smiles
and warm words of welcome. The very women
who had averted their eyes from her now came
hurrying to ask her how she was, and when she
was returning to work. The security man who had
taken her membership card and pass from her handed
them back with a smile, and told her that Ivor Jones
would join her very shortly.

She felt her heart begin to pound when the stocky
figure in the familiar dark suit and roll-neck sweater
came and took her hand between both of his.

'It's good to see you again, Sister Keegan.' His
keen blue eyes turned to the two boys, and he
shook them both by the hand. Then he turned to
a tall, coloured youth behind him, who was dressed
in the dark grey, hooded tracksuit of the Ironsides,
and instructed, 'Take these lads down to the youth
centre and show them around.'

The youth grinned and saluted. 'Yes, Mr Jones.
Come on, boys.'

Robert and David followed him willingly.

'Me name's Dean,' he told them as they made
their way towards the big red-brick drill hall some
hundred yards distant from Cromwell House, and
added proudly, 'I'm a troop cornet in the First
Ironside Squadron.'

His companions stared curiously at him, and he
grinned and enlarged upon that statement. 'In the
youth branch of the movement we're divided into
squadrons, and each squadron has got different
troops in it.'

289

'Like a cavalry regiment?' Robert reacted uncertainly to the information. 'But that's like being a soldier, isn't it?'

The tall youth shrugged carelessly. 'I suppose it is in a way. But we don't have to do drill or anything like that. It's real good fun. We've got karate classes, and judo and boxing. And we've got football and rugby teams. And we have a disco every night if we want it, and our own coffee bar, and there's pool tables and that.'

'Are there many girls in your club?' David's newly-awakened interest in the opposite sex was lately beginning to dominate most of his waking and sleeping hours.

'Oh, yeah, we got dozens,' the tall youth answered, and sketched a silhouette in the air with his hands. 'And some of them are well fit, I'll tell you!'

David looked envious, and the youth laughed and winked at him. 'I'll introduce you to a couple of 'em when we get to the club. But I reckon they'll be a bit too old for you. The ones your age 'ull still be in school, so they won't be here until tonight.'

Robert, the more seriously minded of the twins, questioned gravely, 'Don't you go to school, then?'

Dean shook his head. 'No, I left last year. I'm on the YTS.' He saw the younger boys' puzzled expressions and explained. 'Youth Training Scheme. It's bloody crap, so I spend most o' me time here. But Mr Jones says that the movement's going to start its own YTS shortly, so I'll be joining that instead of the one I'm doing now.'

'Don't you get into trouble for bunking off?' Robert questioned.

'No. The bloke I'm on the YTS with belongs to the movement, so he don't mind me being here

290

instead. There's a lot of us who're on the social in the Ironsides. It gives us something to do.'

They entered the cavernous drill hall, and found it resounding with noise and bustle. Different activities were taking place on all sides, under the supervision of older men and women who were dressed like their guide in dark grey hooded tracksuits emblazoned with the gold motif of the Ironside trooper.

'I read in the papers that the Ironsides have fights with drug-dealers.' Robert was staring at a karate class going through their katas, and his eyes were shining with excitement. 'Is it true, Dean? Have you had fights with drug-dealers?'

The youth's white teeth gleamed in his dark face.

'Yeah, dozens o' times,' he boasted artlessly, 'And muggers and shoplifters as well. Our troops go on patrol round the shops on Meadowpark and with the observation patrols. And down on the Rec. as well. I've had dozens o' fights.'

'You must be very tough!' Robert exclaimed admiringly, accepting the youth's lying exaggeration at face value.

Dean flexed his arm and patted his bicep. 'We keep fit in the Ironsides. We have to, because we never know when we might be having bother. But we all stick together, so we always win.'

By now both younger boys were regarding him with a fast-growing hero-worship, and aware of their admiration he felt kindly disposed towards them. He jerked his head. 'Come on.'

He led them down a corridor and into a small room furnished simply with a table and some straight-backed wooden chairs. There were cupboards lining its walls and from one of these he pulled out some cans of pop and small packets of biscuits.

'Here.' He handed each boy a can and a packet of biscuits, then produced a pack of cigarettes and lit up. He offered the pack to the boys. 'Do you want one?'

There was awe in their eyes at his casual attitude towards something that was strictly forbidden in their school.

'No, thank you. We're not allowed to smoke,' David told him. Then he asked, 'Won't you get into trouble if you're caught smoking here?'

'Nah. Mr Jones don't mind us older kids smoking, just so long as we don't go robbin' for fags. He says that we're frontline soldiers, and a frontline soldier is entitled to something to steady his nerves.'

Both younger boys' eyes widened, and Robert told him, 'Our beaks at school go mad if they catch anybody smoking. Two boys were expelled for it last term.'

'Mr Jones 'ent like that,' Dean stated emphatically. 'He's great! He talks to us like men, because he says that we are men. He says that we're the soldiers of the Lord fighting the battle against evil, and that the Lord don't mind his soldiers having a bit of fun. Just so long as we don't harm anybody else.'

He tilted back on the chair's rear legs and took a long draw from his cigarette, then puffed out a string of smoke-rings, and the two young boys drank their cokes and munched their biscuits and stared at their dashing new hero with bedazzled eyes.


Back in Cromwell House, Lisa Keegan was radiant with happiness. Ivor Jones had taken her into Tabernacle Cottage for a long private talk, in the course of which he had told her that she had been perfectly right to take him to task about the tattooed boys. Then he had spent some time explaining his reasons for ordering the action, and she was gradually convinced that he had had no other option in this particular case.

Afterwards they had sunk to their knees and prayed together for a long while. She had never felt so exalted before in her entire life; it was one of the most moving experiences that she had ever known. Then, afterwards, he had entrusted her with a momentous task. She was to be the lead speaker at a rally of Cromwell Movement women and old people which was to be held on the Meadowpark Recreation Ground on Sunday evening during the coming weekend.

Greatly honoured, she left Tabernacle Cottage feeling that she was afloat on a sea of happiness; a happiness that was only enhanced by the affectionate greetings her boys gave her when they returned from the youth centre. As she drove them back to their school they babbled excitedly about the visit, and begged to be allowed to join the Ironsides.

'Yes, you can join,' she promised them, her heart full of gratitude that she had regained her sons. And she happily visualised them becoming ever closer as in concert they would all serve Ivor Jones through the coming years.

# Chapter Thirty-Four

Winston Otway grabbed the naked girl's long blonde hair with both hands and rammed his penis deep into her anus, ignoring her struggles and screams of pain. With brutal urgency he drove into her until, gasping and crying out himself, he achieved orgasm. Panting heavily, he withdrew from her body, and ordered harshly, 'Wash me.'

Her eyes streaming with tears, Jenny Chapman fetched a bowl of warm water, scented soap and soft towel from the bathroom, and carefully soaped, washed and dried the man's private parts.

He stared down at her bent head with cruel contempt, and when she had finished told her, 'Clean yourself up, bitch, and get dressed. Wait in the kitchen.'

Silently she nodded and hastened to obey.

The huge man yawned and stretched luxuriously, then dressed in silken underwear, a smart three-piece dark suit, white shirt and silken cravat. He pulled silk socks on to his feet and slipped on his expensive hand-made leather shoes. Then he stood staring at himself admiringly in the full-length mirror, while he adorned his wrists and fingers with heavy gold bracelets and diamond rings.

Next he went into the opulently furnished living

room, where he selected a long, fat cigar from an ebony and ivory box, poured a large malt whisky and settled himself comfortably in a luxuriantly upholstered leather armchair. He operated a remote control and a lilting reggae beat filled the room.

Otway savoured the fragrance of the cigar, and sipped the smooth, smoky-tasting whisky appreciatively. The music soared melodically and the glowing tip of the cigar moved gently in concert with the catchy rhythm.

For some time the huge man remained cocooned in a private world of sensory pleasures. Then the music died away, and he flicked the long ash of the cigar into the onyx bowl by his side, and drained the dregs from his glass.

He rose from his chair and Jenny Chapman, who had been sitting in the kitchen waiting for this moment, hurried out to him.

He jerked his head at her and she went into the bedroom to reappear almost immediately with his long fur coat and broad-brimmed hat.

He scowled at her puffy, tear-reddened eyes, and growled. 'Get yourself looking good for when I get back, girl.'

She nodded submissivly. 'I will, Winston.'

'You'd better.' With that parting threat he left the penthouse flat, and she sighed with heartfelt relief and burst into a fit of weeping.

Downstairs in the foyer of the luxury block his driver was waiting, together with the uniformed doorkeeper.

'Good evening, Mr Otway.' The doorkeeper greeted him with an obsequious smile. 'You'll be glad of your coat tonight, sir. The weather's turned really parky.'

Otway smiled and joked. 'What would I do without your weather forecasts, Mr Jenkins?' He slipped a banknote into the man's ready hand, and told him, 'You keep a close eye on my place now.'

'I will, Mr Otway, sir. You know you can depend on me to do that,' the doorman assured him fervently.

Otway swaggered out of the door that the man hastened to hold open for him. He got into the rear of his stretch limousine and told the driver, 'I'll have a look at Edgeton, then go on to the club.'

'All right, Big Man.' The young coloured man nodded, and the long car purred away from the block of flats.

Otway's mellow mood was soon overlaid by burning anger as the limousine slowly cruised through the streets of Edgeton. Instead of tawdry, painted women and girls walking their beats, and kerb-crawling punters, there were only banner-carrying groups of men and women muffled against the cold night air parading beneath the bare branches of the leafless trees, and on the corners policemen stared hard at the long limousine purring past them. Otway cursed sibilantly as he passed the black banners with their gold motif of a helmeted Ironside trooper, and consoled himself that very soon he would be wreaking a bloody revenge on the man who was ruining his business.

He had redeployed his team of girls around the city centre and in the semi-derelict industrial area which bounded the centre on its southern side, but lacking the discreet anonymity and easy access to the rooms of Edgeton, these areas were not half as profitable. Also, many punters had been frightened off by the Cromwell Movement's campaign and the immense amount of publicity it had generated. Otway's drug-dealing operations had also been hit by the Cromwell Movement, whose observation patrols now seemed to pervade the width and breadth of the city. Initially some of the patrols had received rough handling from angered drug-dealers, but recently they had been augmented by strapping teenage Ironsides led by older, tough-looking men ready to fight back, and some of the drug-dealers had been badly beaten.

Otway knew that the crisis point was rapidly approaching, when he must either reassert his domi-nance of the streets or lose all credibility. Already 'Yardie' gangs were eyeing his territory greedily, and old rivals were again readying themselves to challenge him.

The difficulty in dealing with the Cromwell Move-ment was the amount of public support it was attracting, and the apparent readiness of the police to side with it. Three of Otway's best men were even now remanded in custody awaiting trial for an affray with Cromwell Movement members.

All these facts passed constantly through the big man's mind as he was driven slowly through the Edgeton streets, and his mood became savage.

Winston Otway was a very shrewd and cunning man, highly intelligent and utterly ruthless. Recently he had made a close study of Ivor Jones. Darren Maclure had told him that his mother, Wisdom, was a ranking member of the Cromwell Movement, and that through her he, Darren, could find out a great deal about Jones. Otway had listened very carefully to all that Darren Maclure had been able to tell him, and had drawn one conclusion above all others. Which was that without Ivor Jones, there would be no Cromwell Movement. That if Jones was removed, then the movement would wither away as quickly as it had risen and flourished. Otway had obtained from Darren videotapes of Jones addressing a rally of his supporters in Cromwell House, and he spent many hours playing the tape over and over again. Too shrewd to underrate his enemies, nevertheless Otway's customary opinion of people was contemptuous. He had yet to meet the man who was his master mentally and physically. But as he studied Ivor Jones, he was forced into a grudging respect for the man. He found himself admiring the gift Jones possessed to cast a spell over his audiences, and to play upon and direct their emotional responses to his impassioned words. He also admired the way that Jones handled his new-found fame and prominence. The man had not made the mistake of changing his lifestyle to a more opulent mode of existence. Instead he had become even more austere and puritanical in diet and dress and way of life. But at the same time he had not pressed his members to follow his example, nor made any criticism of those members who lived well and lavishly. But despite this, Darren Maclure informed him, many members of the Cromwell Movement were beginning to follow their leader's example, and to ape his sparse and disciplined lifestyle.

'Jones is a smart man,' Otway conceded readily. 'But get rid of him, and the rest will fall.'

The problem was to actually get rid of Jones, however. He was closely guarded at all times, and his public appearances outside the defended confines of Cromwell House had lately become few and far between. Darren Maclure had told Otway that the Security Section had recently been increased in numbers, and the protective measures at Cromwell

House had been made more sophisticated and effective with surveillance cameras and sensor equipment. Darren also said that he thought the Security Section possessed fire-power, even though none of the men were ever seen to be in possession of weapons. What was certain was that the members of the Security Section were all fit and tough and highly trained in unarmed combat.

Winston Otway had pondered on what he had been told, and had concluded that to kill Ivor Jones he would need a top professional hit-man. There were plenty of half-crazed drug addicts who would be prepared to try to take out the leader of the Cromwell Movement in exchange for an assured free supply of 'smack' or 'crack', but Otway was not prepared to risk his own freedom by entrusting such a difficult task to a junkie. Junkies could not be trusted to keep their mouths shut, and could all too easily mess up the assignment. Some of his enforcers were also keen to personally dispose of Jones; Leroy Murchison in particular constantly begged to be allowed to try again. But Winston Otway knew that should a man of Murchison's type be caught, he would say anything at all the police wanted him to say in order to save his own skin.

In the comparatively short time that he had had Darren Maclure working for him, the young man had proved utterly reliable and completely ruthless in carrying out Otway's orders. So Otway had talked to him about possible ways of disposing of Ivor Jones.

The young man had proposed that the movement's leader be dealt with in a spectacular fashion by a bomb attack against Cromwell House, which would not only kill Jones but also the man's lieutenants. Such a devastating blow would serve as a warning to any others who might be considering a challenge to Otway's dominance. Maclure said that he had the necessary contacts to recruit an expert bomb-maker, and to carry out the actual attack.

Otway had considered the proposals briefly, and then enthusiastically concurred.

Now, tiring of riding through Edgeton, Winston Otway told the driver to take him to the club where Darren Maclure would be waiting for him.

The pounding beat enveloped him as he entered the dark interior, where dancers gyrated sinuously on the floor and the acrid herbal smell of 'ganja' was thick on the air.

Darren Maclure was sitting with Leroy Murchison and two young girls at a table, and both men rose to their feet when the big man loomed over them.

Fists touched, hands twisted, fingers entwined.

'Respect, Big Man.'

'Respect, Darren.'

'Respect, Big Man.'

'Respect, Leroy.'

The girls were dismissed, together with Leroy Murchison, and the young man went reluctantly, with an envious backwards look at Darren Maclure who was now the accepted aide and close confidant of the Big Man.

'What you got for me, Darren?' Otway's great head was almost touching the younger man's, and his red-rimmed eyes glittered greedily beneath the broad-brimmed hat.

'I've got a good one, Big Man. A Paddy. Done some jobs for the IRA. He's waiting for me now.'

Otway considered briefly, then nodded. 'Yeah, it's

best to use a honky for this. If we use a blood and something goes wrong, it could point a finger at us. When will the stuff be ready?'

Maclure shrugged. 'Any time now. But he wants something up front.'

Otway frowned. 'If he gets something up front, what's to say that he won't just disappear? If he's IRA he could fuck off back to Belfast or Dublin and we wouldn't be able to touch him, would we? I don't want to go to war with the fuckin' Paddies. They've got more fire-power than we have.'

Again Maclure shrugged. 'Well, he won't finish the job without something up front, Big Man. But if you're not happy with that, then I can keep looking around for somebody else.' He sighed regretfully. 'This guy's good, though. One of the best. We'll be lucky to find another one who can do the business like he can.'

'How much does he want up front?'

'Two and a half.' Darren Maclure grimaced light-heartedly. 'You've got to allow for inflation these days, Big Man.'

Winston Otway chuckled huskily. 'Try telling the fuckin' punters that, my man.' He nodded. 'Okay. Two and a half it is. But you stay closer to that honky bastard than a prick inside a cunt.'

'I will, Big Man.'

Otway rose to his feet, and Maclure asked, 'You're not going, are you?'

'Yeah, I got to meet somebody.'

'Shall I come with you?'

'No need, Darren. See you tomorrow.'

The huge figure swaggered away, and admiring eyes watched him go. Then the supplicants came clamouring to Darren Maclure.

'What d'you say, bro? Did the Big Man go for me joining?'

'Hey, Darren, respect! Did you ask the Big Man about what we was talking about?'

'Darren, what did the Big Man say? Is he going to give me the old price, or what?'

Maclure answered each supplicant with polite prevarications, but softened their disappointments by urging them to have a little patience, saying he was sure that he would be able to persuade the Big Man to change his mind eventually.

He accepted the wads of banknotes passed discreetly to him by the supplicants, and thought how ironic it was that he was making as much money in short weeks as a pimp and drug-dealer's enforcer, as he had made in long years serving his Queen and Country and putting his life on the line. He was also being treated with considerably more respect than when he had been in uniform. He was honest enough to admit to himself that, were it not for the fact that his beloved brother had been murdered by drug-dealers, he could be tempted to accept his present way of life. But his lust for revenge overlaid all else in the final analysis.

Leroy Murchison came back to him, bringing the two young girls.

'Hey, Darren, man, let's take these two bitches back to my place and have some fun.'

With assumed regret Maclure shook his head. 'I can't, Leroy. The Big Man wants a job doing.'

'Can I come?' the younger man demanded eagerly, and his face fell when Darren shook his head.

'Not this time, man. I'll catch you tomorrow.'

Maclure left the club and went to his newly acquired Ferrari sports car. Again the irony of his situation struck him forcefully as he remembered the battered second-hand saloon he had driven while in the Army.

He travelled to a large public house in the city centre, a place of passing strangers who came in for quick refreshment from the nearby coach, bus and train stations. The man he sought was sitting unobtrusively waiting for him in the packed saloon bar.

William Ignatius Conran was small and frail-bodied, the product of a mixed Protestant/Catholic Ulster marriage. His hair was a gingerish, unruly mop topping a thin, pustuled, pallid face. He constantly picked at half-healed sores on his chin, and his mannerisms betrayed extreme nervous tension. But for all his unprepossessing appearance, Conran possessed an unusual talent: he was an expert bomb-maker.

Darren Maclure had met Conran while serving in Northern Ireland. Conran had then been a part-time soldier with the Ulster Defence Regiment. The curious, uncertain friendship formed between them had been cemented when Darren Maclure helped Conran to escape the consequences of a bungled attempt at robbing some South Armagh paramilitaries of some extortion money, which they had obtained.

Now Conran made a precarious and uncertain living as a small-time criminal.

Maclure bought two pints of beer and carried them across to the table where the Irishman was sitting. As he placed the glasses on the stained wood, Conran questioned, 'Did your man go for it?'

Maclure nodded, and when he was seated said, 'You get two and a half up front.'

The little man crowed happily. 'Two and a half. By Jasus, that's not bad, is it! Twenty-five hundred quids. That'll do me for starters.' He sought confirmation. 'And I get the other half when the job's done, do I?'

Maclure nodded and grinned. 'Just make sure that you get well away from here to spend it, William.' He lifted his beer and took a long drink, then laying it down said, 'Right, I'm away. Stay close to your hotel until I get in touch with you.'

'I will, Darren,' The Irishman assured him, then asked tentatively, 'Would you be having a few quid you could lend me, to see me through till I get the smackers?'

Maclure chuckled wryly, and passed a thin sheaf of banknotes across to the other man. 'Here. I'll deduct this from your pay. But watch the drinking, William. I don't want anything to go wrong.'

'Jasus, you know you can trust me, Darren. I'll be there on the day of the race, don't you fret yourself about that.'

In his car again Darren Maclure drove around the city, turning and back-tracking until he was satisfied that he was not being tailed. Then he drove sedately to one of the richer suburbs where the phone kiosks had not all been vandalised, and called Tabernacle Cottage.

When Jones answered, Maclure told him, 'It's all set up, Mr Jones. Just let me know when you're ready to go ahead.'

'Well done,' Ivor Jones answered, and replaced the handset without another word.

## Chapter Thirty-Five

The small lamp-bulb flashed, and Darren Maclure applauded sincerely.

'Brilliant, William! Bloody brilliant!' But then he frowned slightly and asked doubtfully, 'But will it work at a distance? Will it operate through walls?'

'O'course it will, you thick idjit.' The little man brandished the small, flat, rectangular box underneath Maclure's nose. 'This is a transmitter, a radio transmitter. And radio waves pass through solids. It's not a bloody video programmer, it doesn't operate on infra-red rays. Just watch now, and I'll set it off from out in the bloody street.'

He busied himself momentarily with the arrangement of wires and transistors in the open shoebox, then left the room. A couple of minutes later the lamp-bulb in the shoebox flashed on once more, and Darren Maclure smiled with satisfaction.

When the other man returned he told him, 'You're a bloody genius, William. This thing's wicked!'

'Aghh, it's simple enough when you know how. But I get paid because most people don't know how.' William Ignatius Conran beamed happily, and raked with his dirty fingernails at the half-healed sores on his chin until he fetched trickles of blood from them.

'Right then, how soon can you let me have them?' Darren Maclure wanted to know.

Conran rubbed his fingers and thumb together. 'I need the readies. The stuff's waiting for me to pick up, but it's strictly cash on the nail with them boys.'

'Don't worry, you'll get enough to buy what you need,' the younger man assured him. 'But how soon will they be ready?'

'It's four you want, isn't it?' The little man rubbed his mop of ginger hair and screwed up his eyes in calculation. 'I can have them all ready for you by tomorrow. There'll be a separate control transmitter for each, preset on a different frequency. Just to make it simple, I'll number the transmitters and the boxes so you won't get them mixed up. All you'll have to do is to switch on the bomb before you plant it. Then when you're ready to rock and roll, you switch the wee transmitter on, press the second switch whenever you want, and bingo! You have lift-off.'

'Okay.' Maclure was satisfied. 'How much do you need to pay for the stuff?'

'A grand . . . It's the best quality hi-tech I'm using.'

Maclure handed over the cash, and then left the hotel room with a final warning.

'Don't try fucking me about now, William. Because if you do, I'll come after you no matter where you are.'

'Go fuck yourself, will ye!' the small man swore angrily. 'I'm a pro', aren't I? I don't fuck me customers about.'

'Right then, I'll see you here tomorrow afternoon.' Darren Maclure took his leave.

From the hotel he drove directly to the main

railway station, and left his car parked there. Then he walked to the big public house that the travellers favoured. In the saloon bar he found Jenny Chapman in company with another older prostitute, and one of Winston Otway's team of minders.

The young girl, dressed in a micro-skirt and a low-cut sweater which displayed the top halves of her firm rounded breasts, looked fearful and drawn-featured. This was to be her first turnout on the streets. Winston Otway was growing tired of her, and had decided that it was time she began to earn him some money. As always when turning out a new girl, he sent along an older, more experienced prostitute to act as her guide and mentor, and also a minder to ensure that the new girl did not try to run away.

The minder greeted Darren Maclure effusively, knowing that he was the close confidant of the Big Man.

'Respect, Darren. Anything you need, bro?'

'I want to try the new bitch before her cunt gets worn out,' Darren Maclure told him. 'I won't keep her long. Where's the room?'

'Up the back stairs, number eight.' The minder grinned enviously. 'I'd like a taste of it meself. But you know what the Big Man's like. You can't mix business with pleasure when you're on the job.'

The older girl smiled invitingly at the handsome newcomer. 'I'd give you a better time than her, sweet thing.'

Maclure scowled menacingly at her. 'I fancy fresh meat, not stale tripe.'

She tossed her head angrily, but knowing his reputation for ruthless violence did not dare answer back.

He took Jenny Chapman's slender arm and led her away. She came without resistance, but he could feel the tension in her body, and read the fear in her eyes, and he pitied her from the bottom of his heart.

When they entered the stale-smelling room, furnished only with a battered double bed covered by a dirty, stained red blanket the young girl asked timidly, 'Shall I take me clothes off?'

He shook his head.

'Do you want me to suck you off, then?'

'No. I just want you to sit down and listen to me very carefully, Jenny.' He was feeling tense and nervous himself, because he was about to take a very grave risk. If he had judged wrongly, then he knew that all his nerve-straining pretence of the past months would be rendered a complete waste of time. And that he would put himself into real danger.

'Do you want to get out of this, Jenny? To get away from Big Winston?'

Her heavily-mascara'd eyes widened, and doubt and fear showed in her expression. 'Has Big Winston told you to ask me that?' she faltered.

'No,' he denied vehemently. 'He knows nothing about this. You have to trust me, Jenny. I'm a friend, believe me. I hate what these bastards are doing to you. You know what they did to your Mum, don't you.'

She shook her head. 'No. I haven't seen me Mam since I left home. They wun't let me even write to her.'

'She got beat up by Big Winston's boys. They fractured her skull and she's had to have an operation. She's never going to be really right again, Jenny, because of what they did to her.'

'It 'ent my fault,' the girl burst out guiltily. 'I

never told 'em to do anything to her. It wasn't me!'

'I know that, Jenny. And your Mum knows that as well. But she's worried to death about you, and she wants you to come back home to her and Tina.'

'Is Tina all right?' the girl asked anxiously.

'She's all right at the moment, but Leroy Murchison reckons to go after her. He's going to treat her the same way that he's treated you, Jenny.'

'He's a bastard!' she cried out, and tears shone in her eyes. 'I'll kill him if he touches our Tina. She's only a babby.'

'How about what Big Winston will do to your Tina when he gets hold of her, Jenny? Have you thought about that?' Darren Maclure forced himself to be cruel. 'I know what the bastard's done to you. Just think about him doing the same to little Tina. And after he's finished with her, then he'll put her out to work on the streets, the same as he's done to you.'

'I wish he was dead!' She broke down, sobbing and moaning. 'I wish they was all dead . . . And I wish I was dead meself . . .'

Very gently he pulled her towards him and cradled her shaking body in his arms, whispering soothingly to her. 'There now, don't cry, Jenny. I'll help you. I'll save Tina from them; and I'll help you to get away as well. There now, don't cry, honey. Don't cry. I promise I'll help you and Tina and your Mum to be together again. Together and safe from these bastards.'

She lifted her woebegone face, the mascara running streakily down her tear-wet cheeks, and whimpered, 'What can you do to help us? They'm too tough. They'll kill you.'

'Don't you worry about that,' he told her firmly,

his manner radiating a confidence he was far from feeling. 'All you have to do is exactly what I tell you. And then by tomorrow night it'll all be over, and you'll be free, and Tina and your Mum will be safe. You want that, don't you? You want to get away from these bastards?'

'Oh, yeah.' She sobbed bitterly. 'Yeah, I do.'

'Right, then. You will get away from them, I promise. Just trust me, and you will. Now dry your eyes, and do your face up a bit. And don't so much as breathe a word about what I've said to you.'

Obediently she did as he instructed, and repaired her ravaged make-up. He looked at her tear-reddened, puffy eyes and told her, 'If they ask you why you've been crying, you tell them that I was real rough with you; that I hurt you, and that's why you've been crying. Understand?'

She nodded silently.

As they went from the room, he smiled and touched her cheek tenderly. 'I'll come back here tomorrow night and tell you what to do. Just be brave, Jenny. Trust me and you'll soon be back with your Mum and Tina.'

A dawning hope was in her eyes and she whispered, 'I do trust you, Darren.'

'OK. Now just do whatever they tell you to do tonight, and don't upset the bastards. Keep it in your mind that tomorrow night will be the last time you'll have to do anything for them.'

When he delivered the girl back to the couple in the saloon bar, the older prostitute stared hard at Jenny's reddened, puffy eyes and burst out angrily, 'What's you bin doing to her? Why did you have to treat her bad?'

'Rasss bludclahh! I just give the bitch a good

310

riding, that's all. She loved it.' He jeered, and winked at the minder. 'She got a nice tight little cunt, bro. Make sure you get into it yourself before the punters widen it out.'

Then he swaggered away.

Later that night, taking all precautions to make sure he was not being followed, Darren Maclure drove to one of the large multi-storey car parks in the city centre. There he met William Rimmer; they talked for some time and then went their separate ways.

Maclure checked that the prostitutes who comprised Big Winston's stable were working their new beats, then journeyed to the club near the city centre which was Winston's operational headquarters and the social gathering place of his gang members and hangers-on.

In the early hours of the morning Darren watched from a corner as an exhausted-looking Jenny Chapman was escorted in by her minders, and Big Winston totalled up the money she had earned from the punters that night. She had done well, and the big man smiled and tossed her a few pounds of her earning.

'Here, kid, buy yourself something nice.'

Even at a distance Darren could see the relief in her expression that for tonight, at least, it did not appear that she would be savagely beaten for displeasing her master . . .

In that instant all Darren Maclure's inate doubts as to the morality of what he was preparing to do to these people here abruptly disappeared, and he experienced a fierce impatience for the intervening hours to pass quickly so that he could act.

# Chapter Thirty-Six

It was early in the afternoon when Ivor Jones and William Rimmer met in Tabernacle Cottage to finalise the plans for the pre-emptive strike against Winston Otway. Jones listened intently as Rimmer reported on his previous night's meeting with Darren Maclure, occasionally asking a brief question.

'It's Conran who is supposed to plant the bombs inside Cromwell House?'

Rimmer nodded. 'He's going to apply for membership at the Sunday night service here. He'll look the place over then, and as and when he gets the opportunity he'll plant them.'

'How does Maclure intend to get his bomb inside Otway's club?'

'He's going to use the Chapman girl. She'll carry it in in her bag.'

'What about the transmitter?'

Rimmer looked a little irritated. 'I've told Maclure that it's too risky for him to keep it on him when he goes into the club, in case something goes wrong and the girl gets caught with the bomb on her. Otway will have everybody searched if the bomb's found. It would be best if I keep the transmitter with me in the car, but Maclure wants to do it his way. I think he's taking the job too personally myself, but he won't listen. Perhaps you could have a word with him about it?'

Jones pondered for a few moments, then reluctantly shook his head. 'No, it's the lad's prerogative to do the job how he sees best, Will. He knows what he's doing, so let him be.' Then he questioned. 'Who's going to pick up Conran?'

'Sinclair and Philpotts.'

Jones frowned thoughtfully. 'It might be tricky. They could be seen going into the hotel, or leaving.'

Rimmer shook his head dismissively. 'It'll be all right. There's a fire escape at the end of the landing on Conran's floor; they'll use that. It can only be opened from the inside, so Maclure is going to slip the catch on it when he leaves Conran.'

'How about the other residents on that floor? If Conran manages to kick up a racket, they could raise the alarm.'

Again Rimmer shook his head. 'It's a bloody dosshouse. There's ructions most nights. Nobody will take any notice of any disturbance.'

Jones appeared satisfied. 'Tell them to be sure that the room is left as if Conran's just done a runner to avoid paying his bill.'

Rimmer mock-glared. 'Ivor, there's no need to teach your granny how to suck eggs.'

Jones chuckled, and accepted the light-hearted rebuke without comment.


It was late afternoon when Darren Maclure went to see William Ignatius Conran at the sleazy back-street hotel. The Irishman was half-drunk, and Maclure scowled angrily at him.

'I told you to take it easy on the drink.' he accused.

Conran waved away the angry words. 'I've only had a few. There's no need for youse to shout your mouth off. They're all ready. Now where's the up-front money?'

'Later,' Maclure snapped. 'Where are they?'

Conran pulled open the bottom drawer of the rickety dressing table and pulled out four shoeboxes and four small, flat, rectangular transmitters, and laid them in two neat parallel rows upon the bed.

'There now, aren't they beautiful,' he declared, and his drink-reddened eyes moistened as he stared down at the lethal artifacts with the fond gaze of a loving father. 'These are my babbies, these are. Little beauties aren't they! See here now. Just take a look at them.'

He opened the shoeboxes to display the ingenious circuitry, and batteries cocooned within the murderous explosives and six-inch nails.

Darren Maclure nodded. 'They look as if they'll do the business.'

'Do the business!' Conran exclaimed. 'They'll do the business all right, my boy. One o' these babbies 'ull blow anybody within a hundred yards to fuckin' hell and back.'

'Show me how they work?' Maclure demanded, and the Irishman grinned slyly.

'Why do you want to see that? Are youse thinking o' taking the rest of the job offa me?'

'No chance!' Maclure denied emphatically. 'But my boss wants to see one of these for himself, before he comes across with the up-front money. And I need to be able to show him how they work, don't I?'

The Irishman thought this over, and then accepted. 'That's fair enough. But take care, now, that you don't blow yourself and him fuckin' sky-high!'

314

He demonstrated the switches which would activate the bomb and the transmitter, and the second transmitter switch which would detonate the bomb. 'Simple, aren't it? A fuckin' monkey could work it. And it's safe too. There's no way you could set it off by accident. I'm a fuckin' expert, I am. There's no home goals ever bin scored wi' my babbies.'

'Which one can I take to show him?' Maclure wanted to know, and Conran selected a transmitter and bomb.

'Now listen, William, when I come back with the money I want to find you sober. And I want you to stay sober until you've finished the job. It'll be no use you going to join the Cromwell Movement next Sunday if you're half-pissed, or if they can smell the drink on you. They're not the bloody Sally Army; they don't take in drunks to redeem them.'

'Aggghh, Jasus, give it a rest, will ye! I'll stay off the drink from now on!' Conran reacted irritably.

'Just make sure that you do,' Maclure warned. 'I'll see you later.'

'What time?'

'Probably around midnight.'

Maclure left the little Irishman sitting on the end of the bed staring lovingly at the three remaining bombs and transmitters.

As soon as he was alone, however, Conran raised two fingers in lewd salute to the closed door.

'Fuck youse, you black bastard! I'll take a drink whenever I feel like it.'

Then he rummaged under the mattress of the bed and pulled out a full bottle of whisky.

* * *

315

It was early evening and Darren Maclure was waiting in the saloon bar. Jenny Chapman came in with the older girl and the minder, who grinned when he saw Maclure and joked, 'Hey, man, if you're going to be a regular customer she'll have to start charging you.'

'No, she won't.' Maclure laughed easily. 'The Big Man's give me a free season ticket for this bitch.'

The older girl scowled angrily at him as he led Jenny away, and she muttered to the minder, 'He's a fuckin' mad dog, him. He give the poor little cow a real hard time last night.'

The minder grinned broadly and shrugged. 'O' course he's a fuckin' mad dog! That's why the Big Man thinks so much of him. Just don't let him hear you say it, though, because I 'ent going to try and stop him from kickin' the shit out of you.'

Up in the sleazy room, Maclure was cradling the weeping Jenny Chapman in his arms, fury burning in his dark eyes as he listened to her faltering account of what had happened when the club closed and Winston Otway had taken her back to his flat.

'He brought bloody Leroy back, and two or three of the others, and they was all pilled up to the fuckin' eyeballs. And then Big Winston made me strip, and they all kept having me, one after the other. And then they did some terrible things to me, Darren. Terrible. They just kept on and on, and they really hurt me. It feels like I'm torn to pieces inside. They was shoving all sorts o' different things up me, the bastards was!' Her sobs repeatedly choked her words, and her slender body trembled violently. 'I can't stand it no more, Darren. I'll bloody well kill meself! I can't stand no more.'

'You won't have to stand it any more, honey.' He stroked her hair and shoulders. 'After tonight you'll be free of them. Just trust me.'

When she had calmed sufficiently, he told her, 'Now listen very careful, Jenny. You've got to do exactly what I tell you. *Exactly.*'

'I will.' She nodded, staring at him trustingly, her face reminding him of that of a young child.

'Here.' He took the bomb from under the bed where he had hidden it earlier and pushed it to the bottom of the big capacious shoulder-bag she had with her. All Otway's girls carried this type of bag to keep their condoms and personal effects in, and usually a knife as well for their own defence should a punter turn violent.

'Now remember. When they take you back to the club, you'll go to Big Winston's table, like all the girls do, and he'll take the money from Tommy, like he did last night, and count it out. While he's doing that you just act casual, put your bag down by the side of his table, and ask him if you can go and take a leak. When you come out of the piss-corner, I'll be waiting for you. We'll just walk nice and easy out of the club.'

There was fearful doubt in her eyes.

'Big Winston won't let me go out like that.'

'Oh yes, he will. Because while you're in the piss-corner I'm going to ask him if I can knock a quick round off with you, take you to my place for an hour. He'll say it's okay; he always does whenever I want to take one of the girls to my place.' He paused, and smiled confidently. 'Trust me, Jenny. It'll be just like I say. And then, once we're away from the club, you'll never see any of the bastards again. You'll be free, and you'll be safe.'

'Oh, thanks, Darren. Thanks!' She wept in gratitude, and threw her arms around him to hug him fiercely.

Later, when they returned to the saloon bar, the older girl saw immediately that Jenny had been crying. And despite her fear of Maclure, she hissed 'You fuckin' bastard! What you bin doing to this poor little cow? It's right what they calls you. You're a fuckin' mad dog!'

The minder rolled his eyes, and stared aghast at the furious woman. 'Are you fuckin' crazy?' he breathed. 'Are you fuckin' mental?'

Darren Maclure only laughed contemptuously, and winked at the minder. 'It's all right, Tommy. I'm in a gentle mood, man. She's got real lucky tonight, this mouthy slag has.'

Then he swaggered cockily away.

William Conran was lying sprawled across the bed, snoring loudly, the whisky bottle lying empty beside him. The two big men, neatly dressed in dark suits and overcoats, exchanged grins of contempt. Then one of them carefully gathered together the three bombs and transmitters, and stowed them away in a large shopping-bag. The other man turned the senseless Irishman on to his face, knelt to straddle the narrow shoulders, gripped the sweat-soaked head between huge leather-gloved hands, and with a swift heave and twist snapped the thin neck. As vertebrae cracked audibly the Irishman's body jerked once, then sagged into limp stillness. The two men carefully searched the room, packing the dead man's few clothes and possessions into his cheap holdall. Then the killer slung the body over his massive shoulder with an ease that demonstrated tremendous physical strength while the other man checked that the landing was empty.

318

He nodded and the two of them moved swiftly and silently to the fire-escape door, passing through it and leaving it securely closed behind them. As they stepped down the fire escape a dark van purred to a halt beneath them, and its rear doors opened. They got into the shadowed interior, the doors closed, and the van slid away into the night.

The club shook to the frenetic beat of the ear-deafening music. Sweaty bodies heaved and gyrated on the floor, voices shouted in an effort to be heard and wild laughter came from gaping mouths. The acrid fumes of 'ganja' mingled with the smells of human sweat and cheap perfumes.

Darren Maclure sat at Winston Otway's side, sipping his iced white rum and watching the succession of men and women who came to pay court to the Big Man. Because the room was so hot he had taken off his stylish raincoat and hung it near the entrance; the transmitter was in its inside pocket. Then his heart beat faster, and his mouth dried nervously as he saw Jenny Chapman being pushed through the heaving crowd by the man and woman.

'Respec', Big Man. Respec', Darren.' The minder's big white teeth gleamed as the flickering strobe light flashed erratically across his dark face, and he handed a sheaf of banknotes to Otway.

Darren stared hard at Jenny, who appeared dazed with exhaustion, her eyes looking like black holes in the pallid mask of her face. Her hair and skin were soaked with the rain that was falling outside. Then she leaned down to shout into Winston Otway's ear.

'Can I go and have a pee?'

He nodded carelessly, and she slipped the large bag from her shoulder and laid it by the side of the small table.

Outside in the darkness, William Rimmer sat in his parked car some thirty yards from the club entrance, partially shielded by the row of cars parked in front of him. The falling rain forced him to keep his windscreen wipers switched on so that he could see the entrance clearly.

He watched Jenny Chapman and her escorts enter the club, then started his engine. The plan was for him to wait until he saw Darren Maclure and the girl come out again. He would then pick them up and, as they drove away, Maclure would trigger the bomb.

Leroy Murchison stood in the club entrance and cursed the rain. For a moment he was tempted to abandon the errand which would take him out into the cold, wet darkness, but then he saw Maclure's stylish raincoat hanging from its hook. He grinned, and reached out for it. He knew that Darren hated anyone else to wear his clothes, and this knowledge added spiteful savour. Leroy felt the soft silk lining envelop him, and his grin widened.

'You bludclahh, Darren, you fuckin' know how to dress,' he thought admiringly. 'This is cool gear.'

He felt the hard outline of the transmitter in the inside pocket, and took out the rectangular plastic box, frowning curiously at it.

'What's this, then? A fuckin' new sort of phone?'

'Leroy?'

He heard his name being shouted, and looked up to see Darren Maclure's angry scowl bearing quickly down on him.

Murchison laughed. 'Be cool, Darren, man. I

won't hurt your coat. What's this?' He held out the transmitter and triggered the switches . . .

The club's windows and door blew outwards in a flaring, roaring explosion and Rimmer's car was jolted fiercely by blast. For a moment he was transfixed by shock and horror; then he recovered and, gunning the engine, sped away. He was more than a mile distant when the first police cars and fire engines went racing with howling sirens towards the flaming, shattered club.


Ivor Jones was waiting for him back at Cromwell House. When he saw Rimmer's grim features, his face mirrored his own instant concern.

'Where's Darren and the girl?'

Rimmer shook his head. 'They've got to be dead. There was a premature blast; the fuckin' bomb must have been faulty.'

Jones flinched, and for a moment sharp visual images of Darren Maclure's handsome face filled his mind. Then an inner voice urged, 'Keep a grip on yourself, Ivor. You're fighting a war here. You can't allow yourself the luxury of feeling just yet.'

He drew a long rasping breath, and forced his brain to work.

'How about Sinclair and Philpotts?' Rimmer was asking.

'It went okay,' Jones informed him. 'They should be well on their way to Wales by now.'

William Ignatius Conran's corpse was to be buried in one of the vast plantations of the Forestry Commission deep in the Welsh hills.

To one side of the vestry there was a powerful radio receiver tuned to the police network, and a stream of crackling messages concerning the bombing was now coming from it.

Both men listened for a few minutes, eager to learn if there had been any survivors of the blast. From the content of the police messages it appeared that most of the people inside the club had been killed outright. There were very few survivors reported, and all of these were critically injured.

When he had heard enough Jones switched the receiver off, telling his companion, 'We'll get the full sitrep from Matthews soon enough.'

'What's next, Ivor?' Rimmer was keen for more action.

Jones nodded appreciatively. His old friend was a consummate soldier. In war the loss of your own men had to be accepted; the battle must continue to be fought, and the grieving put aside until the action had ceased.

'We clean up what's left of Otway's organisation. I'm going to have Lisa Keegan lead a march around the town centre after the rally on Sunday. Same routine as before: drive the whores from their beats. But this time I want some Ironsides to go with the women and old people. Any pimps or whores who try to kick up rough can be dealt with on the spot . . . Given a good kicking. Also, on Friday and Saturday nights I want to deploy the toughest and fittest Ironsides outside the city centre pubs and clubs, in squads commanded by Security Section men. Their orders are to keep a low profile and watch to see if any police officers get into difficulty when the usual brawls start at chucking-out times. If any of the police do get into difficulties, then the Ironsides are to go to their aid immediately. They'll be wearing uniform of course, and I'll have a word with Chris Thompson to see if we can get a few people with video cameras with the squads, so as to get maximum publicity if there is any trouble.'

'Do you want me to go along as well?' Rimmer asked.

'No. I want you to activate one of our "sleepers".'

While recruiting the Security Section from among the ranks of embittered ex-servicemen, Jones and Rimmer had also contacted several old comrades whom they knew and trusted. Unknown to the others, each man had been individually approached by Jones and Rimmer and given a proposition – that they would be paid an on-going cash retainer to be ready when needed to perform certain covert tasks. They would have no open connection with the Cromwell Movement, but would continue with their normal day-to-day lives. In effect they would be terrorist-style 'sleepers', only activated at intervals for a specific operation.

Now from an inside pocket of his dark jacket Ivor Jones produced a thick envelope. 'There're the details of known sex offenders and child molesters. I want their homes fire-bombed. Use one of the "sleepers" to do the work.' Jones steepled his fingers and rested his chin on their tips, then spoke musingly as if voicing inner thoughts aloud. 'I want to test the water. I want to see how the public react to the fire-bombings, and I also want to force the police to investigate the Cromwell Movement. Although there's nothing to connect us with tonight's action, it's obvious that we shall be prime suspects if there's a sustained campaign of fire-bombing. So they'll have to investigate us, won't they? I shall co-operate fully with them, of course; they will be given access to everything that concerns the movement. I want the

323

public to see that we are innocent and pure in heart. I also want to cause the Chief Constable the maximum embarrassment. He'll look very churlish, won't he? Empowering an investigation into a movement that deploys its finest young men and women to help his force!'

The other man looked doubtful. 'Wouldn't it be better if we waited for the fuss about tonight's bomb to die down a bit, before we start fire-bombing?'

Jones shook his head and declared emphatically, 'No, it wouldn't be better. Time's not on our side. We have to increase our momentum, keep our enemies off balance and confused. I know that I'm taking risks with this, William, but we're playing for very high stakes, and to win I have to take high risks.'

'Yes, but . . .' Rimmer's words were cut short.

'No! Don't argue with me, William.' Jones appeared to be growing angry. 'Just do as I say. I know what I'm doing.'

After a brief moment of hesitation, Rimmer nodded submissively. 'Very good, Ivor.'

'As soon as you've activated the "sleeper" I want you to go up to Newcastle, get together with the Cromwell cadre there and start looking about for suitable premises for a Cromwell House. Make sure that while the fire-bombing is taking place, you're very definitely and publicly in Newcastle. At the same time, I'm going to be travelling around the other cadres. I'm almost ready to begin the activation of some of them, so I want to have a close look at them all, to help me decide where we open up next.' He made a gesture of dismissal. 'Right, then, William, you've done well tonight. Why don't you go to the social club and have a drink?'

'Thank you, Ivor.' The man turned away, then

halted and swung back again, to ask with a troubled expression on his face, 'What about Wisdom Maclure?'

'What about her?' Jones frowned slightly.

'Well . . .' Rimmer grimaced uneasily. 'Supposing the police identify Darren Maclure. They'll be round to see her, won't they? She's a nice woman, and I wouldn't like to think of her getting such a shock. She needs to have the news broken to her gently. And there's the Chapman woman as well. There might be enough left of her girl to be identified; the shock could finish her off, couldn't it?'

For a brief instant Jones' fiery eyes clouded, as remorse overwhelmed him. Then he distinctly heard God's voice in his ear, speaking to him sternly.

'It had to be done, Ivor. There was no other choice possible but to strike first at Otway. Darren Maclure and Jenny Chapman are casualties of war. They're not the first young lives you've seen taken in battle, and they won't be the last.'

Jones nodded, and muttered aloud, 'Yes, they are casualties of war.' Then he became aware that the other man was peering curiously at him, and he flustered, 'No need to stare at me like that, man. I was only thinking aloud.'

In that brief instant he recovered his poise, but his expression was still filled with sadness.

'You're right, of course, William, and your concern for poor Wisdom and the Chapman woman does you great credit. I'll go and see both of them straight away. It's very hard to have had to send those two poor young people to their deaths, but this is war, and at times we have to sacrifice our own soldiers to gain the victory. But when we've won, then we'll make sure that both of them are remembered and honoured for the part they've played in our victory. They'll be acknowledged as heroes of the Cromwell Movement, both of them . . .'


It was past midnight when Ivor Jones knocked on the door of Wisdom Maclure's flat on the Meadowpark Estate. When the light came on and he heard the shuffling of her slippered feet, he called softly to reassure her.

'It's Ivor Jones, Wisdom. Can you open the door, please?'

She was wearing a woollen dressing-gown, and her hair was tied in old-fashioned wire-and-paper curlers. Her eyes saw his sad face, and an awful knowledge invaded their darkly shimmering depths.

'It's my Darren, isn't it, Mr Jones? Something bad's happened to my Darren.'

He nodded slowly, and told her gently, 'I'm sorry, Wisdom. I'm so very, very sorry.'

Her pleasant features crumpled into a tragic mask and she shuddered violently and swayed. He moved to take her in his arms and led her to the small sofa where he sat down beside her, still holding her firmly.

'Wisdom, my dear, I've received some information from a friend of mine who is in the Police Force. He said that there has been an explosion at a club near to the city centre. A great many people have been killed, and he fears that Darren is among them.'

'Oh, God! God! Why did you take my Darren from me, God? Why? Why?' The woman keened and began to rock herself backwards and forwards in her terrible anguish, all the time repeating, 'Why did you take my lovely son, God? Why? Why did you take him from me? Why? Why? Why?'

Faced by this good woman's heartbreak, Ivor Jones felt himself once again assailed by bitter remorse. But then God's voice spoke to him, remonstrating with him, castigating him for his weakness, reminding him that they were engaged in a savage and pitiless war in which these sacrifices must be made, maybe time and time again. God was merciless in his chastisement of Jones' weakness, until Jones hardened himself once more and was able to accept that as the General of the Lord, he must be like a man of steel and show no weakness himself nor accept any weakness in those he commanded.

But for all that steely reinforcement of his resolution, Ivor Jones still could not bring himself to leave Wisdom Maclure alone with her tragedy; and so he continued to sit with her throughout the long weary hours of that night, murmuring words of comfort to her, until with the first paling of the dawn she fell asleep in his arms. Even then he sat on, reluctant to disturb her restless slumber, and his fiery blue eyes were gentle as he gazed down at her grief-ravaged face.

'Darren and Jenny Chapman died for the Lord, Wisdom,' he explained to the sleeping woman in his mind. 'They both died so that the Cromwell Movement can march on to victory. I promise you that their deaths will not be in vain . . .'

# Chapter Thirty-Seven

The blast that killed Winston Otway, Darren Maclure, Jenny Chapman, Leroy Murchison and thirty-eight other people, and left another nine badly injured, reverberated through many other people's lives. For more than a week it remained headline news, and television teams and newspaper reporters swarmed to the city.

Because the vast majority of the killed and injured were of Afro-Caribbean origin, it was widely surmised that white racist extremists were responsible, and Archie Campbell, the firebrand Member of Parliament for Brixton, called upon the government to provide armed protection for the coloured ethnic communities. Isaac Paulson, the Member for Cheltenham West, pointed out that the bombing could have been the work of 'Yardie' gangsters, and was immediately attacked by the race relations industry for his anti-coloured bias.

Then the police issued a statement that, according to their Bomb Squad officers, the device used in the club was thought to be a a very sophisticated type utilised extensively by the IRA. This put the race relations industry into something of a quandary, because they were uncertain whether or not that statement might be construed as implying that the intellectual and technical capacity of West Indian 'Yardie' gangsters were not of sufficient quality to enable them to manufacture such a bomb. While they were still internally debating this issue, the Cromwell Movement's Women and Old People's Rally, followed by a march around the city centre, took place on Sunday evening. There were several violent confrontations between pimps, prostitutes and aggressive young Ironsides, resulting in stabbings and other injuries to both sides. The police made arrests, and then found to their embarrassment that some of the Ironsides whom they were charging with assaults on pimps and prostitutes were the very ones who had helped their officers during the customary savage brawls outside the clubs and pubs on the previous Friday and Saturday nights.

Then the fire-bombings against the homes of known sex offenders began. In three successive nights, thirteen houses and flats were set alight.

The news media were quick to tie in together these fire-bombings and the bombing of Otway's club as the work of a group of vigilantes. One banner headline in a popular daily tabloid summed up the general conclusion when it screamed:


## 'VIGILANTES MAKE CITY
## A HELL FOR SINNERS!'


Charles Blair, CBE, Chief Constable of the City Force, summoned an emergency meeting of his senior officers. He entered the room where the men stood waiting for him, ranged down both sides of the long table, and taking up his position at the head of the table he stood scowling into each man's eyes in turn.

He lifted the front page of the tabloid newspaper with its glaring banner headline, and shook it out before him so that they could all see it clearly. Then he laid it down on the table, and demanded acidly, 'Now, gentlemen, just what is going on in this city? Sir Cyril Wilkinson has been on the phone to me every day for the last week, and he is not happy. He is not happy at all!'

Sir Cyril Wilkinson was the Permanent Under-Secretary in the Police Division of the Home Office, a man whose influence could make or break the careers of top-ranking policemen throughout the country.

Blair smashed the flat of his hand down on to the sheet of newspaper. 'And I'm not happy either, gentlemen. Thanks to garbage like this report, this city is now regarded as being in the grip of virtual anarchy. And we, as a police force are regarded as incompetent fools who have lost control.'

There were ejaculations of protest from among his audience, but Blair ignored them, and went on heatedly.

'We have had more than sixty people killed and injured by bombs, arson attacks and affrays during this last week, and you lot are running around like headless chickens. And the responsibility for your incompetence is being laid at my door.'

A couple of the men standing at the table could not help but smile inwardly with malicious pleasure. The Chief Constable was referring to a cartoon which had appeared that morning in one of the tabloids depicting him dressed like the Emperor Nero, fiddling furiously, while all around him the city was burning.

Blair stared hard at the faces before him, as if daring any of them to show the slightest trace of any other emotion but concern and anxiety. Apparently satisfied with what he saw, he nodded slowly and, in a more even tone, requested, 'Would you all sit down, please, gentlemen.'

There was a brief scraping of chairs and settling of bodies, and then he continued.

'Before we start I'm going to warn you all. In fact not warn, but guarantee, that unless you obtain satisfactory results in the very near future, then heads will most certainly roll. And no one will be immune from the axe.'

With that dire prediction, he himself sat down and the meeting began.

As was customary he listened to reports on the situation from each man in turn, beginning with the most senior and ending with the most junior ranked. Then he began to call on individuals.

Detective Chief Inspector Henry Thomas was questioned about his department's lack of progress in the investigation of the bombing at Otway's club, and the series of fire-bombings.

Chief Superintendent Richard Barker was called upon to account for the uniformed branch's failure to prevent the affrays that had taken place during the Cromwell Movement's march around the city centre on the Sunday evening.

Both men were career policemen who wished to reach the very top of their chosen profession. Therefore both were unwilling to take the blame for what had happened, and so blamed their immediate underlings for the failure to obtain satisfactory results.

Those underlings sat smarting at the injustice of

this blatant buck-passing, but when in their turn they were called upon by the Chief Constable to account for their failings, they each in turn laid the blame on *their* own immediate underlings.

Blair sat frowning while each man said his piece, and then when he had heard them all he stated, 'The Cromwell Movement, gentlemen. I want to know all about the movement, and this man Ivor Jones.'

Again, in order of precedence he called on the commanders of the various departments to relate what they knew about the movement and its leader. Taking their lead from the first speaker, Chief Superintendent Richard Barker, the other senior ranks – while admitting that there was no solid evidence to prove that the movement was responsible for the bombing and arson attacks – still stated their conviction that the Cromwell Movement was the instigator if not the actual perpetrator of those incidents.

When the last man had finished speaking the Chief Constable addressed the meeting.

'Very well, gentlemen. I accept what you have told me at face value. I want a thorough investigation begun immediately into the affairs of the Cromwell Movement. I want you to shake the Cromwell tree and see what falls from it. I want the movement gone over branch by branch and dissected until every single segment of every leaf of it is laid open to us.'

There were enthusiastic nods and murmurs of agreement, and it was at that point when, at the very end of the table furthest from the Chief Constable's chair, a solitary arm was raised.

Blair frowned, and barked sharply, 'Do you want to say something, Inspector Miller?'

Inspector Alexander Miller rose to his feet. 'Yes, sir, I do.'

His lean, youthful features wore an expression of contempt as he briefly glanced at his superiors sitting between him and the Chief Constable.

Blair nodded permission for him to speak.

'Before we begin to investigate the Cromwell Movement, which will undoubtedly give rise to a great deal of media publicity and speculation as to their involvement and guilt in these recent sad events, I think that we should give careful consideration to all the possible implications of such an investigation, sir.'

Blair regarded the tall young man speculatively.

'Speak plainly, Inspector,' he instructed quietly. 'I want you to be perfectly frank with me. There will be no repercussions for anything that you might say here.'

'Very good, sir.' Miller radiated confidence. He was well-spoken, and well-groomed, physically fit and hard. His uniform was immaculate, his posture that of a guardsman. He could have served as a publicity model for the ideal police officer. 'With all respect, sir, I would ask you to consider the overall crime figures in this city for the period since the Cromwell Movement has become active in its crusade for law and order, in comparison with the figures for the period immediately preceding the movement's rise to prominence.' He paused to lift a briefcase from the floor on to the table, and then went on, 'I have the computer readouts with me, sir . . .' He again paused briefly, and then added diffidently, 'I've also obtained a report on what occurred during a recent meeting of certain influential members of the Police Authority, sir. That meeting was held secretly, and certain statements were made during it that I'm sure will be of great interest to yourself.'

333

He waited respectfully for an answer. For a brief instant uncertainty showed in the Chief Constable's eyes. Alexander Miller was accepted as a high-flyer in the City Force, and was personally known to Blair. Although the young inspector was still very junior in rank, he was already being accepted as a certainty to achieve very high rank – possibly the very highest attainable. Miller's family was both wealthy and influential, and not merely on a regional basis, and this fact alone made it politic to give him a full hearing, and to allow due weight to what he had to say.

Charles Blair hesitated only momentarily as all these considerations flashed through his thoughts. Then he graciously gave permission for the young inspector to speak.

Miller smiled gratefully, that smile concealing the savage contempt he had for the man who was holding the rank he so hungrily coveted for himself.

'Thank you, sir.' He extracted some papers from the briefcase and laid them down on the table in front of him. 'Sir, gentlemen, the computer readout shows a quite remarkable diminution in reported offences of all types in the city during the period since the Cromwell Movement has conducted what it terms its "Crusade against Crime". Our force's arrest and summary conviction rate has almost doubled during that same period, directly as a result of the information we have been receiving from the members of the movement. Also, particularly during the last weekend, movement members have gone to the assistance of police officers who were being assaulted, and have actively aided our officers in making arrests of violent offenders. These incidents

334

received extensive media coverage, and evoked a great deal of favourable comment.'

He lifted up a section of the papers in his hand and held them out before him. 'These are copies of the report concerning the secret meeting of the Police Authority members. I would prefer at this time not to tell you how I came into possession of this information. But when you have had the opportunity to read the contents I think you will agree with me when I say that in my opinion it would be impolitic on our part to carry out any high-profile investigation of the Cromwell Movement at this moment in time.' He tapped the sheaf of papers with his free hand. 'The people present at this secret meeting were unanimous in their praise of the Cromwell Movement. They were also unanimous in their praise of the way the police had protected the movement, and co-operated with the movement's observation patrols. They agreed that if we, the police, should continue to allow the Cromwell Movement to aid us in our efforts to maintain the law, then they would use their utmost endeavours to increase our budget, and to allow us all that we so desperately need in the way of new equipment and increased recruitment.'

Miller's gaze swept along the double row of intent faces, and came to rest on the face of Charles Blair.

'With all respect, sir, I would request you to carefully consider the evidence presented within these papers, before ordering any intensive investigation into the Cromwell Movement. It is my opinion, sir, that at present the movement is proving to be a most valuable asset to our force. We should be looking at ways in which we can utilise them more fully to aid us in our task, not alienating them by investigating their affairs. Any present criticisms levelled at this force by the media, or by the Home Office, can be very easily countered by releasing the computer figures I have here for public scrutiny. Because on these figures we are by far the most successful police force in the country at this time.'

Charles Blair pondered briefly, and then asked, 'How many copies of these figures do you have, Inspector Miller?'

Miller's eyes gleamed triumphantly. 'Enough, sir.'

'Pass them around the table, then, and let us all have a look at them,' Blair ordered, and the young inspector was quick to comply.

The computer readout made impressive reading, and spirits visibly rose around the table.

Charles Blair was conscious of this fact, and the figures also impressed him much more than he cared to admit. But he was reluctant to be seen to do a U-turn; so he compromised, by ordering Detective Chief Inspector Henry Thomas to detail his most experienced and competent man to initiate discreet enquiries into the affairs of the Cromwell Movement.

'I've the very man for it, sir,' Henry Thomas assured him. 'Detective Sergeant Matthews. He already has a dossier on the movement.'

'Very well, put him on it. But emphasise to him the necessity for discretion,' the Chief Constable instructed. Then, after closing the meeting, he asked Inspector Miller to stay behind.

When the two men were alone, Blair told the younger man, 'I want you to set up a meeting between myself and Ivor Jones, Inspector. But that meeting must be held in complete secrecy, and for the present only you and Jones are to be party to it. It must remain strictly confidential.'

336

Miller nodded. 'It will, sir. You can trust me.'

Charles Blair clapped the other man on the shoulder. 'I've been watching your progress in the force with great interest, Alexander. And with pleasure also, I might add. I feel that there is a great need for young and eager officers of your calibre to be given accelerated promotion. The senior ranks of this force are presently filled by old and tired men, who are too reluctant to adopt new ideas and methods. I intend to reform this force, and I need men like yourself to assist me in that task.'

'Thank you for your confidence in me, sir.' Miller appeared gratified. 'I hope that I shall never give you cause to doubt either my professional competence or my personal loyalty to you, sir.'

They exchanged a long look, each seeking – and finding – what he hoped for in the other's expression.

Blair smiled with satisfaction. 'I feel that we understand each other very well, Alexander.'

'Yes, sir. I'm sure that you're right.'

When they separated, each man felt content that an unspoken bargain had been sealed between them.

# Chapter Thirty-Eight

George Faraday was presiding over the meeting of the Planning and Resources Committee, composed of the senior members of his majority party on the City Council. This body was the overall management committee of the city. To deal with the problem of the Meadowpark Estate, Faraday had persuaded his members to set up a specialist sub-committee with himself as its chairman, and it was today that the report of that sub-committee was to be received by the Planning and Resources Committee.

Faraday's secret co-operation with Ivor Jones had been remarkably successful during its relatively short span of time. Crime and vandalism had diminished dramatically on the estate, and already eighteen shops had been reopened and rented by both new and old tenants. Many of the most notorious trouble-makers had been frightened into leaving by the actions of the so-called vigilantes, and although there were still numerous problem families remaining, their worst excesses of behaviour seemed to have been cowed, and few complaints concerning them were being received. The drug-dealers and gangs of hooligans, the perverts and vagrants no longer infested the Recreation Ground, and young children and their mothers were once more to be

338

seen playing on the refurbished swings and round-abouts there.

The report was received with plaudits and con-gratulations from the members of the main committee, and Faraday preened himself before their vociferous praises.

'Of course, gentlemen, this will also be of tremen-dous help to the Council financially. Meadowpark Estate was draining us bloody dry. If this keeps up, we'll be well into the black by this time next year.'

'Then it'll be a benefit to those buggers from Sandton Road, won't it, Mr Chairman?' Andrew Popplewell, a rotund, red-faced man, pointed out sourly. The 'buggers from Sandton Road' he referred to were the present majority party's political rivals.

Faraday smiled benevolently at his old friend, Popplewell, whom he had previously primed to make this point. Then he sighed heavily, and nodded.

'Yes, you might well be right there, Councillor Popplewell. The elections are less than two months away, as you all well know. And after the Budget which that bloody clown down in London brought out, we'll be lucky to hold on to a single ward in this city. We're all being tarred with the same brush, and we local politicians are being blamed for what those bloody incompetent fools in the parliamentary party are doing.'

There were frowning nods of agreement from all around the table.

Faraday stared keenly at each man in turn. He knew most of them very well indeed, and judged that the majority – for all their protestations of selfless desire to serve the community – were sitting on the council for the very same basic reason that he himself had for being there: the purely selfish desire for personal aggrandisement and the wielding of power and influence.

During the last few months Faraday had seen which way the political winds were blowing, and he judged that only a miracle could keep his party in power nationally at the next election. It would need a whole series of miracles to keep himself in power locally in the forthcoming local government elections in May if he retained his present political allegiance.

But he believed that one miracle at least had already been granted to him – and that was his secret alliance with Ivor Jones. The man's burgeoning popularity throughout the city was nothing short of phenomenal. Faraday was certain that if the Cromwell Movement put up candidates in the imminent local elections, it would win easily in at least half of the wards, and might possibly triumph in all of them.

He had kept in constant covert contact with Ivor Jones, and although the man had never mentioned the possibility that he might enter candidates for the Council, it was all too likely that he would be considering doing so. Faraday wanted to ensure his own continued political survival, and indeed continued advancement, and now he was of the firm opinion that he could best ensure that survival and advancement by throwing in his lot openly with Ivor Jones and the Cromwell Movement. But being the wily old campaigner that he was, Faraday had no intention of burning all his bridges behind him. These men present tonight were his political powerbase, and he wanted to carry at least some of them with him.

He decided now that there was nothing to be

gained from prevarication, and so he spoke out bluntly.

'It's my opinion that after the first Thursday in May there won't be a single one of us left sitting here. We'll all be out on our arses. Unless . . .' He let the final word hang.

It was Popplewell who plucked it out of the air.

'Unless what, Mr Chairman?'

'Unless we dissociate ourselves publicly from the insane policies of the present Cabinet.'

Surprise and puzzlement was the general reaction shown on the faces around the table, but there were several who nodded agreement, and a single young councillor named John Clare who instantly divined Faraday's drift.

He held up his hand. 'Mr Chairman?'

'Yes, Councillor Clare.' Faraday nodded permission.

'Mr Chairman, am I correct in assuming that you're considering changing your political allegiance?'

Mutterings of outrage and protest greeted this accusation, but Faraday only smiled, and nodded.

'In a sense, you're correct, Councillor. But I'd prefer to describe it as a slight realignment of my political allegiance.'

'I reckon you'd best make yourself perfectl;y plain, Mr Chairman,' an old diehard party member grunted scowlingly.

'I intend to do just that, Councillor Jobson,' Faraday snapped curtly. 'Now, let's be honest with each other for a change, shall we? We're all of us here for our own advantage.'

He ignored the outcries of protest and indignation that greeted this statement, and went on, 'If we don't do something really quickly about dissociating

341

ourselves as a group from the policies of the present government, then we can all kiss our seats on this Council goodbye. If we're to survive, then we've got to act daringly, and we must do something that will win us instant public support. We have to take a risk, gentlemen, or we'll all go under in May. We can't afford to sit tight and hope for the best any longer; it's too late for that now. The bloody ship's sinking fast, the bottom's falling out of it.'

Again it was young John Clare who spoke out. 'What you mean, Mr Chairman, is that we have to abandon the ship we're on, and get aboard another one straight away.'

Faraday nodded. 'You've got it in one, Councillor.'

The younger man smiled shrewdly. 'And will I have it in two if I say that you're going to suggest that the ship we should get aboard is named the Cromwell Movement?'

Faraday chuckled and nodded again. 'You've got it in two, Councillor!'

There was an instant of shocked silence around the table, then a sudden babbling of voices, some supportive, some derogative, some jeering, some applauding, some protesting, some agreeing.

Angry disputes raged back and forth across the table, and George Faraday sat back silently in his tall chair and watched and listened with a gleam of contempt in his eyes. Then he leaned forward and hammered the table-top with his fist, shouting, 'Order! Let's have some order!'

Gradually the noisy arguments died away, and Faraday nodded curtly.

'Thank you, gentlemen. Now what I propose we do is this. That we, as the governing council make a public statement that we can no longer associate ourselves with the present government's policies on law and order, and taxation. That we as the governing Council fully endorse and support the aims of the Cromwell Movement, and that we intend to give financial aid to the movement to enable it to expand its work among the unemployed young people of our city.'

'Hmmpphhh!' Councillor Jobson emitted a loud snort of disgust. 'Use public money to help young layabouts and thugs? It's a disgrace!'

Faraday ignored the interruption, and went on, 'That we as a Council also intend to give financial aid to the Old People's Care Association, which is to be set up as a joint venture between this Council and the Cromwell Movement.'

Certain of the more quick-thinking councillors were beginning to nod approval, perceiving the advantages to be gained by this type of alliance with the Cromwell Movement. But others, such as Councillor Jobson, were hostile.

'Where's the extra money going to come from?' he demanded to know. 'We're already cutting things to the bone.'

For the first time Faraday allowed a flash of irritation to show, as he snapped, 'For God's sake, Councillor Jobson, will you let me finish what I'm saying? I'll tell you where the extra money will come from; it's going to come from cutting out all those other grants that we make to various pressure groups and local interests. We'll cut the social services budget; we'll close the special homes for problem children to begin with, and get rid of all the damned social workers who staff them. There'll be no more foreign holidays for young thugs and social workers at public expense; no more grants made to support ethnic groups and social clubs; no more lesbian and gay aid; no more arty-farty project grants to some idiot to slosh buckets of paint on walls and call it a soddin' mural. There'll be no more rip-offs from the public funds in this city either. And we'll set the example ourselves by cancelling all Council social functions and Councillors' fact-finding trips. We'll cease drawing our subsistence and travel and expenses allowances. We'll order a comb-out of every Council department, but concentrate on the top echelons. There's no sense in making a dozen street-sweepers and dustmen redundant, when we can achieve the same amount of savings by getting rid of one inefficient manager. And there'll be no more golden handshakes to our executives either, when they get the chop for making balls-ups. Also, the salary levels of all top executive and managerial staff will be frozen indefinitely, and in some cases reduced: there's too much public resentment being voiced at present about fat cats on our payroll . . .'

Hands went up and permission to speak was sought, but Faraday refused to give way and went on relentlessly.

'Do you know why Ivor Jones is going from strength to strength in this city, and now throughout the country? Well, I'll tell you why. He's living up to his own propaganda. He's living like a puritan, practising what he preaches. If we're going to retain power here, then we must be seen doing the same. We've got to be seen to be making the same sacrifices that we intend to demand others make.'

Now his voice subtly altered, and a note of cajolery entered his tone. 'We've got to take short-term pain, to make long-term gain, gentlemen. The gravy-train will soon be running along the tracks again, if we bring it to a standstill for a short time now. But make no mistake, if we aren't seen to alter, then we might as well get up and go right away. Because we'll certainly be kicked out next May if we don't!'

He leaned back in his tall chair and instructed them quietly, 'Just think about it for a while, and then we'll take a show of hands on my preliminary proposals, just to see where the land lies.'

After a few minutes the show of hands was called for and Faraday carried the vote by a small majority. As he expected, Councillor Jobson and his clique opposed. Popplewell, John Clare and most of the younger councillors supported.

Faraday was satisfied with the support he had. If anything, it was a greater number than he had hoped for.

'Very well, gentlemen. We all know where we stand now. I shall issue a public statement on behalf of my own supporters detailing what we propose to do, and the agenda we shall act on if re-elected. You other councillors must act as you see fit. I think it's plain that we've come to the parting of the ways, don't you?'

The meeting dissolved in considerable acrimony, and George Faraday, Andrew Popplewell and John Clare went off together to a quiet public house. There they sat and talked for some time, and settled on the format of the statement they would jointly issue to the press.

Then John Clare asked, 'Tell me, Mr Faraday, have you already come to an agreement with Ivor Jones about what we're going to do?'

George Faraday hesitated, then grinned bluffly and spread his hands wide. 'Well, not exactly, John. But

345

I'm sure that Jones will jump at the chance of joining forces with us. I've already arranged for a meeting with him when he returns from his present tour.'

He saw the instant doubt in the faces of his companions, and suddenly threw back his head and roared with laughter. Then he challenged them, 'Have you got tickets for any other boat?'

Rueful grins creased their faces, and both men shook their heads.

'None of us has,' Faraday stated bluntly, but laughter was still bubbling from him. 'In fact, we haven't even got a bloody lifebelt between us, have we? So it's sink or swim, lads, and I'm going to swim towards Ivor Jones, and hope to Christ that he chucks me a line.'

He began to roar with laughter again and, infected by his gallows humour, the other two men started to laugh too.

# Chapter Thirty-Nine

For Chris Thompson, there were not enough hours in the day. Never before in his life had he worked so hard and so long. And never before had he been so poorly rewarded financially for his efforts. Paradoxically, for a young man who had always been extremely materially minded, his present shortage of personal cash did not worry him in the least. In fact, he had never been happier or more contented. His loyalty and commitment to Ivor Jones and the Cromwell Movement was now absolute. In return, Jones displayed his trust in the young man by taking him increasingly into his confidence. Thus Thompson was aware of many of the covert actions of the Security Section, although taking no part in those actions himself. Instead, he was being given his head in other directions; he was becoming accepted as the 'ideas' man of the movement, as well as its press and publicity officer.

As a propagandist he was doing a superb job of presenting the desired image of the movement to the world at large, and he had quickly established a network of contacts throughout the national and local news media whom he kept supplied with an endless flow of colourful stories and reports about the movement's activities.

He was now accompanying Ivor Jones on this latest series of visits to the various Cromwell cadres situated around the country. As always, Jones used Chris Thompson as a shield between himself and the media reporters. It was a policy that they had discussed and formulated during long conversations. Thompson had realised that it would be a grave mistake for Jones to allow himself to become easily available to journalists and television pundits. In too much personal exposure to the media, there was a danger of having the public come to look upon Jones as just another publicity-hungry, self-serving opportunist who had latched on to a formula for self-aggrandisement. Instead Jones remained aloof from the media, but not hostile or arrogant in his attitude towards those who sought to interview or photograph him. His refusals to be interviewed or to appear on television chat shows were made politely and pleasantly, and his given reason for those refusals was always that he regarded himself as being merely a working member of a great movement, and that there were many members of that movement more deserving of publicity than himself.

Within the movement itself, however, Jones was much more approachable. Any member, even the most recently joined or the most humble, could always tell him about their problems. He would listen gravely to them, his fiery blue eyes fixed upon theirs, his weathered features displaying interest and concern, and the speaker would leave feeling that he had a true friend and helper in Ivor Jones.

At the constant rallies and meetings of the movement, Jones would display his consummate mastery of rhetoric and crowd arousal. Always he repeated his main themes: the right of ordinary people to live their

lives without fear . . . The right of ordinary people
to defend themselves against those who would harm
them . . . The right of ordinary people to plain and
simple justice.

The tour of the Cromwell cadres was triumphantly
successful, and their clamorous demands that Ivor
Jones activate their branches were growing too stri-
dent and pressing for that activation to be deferred
for very much longer. But finance was becoming a
problem. It was apparent that the initial joining and
membership fees were insufficient to cover the fast-
increasing expenses of the movement as a whole.

It was Chris Thompson who came up with an
answer to this problem. He proposed the establishment of a 'war chest'. Each and every movement
member would contribute ten per cent of their income
to this fund. Simultaneously the Cromwell observation patrols and the Ironside protection squads
which guarded shop and private premises would now
be metamorphosed into a commercial company, to
be titled, 'Cromwell Guard'. This company would
undertake to maintain the security of residential and
business premises for a fee to be paid by those who
wanted its services.

It proved highly successful. The proven ability of
the Ironsides and the observation patrols to protect
premises made people very reluctant to have that
protection withdrawn, and so the vast majority paid
willingly. Those who refused to pay found that their
premises almost immediately become vulnerable targets to criminal predators once more, and very soon
they too paid the fees for the security cover of the
Cromwell Guard.

Chris Thompson displayed considerable business
acumen in persuading a commercial communications

company to equip the Guard with mobile phone circuits at nominal rates, in return for the publicity this use of their equipment and network generated.

A new uniform was also designed, to get away from the image of second-hand police uniforms and big peaked caps which had become the hallmark of the long-established private security companies. The Cromwell Guard wore dark grey berets badged with the gold emblem of the Ironside trooper, above High-collared French-style blousons and well-cut trousers tucked into paratroop boots. And many young and old men and women clamoured to wear this dashing new uniform.

Another new venture also took wing. The Cromwell Movement contracted with the Department of Employment to train long-term unemployed teenagers and adults in community service skills – a euphemistic term which could cover a multitude of applications.

After a period of negotiation the Department agreed, and the Cromwell Movement became registered as employers of labour. Immediately carefully selected adults and teenagers from the various Cromwell cadres around the country were brought to the city and given intensive training and indoctrination courses in movement work and mores at Cromwell House. Their subsistence and accommodation, funded by the Department of Employment, was found by Cromwell Movement members in the city.

As the cold, inclement weather of winter gave way before the advance of spring, Ivor Jones and his close associates could feel more than satisfied with the progress they were making towards their eventual goal.

Only one matter troubled Jones, and that was that as the movement membership increased, so did the necessity for a more recognisable structure of command. It was also time, he felt, to launch the movement's own official journal. He decided that both matters could be dealt with at one and the same time, so a couple of weeks after his return from the tour of the cadres, he summoned his closest aides to a meeting at Tabernacle Cottage.

William Rimmer, Chris Thompson, Lisa Keegan and Wisdom Maclure were all present, plus several senior members of the Security Section and the Ironsides.

After congratulating and praising those present for their sterling work performances during the past months, Jones spoke directly to Chris Thompson.

'I want you to immediately purchase the necessary equipment, and recruit the necessary staff to begin publication of our own official journal, Mr Thompson. It will be titled *The Vanguard* and you will be responsible for the layout and material, subject to my approval of course. I want a lively magazine, Mr Thompson. It must be a professional publication in every aspect; nothing amateurish in presentation and format, because I intend that it should also go on offer for sale to the general public. Can you handle this assignment?'

The young man nodded happily. 'Yes, Mr Jones, we'll have the glossiest magazine any publisher could ever wish for.'

'Good! I know that I can rely on you for a quality product.' Jones smiled, and Thompson preened under the compliment.

Then Jones went on, 'I want our members to feel that it is truly their magazine, so have lots of personal profiles and gossip. Plenty of interviews with members – perhaps you could even let them do pieces about how they see the movement and their role in it.'

The smile left his face and he looked grave.

'On the more serious side, I want every edition to carry stories of the latest crimes and outrages committed in this country. I want interviews with the relatives of victims, and with the victims themselves whenever possible. I want the gory details of the crimes, with full-colour photographs whenever possible. I want any lenient sentences imposed by the courts reported, with pictures and profiles of the offenders who got away lightly. The same goes for any criminals who are obviously guilty, but manage to evade punishment on legal technicalities.'

Chris Thompson began to feel increasingly uneasy, and the look on his face betrayed this fact.

Jones frowned, and challenged, 'Do you have any difficulty with that, Mr Thompson?'

'We'll be accused of catering to ghoulish tastes, Mr Jones. Of indulging in the worst forms of sensationalism. It could damage *Vauguard*'s credibility as a serious journal.'

Jones sighed and asked in a patient tone, 'Tell me, Mr Thompson, how many ordinary people rush out to buy the *New Statesman*, and then eagerly devour it from cover to cover? In how many pubs and workplaces are its contents talked about and discussed?'

The young man smiled wryly, and nodded. 'I take your point, Mr Jones. The magazine will be presented as you want.'

Jones' blue eyes bored piercingly into the younger man's for some seconds and then, apparently satisfied, he nodded. 'Good, Mr Thompson, good. Get the project moving straight away.'

'I will, Mr Jones,' Thompson assured him obediently.

Jones then spoke to the gathering at large.

'Now that our movement is fully established, and is on the verge of a rapid and extensive expansion nationally, we need to look carefully at our command organisation.

'The Cromwell Movement is the army of the Lord, and every army must have graded ranks and a hierarchical structure. We shall introduce such a structure into the movement immediately, using the first edition of our new magazine to publicise and inform our membership of what is happening.

'For the main body of our movement, the rank titles need not be militaristic. Older members, both male and female, will be titled and addressed as "Elder", the younger members as "Brother" or "Sister". Collectively, the whole will be known and addressed as "The Brethren". We must lay great emphasis on the movement being in effect one great and extended family. And each member, young and old, must be made to feel that he or she is loved, cared for, and protected by the other members of this great family. This family must become increasingly interdependent and self-sufficient within its extended unity.'

Jones suddenly got to his feet and began to pace up and down, as his enthusiasm for what he was saying took greater and greater hold of him.

'I visualise a time in the not-so-distant future when this movement will be able to provide each and every service and necessity for its members. Cromwell hospitals staffed by Cromwell doctors and nurses; Cromwell schools with Cromwell teachers; Cromwell shops and Cromwell tradesmen; Cromwell garages and transport companies. Everything needed by our members will be provided by our members. A self-sufficient, self-contained entity, protected by our own Security Sections which will be expanded. As that expansion takes place, the men will be organised into Defence Squads, and will take military-style rankings: Trooper, Corporal, Sergeant, Squad Cornet and Squad Captain.

'Our youth branch, the Ironsides, will also become more strictly organised than at present. They too will be ranked in their Squadrons as Trooper, Corporal and so forth.'

He came to a standstill and faced his intent, absorbed listeners.

'You who are here with me today are my closest aides; you each of you shoulder many responsibilities. Accordingly, from this moment on you will hold the rank and title of Commandant of the Cromwell Movement. You will be addressed by that title, and you will use it in all your dealings with the membership of the movement and with the public.'

There was a general response of pleasure and appreciation at this announcement, but Chris Thompson's initial reaction was of incredulous amusement.

'Commandant? Me a Commandant?' he thought with an inner smile. 'People who know me will think that I've had a mental breakdown if I use that title when I'm dealing with them.' He visualised how some of the media people he knew would jeeringly react to the new title, and felt distinctly embarrassed.

'I myself shall continue to be addressed as plain Mr Jones.' With that final instruction, Ivor Jones dismissed the meeting and each went about their individual work. Thompson sat at his desk and, chuckling with self-mockery, idly jotted down his new rank.

'Commandant Christopher Thompson . . . Commandant Thompson, Cromwell Movement . . . Commandant Christopher Thompson of the Cromwell Movement . . .'

He wrote out a mock newsflash: '. . . Cromwellian Defence Squads today went into action at Edgeton. Cromwell Movement Commandant Christopher Thompson directed the operation. Commandant Thompson expressed himself as well satisfied with the progress his troopers were making . . .'

The young man pushed himself back in his chair, and said aloud, 'Commandant Thompson, Cromwell Movement.' He smiled wryly, and admitted to himself that the words had a certain ring to them. They would certainly look more impressive on a business card than, 'Chris Thompson, *Gazette* Reporter'.

The urge to mock at his new title was slowly ebbing, as imperceptibly a liking for its martial ring began to invade the young man's mind.

The phone on his desk rang, and he answered it.

'Hello, Chris Thom . . .' He bit off the word and went silent, and the voice on the other end of the line enquired. 'Hello? Hello? Can you hear me?'

Thompson cleared his throat and began again. 'Good morning, this is Commandant Thompson of the Cromwell Movement . . .'

'Oh, Commandant Thompson! Good morning, sir. This is Julien Fothergill of Skytrek Television Productions. I do hope that I haven't chosen a bad time to call, Commandant, but I wanted to enquire about the . . .'

As the voice babbled on Chris Thompson leaned back in his chair and smiled with satisfaction. It was definitely gratifying to be treated with such deference as a Commandant of the Cromwell Movement. He nodded admiringly in acceptance. 'Mr Jones has certainly got something here with these new ranks and titles, hasn't he . . .'

During the course of the day and evening Chris Thompson answered the phone several more times, and with each succeeding repetition of his new rank and title its usage seemed more natural to him. He found himself enjoying the undoubted tone of deference which entered his callers' voices when he announced his rank.

By the time he had finished work he was beginning to wish that this new rank brought with it a distinguishing badge or uniform, so that people who saw him would recognise that he held a high position within the Cromwell Movement.

'I'll have to suggest that we introduce something of that sort,' he decided, and his mind filled with visual images of himself wearing a dashing uniform.

'Jesus Christ! I'm acting like a silly kid!' He tried to scoff at his own imaginings. 'This is a civilian organisation, not a bloody army. And I'm a civilian, not a soldier.'

Yet still those images persisted, and when he slept that night his dreams were of men saluting him, and rushing to obey his commands.

# Chapter Forty

The local elections proved a sweeping triumph for George Faraday's breakaway party, the Reform Group, whose candidates won all but three of the city wards. A sizeable number of the Reform Group candidates were newcomers to local politics, and came from a wide variety of backgrounds. Some were shopkeepers, some industrial and construction workers, a couple were local businessmen, and there was a schoolteacher. The one thing that all these newcomers held in common was membership of the Cromwell Movement.

On the Saturday evening of the week following the local elections, a rally was held at Cromwell House for the senior members and officers of the movement.

The great hall was packed to capacity an hour before the rally was to begin. In the main body of the hall the Elders crammed the seats. Row upon row of excited men and women, many of whom were wearing what were fast becoming the popular distinctive garments of the Elders of the movement: the men in dark suits and roll-neck sweaters, their hair close-cut; the women in black dresses with wide white collars, and only the bare minumum of make-up on their

357

faces. Plentifully scattered among the sombrely-clad Elders were the dashing French-style uniforms of the Cromwell Guard. The balconies were crammed with young Ironsides in their dark grey tracksuits and bomber jackets, and hanging from the railings of the balconies were continuous lines of Ironside trooper flags.

On the raised pew to the side of the pulpit where the Chapel Elders had once sat, the Commandants of the Movement were now seated. They all wore their own newly designed uniform of dark grey tunics and trousers, without emblems, the women wearing skirts and black silk stockings instead of trousers. The uniforms were simple and austere, but expertly tailored from the finest cloth.

In the vestry room Ivor Jones, dressed in his old dark suit and roll-neck sweater, sat listening to the murmurous humming of massed voices coming from the hall. Although he was well aware of the ever-intensifying, impatient expectancy of the crowd, he was in no hurry to join them. He was waiting for God to come and talk to him.

For many minutes he waited patiently, and then he smiled in welcome as the familiar voice filled his hearing.

'Well, Ivor, this is a big night, isn't it?'

Jones nodded, then shrugged his broad shoulders and stated confidently, 'There'll be bigger ones to come.'

God chuckled appreciatively, and agreed. 'There certainly will be, Ivor. But this is still something of an occasion, isn't it?'

'Yes, it is,' Jones smilingly conceded.

'What are you going to tell them tonight, Ivor?' God wanted to know.

'I'm going to announce the immediate activation of four Cromwell cadres: one in Scotland, one in the North of England, one in the Midlands and one in the South. Four new battle-fronts are opening. The movement is truly on the march, Lord!'

'It certainly is,' God affirmed admiringly. 'You've done well, Ivor. Very well indeed.'

'Thank you, Lord.' Jones was truly gratified by the admiration in the Lord's voice. 'But I know that I owe my success to you.'

'You deserve this success,' God assured him; then a warning note entered his voice, 'But be careful of George Faraday, Ivor; he is too ambitious and greedy for power. And don't trust Charles Blair either; he's willing to let you do his dirty work for him now, but he could turn against you at any time.'

Jones smiled confidently, and his fiery blue eyes were hard and merciless. 'Don't worry, Lord. I know them both for what they are. But what they should be remembering is the story about the monkey who sneaked a ride on the back of the tiger!'

God roared with laughter. 'I know that story, Ivor. The tiger runs out of the jungle into the plains, knowing that the monkey can't run fast enough to get away if he jumps off the tiger's back.'

'Exactly!' Jones nodded, and chuckled. 'And just guess who the tiger is, and who the monkeys are?'

Again God's laughter roared out.

From the hall a low-pitched unified chant had started up, and Jones said, 'Just listen to them, Lord. They're excited because we're winning the battle against evil in this city. Just imagine how much more excited they'll be when I tell them that we are opening new battle-fronts; that we are going to go to war against the thugs and criminals throughout this entire nation.'

The massed voices were chanting in unison.

'We want Mister Jones . . . We want Mister Jones . . . We want Mister Jones . . .'

Feet began stamping in rhythmic double punctuation to the name: 'Mr Jones! Mr Jones! Mr Jones! Mr Jones . . .'

The stamping became heavier and faster, the voices stronger and louder, and another name was beginning to be heard.

'You'd better get out there, Ivor, before they bring the roof down,' God advised.

Ivor Jones stood up and walked out into the hall, and as he mounted into the pulpit and lifted his arms in salute a thunderous roar of acclamation greeted his arrival, and the echoes of the name they bellowed reached far out from the hall and across the rooftops of the city.

'CROMWELL! CROMWELL! CROMWELL! CROMWELL! CROMWELL!'

Warner now offers an exciting range of quality titles by both established and new authors. All of the books in this series are available from:
Little, Brown and Company (UK),
P.O. Box 11,
Falmouth,
Cornwall TR10 9EN.

Alternatively you may fax your order to the above address. Fax No. 0326 376423.

Payments can be made as follows: Cheque, postal order (payable to Little, Brown and Company) or by credit cards, Visa/Access. Do not send cash or currency. UK customers: and B.F.P.O.: please send a cheque or postal order (no currency) and allow £1.00 for postage and packing for the first book, plus 50p for the second book, plus 30p for each additional book up to a maximum charge of £3.00 (7 books plus).

Overseas customers including Ireland, please allow £2.00 for postage and packing for the first book, plus £1.00 for the second book, plus 50p for each additional book.

NAME (Block Letters) .........................................................

ADDRESS...........................................................................

..........................................................................................

☐ I enclose my remittance for _____

☐ I wish to pay by Access/Visa Card

Number  ☐☐☐☐☐☐☐☐☐☐☐☐☐☐☐☐☐

Card Expiry Date  ☐☐☐☐